WHO KILLED JUNE?

A novel by
Richard J. Marco

PublishAmerica
Baltimore

ISBN: 1-4241-3107-3
PUBLISHED BY PUBLISHAMERICA, LLLP
www.publishamerica.com
Baltimore

Printed in the United States of America

This book is dedicated to my children—
a daughter and three sons, who have collectively
given me much pleasure and many grandchildren.
Without them, life would have little meaning.

CHAPTER ONE

Pat Joseph, a lawyer in his late middle years, was comfortably satisfied with his life and practice. His office and home were in Milltown, Ohio, a small town some thirty miles south of Cleveland, from where he and his wife migrated when their children were still of school age. Now Joseph was past the age of waiting for a million-dollar client or a case that would seal his fame. He sat in his office, feet propped on the waste basket beneath his ancient scarred oak table, remembering when he could get his feet all the way to the table's top. Now, his rounded paunch made the effort uncomfortable. He recently joined the town's new Recreational Facility gym in an effort to lose weight, or at least reduce the size of his waist. He discovered that working out and skipping an occasional breakfast didn't work—nothing worked. *God designed me plump,* he thought, *so why fight it?*

Over the years many clients had been interviewed across the beat-up table behind which he sat. He purchased the table for five dollars in Cleveland, when the Public Library decided it had outlived its usefulness. It served him well—somewhat in the nature of a security blanket. It was carefully placed so Joseph could see out of his office's large front window to observe the happenings on the uptown square. He never failed to appreciate the charm of Milltown's square, with its brilliant white gazebo, stately oaks, ash and plane trees, through which brown, red and black squirrels scampered. The square was surrounded by century-old buildings, similar to the one Joseph occupied. The building owned by he and his wife was now named *The Joseph Building.* It was located in the middle of the block on the south side of the square.

A church and the library were located on two corners of the square, framing the courthouse. The west side of the square held various retail establishments, while banks, an ancient hotel, restaurants and a long outmoded firehouse encompassed the north and south sides. The buildings, the gazebo and the nearby school all guaranteed activity every day of the week, providing continuous entertainment for the elderly lawyer.

Joseph was particularly pleased, and somewhat surprised, by the care the City took of its square. Flowers were planted at each corner in a succession that guaranteed blooms all during the growing season. The earth in each flower bed was carefully spread with mulch to inhibit the growth of weeds—weeds were never allowed to mar the beds. Even the children scampering through the park each day carefully avoided stepping on the flowers…adults, young and old, were careful where they placed their chairs or blankets during the Friday night band concerts so as not to cause damage. Judiciously placed trash receptacles kept litter from finding its way to the ground. Old-timers and newcomers alike took pride in the square and cared for it like the precious jewel it was.

Looking at the square, Joseph thought of the time, not long ago, when the sidewalks surrounding it were of classic sandstone. Over the years, the stone became worn, cracked and badly treated by Ohio's freezes and thaws. When the walks could no longer be repaired, the uptown merchants and the agencies dedicated to the preservation of the square demanded that the walks be replaced with the original style of sandstone. The city administration objected strenuously because of the cost and difficulty of care. They wanted the more permanent and less costly concrete. The arguments that raged were finally resolved by compromise. The city installed concrete sidewalks, but in front of each business and office, a small two-foot square of sandstone was embedded in the concrete.

Joseph found this amusing, remembering something similar occurring on one of the old residential side streets just off the square. Originally paved with cobblestone bricks that became worn down to the point where they had to be replaced, the city intended to repave the street with concrete. The residents demanded the original type of cobblestone be utilized. They won. It was the only street in Milltown—and probably Ohio—that wasn't either concrete or blacktop. Joseph was pleased with his neighbors, who were dedicated to preserving those things that made his town special.

Across the square from Joseph's office sat the old Americana Hotel, where permanent and transient residents during the spring and summer months sat in bent-wood rockers on the covered porch wrapping around the building providing ready access to the square's activities. The increasing good weather caused checker boards to appear along with some of the old-timers. Joseph thought, *Nothing untoward can happen while these good people are keeping watch. Maybe someday, I'll occupy one of those rockers. Wonder if the square looks much different from that side.*

Between the hotel and the deli where Joseph usually ate lunch was Melton's Meat Market, where cuts of meat were found in the refrigerated glass case or prepared as customers' directed—but never in shrink-wrapped cellophane. Several other stores surrounding the square carried clothing, flowers, hardware, pharmaceuticals, hobbies—all dispensed with a personal touch—the salespeople knowledgeable about their customers' needs, wants and names. Second floors housed offices and an occasional residential apartment. The second floor of one of the buildings was occupied by an almost defunct service organization with an odd-sounding name whose members actually owned the building, never to be used for any other purpose.

The plate glass window through which Joseph watched the day's activities was adorned, in large gilt letters, with the arched declaration *Patrick Joseph, Attorney at Law.* Behind the window was his office, partially paneled—the paneling darkened with a patina of age—and containing a fireplace no longer used. The ceilings were high and of the old-fashioned pressed tin. The walls, where not paneled, were painted a soft eggshell color. Joseph's various diplomas, pictures of grandchildren and presidents long dead adorned the walls, while a case built for that purpose housed his collection of glass and ceramic pigs. All taken together, everything lent a comfortable air to the room—at least Joseph found it so—as perhaps did his clients.

The contented lawyer noted it was a gorgeous spring day—not really unusual for Ohio—with the sun shining on the budding leaves and greening lawns. Probably the farmers would say it was either too wet or too dry for planting, but Joseph didn't care. It was a beautiful day. He did miss the serenity and quiet that prevailed when he first moved to Milltown, years earlier, since spoiled by pilgrims from Cleveland and Akron. Like most migrants, he believed immigration should be outlawed once he arrived. Nothing he could do about it now.

Joseph was short, plumb and bald, none of which bothered him much. Food—especially Italian cooking—was a passion that contributed to his round appearance. Despite his age, his remaining hair, a slightly unkempt curly fringe surrounding his bald pate, was as black as it ever was and usually needed a trim. As a concession to the passage of years, some grey invaded the neatly trimmed bushy mustaches resting beneath his generous nose. Eyebrows, black as his hair, were full and had a mind of their own, operating independently of each other—the left rose into a permanently furrowed brow and the right lowered—when questioning the credibility of a witness or when Joseph was otherwise displeased. His bright eyes were hazel colored, but the coloring was seldom noticed because of a perpetual squint. Friends said that the lines spreading outward from his eyes were laugh lines—those not knowing him well called them frown lines. In any event, the wrinkles were permanently etched but did not detract from his appearance. He was often referred to as intimidating by those having little contact with him, but children and friends knew he was truly a gentle, sensitive soul—somewhat insecure and a little shy.

Pat Joseph and his wife, Mary, moved to the pleasant suburb of Cleveland from the ethnic intercity after attending a Sunday morning Mass while passing through Milltown. As they were leaving the church, the pastor reached for and shook Joseph's hand saying, "We're always pleased to have visitors. Welcome, and please come again."

Later, at breakfast, Mary said, "You know, Pat, we've been going to Mass at St. Pat's for years and no one knows us, or anyone else. We really should think about moving to a town like this, where at least the pastor knows the difference between visitors and parishioners. It would be good for the kids too—I know."

They had four children, the oldest a girl, followed fairly quickly by three sons. Joseph had no concern about his name being carried into the next generation. When asked, the children seemed equally excited about the move—the only one not so sure was Joseph. He was never comfortable with change.

Within six months, acreage was purchased, a saltbox house designed by Mary, and built by a contractor she picked. The move to Milltown was accomplished before Joseph even got used to the idea of moving. Not being happy about the one-hour commute to Cleveland every day, and recognizing the inevitable, Joseph finally conceded and moved his practice to Milltown. Some of his clients followed and, since Milltown was the county seat, Joseph had little difficulty in rebuilding a comfortable practice. He was thinking about all these things as he contemplated the changes in his life since.

Several months earlier, Joseph had tried and won a murder case—his first since coming to Milltown. He still basked in the glow of a hard-earned acquittal secured for a middle-aged lady for whom he had developed a real fondness. He hadn't told the client it was the first major criminal case he tried in Mills County. He had tried several such cases in Cleveland, but the busy attitude of the courts and the Prosecutor's Office depersonalized all of the participants, making it impossible to get overly involved with clients or cases. Somehow, it was different in Milltown, and Joseph was aware that such a case would become an integral part of his life. Before reluctantly agreeing to represent her, he had been content with his somewhat provincial practice. He hadn't wanted to try a murder case, but felt obligated to once his probing revealed what he believed to be the true facts. The inquiry led to an unshakable conviction that the police failed to investigate the crime adequately. Now, filled with his success, he thought, *Maybe I'm not a bad trial lawyer. Always wanted to try a major criminal case, but never thought I was good enough. Scared of the responsibility I guess.* The thought caused him to laugh aloud. The passing feeling of accomplishment did nothing to eliminate Joseph's sense of insecurity.

The publicity surrounding the case resulted in an influx of new clients—especially criminal defendants. Although Joseph was pleased with the adulation, he wasn't sure he liked all the work. Fortunately his associates, including his sons, were able to carry most of the load. *The secret of family success is to have sons to work the fields while the old man rests and reaps the benefits.*

An early riser by nature, Joseph continued his habit of arriving at the office earlier than anyone else. It gave him a chance to read the newspaper without the unceasing ringing of the phone or other interruptions with which his days had become full. He looked forward to news about crimes in the area...even though he wasn't pleased that the crime rate had grown unceasingly since his arrival in Milltown.

Looking at the masthead of the newspaper spread before him, Joseph was again reminded that the century-old brick building owned and occupied by him—actually owned by him and his wife, Mary—had previously been the home of the *Milltown Reporter.* It irritated him, but only moderately, that the locals still thought of it as the *Reporter Building.* With increasing interest, he read the lead article beneath the headline.

POLICE INVESTIGATE MILLTOWN HOMICIDE

MILLTOWN—Police are investigating the apparent stabbing death Saturday morning of a 31-year-old woman. Police were called at 6:25 a.m., shortly after the body of June Westlock of 234 North Stubb Ave. was discovered in the laundry room of her home. She was found with multiple stab wounds in the torso. The coroner concluded she probably died of those wounds. Police do not yet have a motive for the homicide. All of the evidence was to be turned over to the State's Bureau of Criminal Investigation. Police would not elaborate on their findings except to say that Westlock's 8-year-old daughter was asleep in one of the bedrooms of the home at the time the body was found. A call was received from the deceased's estranged boyfriend, Clarence Knedder, at 6:25 A.M., who reported he found the body. Although police said there were several leads, no one has been charged as yet. Knedder is apparently not a suspect at this time.

Even though earlier than normal starting time, Joseph called, "Della, are you here?" Her office was just outside his door so, as usual, he ignored the intercom.

Long-suffering Della Raven, his attractive secretary, walked into Joseph's office smiling. "Yes, I'm here. What do you need, Pat?"

Both had taken a great deal of ribbing about her name and its association with Earl Stanley Gardner's fictitious *Perry Mason*—even more so now that Joseph had actually tried a murder case. Della was actually her given name—her married name, Raven. Tall, slender and full-figured, with hair as black as her name suggested, combed neatly in a current style. Her fresh looks and unlined face belied her age—she being a contemporary of Joseph. Joseph was extremely fond of her and she of him, even through there was no romantic basis for that affection. She, her husband, Joseph and his wife were good friends and socialized on a regular basis.

"Della, I hope the coffee's on," he griped as she walked into his office and handed him a cup, black the way he liked it, and pecked him on the cheek.

"Are we feeling grumpy today?"

Mumbling, "Thank you," he tried to keep from smiling as Della slipped comfortably into the client chair across from him. "Not really grumpy. But you know, I'm concerned the office is going to hell. I can never find anything. The girls have taken to wearing pants to work. Don't they want to look like women instead of undernourished boys?" He was referring to several of the office secretaries and the receptionist. "And the boys...they come to the office in sweaters and jeans instead of shirts, ties and jackets," not mentioning that he was talking about his own sons.

Della would no more appear in the office without proper attire than she would nude, yet she was able to accept, more easily than Joseph, the young people's need for independence. "I told the girls they could wear slacks so long as they were neat and clean—not too tight. They don't look bad. The boys took it on themselves to dress casually when there is no need for court appearances. You want to say something to them—go right ahead."

Pat Joseph had no intention of saying anything to anyone. He would leave that up to Della—and bring in Mary if necessary. Changing the subject, "By the way, Della, have you read this morning's paper?"

"No, why?"

"There was a stabbing death on the north end of town. A June Westlock. Know her?"

She responded with a slight frown, searching her memory for the name in her mental list of clients, "I don't think so," as she sipped her coffee. "We did a deed, or something, for someone named Westlock a couple of years ago, but nothing recently that I know of, and no June Westlock."

Joseph proceeded to read the article to her, after which Della said, "You aren't really thinking of getting involved, are you?"

Although Joseph pictured himself doing great things in the courtroom, he knew he wasn't up to handling another murder case just yet. He would never admit that to anyone, much less himself. "I don't think so. I don't know any of the people in the article except for Knedder. I think we handled a little traffic matter for him some time ago. Besides, even if I wanted to, Mary would have a major fit. She doesn't want me to deal with any more high-visibility cases. She says she can't go grocery shopping without someone asking her about my last case. It's just…I'm curious about what happens in town."

Turning back to the paper and sipping his coffee while Della began to spread files on his desk, he asked, "By the way, do you remember that nice young fellow that worked for the *Reporter*? I think his name was Stan something. He covered the other trial. Maybe I could satisfy my curiosity by talking to him."

"Yes, I remember him. His name is Stan Marten. Nice young man. I have his number in my Rolodex. But, Pat," Della used his first name only when there was no one else within hearing distance, otherwise she insisted on the proper Mr. Joseph, "you really don't have the time to waste on this. I don't like—don't want you to get involved in another murder case. It takes too much out of you, and nothing else gets done around here. You have more than you can handle now. Besides, it wears you out." She was as concerned about his health and well-being as Mary.

"Never mind," Joseph growled. "Just get him on the phone for me. I'm curious—that's all."

*   *   *

While waiting for the call to be placed, Joseph sat back and glanced at his collection of ceramic, glass and metal pigs. Mary always had a substantial accumulation of animals at their home—usually rescue animals needing a home or loving care She had no objection to horses, goats, dogs or cats moving onto their thirteen-acre homestead, but drew the line at pigs. She wouldn't allow a live pig anywhere near her home…not even the small pot-bellied one Joseph wanted. Hearing of Mary's unalterable position, one of Joseph's neighbors jokingly gave him a cast iron piggy bank, that Joseph settled in a place of honor at his office. Thereafter, his friends saw to it that his office and home were filled with a constant flow of inanimate pigs. Joseph would say appreciatively, "Thank you. I have a particular fondness for pigs. They're the most intelligent of beasts and I've never seen one without a smile on its face. Not always pleasant smiles, but at least they smile." His yen was partially satisfied by collecting and displaying the unending source of ceramic, glass, wood and metal pigs.

Della, having reached the reporter at the newspaper, buzzed Joseph, expressing her displeasure in cold, formal tones. "Stan Marten's on the line, Mr. Joseph."

Joseph met the reporter while trying the Mountain City murder case. They became friendly. Stan Marten was the only reporter with whom Joseph felt comfortable—he believed he could confide in him. When Joseph said something was off the record, it stayed that way. Stan, young, slight and blessed with a full head of curly reddish hair, had recently received his journalism degree from Akron University. His first job out of school was covering the courthouse beat for the *Milltown Reporter.* He intended staying there only until his writing was recognized in a major

13

market like Cleveland or Akron—maybe the *Plain Dealer* or the *Akron Beacon Journal*.

"Hi, Stan. Pat Joseph here. Read your story in the *Reporter* this morning and, as always, was pleased with your coverage. You're really quite good. Wondered if there is anything new."

"Thanks. I assume you're talking about the Westlock stabbing? Why you asking, Mr. Joseph? Something I should know?"

"No…no…Stan," Joseph laughed, "nothing like that. Just curious. I'm not ready to try another murder case—the last one exhausted me. I don't want to do another one anytime soon. But there aren't many killings in Milltown. I don't like that kind of thing, or scandals, happening in my town. Haven't started my usual daily grind yet and the article made me think about you. We haven't talked for a while. Thought I'd ask you about it—really just an excuse to talk to you. Mostly just inquisitive, I guess."

"Well, Mr. Joseph…" Like most everyone, the reporter found it difficult to call Joseph by his given name. The only people who used his first name were receptionists and aides in doctors' offices—which irritated Joseph. "Pretty much everything I know is in the story. The police really don't believe her boyfriend had anything to do with it, even though it seems he had the best opportunity and, as a matter of fact, a rather strong motive. What they're looking at is a possible drug connection. It seems Westlock was seen Saturday night in the company of a young fellow down on Forge St.—probably looking for drugs. She was going into Cockroach's house."

Cockroach was a well-known local small-time hood whom Joseph had once successfully represented in a misdemeanor drug case. A strikingly handsome, if somewhat hard-looking, black man, he seemed to be involved in most of the drugs that hit Milltown as well as being the best-dressed fashionable resident of Forge Street, who always drove large new cars. He lived in an older, seamier part of town and the source of his income was not discernable to anyone. Forge Street was formerly the center of Milltown's industrial district—the factories long since closed and abandoned. The area required a great deal of attention by the police—and worry to Joseph. It seemed no one could keep drugs from finding their way into the community, in spite of the fact that most of Milltown's residents denied their existence.

"Do they know who the young fellow is?" Joseph asked.

"Not really, Mr. Joseph. He was described as being a white guy, rather small, slight build, dark hair. June and her live-in boyfriend, Knedder, spend a lot of time in the area with their druggy friends…especially Jimmy Takas. Jimmy and Knedder are always together and the cops believe the description fits him. He's a heavy user and always seems to be on the periphery of the local action. Knedder's and Takas' name are frequently on the police blotter. The street talk is that June's not a big user, but heavy into dealing or supplying. They say she's always got something available for friends—gives away a lot. Not sure where she gets the money to buy the quantity of drugs she seems to have—probably from Knedder. Anyway, she's known as being generous with it and, as a result, has lots of friends. Don't know if it's true or not, but that's the talk."

Joseph's heart skipped a beat, an immediate hollow feeling settling in his chest. He didn't know young Jimmy Takas personally since grown, but had seen him regularly as a child running around the church hall, where his mother worked in the kitchen. Mrs. Takas cooked for all the special affairs at the church Joseph and his wife attended. A grandmotherly type, Mrs. Takas was in charge of the kitchen—her children always there and always underfoot. Joseph remembered Jimmy as a bright-eyed energetic child, small and spindly for his age, but always running. Joseph recalled seeing him flashing through the church hall, hair in his eyes and tiny wire-rim glasses slipping down his nose. He was sure Mary knew the family well and felt certain she would not want him to be involved.

Joseph swiveled his chair around and gazed at his pigs resting on the shelves especially reserved for them behind his desk. As usual, the pigs were smiling, but the smiles weren't particularly chipper…in fact, his pigs had a mocking look on their usually pleasant faces.

Joseph said, "Thanks, Stan. If you hear anything more, please give me a call. I might know the Takas boy. My wife would have a fit if I got involved. Take care."

"So long, Mr. Joseph, and I'll ask the same. If you hear anything, please let me know. I don't usually cover the police beat, but I was the only one available Saturday morning and got the assignment. I try to do a good job."

"You always do," Joseph said as he hung up the phone.

Della, standing in the doorway, did not have a pleasant feeling. She walked into Joseph's office with a stack of files and her notebook. "Are you ready to do some work?" she asked somewhat petulantly.

Joseph, in an effort to appease her, said, "Sure, sit down. Let's go over the files you have. Maybe when we get through we can walk over to the deli and grab a cup of coffee and a donut."

CHAPTER TWO

No matter how he tried, the elderly lawyer couldn't quit thinking about the young lady who was stabbed to death in his adopted home town. Perhaps the changes in his community weren't inimical to Milltown only—maybe other cities and towns bore the same agony—suffered from the same kinds of occurrences while their residents slept—learning of the atrocities only in the morning papers.

Joseph couldn't understand the lure of drugs. In his naïveté he didn't pretend to comprehend that, for reasons not apparent to him, there are those who prefer illegal to legal, night to day. *Normal people,* Joseph gave free rein to his thoughts, *try to avoid the dark whenever possible—others I don't understand seek the darkness. Maybe it's because at night there are always choices...to be seen or not...to sulk, walk or run. To live in the shadows or under the streetlights...to steal or not...to enter open garages or backdoors or not...to do drugs openly or in hiding. Perhaps there is some genetic similarity in those that exercise the preference of night to day. Whether there is or not, there always seems to be a congruence in the activities of the people that live in the night—the night walkers.*

Day's light does not give the kind of choices that darkness does. The sun, even when obscured by clouds, beats down light and surrenders alleyways, cubbyholes, and dead ends to casual observation by anyone who looks. The single saving grace of day is that people rarely see what's happening around them. Most walk with their heads lowered, watching the ground as if it will yield some important secret—heads bent in solemn silence—afraid to make eye contact with other human beings, afraid to see something out of the ordinary—something that would require involvement. Such people would rather walk through life on a track like the old-fashioned cars at Euclid Beach amusement park, that no longer exists except in my memory.

But the chance of observation, as attested by the growing television shows featuring voyeuristic video cameras labeled "realistic programing," grows greater every day. This, along with the small number of walkers that look where they should not purposefully, hoping to catch someone in an embarrassing, illegal or humiliating circumstance, is scary. These few are eager to tell what they see.

Joseph's thought process continued, *By nature, night users do not want to be seen even by those like them. So it's no surprise that those wanting invisibility live by night and sleep, when possible, during the day. Those that live in the dark are a breed. They are called nightwalkers. They see forms in the dark but try not to recognize faces. They honor each other's privacy and never seek to determine each other's business. They abide the law during daylight hours and use the dark to hide their activities, usually beyond the law—but that is where they live, in the land of marijuana, heroin and cocaine—for smoking, shooting, free-basing or snorting,—or whatever illicit activity available or popular at the moment. Neighborhood parks designed and built for daytime play filled with the shrieks of happy children, after the setting sun become retail pharmaceutical outlets for the night walkers.*

* * *

It was on a fine April morning—Friday, April 4, to be exact—one such night walker began the day as though it weren't her last. June Westlock, as was her custom, slept as late as possible, waking reluctantly to the ring of her alarm at about ten o'clock in the morning. She stretched, scratched and finally walked into the bathroom for her morning ablution, which included popping several pills to alleviate the morning headache and rinsing her face with cold water to diminish the red in her eyes.

She soon felt composed enough to awaken her eight-year-old daughter, Shelley, and prepare a hasty breakfast for her. June loved her daughter. She was the result of June's longtime relationship with Clarence Knedder, a black man who lived with June off and on for the past several years. June intended to take her daughter to work with her, it being spring break, Shelley didn't have to go to school.

June couldn't handle breakfast following her indulgences of the night before. She rarely had an appetite for food in the mornings, and certainly no appreciation for how lovely the day. A little over five feet, five inches tall, she was slender and had skin never touched by the sun—white as alabaster and not yet lined except for a slight tracing drawn from her eyes. Naturally blonde, her hair was long and usually worn down, framing her thin face. Her eyes were cornflower blue, but this morning the whites still streaked with red. She found it difficult to keep them open.

While Shelley ate, June phoned her sister. "Beth, can you pick me and Shelley up? Car's broke down again. Need a ride to the store."

The only job June ever held was as a part-time employee in her parents' bakery, usually two or three days a week. But, unfortunately for her lifestyle preferences, she was required to work on weekends. She didn't like having to work, but relied on her parents for sustenance and her friends for support. The store was in Braden, a suburb of Cleveland about four miles north of Milltown, peopled mostly by solid blue-collar workers who commuted to the Ford and Chevy plants in its northern parent city.

On those days that June worked when Shelley didn't have school, she brought her daughter to the bakery. By doing so she could avoid paying a babysitter; and besides, Shelley, a bright, articulate and loving girl, enjoyed the bakery smells, the customers, and her grandparents. Her grandparents, despite their racial biases, adored their granddaughter.

"No problem. Pick you up in about a half hour."

"Thanks, see ya."

Beth, her slender frame settled at the kitchen table in her parents' home, her long blond hair as natural as her sister's, but a shade darker, gathered into a ponytail. As she sipped a cup of coffee, she thought, *Should I make a piece of toast for myself?* But, like her older sister, she didn't do breakfast well. She pushed up from the table, carried her dirty cup to the dishwasher, and went to the bedroom she occupied to dress. Her parents had left for the bakery long before Beth awoke.

Beth Westlock, looking like a younger, darker version of her sister, arrived at June's house a little before eleven. They rode to the store together without saying much to each other. Neither felt much like talking, Shelley making it easy on them by, as little girls her age do, her perpetual chattering. The day progressed quietly, except for the usual Friday run on baked goods.

In the middle of the afternoon, Beth answered the phone, "Braden Bakery, Beth speaking. How may I help you?"

The call was from Jimmy Takas, "Hi, Beth. Is June there?"

He sounded anxious and had no time for small talk.

"Hold on, I'll see."

Punching the hold button, she called, "June, it's Jimmy Takas. You want to talk to him?"

"Hell no! I don't want to talk to him. He's a pain in the ass," looking around to see if her parents could overhear. She was, even at this age, concerned about her parents' approval. They weren't near. "Always wanting somethin' from me or Clarence," referring to her longtime live-in boyfriend, and father of Shelley, from whom she was currently estranged.

Beth picked up the phone, pressed the flashing button, and said, "She's not here, Jimmy. I'll tell her you called."

"Okay, thanks. I got to talk to her. It's kind of important. I'm at work so she can't call me back. But tell her I called and I'll catch her, or Clarence, tonight—probably at *Tracks*."

When the bakery closed at six o'clock, June and Shelley went home with Beth and their parents. They enjoyed their usual Friday family dinner, as always, accompanied by pleasant conversation. The sisters, despite their other activities, really enjoyed their parents and each other. After dinner, June said, "Beth, could you take me home, please? I promised Shelley she could go bowling with her friends tonight. Like to drop her off on the way—at the bowling alley. She and her friends are gonna have a bowling party. She don't have to get up early, so I told her she could stay out till eleven."

Bidding the older Westlocks goodnight, the sisters said simultaneously, "See you in the morning."

The older couple was already yawning and showing signs of preparing to retire. They would be at the bakery by four thirty the next morning.

Beth and June left, stopping at the bowling alley as promised. June instructed Shelley to be out front on time. Even though the bowling alley was within walking distance of their house, June didn't want her daughter on the street so late at night. Like most parents, she didn't want her habits to rub off on her daughter.

Beth took June the rest of the way home and left, having her own plans for the evening. June enjoyed a cold beer while changing from her uniform into the customary too-tight jeans and T-shirt that showed off her slender, attractive figure. She looked out her front door and noted her friend and across-the-street neighbor, Casey Patterson. As was expected on warm evenings, she was sitting on the front porch of her house. It was unusually nice for this early in the spring. June grabbed a couple of beers and trotted across the street to her friend's house.

"Hey, Casey," June said, "Want a beer?" handing her a bottle that Casey gratefully accepted. "Car's in the garage again. Can you give me a ride over to Forge Street? Need to see someone—pick up something."

Forge Street wasn't far—just across town, but June wasn't into walking, and her chore didn't lend itself to being on the street too long.

Casey had nothing better to do, "Sure. Let me get my keys."

Bringing their beers with them, and sucking on the bottles as they went, they drove to Forge Street. June pointed out the house where she wanted Casey to stop, even though Casey had been there several times before. It was an old, not too well-cared-for house, painted long ago with a green paint that must have been bought at a store-closing sale. Casey stopped in front of the house and waited in the car, keeping the motor running. She didn't know who lived there, but certainly knew the purpose of the call.

"Be right back," June said as she jumped out of the car and ran up to the front door of the house.

Standing on the rickety porch, she knocked lightly on the door frame. No sense calling too much attention to her presence. The porch light was out, but Casey could see by a light shining through the open front door an African-American woman she had never met speaking briefly with June. She went back into the house while June waited on the porch, moving about nervously, until a black man came to the door and exchanged a small package with June for something that was clutched in her hand. He went back inside, closing the door behind him.

One positive aspect of the drug world is that racial prejudice takes a backseat to other needs. Those involved in the seamier world of drugs learn quickly that there is no rational basis for bigotry.

June ran back to the car, jumped in, and said, "Let's go."

As Casey pulled into her drive, June said, "Thanks a million. I owe you. I'll stop by later—may be we can share…" Casey knew what she was talking about and looked forward to the possibility with anticipation. "If you're gonna be around all evening, I'll need a ride later. Got to stop at Brenda's house," a mutual friend of theirs, "and pick up Shelley on the way back."

"Sure. I ain't doing nothing tonight. Probably be on the porch. Just call, or walk over."

*   *   *

Returning home, June took care of the chores she hadn't been able to attend to earlier that day…making her and Shelley's beds and washing the few breakfast dishes Shelley used. After she was finished, June walked over to Casey's house, carrying a couple more bottles of cold beer. Sitting on the porch swing with Casey and enjoying the beer, and looking around to see if anyone were in earshot, she offered to share a marijuana cigarette.

"Want to share a joint? We can go by Brenda's after and pick up Shelley on the way back. Okay?" Brenda Blanton was a friend with a daughter Shelley's age.

"Where we got to pick up Shelley?" Casey asked, taking a puff on the small cylinder June handed her, allowing the smoke to drift from her mouth, sucking it into her nose and deeply into her lungs. She held it in as long as she could, creating a fine, relaxed feeling.

"She's at the bowling alley. Promised I'd pick her up by eleven."

"Sure. No problem. I wasn't gonna do nothing tonight. So nice out I'd just spend the evening on the porch anyway."

On the way, they stopped at a nearby convenience store to pick up a six-pack. Casey parked in front of the apartment building where Brenda lived. It was in an area of town that was newer than where they had been earlier, but with no better reputation. The police were kept busy just watching.

June said, "Come on—we'll grab a beer and another joint. I really got some good stuff tonight. Got some powder to lace it with. "

Climbing the outside stairs to the apartment, June knocked on the door and walked in. Brenda was sitting at the kitchen table smoking a hand-rolled cigarette and drinking coffee.

June rambled, a relaxed smile on her face, "Hi. Brought a present for your kid. Got to get home by eleven. Shelley's at the bowling alley and got to pick her up. I don't want to leave her alone too long. Scored a couple of rocks tonight. Wanta share?"

"Sure."

They crushed the rocks, rolled a couple of marijuana cigarettes and mixed the white crystals into the dried leaves. Lighting the cigarettes and drawing deeply, June said, "Ahhh, this is the best I've felt all week. Clarence's been bothering me. Got a restraining order through a friend and the police served it on him. But he's still coming by my house, breaking in when I'm not there. He's been following me around too. Clarence's so fuckin' jealous he's got me a little scared…Clarence's just being a pain—wantin' to see if I'm making it with someone else. So goddamn jealous. I ain't gonna worry about it though. Let's just get spacey…not worry about the bastard."

They smoked quietly for a few minutes, getting giggley. They were feeling so relaxed they hardly noted the passing of time until Brenda's daughter walked in and asked, "Hi, where's Shelley?"

"Oh, shit!" June exclaimed. "Got to get goin'. Promised to pick her up at eleven. She's bowling."

"Don't sweat it. Lots of time," Casey interjected.

June and Casey left, arriving at the bowling alley just as the kids were pouring out the front door. Shelley recognized and ran to the car, a big smile for her mother. She couldn't wait to tell her how much fun she had.

Tall, gangly as only young girls can be, she had the athletic grace into which she would one day grow. Her skin, the color of creamy light chocolate milk, demanded that her cheek be stroked. She had large dark brown eyes in a sensitive face, her head crowned with reddish brown bouncy curls. June should have noticed the beauty she had helped to create, but was occupied with her own needs. All the way home the little girl babbled about her evening and the great time she had with her friends—giggling about her bowling score. June nodded occasionally to pretend interest…her mind otherwise occupied.

When they got home, Casey pulled into her drive. June thanked her for the ride. Then she and Shelley walked across the street hand in hand. "It's late, honey. Better get ready for bed."

Shelley kissed her mother goodnight and went into her tiny bedroom towards the back of the little ranch house. It was filled with dolls, stuffed animals and other little girl things. She crawled into bed clutching a scraggly stuffed bear in her arms.

June undressed in her room and put on a long dressing gown that tied in front, wearing only a short nightie beneath. She went into the living room furnished with cheap furniture and settled into a faux leather couch. She clicked on the television and tuned it to an MTV station, trying to settle down and enjoy the remainder of her earlier high. Too restless to sleep—besides, it was only midnight—she didn't really resent Shelley, but she would like to be able to party when she wanted. Shelley inhibited her to some extent. Hearing a light knock on her front door, she welcomed it…probably one of her friends. *Maybe I can find a little action yet tonight,* she thought.

CHAPTER THREE

Stately old homes lined Main Street, north of Milltown's square, once housing Milltown's more wealthy residents. The homes long since had metamorphosed into offices for lawyers, accountants, insurance salespeople and other similar businesses—everything but the residences for which they had been created. Farther north, small business strips appeared on each side of Main Street dedicated to convenience stores, funeral parlors, beauty shops, pizza establishments and video rentals. None of it was the same as when Joseph and his wife first saw Milltown and made the decision that it was to be their home—the place where they wanted to raise their family.

Still farther north, major shopping centers appeared created for the likes of Wal-Mart, Kmart, Target and Kohl's as well as numerous restaurants and fast food emporiums, all designed to keep Milltown's residents near home—no reason to travel to Akron or Cleveland for shopping.

North of the city limits were open fields and an occasional business dedicated to pleasure. *Tracks*, a bar and restaurant combination on North Main Street a couple of miles past Milltown's city limits, was, during the week, a typical neighborhood bar catering to tired and thirsty workers stopping for a relaxing drink at the end of the day. The bar was separated from the restaurant by a dance floor designed in such a way as to protect those wanting to drink quietly at the bar from those interested in dining. Even so, during the busy meal times, some customers chose to have their meal served at the bar. In this way, a patron's drinking time wasn't diminished by the need to move elsewhere for food. The bandstand, at the rear of the dance floor, could, and on weekends did, accommodate a live band or disc jockey.

On Friday and Saturday nights, younger crowds were expected because of the live rock or country bands. Unfortunately for such patrons, the surrounding open fields were ideal for Township and State Police Departments to supplement their coffers by lurking in wait for those careless enough to operate their motor vehicles after quaffing sufficient alcoholic beverages to test in excess of the legal limit. The fields were also gathering places for litter and trash that wasn't allowed to penetrate the uptown area. It was a different world and the treatment of it was reflected in the attitude of its inhabitants.

On most evenings, the bar was tended by a good-looking young man, named Tony Nuncio. He was all that was needed during the week, but on weekends his duties were augmented by a cadre of attractive young ladies in short skirts and low-cut blouses brought in to service the several tables scattered around the room surrounding the band stand, encourage the sale of beverages and make sure the patrons enjoy themselves. Bouncers in tight T-shirts and jeans wandered through the bar on weekends as well to maintain sufficient order that beverage sales were not interrupted.

Tony's wardrobe consisted of tight T-shirts to show off his washboard abs, sleeves torn off at the shoulder to advertise his biceps and hint at his virility. He and Jimmy Takas were the same age. Jimmy, one of the regulars at *Tracks*, enjoyed being there both during the week and on weekends. Though the two men had been in school together, they weren't friends. Tony, with his dark good looks and swinging lifestyle, was an athlete and popular with the girls. Never quite good enough for an athletic scholarship, he had no desire to attend college anyway. He and his friends, legal age or not, hung out at *Tracks* while still going to school. His goal in life was to own a bar like *Tracks*, where all the good things in life—booze and broads—were available. He began working there right out of high school busing tables, washing glasses and cleaning up. The owner, not a Milltown resident, having noticed Tony's size and athleticism, gave him the opportunity to work as bouncer and finally bartender—the apex of his career objective. Tony also wasn't above making a little money under the table—dealing. *Life is good,* he thought while polishing the gleaming bar that was his domain.

Jimmy Takas, on the other hand, was small, not athletic and would not be very popular with the girls except that he was an exceptionally good dancer, much in demand on the dance floor, if nowhere else. He enjoyed the opportunity to hold girls and feel their young bodies move.

On this Friday night, April the fourth, Jimmy was perched on his favorite bar stool, elbows splayed on the bar, close to the drinks and back to the wall so he could watch the action on the dance floor. His elbows, and those of the multitude of drinkers worshiping at the bar, helped to keep the bar highly polished. Jimmy was always hopeful that he might find on the dance floor what he was on the prowl for—girls and drugs—not necessarily in that order. He was there every weekend and as often during the week as possible. Short and slight, light brown hair parted on the left and long enough in front to hang over his be-spectacled eyes as though trying to hide them. Always well-groomed in the most recent fashion, he wasn't noticeable. He had long outgrown his acned youth that left scarred remembrances. Perhaps it was the memory of that condition that caused him to keep his head lowered while peering through the top of his glasses.

On this particular Friday night, Jimmy paused only long enough for a haircut on his way from work and a brief stop at home to change from his work clothes into something more comfortable—tan slacks, unbuttoned flowered shirt over a silky white T-shirt and black mocassin loafers. On his way out the door he yelled to his mother, "See you later, Ma," and rushed to *Tracks* to begin his weekend. His mother was disappointed because, as always, she had prepared a good dinner for him. As usual, he didn't notice. She said nothing, knowing Jimmy would react badly to anything she might say.

Jimmy saw nothing wrong with being thirty-two and still living with his parents. He impregnated an otherwise nice girl who had a bit too much to drink shortly after his high school graduation, married her and in quick order fathered a second daughter. His wife tired fairly quickly of his irresponsible ways but endured them because of the little girls. Finally, shortly after the youngest child was born she acceded to her mother's demands and informed Jimmy she would no longer to tolerate his erratic conduct and insisted he leave. Jimmy wasn't a fighter so shrugging acquiesced to her demands. His first reaction was to move back with his folks. It never occurred to him that it might be an imposition. He knew his parents adored the two little girls he fathered and would want to have access to them. He was doing his folks a favor by moving back into their small home.

Even though his wife had custody of the girls, Jimmy said he loved them but other things always seemed to interfere with his supporting or visiting them. He did try to see them from time to time, mostly because it pleased his mother and kept her off his back. Like all children, completely unaware of their parents' failings, they loved him. They especially enjoyed visiting with and being cared for by their grandmother. That worked for Jimmy, since their presence didn't impede his lifestyle. Hanging on to a regular job was difficult, so he didn't make all the support payments ordered by the Court. He would make up for it by not seeing the girls, except for his mother's influence. He didn't want to alienate her or jeopardize his living arrangement.

Living with his parents was only slightly awkward. They had, at his insistence, made an apartment for him in the basement of their modest home, and even though they expected him to pay rent, they didn't pressure him for it. Besides, he didn't spend much time there. He went to work when he had a job, came home to change clothes and go out for the evening. He didn't like to take meals with his parents . When he was in their presence for any length of time, they asked too many questions and had too many suggestions on how he could improve himself and his habits. He was satisfied with his life. Work when he had to, get drunk as often as possible and get high when he could afford or scrounge drugs. He never understood why others were critical of his lifestyle—and sometimes wondered why he wasn't completely satisfied with it.

Sitting at the bar where he could watch the room, Jimmy's hands clasped a glass of Long Island iced tea—a favorite drink. He'd already had several as well as a couple of bottles of beer with dinner. He showed little effect from the drinks, except that he slumped lower on the stool, supporting himself more heavily by his elbows. Earlier he had eaten at the bar, *Tracks'* Friday special…fried fish, cole slaw and chips smothered in ketchup. Around ten o'clock, the usual crowd, many of whom Jimmy recognized, started coming in for the noisy music and rowdy talk.

A local rock band was setting up for the night. The leader's girlfriend always accompanied him to his gigs. Jimmy became acquainted with her over the months they had been playing there and would dance with her several times during the evening—the musician considered Jimmy no challenge. He danced with a number of other girls as the evening progressed. He was actually a pretty good dancer. Even though occupied with the music, he surveyed the room for June Westlock or Clarence Knedder, or anyone else who could supply his needs. He was beginning to feel a little desperate.

It was still early. Jimmy knew that sooner or later someone would show from whom he could cadge a rock or two. He expected June to make an appearance. She and her sister usually did on weekends. Jimmy wasn't aware that she was occupied with her daughter on this evening. She always had something, and was usually willing to share. He wasn't particular what kind of drugs—anything would improve the way he felt. The several drinks Jimmy had while waiting already started to work their magic on him—but he felt the accustomed agitation rising.

He called the bartender over, "Hey, Tony. Where is everyone? I need something more than you got."

"You've had enough, Jimmy. We don't allow drugs or anything like that here. My job's important to me. The boss would kick me out in a second if he knew I allowed anything like that to go on here."

It wasn't that Tony was unwilling to earn a little extra cash by getting some drugs for regulars, he just didn't trust Jimmy. Besides, Jimmy was acting kind of queer tonight.

Jimmy was just drunk and desperate enough to be a little bold. "Cut the bullshit. You know who's here I could score from."

Tony turned his back on Jimmy and walked away, not so much to see if another patron needed service, but to get away from Jimmy. Jimmy had a tendency to get disagreeable when he didn't get his way or if he felt someone was holding out on him.

Several drinks later—it was close to one o'clock in the morning—Jimmy had seen a number of people from whom he had been able to inveigle weed or a rock in the past. No one admitted to having anything that Jimmy could buy or beg. Just talking and thinking about it increased his appetite. The need was getting stronger with every passing minute and Jimmy more and more agitated.

Jimmy signaled Tony, "Tony, you seen June? She should be here by now. Always has something."

"Nope. I really don't expect her, Jimmy. It's late. She and Knedder broke up, I hear, and she's got her daughter to take care of. I doubt she has anything you want anyway," Tony responded impatiently.

Jimmy was feeling belligerent, "Bullshit, Tony. I've always been able to score from her and Clarence. You fuckin' know it."

"Look, Jimmy. You've had enough. Go home," Tony suggested as reasonably as he could.

"Don't fuck with me, Tony. I'm goin' get what I want," Jimmy slurred, "and you know goddamn well where it is. I got money to pay for it," and struggled some loose bills from his pocket.

"That's it, Jimmy. You're cut off, and if you don't get the fuck out of here now, I'll throw you out!"

Jimmy started to argue, but as Tony stepped from behind the bar, Jimmy scurried out the door, muttering, "I'll get what I want...fucker ain't gonna stop me..."

Jimmy staggered from the bar and into the parking lot. Looked around for his car and checked to see if the cops were hiding in their usual place. There was a particular highway patrol officer who was mean and loved to bust drunks. He hid behind the building most nights. *No one in sight,* Jimmy mumbled, *Must be somewhere else busting someone's balls. Sure don't need another D.U.I.*

Jimmy searched his pockets for keys, carefully unlocked his car door and found the slot for the ignition. Checking around again—he knew the cops usually hung out in the parking lot or hid in the nearby field waiting to pounce—he started his car and headed south on Main Street, intending to get off the main drag as soon as possible. He knew where June lived, just East of Main on North Stubb. He'd been there lots of times—usually doing one type of drug or another with June's live-in, Clarence Knedder.

Jimmy drove carefully, as drunks do, and found June's house with no difficulty. It was a small three-bedroom basement-less ranch, probably built shortly after World War II. The lap siding, much of which could use repair, had once been painted white but, over the years, faded to a dirty grey. It was badly in need of paint and a little loving care. The front windows were flanked by non-functioning shutters that had once been a vibrant red—now dulled with age, also in need of repair. One hung loose and looked as though it had been that way for some time. The small front yard was in grass, but the house lacked shrubs or flowers. It was just a small rectangular box where someone lived—it was not a home. A bright mercury vapor light from a neighbor's backyard shone on the detached garage at the rear of the lot, so Jimmy pulled only a short way into the drive to stay in as much of the shadows as possible.

Turning off the motor, he walked carefully up the walk to the front door. Stepping on the small functional concrete stoop, not big enough for anything but a single flower pot to decorate…if anyone wanted to…no one apparently did…he looked in the small eye-level square window in the door. He knew someone was home. He could see lights inside. June's daughter must be asleep in back.

June answered Jimmy's knock—the doorbell didn't work—dressed in a robe. *Look like it's all she got on,* he thought as she stood in the door with the living room light behind her. Her sexuality didn't move him—other appetites were working.

Yawning, June said, "Hi, Jimmy. Come on in. What you doing here so late?"

"Where's Clarence?" he slurred.

"He don't live here no more…I kicked him out…tole him to stay away."

"I need a couple of rocks or somethin'." He could smoke them in a marijuana cigarette, or if he snorted a couple of lines, it would fix him up all right. The need was great.

"I don't got anything in the house, Jimmy. You know I don't want anything around my little girl."

"Oh, bullshit. You always got somethin'. How many times Clarence and I party here with you? I know you do. I really need something tonight. Can't see my kids this week and…girlfriend cut me off. I really need somethin'!" He pushed his way past June and walked toward the linen closet in the hall. That was where she always kept the fixings.

June blocked his way. She didn't want him anywhere near her daughter's bedroom, saying, "I told you I don't got nothin'. Hoped you might. I could use a jolt myself," she suggested hopefully.

Jimmy turned and grabbed her by the shoulders. "I need somethin'…now!"

She wasn't in the mood for his drunken persistence. June was as tall as he and could have easily pushed him away, but didn't want to make a fuss and wake her daughter. "Take it easy, Jimmy. Maybe we can get something. Why don't you go over to Bub's? He usually got something." as she walked him toward the kitchen pointing out the kitchen window. "See, his lights are on. Probably on the stoop. It's such a nice night. I'll call and tell him you're coming over. Check there," she babbled nervously.

Bub Draco lived around the corner on Franklin Ave. His house could be seen from June's backyard. Like most of those living in the neighborhood, he came alive after dark—night people. He had a day job, but spent most evenings working on or riding his motorcycle. He wore biker garb, muscular arms growing out of a well-worn leather vest, captain's hat sitting on the back of his head allowing free rein to his black curls. He was sitting on his front steps sucking on a long-stemmed beer bottle and talking to a neighbor, who appeared equally as rough.

Jimmy scurried out the front door of June's house and ran to the corner…his need sobering him enough to steady his legs. He crossed the street and saw Bub and another man sitting on the stoop holding on to brown bottles lifted occasionally to their mouths.

Running up the front walk of the house, Jimmy called, "Bub, I need some coke—you know…a little crack."

"What the fuck's wrong with you, man? Talking like that here. My kids are watching TV in the house. I don't do that stuff and, even if I did, there's no fuckin' way I'd give you any."

"I got money, man. I'll pay. I really need somethin'," reaching into his pocket.

"Get the fuck out of here. I don't got nothing." Bub said threateningly as he stood and moved towards Jimmy.

Jimmy yelled, "Well, go get some, man. You know who's got it. Get me some."

As Bub climbed to his feet threateningly, Jimmy, slurring his words, muttered, "Aw, shit. Maybe I'll just kill myself…don't got nothing…can't see my kids…nothing…" backing towards the sidewalk.

Ignoring the tirade, Bub stalked towards Jimmy, muscles rippling, talking quietly enough so only Jimmy could hear. Even in his drunken state, Jimmy knew he was in trouble. "I told June I didn't have anything and, even if I did, I ain't gonna share with you. Whatever I get, I need for me and my *friends*. Take June—go see Cockroach. You got a car. She knows where he lives—get the fuck outta here!"

Open hands in front of him, palms out to stop the advance, Jimmy sniveled, "I didn' mean nothing, man. June sent me over. Said you got stuff. Sorry, man. I didn' mean nothing." He backed towards the sidewalk. As soon as he could, he turned and ran towards June's house.

The lights in the living room were out except for the dim shine of the television screen—the door closed. Jimmy banged on the door, "You fuckin' cunt. Let me in. He was gonna kick my ass. You knew it. Let me in!" Jimmy screamed.

June, neither fearing Jimmy nor wanting her daughter awakened, opened the door.

Bub had called as Jimmy scurried down the walk, saying, "Take him over to Forge Street. Get him a fix if you want any peace tonight." He'd seen her there earlier talking to Cockroach, who was a constantly reliable source—the neighborhood supplier. "I got some from Cockroach tonight. Send Jimmy there."

"Okay, asshole," June said to Jimmy as she opened the door, "Drive me over to Forge Street—Cockroach's house," stepping out and pulling the door closed behind her. She hadn't dressed, still wearing only the light robe over her short night dress.

Not trusting her completely, Jimmy followed June to his car, found the key still in the ignition, started the engine and backed rapidly from the drive. He crossed Main Street into the older part of town and found Forge Street without difficulty. By this time, it was nearly two o'clock in the morning and he was sober enough to watch more carefully for cops. He followed June's instruction and stopped in front of the house halfway down the block. The porch light shone a pale amber and lights were lit throughout the house. A number of the houses on the block showed light. Night people.

June walked up to the door while Jimmy waited impatiently, motor running. He couldn't hear the conversation but saw June talking to the attractive black girl who appeared at the door. She kept shaking her head. Finally June shrugged and returned to the car.

"She don't have nothing, Jimmy. Cockroach ain't home yet and she's afraid things are getting pretty hot. He only had a little bit tonight and it's gone. She used up what she had. Can't get no more until Cockroach gets home. I know she's telling me true."

Jimmy was beginning to lose his temper, "I don't believe her or you, cunt. You always got enough for yourself. I want mine."

He raced the motor as June got into the car and hurried back to her house, arriving there quickly. June jumped out of the car and ran to the front door. As Jimmy walked up to the house behind her, he noticed movement on the porch across the street. *Someone's sitting there smoking,* Jimmy thought so kept his hands to himself, even though he wanted to get all over June.

They entered the house. June tried to close the door behind her before Jimmy could enter. He pushed her out of his way and slammed the door behind him. June scurried across the room and picked up the phone from the small table next to the couch. Jimmy grabbed for her and she ran into the kitchen, knocking over a large floor wicker basket with dried flowers in it. Jimmy followed…. He was going to get something tonight.

*   *   *

At twenty-five minutes after six on the morning of April 5, June Westlock's estranged boyfriend, Clarence Knedder, sitting on the edge of the couch in the living room of the North Stubb home, dialed 911.

"What is the emergency?" Dispatcher Sharon Walls asked in a calming voice.

"Please send the cops! It's awful! Please send the cops…."

"What is the problem?"

"It's on North Stubb! Send the cops!"

The operator had already picked up the street address from her screen. The shift supervisor, Sergeant Hilary Dale of the Milltown Police Department, was slouching in front of the dispatcher's desk visiting with her and waiting patiently for his shift to end so he could go home for a much-needed good day's sleep. They'd worked together for several years…mostly on the night shift. With little else to do, they would on occasion chitchat about nothing important. Just a way to make the night go faster.

Sergeant Dale was tall and broad shouldered with a slim waist advertising his more than irregular visits to the gym. Craggy features, bushy eyebrows sitting squarely over icy-blue eyes and beneath his shaved head made him an intimidating figure. It stood him in good stead as a police officer, but belied his intelligence and gentle nature. His stern appearance discouraged most from commenting on the poetry of his name.

Sharon Walls motioned for him to look at the screen, mouthing, "Looks like trouble."

The North Stubb street address appeared on that screen fairly frequently so was familiar to both of them. He whispered back to the dispatcher, "I know those folks. I'll head there now. If I need help, I'll call."

"I think you'd better get someone to go with you. He sounds real bad," the dispatcher whispered, hand over her microphone.

As Dale rushed from the headquarters building, he almost ran into Rob Stanford, a uniformed patrolman, who was just walking in. Dale said, "There's a problem at Westlock's. Follow me there."

The youthful officer responded, "I was supposed to clock out, but I'll grab my cruiser. Be just a couple of minutes behind you."

The dispatcher tried to keep the caller on the phone, but could get nothing useful from him. Within minutes she was able to hear Sergeant Dale's voice in the background over the phone. Obviously he had arrived at the scene. There was nothing further needed from her, so, after waiting for a few moments to see if Dale would come on line, she disconnected, noting in her log all that had transpired. She had heard no sirens. Since Dale didn't know what he would find when he arrived at June Westlock's home, he used neither siren nor the flashing blue light with which his unmarked car was equipped.

*   *   *

Westlock's home was so close to the police station that Dale arrived there at twenty-eight minutes after six, just three minutes after the 911 call came to the station. *Oh shit!* he thought, *what happened at June's house now?* He knocked on the front door and walked in without waiting for a response. The door was not locked…entering directly into the living room. Dale could see Clarence Knedder, a tall, stockily built black man in his mid thirties, sitting on the couch, face in his hands, sobbing loudly, "She's dead…."

Sergeant Dale knew Knedder well because of many police contacts— the most recent being a court order delivered by Dale to Knedder not to be within five hundred feet of June's house.

Goddamn, what'd Knedder do now? Dale thought, but said aloud, "Who's dead? Where's June? Calm down, Clarence. What's happened? What the

36

hell you doing here? You know June had a restraining order on you. I gave it to you myself last week. You'd better have a goddamn good reason for being here."

Knedder didn't look up, but pointed toward the back of the house. Sergeant Dale, drawing his service weapon, started to walk across the living room toward the bedroom area. "Not there," Knedder said. "In the laundry room—through the kitchen."

Changing directions, Dale followed Knedder's instructions and entered the kitchen noting the disarray, walking through it to an arched passageway leading into the laundry room. It was beginning to get light out. It looked like it would be another nice, sunny northern Ohio day. The backdoor to the house opened directly into the laundry room area but was now closed and chained. No light penetrated from outside. It would have been pretty dark in there except for the naked light bulb hanging over and shining down on the dead, almost naked body of June Westlock. The string pull that operated the light had a shines-in-the-dark skeleton as a macabre ornament dangling several feet above June's face.

Looking through the arched doorway into the laundry room, the sergeant saw June lying on the floor in a pool of blood. Her robe was open, revealing an expanse of marble-white skin flawed by stab and puncture wounds...some surrounded by dried blood—some bluish in color...that appeared to have been inflicted by a knife or other sharp weapon. Dale had known June for years...she was as close a friend as he could have on the dark side. He liked her. As he observed the viciousness of the attack on her, he could feel his gorge rise. A police officer with more than ten years' experience, he had seen many accident victims with serious injuries, but he had never seen someone he knew as well as June intentionally mutilated this way. Not many deliberate killings at all in Milltown.

There was no doubt in his mind she was dead. Looking around and seeing no immediate danger, he holstered his weapon and carefully reached across the bloody floor and tried to find a carotid pulse. Nothing—her smooth skin was cold to his touch.

He stepped back though the arch and looked at Knedder, who was still slumped on the edge of the couch, face in his hands, sobbing loudly.

"What the fuck'd you do? Why'd you do her like this? Did you touch her?"

Knedder shook his head from side to side, mumbling into his hands, "No! nooo! She wasn't breathing. She's naked and there's blood all over—"

"You find her, or kill her? How long you been here?" Dale demanded, face reddening, anger rising.

"I don' know what time I got here. I don't got no watch. I found her like that," gesturing towards the back of the house.

Remembering what he was and why he was there, despite the emotional impact, the sergeant determined to handle the matter as professionally as possible. Taking a long, calming breath, he decided not to ask any more questions until Knedder had been Mirandized. The Supreme Court said, in a case identified as the State of Arizona versus Miranda, some years earlier, that nothing a defendant said could be used against him in a court of law unless he had been advised of his Constitutional rights and warned that whatever he said could be used against him. These came to be known as the Miranda warnings. The warnings were printed on a card every police officer carried. Extracting the card from his pocket, Dale began, "You have the right to re—"

Just then the sergeant heard an approaching siren. He didn't yet see the red and blue lights flashing on the roof of Patrolman Stanford's police car but decided to wait at the front door instead of continuing with Miranda. Within seconds, Rob Stanford, the uniformed officer Dale had spoken to earlier, arrived at the scene. Patrolman Stanford, Dale knew, did everything by the book. He was pleased with the young fellow's professionalism and intended to ask him to take Clarence into custody, Mirandize him and transport him to the station.

As Patrolman Stanford walked through the front door, Harold Thuman, Mill County's newly elected prosecutor, tried to follow him in. Thuman, dressed in jeans and a light jacket, appeared slightly disheveled. The youthful prosecutor was tall, well built and handsome in a rugged way, except for some softness around the middle and darkening pouches beneath the eyes. His dark brown hair was slightly unruly and shot through with just the right amount of grey to give a distinguished appearance. A shock of hair hung down over Thuman's right eye and looked as though it might be trained that way. Eyebrows, jet black, formed a single dividing line between forehead and nose. Currently unmarried, he usually dressed in well-tailored suits, starched white shirt and power tie as though a uniform. He did not appear his usual self, so it took a moment for Dale to recognize him.

Dale reached his arm in front of Thuman and blocked the way into the residence. He noticed that the almost covered right eye was blinking fairly rapidly. "Why are you here, Mr. Thuman?" Dale asked.

"I and was just getting up—had my scanner tuned to the police channel and heard the call. Decided to go on station and was on my way when I heard the siren, so followed it here. Thought I'd better look in and give a hand if I could," he replied.

Dale wondered, *Wonder why's he up this early? Last prosecutor never took this kind of interest in our work.. Hope he's as good as he is ambitious*, asking instead, "Are you all right?"

"Yes, of course. Why?"

"Well, looks like you might have something in your eye," Dale gestured towards Thuman's face.

"No...no...oh, that's just a little tic—when I'm tired. Got some medicine for it—but left it home."

Dale, his hand still obstructing the way, explained, "Can't let you go in though, Mr. Thuman. Got to secure the scene for the detectives."

"I'll just look around. I'll likely have to try this case—always like to get a feeling about a crime scene and whatever happened here. Maybe help with your investigation," Thuman pressed.

"You know better than that," Dale said, taking Thuman's arm and ushering him out the front door, pulling it closed behind him. "It'd be my ass...be in plenty of trouble if I allowed the crime scene to be contaminated. You know that. Don't want to give some slick defense lawyer the chance to fuck up this case."

Dale stood with Thuman on the front stoop waiting for the detectives to arrive, saying nothing to one another. Dale was uncomfortable and would be relieved to turn the investigative responsibility over to the homicide detective. He was also anxious to be rid of Thuman, thinking, *I'm never comfortable with a civilian on the scene—Thuman hasn't had police training as far as I know…Don't want to get in trouble with him or my superior. Hate this shit.* He waited, appearing unperturbed, wondering, *Why did Knedder have to do her like that?* as other police vehicles, detectives and emergency units began to arrive.

The flashing police lights and the arrival of other official-looking vehicles—all with the appropriate sounds and lights—began to attract the neighbors. A crowd began to form outside the little house—many of the people looked like they had not yet been to bed. Night people curious about one of their own.

CHAPTER FOUR

Saturday morning Jimmy Takas woke in his own bed. He had no memory of how he got there—or of how he got home for that matter. It was almost noon. He was still wearing his trousers, one shoe and both socks. It was the ringing of the telephone that aroused him. Since it kept ringing, he assumed no one else was home to answer it. Reaching for the extension on the nightstand next to his bed, he picked it up, mumbling, "Hello."

"Jimmy? This is Laura."

It took a moment, but he finally was able to put the name to his ex-wife's voice.

"We need to talk, " she added.

Fighting through the familiar morning grogginess and headache, Jimmy tried to put her off, "Laura, I just woke up and I don't feel so good," but she insisted. She sounded queer, he thought.

Finally, "Laura, what's the matter with you?" he asked impatiently.

Laura responded, her words stumbling across each other, "Haven't you heard? The police called this morning—looking for you. June's dead. Somebody killed her. They said you was with her last night. She died sometime last night. They want to talk to you. Were you there? Do you know anything about it?"

Jimmy broke out in a sweat and, unexpectedly, started crying—surprising himself. His head was so fuzzy he had no actual memory of anything that happened the previous night. A vision of something bad flashed through his mind. He didn't know what. He remembered something about blood on his shirt. It was all so hazy.

Concerned by his sobbing, Laura said, "Jimmy, Sergeant Dale called this morning. He's looking for you. Wants to talk to you. He said you was with her last night. Were you? Tell me!"

Jimmy was unable to compose himself sufficiently to talk to his ex-wife, so he muttered, "Goodbye," and hung up the phone.

* * *

In a daze, Jimmy walked into the bathroom, splashed cold water on his face and took several deep breaths. Finally he felt capable of talking without starting to cry again. He thought, *What the hell's wrong with me?* He returned to his bed—a surplus military army cot—sat on the edge of it and picked up the phone. Holding it in his hand, he looked around the room, noting its dishabille. It was furnished with used pieces picked up at the local Goodwill store and containing only such memorabilia as his mom had collected from Jimmy's school days. None of it meant anything to Jimmy. Taking a deep breath, he called Laura back.

"Laura, tell me again what happened," he asked in a calmer voice.

She responded, "Jimmy, June is dead. Someone killed her. You got to call the police. Sergeant Dale said he has to talk to you. That's all he would tell me. I didn't tell him that you were living with your mom, but I'm pretty sure he will find out quick enough. You'd best give him a call."

Jimmy hung up the phone and sat on the edge of his bed thinking. He lit a cigarette and smoked it down to the filter. He lit a second, took a deep breath, called the police station and asked for Sergeant Dale. "This is Jimmy Takas. You want to talk to me?" he asked when the sergeant came on the phone.

"Sure do. Will you come in voluntarily, or do you want me to send a car for you?"

"Nah…I can come in. Do you want to see me now?"

"Well, why don't you just tell me where you are," the officer said, unnecessarily since the name and address that he wasn't familiar with flashed up on his computer screen. He wanted to see if Jimmy would be truthful.

"I'm at home—living with my folks. But I'll come down as soon as I get washed up and dressed. Slept in a little," trying to laugh without much success—wanting to keep it light.

Jimmy showered and dressed in clean jeans and T-shirt, arriving at the police station some thirty minutes later. Sergeant Dale was waiting for him. He directed Jimmy back into the recesses of the station, where Jimmy had never been. He opened a painted metal door leading into a small room, the walls of which were concrete block painted an institutional light blue. The room was furnished with a metal table bolted to the floor in front of a backless stool, also bolted down. Jimmy was instructed to sit on the bench. There was hardly enough room for Jimmy to squeeze past the table and seat himself as instructed.

The only other piece of furniture in the room, a straight-backed chair, was pulled up to the other side of the table nearest to the door. Sergeant Dale seated himself in that chair, effectively blocking egress from the room. Jimmy felt more than a little claustrophobic.

"Okay, Jimmy, got any idea why I have you here?" Dale started.

"No, not really, except Laura called me and said something about June being killed," choking on the last word. "But I don't know what that's got to do with me."

Ignoring Jimmy's remark, the sergeant said, "We found June Westlock this morning—stabbed to death."

Jimmy responded, "Phew…yeah? Like I said, got a call from my ex. She just told me June was dead and you wanted to talk to me 'cause I seen her Friday night. She didn't tell me she was stabbed."

"She was killed in her house. We're talking to everyone we know was with her last night." Sergeant Dale continued, "Before we talk about last night, I need some background information."

He then asked Jimmy for his full name, the correct spelling, his birth date, social security number, address and place of employment—all the basic information needed for the standard police report dictated by the form Dale spread on the table before him. Jimmy wanted to read it upside down, but was fearful of looking at it.

Finally Jimmy asked, "You know all that shit about me—why you asking me that stuff?"

When Dale stared at Jimmy without responding, the nervous young man provided the requested information in a monotone, never looking up from his hands folded on the table before him, hair hanging over his eyes.

When Dale had finished filling in all the blanks on the report form, he said, "Whenever I have somebody on station, I have to read them their rights. You're not under arrest or anything, I want you to understand that. You can leave anytime you want. No one can stop you."

Jimmy was aware that the facts did not comport with the words. There was no way he could get past the sergeant, so he said, "Um, okay."

"Now do you read, write and understand the English language?"

"Why are you asking me these questions? You know me. Are you recording this?"

Again ignoring Jimmy's question, Sergeant Dale said, "We know you were with June last night. She was killed and we know you were there. Just answer my questions and then tell me what happened." He adopted a much more aggressive manner and authoritative tone.

Jimmy was getting more and more frightened. At first he tried to deny being at June's house…then said he didn't remember much…he'd been drinking an awful lot. Finally he admitted going to her house after leaving *Tracks*, where he had "enough to drink that I wasn't real sure of what was going down." He explained he was looking for Clarence. "June tol' me he don't live there no more so I left. That's all I know."

Dale looked at Jimmy long enough for Jimmy to feel even more uneasy than he had. Then placing a small tape recorder on the table, he pointed toward it and said, "Jimmy, we record all our talks. It's routine. Now cut the bullshit and give me some straight answers."

"I don't like this very much," Jimmy squirmed.

Dale slipped in the Miranda warnings, saying, "Look, Jimmy, if you feel threatened for some reason, you can always call a lawyer. If you can't afford a lawyer, one can be appointed for you. You have the right to remain silent and anything you say can be used against you in court. Anytime you want to stop the questions and talk to a lawyer, just tell me and we'll stop. If you want to answer some questions now, you can stop me at any time. Do you understand all that?"

"Yeah, unhuhn."

"If you're okay with all this, just sign this form," handing Jimmy a pen and the Miranda rights form he took from the file folder into which he had slipped the questionnaire he had filled with Jimmy's vital statistics.

Jimmy, not knowing what else to do and feeling the pressure of Dale's stare, scribbled his name on the paper without reading it. Dale didn't care, the form had Jimmy's signature.

"Now, Jimmy," Sergeant Dale continued a little more kindly, "please tell me everything you did Friday night starting at, say, about seven o' clock in the evening."

"Uh, okay. I went to *Tracks* right from work. Well, I got a haircut first and changed clothes. Got there, I don't know, about five thirty or so. Wanted to be there for happy hour and Friday night's fish special. Had a couple of beers and dinner. Then I drove over to the house of my buddy and no one was home. So—"

Dale interrupted, "What buddy and where does he live?"

"His name is Roger and he lives out in the Township, but he wasn' home...."

Dale made a note of the name as Jimmy continued, "So I went home, took a shower. Wanted to wash my hair 'cause I had a haircut and wanted to get the clippings out. Talked to my mom for a few minutes and then left again."

"What time did you get home?"

"Oh, about seven thirty or eight o'clock. Anyway, since Roger wasn't home, I thought he might go to *Tracks*. We almost always go there on Fridays. I went back to *Tracks*. He wasn' there. Had a few more drinks— Long Island ice tea—danced with a couple girls. They like to dance with me—I'm a pretty good dancer."

"How long did you stay there?"

"Oh, I don' know…. Maybe till one or one thirty. Then I went over to Clarence's house. June was there. Said he wasn' home. She'd kicked him out sometime—I don't know when. Anyway, he wasn't home—hadn't been there for a while. So I went in for a couple of minutes, sat down and just, you know, talked. That's about it. Then left."

"Come on, Jimmy. You went there for drugs. We know June has drugs, or can get them. That's why you went there," Dale said, exasperation creeping into his now roughened voice.

"No. I told ya. I was looking for Clarence."

"Bullshit. Is that why you went over to Bub's house?"

Jimmy wondered how much the sergeant knew about his evening. Maybe he knew more than Jimmy did—his memory was so foggy. "I was looking for Clarence," Jimmy whined.

The questioning went on for several hours, Jimmy getting more and more nervous, the sergeant's voice droning on in a hypnotic manner. Out of the blue, Dale asked, "Do you think Clarence has it in him to kill someone?"

"I, uh…can't see him doing that. He's such an easygoing guy. No…no, I can't see him doing that."

Back and forth the questions went. "What did you have to drink at *Tracks*? Who was tending bar? What time did you leave? Who did you see?" and finally, "Look, there were only two people at June's house last night. One of you killed her. Was it you?"

"No! No! I couldn't do that!" almost whimpering, tears beginning to fall.

"Would you be willing to take a polygraph test?"

"What's that? A lie detector test? Sure."

"Okay. Don't leave town. I got lots more people to talk to and I'll want to talk to you again."

Relief flowed through Jimmy—he was being allowed to leave. "Sure. Sure. Just let me know. I ain't going nowhere."

* * *

Dale and the other officers interviewed all of the persons Jimmy named and confirmed as much of his story as they could. Suspicion growing, Dale knew he had to talk to Jimmy again, so three days later, he had Jimmy picked up at work and brought into the station. Jimmy had been kept under loose surveillance, enough so that Jimmy was aware of seeing police cars wherever he went.

"Jimmy, I talked to lots of people who saw you on Friday night and Saturday morning. We know a lot more about June's killing now. I need to ask you some more questions."

Jimmy sat on the same bench in the same concrete block room, it felt cold, but he was sweating, a stone settling in his stomach. "I don't know what I can add to what we already talked about."

"How was your day at work?" Dale asked innocently.

"The usual. It's hard work and I'm always skinning up my knuckles. You know, working on old motors, wrenches slip and screwdrivers are like chisels. Look at my knuckles."

"Okay. I have to tell you again you aren't under arrest and I did advise you of your rights before. Right?"

"Yeah."

"Okay. The other day we talked about you taking a polygraph test. Remember?"

"Un-huhn," unsettled.

"Okay. I can set the test up for tomorrow."

"Well, I got to work and I hear those things...I don't know...aren't reliable."

Dale interjected, "They're pretty accurate. Besides, they can't be used for or against you in court. They're just a...you know...tool."

"I don't know. You asked me to take a blood test. I went to the hospital like you tol' me to. They took some of my blood. It hurt. When you guys gonna leave me alone?"

"Look, Jimmy, you pass the test and I'm satisfied you been honest with me, I'll never have to talk to you again."

Jimmy said, "I don't want to be no trouble or nothing. But I don't trust those things. I thought you were through with me and now you make me come back here. I can't believe the things you're telling me. I just wanna go back to work. I'll get fired if you don't let me go. Got support payments to make," his whining voice almost pleading.

"You can leave pretty soon, Jimmy. Just a few more questions. Tell me again what you did Friday night. Start after you left work…."

Jimmy sighed and repeated the story several times, always in response to Dale's demands to "Tell me again."

After several hours, Jimmy finally admitted that he had gone to June's house in the early morning hours to get some drugs. He didn't know that June had kicked Clarence out and thought he would be there. "He's always got something." June told him she didn't have anything at home and sent him to a neighbor, saying she would call and tell them to have some stuff ready for him. Jimmy's drug-induced paranoia was deepening and when he got to the neighbors, his need was great. He had little memory of the conversation there except that they wouldn't give him anything. "The guy there scared hell out of me so I left pretty quick."

When he got back to June's she took him to somebody's house. "I don't even know whose house, or exactly where it was, except it was on Forge Street." She promised him drugs would be available. "They said they didn't have none, so I took her back home and left."

"How often did you go to June's house to do drugs?"

"Uh. Quite a bit actually—but I thought it was Clarence's house. She didn't sell or nothing—just always had some. I'd give Clarence money once in a while to help buy the stuff. We'd party there maybe once or twice a week."

"Where in the house did you 'party?'"

"Uh…usually in the laundry room. She'd cut some lines on the dryer or we'd freebase it on a spoon or in a test tube she kept with her stash."

The questions kept coming. "Did you touch anything else in the kitchen? Were you playing with knives? Do you own a knife? Did you lose your cigarette lighter?"

To the last question, Jimmy answered, "Yeah, I must've misplaced my lighter. It was a little, like, Cricket lighter. Don't know where, or when, I lost it."

Looking closely at Jimmy, Dale said, "It was next to June's body, Jimmy. Did you drop it there?"

Jimmy's eyes widened, sweat popped out on his forehead and his hands felt suddenly clammy. "Gee, I must've left it at her house some time ago. Maybe she used it for freebasing. Don't know when I lost it. Know I didn't have it for a long time."

More questions followed. Finally the door opened and Lieutenant Richard Tells, a tall, balding man with a substantial girth, stuck his head in. "Anyone hungry? I'm going to McDonald's and can bring something back."

Dale said, "Yeah. I can use something. You, Jimmy?"

"No, no...I just want out of here. Got to get back to work."

"Pretty soon. Just a few more questions."

Tells was gone for some thirty minutes. When he returned he had a sack of hamburgers, fries and coffee. "Who wants what?" he said, sitting on the corner of the table next to Jimmy. Looking up, Jimmy felt completely intimidated, more by the size of the big man looming over him than the questioning. He had kind of gotten used to Sergeant Dale.

Jimmy said sulkily, "I don't want nothing—except to get out of here—back to work." He'd been there more than three hours.

Tells turned toward Jimmy and said in a voice much less kind than that used by Dale, "Jimmy, this is what we know. You went to June's house looking for drugs. She didn't have any. You drove her, in your car, to Forge Street. Couldn't get anything there. Took her back to her house. Went in—had sex with her—and left her dead on the laundry room floor. Your lighter was next to her body and your fingerprints in her blood on the dryer. You killed her and aren't man enough to admit it."

Jimmy jumped as far to his to his feet as he could get, crammed in as he was behind the metal table, crying, "No! No! That isn't true! I couldn't do nothing like that! She was my friend...." The last sliding into a sob.

Tells, hand on Jimmy's shoulder, pushed him back onto the bench. Cringing, he sat, face in his hands, tears streaming as he sobbed aloud.

Neither Tells nor Dale showed any sympathy. Dale said, "We offered you a polygraph test. If you're telling us the truth, you'd want to take it. We'll set it up for tomorrow morning."

"Let me think. I'll call you in the morning if I can make it," Jimmy whispered.

"Jimmy, we don't have many murders in this town. We don't know if you intended to kill June or not, but we know you did. We're giving you a chance to make it right. You'd best take it. It's time for you to be a man."

"This is like a fairy tale…a bad dream…. Let me think. I'll call you…."

"I don't believe you, Jimmy. But I have to let you go for now. Can't hold you so I'm going to let you go, but you'd better stick around. I'll want to hear from you first thing tomorrow morning. In the meantime we'll be keeping an eye on you. We'll be watching you. Running away or suicide isn't the answer. You won't find it in drugs either. Tell us what we want to know. You'll feel a lot better."

Looking at the sergeant, Jimmy said, "I ain't gonna do any of those things. Just let me out of here. I promise I'll get back to you tomorrow morning. Is it okay if I hit it now?"

"Go ahead, Jimmy. See you tomorrow."

Jimmy, completely traumatized by the conversation, left the police station and drove home, totally unaware of his surroundings. As though waking up, he found himself in his driveway—his parents weren't home. It came to him what he had to do. He walked into the house, down the stairs to his basement apartment, showered, changed and packed his few possessions into a gym bag. He returned to his car, looked around to see if anyone were watching, and left heading south, thinking, *Maybe I can get to Florida—get work there*…. When he got to Lexington, Kentucky, he stopped and called Laura, saying, "I'm leaving. I don't know what happened but the cops won't leave me alone. Say goodbye to the girls for me. I love you."

She could hear him crying.

CHAPTER FIVE

Joseph was pretty adept at kidding himself, so convinced he wanted nothing to do with the June Westlock stabbing case, he was nonetheless engrossed in the coverage, just, as he told himself, *being curious.* He snatched the paper each morning on his way to the office and couldn't wait to read the continuing saga. Milltown had not had what was considered an unsolved murder in years; that is, except for the Mountain City case Joseph tried the previous year. The killing of June Westlock was the subject of daily conversation at the grocery stores, lunch counters and beauty parlors, especially at the *Round Table*, where Joseph usually took lunch...the town agog.

The *Milltown Reporter* printed, under Stan Marten's byline, in its almost daily coverage of the case during the week following the murder:

MILLTOWN - The drapes were drawn across the living room window, but a light was burning inside the Milltown home of June Westlock, age 31. The window bore a crime watch decal. The neighbors keeping a gruesome vigil talked quietly among themselves. A young lady holding an infant in her arms said, "Every time I look over there I can't believe it happened. This is awful. That light was never on. The TV was on all the time but no light."

It has been two days since the body of Westlock was discovered in the laundry room of her home. The neighbors still can't believe that the calm of their North Stubb Ave. neighborhood has been shattered. "My wife's spooked...she wants to move," said one of the neighbors.

An autopsy by the Cuyahoga County Coroner's Office determined that the cause of death was a knife cut that severed the aorta, the main artery carrying blood from the heart. The Coroner's Office has not yet established the time of death. Lieutenant Richard Tells of the Milltown police reported that the investigation is continuing and that there are several suspects.

The comings and goings of the police and the yellow "Do not Cross" tape across the front door make the death all the more disturbing. The neighbors watched as the police removed Ms. Westlock's washer and dryer and a rolled-up piece of carpet from the home.

Ms. Westlock was described as a pleasant woman who spent most of her time with her daughter or working at her parents' bakery. Her daughter was asleep in the home at the time of the killing and was apparently unaware of the death. Ms. Westlock's body was discovered by Clarence Knedder, her estranged boyfriend. Knedder is the father of Ms. Westlock's daughter. Ms. Westlock had secured a restraining order against Knedder several days before she was killed. He was charged with criminal trespass after he found the body, and released on bond. Knedder said he was living with his sister on Forge St. in Milltown.

Joseph took a proprietary interest in Stan Marten's work, and was pleased that the *Milltown Reporter* allowed him a byline. After reading the article at his desk, Joseph called Marten without asking Della for his number—Joseph had by this time memorized it. *I've been taking enough abuse at home,* Joseph thought, *I don't need Della to jump all over me too.*

"Hey, Stan, nice article. Glad to see they're using your byline. Well deserved. Anything new, besides what's in the paper?"

"Hi, Mr. Joseph. Thanks. No, nothing that I know of. I think the police are close to locating Takas though. They seem pretty sure he's the killer. Have you heard anything? Do you know Takas, or anything about him?"

"I knew him when he was a kid. Through his mother. She was in charge of our church kitchen—cooked for all the doings. Little Jimmy was always there—always underfoot. Seemed like a nice boy though. Don't know what he grew up into. If I hear anything, I'll give you a call. Trust you'll do the same."

"No problem."

After a few pleasant minutes of conversation, Joseph hung up the phone, put down the paper and reached for his coffee cup. It wasn't there. "Della, where the hell is everyone?"

Della Raven walked in, carrying Joseph's coffee and her note book. "It's going to be a busy day. Can you drag yourself away from the paper and your morbid interest in the Westlock killing long enough to do some work?"

"God," he commented, "you're getting to sound more like Mary every day," as he reached for his cup.

"Well, everyone else is working pretty hard here in the office—you're the only laggard. The kids are busy twenty-four/seven."

"What the hell does that mean? Twenty-four/seven? Doesn't anyone speak English anymore?" he groused.

Della smiled, sat in the client chair and opened her book. "First, you have to…"

* * *

Joseph had slipped the *Milltown Reporter* under his desk when Della walked in, even though he was unable to put anything past her. As soon as she left, he checked the *Cleveland Plain Dealer* and the *Akron Beacon Journal* to see if they had picked up the story. Of course, they had. After reading the articles and learning nothing new, Joseph pulled the files Della had deposited on his desk to the center of his work table and tried to concentrate on the documents they contained. Probate and real estate work were always there, always needed handling, almost always very boring, but they did pay the bills. He tried to put June's death and the possible Takas involvement from his mind, yet had trouble concentrating on anything else. Finally he took his jacket off, rolled up his sleeves and resigned, set to work—boring.

Even though Joseph scoured the papers for the next several days, there was nothing about the killing. A week went by, and finally, on the following Tuesday morning, the *Reporter* stated in its bold page one headline:

ACCUSED MILLTOWN MURDERER CAN'T BE FOUND

MILLTOWN—Police have charged a 32-year-old Milltown man with the stabbing death of June Westlock, a Milltown woman, but he apparently left town after being questioned by the police. An arrest warrant has been issued for James (Jimmy) Takas who police say killed 31-year-old Westlock. Takas had been living with his parents in Milltown but his present location is unknown. The police declined to assign a motive for the killing, or how they determined that Takas was responsible for the death, but sources close to the investigation said it was a drug-related killing.

Westlock, officials said, was stabbed thirteen times and died from a wound through the back that severed her aorta. Her eight-year-old daughter apparently slept through the struggle in a bedroom of the one-floor home.

The body was discovered by Clarence Knedder, Westlock's estranged boyfriend. He was charged with criminal trespass based on a request made by Westlock that he be kept away from her home. The prosecutor has dropped those charges. Knedder and Westlock had lived together off and on for a period of years and he claims to be the father of her daughter.

Takas, a white male about five feet, eight inches tall and of slight build, was last seen driving an older-model grey Ford sedan with an Ohio license plate. Anyone with information on Takas' whereabouts is encouraged to contact the Milltown police.

Joseph felt a cold chill race through him as the police finally put a name to the killer. For some reason, it bothered Joseph much more than he thought it would. He knew so many of the people involved, and was especially upset that the mother of the accused was, through their church, a friend of his wife.

I just can't have any part of this case, he thought. *Mary would kill me.* He put the paper down, and called for Della to bring him more coffee and current files.

*   *   *

It was two months since the killing and Joseph had succeeded in burying it in his mind—what with all of the work in the office. A warrant for

Jimmy Takas' arrest had been issued by the Milltown Municipal Court on an affidavit signed by Sergeant Dale, charging Takas with murder. Unknown to anyone locally, Takas was living in southern Florida, where he found a job as a glass installer. With Takas now considered a fugitive, the Milltown police called the Federal Bureau of Investigation into the case.

Even though Jimmy was unable to give background information to his new employer, his employer didn't give it a thought. So much construction was happening in Florida that employees came and went without leaving much impression on the employers. Jimmy was a good worker and caused no trouble on the job. As always happens, fate took a hand. Jimmy was sent out on a job and was stopped for a minor traffic offense. When he could produce no identification, and because of Jimmy's reaction, the police became suspicious, brought him to the station and did a fingerprint check. The warrant appeared on their computer screen. Jimmy was arrested and the Milltown police notified. Jimmy patiently awaited the arrival of Officers Dale and Tells in a Florida jail cell. He had never doubted that he would be found sooner or later.

Sergeant Dale followed Lieutenant Tells into the cell where Jimmy was being held and said, "You told me you wasn't going nowhere. Lied to me, huh?"

Jimmy didn't respond and Dale continued, "You going to give us a hard time and fight extradition or you going to act like a man and come back with us?" indicating himself and the lieutenant.

Jimmy said, without looking at either, "I'll go back with you. There ain't nothing else to do," as he stood to follow them.

"Hold on, Jimmy," Dale said. "We got to do the paperwork all proper."

A local lawyer was assigned the task of representing Jimmy, and did so in a lackadaisical manner, approving Jimmy's consent that extradition be waived. For this he collected a nominal fee from the State. The procedure for waiving extradition was quickly accomplished and Jimmy and the officers were soon on a plane back to Cleveland. A Milltown police car was waiting at the airport and Jimmy, in shackles, was brought from the airport to the Milltown City Jail. He was before Municipal Court Judge Dana Close within hours of his arrest.

The following day, Joseph read:

MILLTOWN—Sitting alone at a table in Municipal Court, accused murderer Jimmy Takas listened quietly as Judge Dana Close set his bond at $500,000 cash. Harold Thuman, newly elected County Prosecutor, appeared on behalf of the county and requested bail in that amount citing the nature of the charge and that Takas had left the county when he learned he was the object of the police investigation.

Takas, 32, is charged with the stabbing death of June Westlock. He was arrested in Miami, Florida, Monday and waived extradition. Westlock was stabbed to death in her home while her daughter slept in a nearby bedroom. Takas left the area about a week after the killing, Thuman said, because he was convinced he was going to be arrested for the crime.

Takas, who had no attorney present, said he would stay in the county with his family. "I don't plan on going no place," he said.

The judge, noting that there was a legitimate concern Takas might leave the area again, set the $500,000 cash bond. He also said an attorney would be appointed to represent Takas, who said he was indigent, having only $4.98 and an ancient Ford Sedan, still in Florida.

A preliminary hearing is scheduled for next Friday afternoon, a court spokesman said, unless the grand jury hands down an indictment before the scheduled hearing date.

*   *   *

In Ohio, when a person is charged with the commission of a felony, he or she is entitled to a preliminary hearing within seven days of his arrest. The purpose of a preliminary hearing is for a lower court judge to determine whether or not the evidence submitted by the State is sufficient to believe that a crime has been committed and that the person charged may have committed that crime. If the judge determines there are reasonable grounds in support of the State's evidence, the person charged is bound over to the grand jury to either hand down an indictment or no-bill the case. If an indictment is handed down, the defendant is brought to trial. But if the charge is no-billed, the defendant is released.

A prosecutor can, and usually does, bypass the procedure by empaneling and presenting the case for consideration to a grand jury before the seven days has expired. This is more often than not done by the State in order to avoid informing the defendant or his lawyer how weak or how strong the State's case is. In this way, the prosecution can adopt whatever spin he wants before the defense counsel is made aware of the facts. For some reason state prosecutors, as opposed to federal prosecutors, prefer trial by ambush rather than giving anything away to the defense. Perhaps it is because they rely on the electorate for their jobs and voters are impressed by convictions. It becomes a number game rather than a search for justice. Prosecutors justify their position by saying, "Defendants have their own lawyers to protect them."

Unfortunately, the cards are stacked against persons charged with a crime by this procedure. Neither they nor their lawyers are permitted access to the grand jury proceedings. If a prosecutor wants to, he can command a defendant's presence before the grand jury by subpoena, and the person charged with a crime must appear without counsel. A grand jury hears only one side of a case, and not all of that. It only hears what the prosecutor wants it to hear. Rules of evidence do not apply, hearsay is allowed and the defendant is not permitted to present anything. The prosecutor has complete control over the proceedings—it has been said that with the control exercised by a prosecutor, he could secure an indictment against a refrigerator.

As expected, Prosecutor Thuman, unwilling to give the defendant an opportunity to hear any part of the State's case, immediately convened a grand jury. The grand jury handed down an indictment within a matter of hours. Hardly enough time for Takas to change into the standard orange prison jumpsuit.

*   *   *

Joseph's office occupied the upper two floors of his building, which really amounted to all the available office space. A conference room and storage space were located on the lower level—formerly called a basement. This he converted into offices for an energetic young lawyer for whom Joseph had developed a fondness. The elderly lawyer had no desire to be a landlord; however, his liking for young Terry Bernow—his name shortened from its original Slavic form—was true to his ethnic origins. Pleased that there was at least one person, other than himself, who expressed pride in his ancestry, Joseph allowed himself to be persuaded to rent the space to the young lawyer.

Even though Terry Bernow had been engaged in the practice of law for only a short time, he was convinced that hard work, long hours and dedication would produce success. He was extremely energetic, tall and slender with dark brown eyes and brown curly hair shot through with grey that belied his youth. Carefully nurtured chin whiskers were also shot with grey and designed to deny his youthful, unlined features.

Joseph was truly fond of young Bernow, but there were things about him that Joseph couldn't understand or approve—such as advertising in the yellow pages. Joseph could never bring himself to do this. It was ingrained in Joseph that publically promoting a lawyer's practice was just not acceptable. During the early years, rules to that effect were stringently enforced by the disciplinary arm of the Bar Association. Now the Supreme Court had taken the position that denying lawyers the right to advertise was an infringement on their First Amendment Constitutional rights of free speech. This resulted in many lawyers advertising their wares as flagrantly as used-car dealers. Not Joseph—but he couldn't deny his young friend the right to do so. He nevertheless reminded him frequently how tasteless he thought it. Joseph's wife, Mary, suggested to Joseph on such occasions that "There is nothing wrong with your having an opinion, it is in the fact that you express it that gets you into trouble."

In any event, Terry's work ethic, consummate cheerful nature and obvious pride in his ethnic origin convinced Joseph to rent space in the building to him that he would have preferred be used for the storage and conference room it once was. He enjoyed the young man, but watching the exuberance with which he attacked each case exhausted Joseph.

Joseph's affection for Terry even extended to inviting him to his Friday afternoon's cocktail hour—a tradition Joseph started years earlier. He believed it important for his staff to get together at least once a week to talk about office matters and to exchange reports concerning their week's activities. It was difficult to find a time when everyone was available. So Joseph began serving cocktails late Friday afternoons. Suddenly, no one had a problem finding time to attend. The cocktails were served in Joseph's office. It was crowded, but no one seemed to mind…everyone had a contribution to make on business matters and often everyone talked at once. The elderly lawyer tried to maintain some sense of order, but was never able to do so. Unable to make anyone listen to him, he called on Della to chair the meeting. The young people were more afraid of her than of Joseph, and she managed to control them in the same way Mary controlled the kids at home—with a smile or frown.

Why doesn't that work for me? Joseph wondered and then shrugged it off as being either a genetic or gender thing.

Terry reported, "I hear Jimmy Takas was arrested in Florida. Sergeant Dale and Lieutenant Tells are down there picking him up. He waived extradition and agreed to come back to stand trial. A couple of my kids are the same age as his daughters. They go to the same school. I met Jimmy's parents at some school function or other. His mom called me and wanted to know if could I help him. I told her I'd see him as soon as he was back here and available. Should be able to see him Monday morning. I'm going to try and see him then. I hear Thuman wants to ask for the death penalty." Turning to Joseph, he asked, "Want to go with me to see him— Jimmy, that is?"

Pausing in his recitation, he looked at Joseph, saying, "I told his mom that I couldn't handle it myself and would ask you to help. They thought it was a great idea. Seems they know you from somewhere, but were afraid to ask you to handle it. Will you go with me?"

Della frowned and opened her mouth to say something, closing it quickly and turning toward Joseph. The room was suddenly silent. Everyone else looked at Joseph, who sat relaxed in his swivel chair, cocktail glass in hand halfway between his belt and his lips. His heart lurched. In spite of his interest in the case, he didn't think he wanted the responsibility of another murder case this soon—if ever. After a lengthy silence, he responded, "I don't think so. Della keeps reminding me how busy I am and that I'm a slacker because I don't pay proper attention to business," he said with a smile towards his secretary. She pulled a face at him, looking relieved, as he continued, "I'm not sure I want to get involved in another case that's going to take so much time."

The rest of the staff was amazed by Joseph's response. All talked at once.

"We can handle things here."

"You got to do this."

"At least think about it."

They didn't seem to understand. Joseph liked his life and the practice, as mundane as both were. No matter how romantic his dream visions of himself were, he hated changes or disruptions. He didn't like conflict and felt totally inadequate to represent a client charged with anything worse than a minor transgression. Butterflies—tremors—chest pains—palpitations all accompanied even the discussion they were having.

Joseph raised his hands to silence them. "All right, I'll think about it over the weekend and get back to you Monday. In the meantime, let me enjoy my Martini without any more babble."

Again Della looked as though she might want to interrupt, but sat quietly. Somehow she didn't look nearly as pleased as she had earlier. Bernow didn't notice the frown she directed toward him as she raised her glass to her lips. It didn't escape Joseph.

The rest of the hour was spent in small talk and Joseph left promptly at five, giving the staff time alone to enjoy each other's company without his stultifying presence.

Driving home in his small pickup truck, Joseph thought about the coming conversation with Mary. It being Friday, he was sure she would want to go to the mall for pizza and shopping. Entering his long, tree-lined driveway, he noted that the trees were almost all leafed out so he couldn't see the house from the road. He began to relax and prepare himself to tell Mary about the day's activities and the request that he become involved in the Takas case. *Mary will be proud of me for refusing,* he thought. She hated for him to be involved in high-profile cases. Every time his name was in the newspaper, she would grouch, "I can't even go to the grocery store without someone asking me about it...."

Mary Joseph, short, with a slender build that belied her age, had short, carefully coifed but uncolored hair that was almost completely grey—Joseph thought it quite attractive. After Joseph explained in detail what had transpired earlier, he fell silent, awaiting her approval of his actions.

She responded to the information in a completely unexpected way. "You what!" Mary exclaimed after listening silently to Joseph's recital. "Pasquale!" She only called him by his given name when really angry. "You know Mrs. Takas is our friend. She's a good person and works hard for the church. We've know Jimmy since he was a baby. Blanche deserves whatever help she needs and you should be ashamed of yourself for saying no!"

"But, Mary...you never want—" Joseph began.

"Don't but-Mary me. You know the right thing to do. I expect you to do it!" Mary scolded.

"Damn it, Mary! Can't you ever make up your mind. First you get mad at me when I get involved in something you don't like and then get mad at me when I don't. Make up your mind, for God's sake."

"Don't you swear at me!" Mary said, shaking a finger at Joseph all the while petting the cat lying peacefully on her lap. The raised voices didn't bother the cat at all. In fact, he seemed to enjoy the entertainment accompanying the attention. Mary didn't miss a stroke and the cat's purring could be heard over the silence following Mary's words.

Joseph shook his head in wonder. He never knew what to expect from his wife, her grey hair bouncing with exasperation. *I don't know why,* he thought, *but she's better looking today than she was the day we got married. Don't think she's gained an ounce. Wished I'd age as well.*

"Okay, okay. I'll call Terry in the morning and let him know I'll go with him Monday," and then, trying to salvage his macho image, "But I don't know if I'm going to get involved or not. I'll make up my mind later. Somehow nothing I ever do satisfies you," Joseph groused.

Her patented "Humphh" was the only response Joseph received.

Joseph quietly changed into casual clothes, got the keys to his pickup truck and waited in the drive for Mary to feed and deliver a few loving words to each of her cats and the dog so they could go and get their Friday piece of pizza. Joseph would stop at Walden Books and pick up a paperback to read while Mary shopped.

Waiting for Mary to emerge, he used the opportunity to give Terry a call at home and let him know he would work with him on the Takas case, if he was still wanted. Terry was elated—Joseph was not.

"What time Monday morning?" Joseph asked.

"First thing in the morning," Terry responded.

"Okay. See you then."

The trip to the mall was uneventful except that Joseph found the most recent David Baldacci book. He enjoyed reading the fruits of the young lawyer author's imaginative mind—each novel differed from the last.

CHAPTER SIX

While waiting for Terry, Joseph propped his sensibly shod feet on the waste basket beneath his scarred table and perused Monday morning's *Milltown Reporter.* Another article by Stan Marten relating to the Westlock killing described Takas' initial appearance before Municipal Court Judge Dana Close. The Court had set a date for the preliminary hearing—not that it would make any difference—and after considering the matter, set bond at five hundred thousand dollars, which also would make no difference. Jimmy had no money and everyone in the community knew his parents couldn't raise bond. Such legal fictions raised Joseph's blood pressure. *Why the hell do we play such games? Everyone knows Jimmy is going to cool his ass in jail until his trial is over—and then probably he'll be in prison. Such crap.*

The Court, as required of it, inquired as to Jimmy's financial situation. He told the judge he owned nothing but an old, beat-up car that was still in Florida. It had no value and Jimmy no longer had a job. His indigency required that the Court assign a lawyer to him. The Supreme Court once proclaimed that no one could be sent to jail without the assistance of competent counsel. This, too, was a fiction that raised Joseph's ire. Usually experienced lawyers refused to accept assignments. Only those just beginning practice were willing to accept appointments by the Court because it paid so little. But it was better than sitting in their offices waiting for a paying client. At least Ohio's Supreme Court recognized a need for some special training before a lawyer could represent an indigent defendant charged with murder. Joseph was certified to accept such cases.

Since Takas has no money or property, he will be entitled to assigned counsel, Joseph thought. *Wonder what kind of promise Terry made his parents. It's unlikely they can afford the legal fees. Looks like we will probably have to eat this one if the Court sees fit to appoint us—hope Mary's satisfied.*

Since Terry had not yet arrived, Joseph flipped through the rest of the paper, noting an article on the editorial page about Thuman, the newly elected prosecutor, who had defeated the incumbent. It was Thuman's predecessor against whom Joseph had tried the Mountain City case the year before. It was still frequently in his thoughts. While Joseph was actually fond of the former prosecutor, he had no love for Thuman, even though he didn't know him well. Thuman had gained all of his legal experience in various prosecutors' offices in nearby counties so wasn't well known in Milltown's legal community. Even so, rumors of the underhanded way in which he secured convictions spread into the county. Joseph had no real experience with him, having met him only on one or two occasions at political gatherings. Joseph didn't like to prejudge people or allow rumors to influence his opinion; nevertheless, the occasions resulted in a feeling of aversion that Joseph was at a loss to explain. He didn't like Thuman, but wasn't exactly sure why. It was just a feeling of being unclean or slimy that permeated Joseph on the rare occasions he had contact with Thuman.

Harold Thuman lived in Mills County most of his life, growing up in one of its southern townships. He had gone to college and law school at nearby Akron University. Although physically imposing, he did not participate in sports or any other type of athletic involvement, limiting his extracurricular activities to debating and politicking. He had little regard for the niceties—his credo, *Win at whatever cost.*

Thuman, for as long as he could remember, intended for politics to be his life. He always knew that one day he would seek public office, just didn't know which. After being admitted to the bar in Ohio, he devoted his entire professional life to prosecution—it being the quickest road to winning elections. He believed, and probably rightly so, that no one would vote against someone who sends bad people to jail. He found the weakest candidate to be the young, attractive Mills County Prosecutor, and then added to her weaknesses by the liberal use of rumor, innuendo and outright lies.

In his early thirties, Thuman's tall and stocky build, with a shock of brown hair always falling across his eyes—his trademark—gave him a boyish look. He encouraged the belief that he was a super hero who would send all criminals to jail and save the public. It was Joseph's opinion that he was more interested in winning cases than justice. Despite the short time in office, the media was aware of the arbitrary changes Thuman made in the Prosecutor's Office. An editorial appearing in the morning *Reporter* declared:

THUMAN MAY NEED TO CHANGE STANCE

An apparent cog has developed in the pipeline of information flowing from the County Prosecutor's Office. Whether it constitutes a problem depends on whether you are an attorney representing the defense or the prosecution. Prosecutor Harold Thuman has decided not to employ an open file policy like his predecessor, when it comes to releasing information to the defense during a criminal trial preparation. He will only release information that he is compelled to under state law, and even then it might require a court order before he will release the information.

Thuman feels his stance is justified, since his priority is to secure convictions, not the concerns of the defense. Delays caused by his arbitrary position require defense counsel to do a more comprehensive investigation. While it may be legally justifiable, it results in defendants spending more time in jail while awaiting trial, increases legal fees and increases the cost of indigent defense to the county. If Thuman's policy results in speedy trial limitations running out, some defendants might be set free who would otherwise have come to trial. Preparation is the key for both sides, and the defense usually is only asking for equal footing on the facts available.

Thuman's stance, however justified, could easily become a waste of time for his own office and defense attorneys. Hopefully, he will see fit to alter his position so that there need not be a fight over the release of every piece of information to which defense counsel would otherwise be entitled. We trust he will use good judgment and recognize that it would be in his best interest as well as his adversaries' to see that justice is conducted in an efficient and timely manner.

Joseph scowled as he read the editorial, thinking, *There is no way in hell he's going to change. Wish he'd read the Code of Profession Responsibility and learn that he is supposed to seek justice, not convictions. No sense wasting time wishing for the impossible.* Looking towards his pigs, he mumbled, "What do you think?"

As expected, there was no response except their usual smiles that Joseph attempted to read. He decided that their sardonic expression bordered on full-blown sneers.

A knock on the frame of Joseph's open door interrupted his thoughts.

Joseph looked up, saying, "Come in, Terry," and, turning towards the door, said with a smile of greeting, "Hi."

Terry walked in, cheerful as always, dressed in a blue sports jacket, tan slacks, white shirt and tie. "Are you ready to walk over to the jail?"

Joseph thought, *He always looks so neat in his clothes. I look like I sleep in mine,* but said aloud, "Yes, I'm ready. Did you read the morning paper?"

"No. Why?"

"This editorial." Tapping the paper, he showed the article to Terry. "Looks like we're going to have a fight on our hands. I'm sure this article will have no effect on Thuman. The paper also had a story saying that Jimmy told the judge he had no money…something about four dollars and a car…. How are his parents going to pay us? I don't think they have much money—both are retired—if we can't get the Court to assign us to the case, we may be working for nothing."

Joseph changed the subject. "You know, Terry, I never liked Thuman. Not that I've ever come across him in court. He's always worked in some prosecutor's office or other in some of the surrounding counties. I understand he's just plain mean. I didn't like the way he ran his campaign here in Mills County—using dirt, scandal and garbage. I know his predecessor had some weaknesses, but she was a nice person. At least when she said something was so, it usually was."

Terry, looking a little pensive, said, "I've heard some of the same things and I've seen him at bar meetings in town—have never really had a chance to get to know him—didn't think I wanted to."

Then returning to the subject Joseph had raised, Terry added, "Anyway, we'll have to ask the judge that draws the case to appoint us. I guess Judge Close appointed someone else, but Jimmy wants us. Since he is entitled to assigned counsel, he can ask the judge that draws the case to assign us. Don't really think it will be a problem getting appointed."

"Naturally," Joseph groused. "Biggest case of the year and there's no pocket." He then called out, "Della, Terry and I are walking over to the jail. Probably won't be back until after lunch. Hold down the fort."

*   *   *

Joseph and Terry left through the front door of the century-old building. As always, Joseph appreciated the sun shining through the trees on the square. They cut diagonally across it, Joseph admiring the young ladies in short skirts and brightly colored summer clothes. Soon enough they would be exchanged for drab winter wear. *At least maybe the kids that wear those low-rise pants—I think they call it "sagging"—will start to wear some decent clothes. I've seen enough navels to last me a lifetime—can't help but wonder how those kids keep warm wearing such things—no respect for themselves or anyone else—How many times have I said, "I don't understand this generation?" How many times did my dad say it about us?*

Coming back from wherever he was, Joseph asked, "How do you want to handle this, Terry?"

"Jimmy is expecting me. I'll tell him you're going to be on the case with me. His mom said she mentioned it and he was pleased. He remembers you from when he was a kid. Maybe you can get his story."

"I'd hoped he wouldn't want me. I need an excuse to stay off the case," Joseph interjected, "but we'll play it the way you planned. Sounds okay."

"Mr. Joseph, if you don't like to take criminal cases, why do you do it?" Terry asked.

"Let me tell you a story." Joseph found it easier to express his thoughts and feelings by telling stories. "Some years ago, I was assigned a case to handle for a young man charged with sexually molesting a couple of kids. They were ages sev… It doesn't matter. They were just children. Anyway, this pedophile was in my office one day while we were preparing his defense. When it got time for him to leave, he stood in front of my desk and said, 'You're working so hard for me, you must really like me.'"

Joseph stared off into space, remembering the incident, then said, "I looked at him standing across from me—a young man—good looking—but charged with a terrible crime…and deservedly so. I said to him, 'Like you? I can't stand the sight of you. I hope, after this case is over, never to see you again. Don't ever misunderstand me. I'm not working for you. I'm protecting your freedoms and rights as spelled out in our Constitution. If the rights of the most miserable, rotten criminal aren't protected, then no one's rights are protected. The Constitution, and what it stands for, is the most important thing in the world to me, and should be the most important thing in the world to every American. I'll represent you, as I must, and do the best I can, but never believe for a minute that I like you, or condone what you've done.' I later worked out a plea agreement for him and, thankfully, have never seen or heard from him again."

Terry didn't say anything, but looked at Joseph with a newfound understanding—and maybe respect.

By this time, they arrived at the jail behind the Old Courthouse. The Old Courthouse still had an ancient tower that contained a working clock. It was attached to the New Courthouse by a second-story walkway.

A new jail was being built on a piece of ground near the city limits. While waiting for the construction to be complete, the Old Jail was still being used. It was behind the courthouse and across a shared driveway that led to an exercise area for the prisoners. Old, rickety basketball hoops with the nets long gone, some rusty free weights without the bars, a couple of weight benches and barely visible painted volley ball courts occupied the open area surrounded by an eight-foot chain-link fence topped with razor-sharp metal coils. The jail was even older than the Old Courthouse—probably eighty years old—and built to accommodate maybe thirty men and fifteen women prisoners. It now held almost twice that and a number of the prisoners were farmed out to surrounding communities at an exorbitant rental while waiting for the new jail.

The Old Jail was built in the days when the sheriff and his family lived in an apartment at the jail. The sheriff's wife was expected to prepare meals and feed the prisoners. Although the current sheriff was divorced, he still occupied the apartment most of the time, but now the county hired and paid for a cook. Surprisingly, the food coming from the prison kitchen was excellent.

Thursdays were pizza day. Most of the lawyers in town, with clients housed for whatever reason at the jail, arranged to call on them around the noon hour on Thursdays. While waiting to talk to their clients, or after completing their visit—so long as it was close to noon—each lawyer managed to stop at the kitchen. The chef generously shared his fresh-baked pizza with the visitors, who had nothing but high praise for him. He enjoyed the admiration—they the pizza.

Walking into the prison office on the lower level, Joseph called out to the secretary-receptionist by name, "Hi, Wanda, Terry and I are here to see Jimmy Takas. I assume he's in."

"He is now. They took him over to Municipal Court as soon as he got here so they didn't get a chance to complete booking him. They're just finishing up now. I'll call back and see how soon you can see him."

Booking is the procedure used to record necessary health and identification information of a prisoner. Although not complicated, the information obtained is typed into computers by corrections officers who don't know how to type—and could care less how long a prisoner has to stand in front of their counter-high desk. The prisoner is then told to stand behind a line in front of a pull-down chart calibrated in inches to show height. Full face and profile photographs are taken of the prisoner while he holds a number placard in front of his chest. He or she is then brought to a little alcove behind the desk, where old-fashioned roller ink fingerprint equipment is kept, fingerprints are taken and then recorded in the computer. A sorry combination of the new and the old.

Once all of this has been accomplished, the prisoner is removed to the prison's general population, unless he's to be brought to court, see his lawyer or be on suicide watch. In such cases, he is kept in special metal cells located adjacent to the booking area the inside of which could be observed through a small opening in the metal door. Whatever the reason, Jimmy Takas was still in the booking area and locked in one of the secured cells.

After a relatively short wait, an officer came to the reception area and accompanied Joseph and Terry through a locked steel door into a small vaulted lobby which contained only the entrance door through which they entered, and a similar door exiting into the prison booking area. Joseph felt sweat trickling down his face with the three of them crowded into the small alcove. They stood in front of the second door, leading into the booking area. It could not be unlocked until the first door was closed and locked. The officer used a large old-fashioned key for these purposes. Once inside, the two lawyers were led back to booking and showed to the cell holding Takas. They were required to pass through a metal detector, empty their pockets and leave their briefcases with the desk sergeant—although Joseph was permitted to keep a legal pad and pen for notes. Knowing both Joseph and Terry, the officers kidded with them through the entire process.

Finally permitted access to Jimmy's cell, they could hear the door clang shut behind them and the lock clicking into place. This sound never failed to create a catch in Joseph's breath and give rise to an alarming claustrophobic feeling. He fought it off, but the sweat on his palms and brow stayed.

Jimmy Takas sat in the cell on the single metal cot, looking lost and miserable, head hanging almost to his knees. All Joseph could see was the top of his head, brown hair straggly and dirty hanging over the boy's eyes, almost hiding the cheap horn-rimmed eyeglasses he wore. He was still wearing the clothes he'd been wearing when brought from Florida, except that his pockets were emptied and turned out and his belt and shoelaces removed. As soon as he was put into population, he would be assigned a bright orange jumpsuit with the words *Milltown Prisoner* in large black letters emblazoned across the back. Next to him on the bunk was a paper that Joseph recognized as the indictment. He hadn't yet seen it and wasn't exactly sure about the charge.

"Hi, Jimmy," Terry said. "I don't know if you know Mr. Joseph. He is going to be helping me with your case. Is that okay?"

Jimmy didn't look up, but responded, "I know him. I don't know if he remembers me. Used to see him at the church hall all the time. It's okay with me if my folks can pay him. They don't got lots of money, you know."

"It's all right with them. I asked and they said they would be pleased if Mr. Joseph would help. But I think we are going to have to ask the judge to appoint us. You don't have any money and your folks can't afford the expense. So we'll try to get appointed to the case. In the meantime, we'll proceed as though we're already your lawyers. Okay?"

No response except an accepting shrug of the narrow shoulders

The cell was about eight feet by ten feet—the walls of concrete block were painted institutional grey. A steel bunk, without mattress, was bolted to one wall. Opposite the bed there was a toilet without a seat behind a low concrete wall to provide a modicum of privacy. There was no other furniture in the room. The entire cell was visible through the small wired glass window in the door. A chill raced down Joseph's spine as he contemplated the possibility of spending a night there.

Takas slouched on the edge of the bunk as close to the far wall as he could get. His hands covered most of the lower half of his face. Joseph could see the glasses sliding down his nose, the dirty hair hanging over as much of his face as it could reach...abject misery.

Joseph and Terry looked around, trying to find a place to sit. Shrugging, Terry finally perched on the open toilet, while Joseph sat on the mattress-less bunk next to Takas. Terry prepared to take notes with the pad and pen they were allowed to keep.

Joseph reached over tentatively and put his hand on Takas' shoulder, saying, "Jimmy, tell us what you know about June Westlock's death." He purposely did not identify her death as murder or, by his question, involve Takas.

Jimmy shrank from the touch, seeming to withdraw further into himself. He was obviously frightened and, at least, a little confused. He appeared to have much to say, but was afraid or didn't know how to say it. He cleared his throat and started, "I really don't remember much...." His voice trailed off into silence.

Joseph allowed the silence to build, saying nothing.

Takas cleared his throat and began again, "I was home and my mom and dad were out. Mom left me some money to get a haircut. I did and went to *Tracks* about six o'clock. Nothing was going on so I had a couple of drinks while waiting for…" Silence.

After a few seconds, Joseph asked quietly, "Waiting for what?"

"You know. Waiting for someone to show up that had some stuff," obviously afraid to put it into words.

Joseph couldn't allow that. "Jimmy, you have to be completely honest with us if we're to help you. You know that you have been charged with murder and the prosecutor wants to ask for the death penalty…."

Jimmy shrank even further into himself.

Joseph continued, "Now tell us what you remember."

Jimmy shuddered and made an effort to sit up straighter. "I wanted some drugs. Cocaine, powder or crack, I didn't care what. I knew I could get marijuana. The kids are using some other stuff to sniff—I don't know what all—but it scares me. But I needed something to get my head straight. I was drinking pretty heavy—had been for some time. I knew June or Clarence would stop at *Tracks*…they always did…and would have something. If not with them, at their house. Me, Clarence and her used to do lines at her house all the time after their kid went to sleep. I had heard she was fighting with Clarence and maybe he wouldn't be around with her, but she could always get something from his sister or Cockroach. I really needed it…." Again his voice trailed into silence.

Joseph didn't break into the silence, again allowing it to build—waiting for Jimmy to continue.

A deep sigh, and then, with a keening sound, he groaned, "I don't remember…I was home in bed…the phone was ringing. It was Laura. She said something about money and then something about June. 'She's dead,' she said. I couldn't believe it. Then I looked down…only had on my pants and underwear…. My T-shirt, I seem to remember, had blood on it. Didn't know where it was. Laura told me the police wanted to talk to me. I said I'd go see them. But I was crying so hard, I couldn't talk no more. I hung up the phone and just sat there. Don't know how long. After a while, I got up, took a shower, then went to talk to the cops.

"Sergeant Dale took me into a small room and began asking me questions. At first I told him I hadn't see June, but he said lots of people saw me with her. I admitted I'd been by her house but went home from there. He went on and on—said I was going to jail for life—said they had proof that I killed her. I couldn't have," he sobbed.

Joseph waited for him to calm down and asked, "What did you do then?"

"When I left the police station I went home. Went to work and did my usual stuff. The cops came and got me at work and took me back to the station and pushed and pushed. Said I had to take a lie detector test. I said I would and they let me go home. No one was there. I thought, *They really believe I killed her.* I didn't want to go to jail, so I took whatever money was around the house, packed some of my stuff in my gym bag and left.

"I didn't know where I was going, but headed south. A couple hours later I called Laura and told her I loved her and the girls and that I was leaving. She cried and said I should come back. I was crying too, but I wasn't going back. I was in Florida when the police found me. I don't know how they knew where I was, but when they came to get me, I said I'd come back. That's all I remember. What are they going to do to me?" He sobbed pathetically, breaking into tears.

Joseph waited for Jimmy's breathing to slow, then asked, "What happened to the bloody T-shirt?"

"I don't know...I don't know.... Maybe Ma washed it...maybe there wasn't one...I don' know!"

Joseph stood and placed his hand on Jimmy's shoulder, forcing him to look up at him, "Look, Jimmy, Mr. Bernow and I will do the best we can for you. You will be indicted and I feel sure that neither you nor your parents will be able to make bond. If you are charged with capital murder, there won't be bond anyway, so you'll be sitting here in jail for several months until the case comes to trial. Mr. Bernow or I will be talking to you fairly frequently, but if you feel you have to see one of us, just tell the jailer, he'll give us a call. Okay?"

No response.

"One of us will be with you whenever you have to be in court. Whatever you do, you have to be completely honest with us or we won't be able to help you. One more thing. You are not to talk about this case to anyone except Mr. Bernow or me. That means the police, anyone here in the jail, your parents…anyone. Do you understand all that?"

Joseph studied Jimmy for a few minutes, then said in a calm and quiet voice, "Jimmy, I think you are bullshitting us, and that's something you can't afford to do. I think you remember a lot more than you're saying. Let one of us know when you're ready to tell us what happened."

For the first time, Jimmy looked up at Joseph pleadingly and sobbed, "You got to believe me. I don't remember. They said I raped her and killed her. I know I couldn't've done none of that to June…." He looked down at his feet, appearing to shrink within himself.

Joseph reached for the paper sitting on the cot next to Jimmy and asked, "Okay if I take this with me?"

Jimmy just nodded, never moving from the same dejected posture on the edge of the bunk.

Terry stood and patted Jimmy's shoulder also, walking out of the cell behind Joseph. As Joseph reached for the door he heard a hesitant, "Mr. Joseph."

Joseph looked over his shoulder and saw Jimmy looking at him, hair hanging in front of his glasses, mouth trembling. Joseph shivered as he looked into Jimmy's haunted eyes…eyes haunted by unreported or un-recalled memories.

"Mr. Joseph, they kept telling me I had to take a lie detector test."

Joseph nodded, turned and walked out with Terry, saying, "Whew, looks like we have our job cut out for us."

*　　*　　*

It was nearing the noon hour when Joseph and Terry finally walked out of the jail's front door. "Want some lunch, Terry?" Joseph asked.

"Sure."

"Let's walk over to the *Hot Dog.*" The *Hot Dog* was a small restaurant featuring many different types of wiener and sausage sandwiches. It was located just west of the square and was one of Joseph's favorite spots—he had so many. They had a root beer float to die for. Served in a tall frosted glass filled half way with their special brand of root beer, the rest of the glass packed with soft vanilla ice cream, smothered with whip cream stacked at least four inches above the glass and topped with sliced almonds. Joseph's mouth watered as he thought about it.

"Okay, Mr. Joseph. We can talk about the indictment there."

It took just a few minutes to walk to the eatery. As they entered, Joseph noted that the lunch crowd hadn't yet arrived. Joseph ordered a jumbo hotdog, smothered in pickle relish, onions and mustard. It had some special name on the menu, as did all of the sandwiches, but Joseph couldn't remember them. He just told the teenage waitress, a daughter of the owner, that he wanted his usual. While waiting for the sandwich, she brought the root beer float. Joseph felt a little guilty about consuming it, but didn't let it stop him, savoring every bite and sip. Terry ordered something not nearly so exotic. *Kids have no taste.*

Sitting in a booth, Joseph and Terry removed and unfolded the indictment served on Jimmy. After glancing at it, Joseph handed it to Terry, saying, "Take a look at the indictment. May as well know what we're up against. Thuman sure didn't waste any time getting to the grand jury. Wonder what's the big hurry—other than he doesn't want to give anything away to the defense. The son-of-a-bitch sure doesn't take any chances…."

The indictment read:

The jurors of the grand jury of the State of Ohio, duly selected, impaneled, sworn and charged to inquire of crimes and offenses committed within the body of Mills County, in the State of Ohio in the name and by the authority of the State of Ohio, upon their oath do find and present that Jimmy Takas, late of said county, on or about the 5th day of May in this year of the Lord and within said county unlawfully and purposefully did cause the death of another: to wit June Westlock, in violation of Section 2903.02 of the Ohio Revised Code, contrary to the statute in such cases made and provided and against the peace and dignity of the State of Ohio.

It was signed by the prosecutor and the foreman of the grand jury.

Joseph said to Terry, "Want to check the penalty section of the Statute? Candidly, I'm amazed he wasn't charged with aggravated murder. Bet you ten to one he will be reindicted before we get to trial. Thuman's bound and determined to try a death penalty case in this county."

"You're probably right, Mr. Joseph. The statute provides a penalty of fifteen to life unless there is a sexually motivated specification, in which case it is life without parole," Terry said, reading from the copy of Ohio's Criminal Law Manual he carried with him. It contained sections of Ohio's Revised Code pertaining to crimes, Rules of Criminal Procedures and other bits of information a lawyer might need in the handling of a criminal case.

*   *   *

Jimmy Takas was arraigned the following morning, Prosecutor Thuman himself appeared on behalf of the State. Judge Clarke had drawn the case. White haired and of an age with Joseph, they knew each other fairly well. Of the two Common Pleas judges in Mills County, Joseph was pleased that Clarke was on the case. Joseph and Terry appeared with the defendant and informed the Court of Jimmy's finances, submitting an affidavit of indigency. Joseph closed his presentation with "Jimmy has no assets and his parents are unable to afford the cost of defense."

After asking some questions of the boy, Judge Clarke turned to Joseph. "Mr. Joseph, I am going to find the defendant indigent and assign you and Mr. Bernow to represent him, if that is satisfactory to him." Seeing Jimmy's affirmative nod, the judge continued, "Is your client prepared to enter a plea to the indictment?

"Your Honor," Joseph addressed the bench, "Mr. Takas acknowledges timely receipt of the indictment and waives the reading of it in open court; however, refuses to enter a plea—standing mute at this time. The reason he is unwilling, at this time, to enter a plea is on the advice of counsel so as not to waive any possible defects in the charging document or the proceedings."

By refusing to enter a plea, the defense can, at a later date, raise any defects in the procedure or charging documents. Even though Joseph and Terry weren't aware of any defects, they wanted to make sure they had sufficient time to review them adequately. In an effort to make sure they missed nothing they chose this manner to preserve the ability to do so. "Since the defendant stands mute, Your Honor, I believe you are required to enter a 'not guilty' plea on his behalf."

Judge Clarke looked at Joseph as though annoyed—he wasn't. "Very well, Mr. Joseph. You don't have to educate the Court on procedures in criminal cases, but I will, as required, enter a 'not guilty' plea on your client's behalf."

At this point Thuman said, "Your Honor, if the Court please, we would like to address the issue of bond. As you know the municipal judge ordered the defendant held on $500,000 bond. We are considering asking for the death penalty, in which case there will be no bond. We are therefore asking that, for the time being, you continue the $500,000 bond."

Joseph stood and said, "We, too, wanted to address the issue of bond. I'm sure Your Honor knows Jimmy's family. They have lived all their lives in the community and have never been a problem. Jimmy has always worked and has had no serious dealings with the authorities. He assured me he would stay with his parents and make himself available to the Court whenever required. I do not think he would be a risk of flight and ask the Court to consider a personal recognizance bond."

Judge Clarke waved both lawyers to their seats. "Yes, I know the defendant's family; however, under the circumstances I will grant the State's request and continue the bond at five hundred thousand dollars."

Joseph, glancing at Thuman, noted the smug grin on his face. *Wonder what's with him and why he's taking such a personal interest in this case,* Joseph thought.

Judge Clarke continued, "Now, there is one other matter to bring up. I am not going to hear this case. I've made a notation on the file jacket to reassign the case to Judge Janet Crider in Courtroom Number One. For the record, you should be made aware of the fact that I have known the

Takas family for some time—Jimmy's parents—and although I believe I can be impartial, I want to avoid any possible appearance of impropriety. For that reason I will not hear this case."

Joseph was not pleased with the judge's decision to dump the case. He was the judge before whom Joseph had tried the Mountain City murder case and had been well satisfied with his handling of it. *Maybe he isn't the brightest of judges,* Joseph thought, *but he is extremely fair, always willing to listen and take the most just position.*

Joseph knew that if Judge Clarke were to recuse himself, the case would be assigned to Judge Crider, a well-respected lady of indeterminate years, who was married only to the law. She dressed conservatively and smartly, was well read and intelligent, but all of her legal experience had been obtained in the local prosecutor's office. Even though she was capable and knowledgeable, Joseph felt her bias would not benefit his client.

"Judge, we have no doubt that you would not allow your familiarity with the Takas family to influence you in any way. The defense would request that you stay on the case. We aren't permitted to judge shop and I don't think the State should be allowed that advantage. No one has ever questioned your impartiality—and I don't think anyone would do so now." Joseph tried to talk Judge Clarke out of his decision, but Clarke was adamant.

* * *

"Shit," Joseph said to Terry, "Judge Clarke recusing himself isn't going to make things any easier," referring to the transfer as he showed the article appearing in the morning paper to Terry.

The major newspapers hadn't yet picked up the most recent events in the story, but Joseph was pleased to note that Stan Marten was continuing to cover the story for the *Milltown Reporter.* He was satisfied it would be reported fairly as he read the article in the paper on the morning following the initial appearance before Judge Clarke:

MILLTOWN—Relying on a little used legal option, Jimmy Takas' attorneys Monday offered no plea on his behalf to a charge of murder, causing the Court to enter a "not guilty" plea. Takas' attorneys, Terry Bernow and Patrick Joseph, assigned by the Court, said this strategy leaves more options as the case progresses. They declined to elaborate. Takas is accused of stabbing June Westlock to death in her Milltown home and fleeing to Florida after being questioned by the police.

Judge Clarke recused himself from hearing the case, stating he was personally acquainted with the Takas family. The matter was reassigned to Judge Janet Crider in Courtroom One. Judge Crider will schedule all future hearings.

Takas, who has lived in the city most of his life, has been held in the county jail since being returned from Florida. He waived extradition and voluntarily returned with the Milltown police. The police refuse to speculate on the motive for the killing; but said it appears to be drug related.

The article went on, at length, to report the history of the case. "Might make it difficult to empanel a jury," Joseph mused.

*   *   *

As Joseph suggested earlier, even before he and Terry got started working up the case, the indictment was amended by a second grand jury. Prosecutor Thuman sought and, of course, was able to secure an amended indictment, charging Jimmy with the additional crime of aggravated murder while Attempting to Commit Rape. "The good news," Terry said, "is he didn't ask for the death penalty. The bad news is that Jimmy can be sentenced to life without parole instead of fifteen years to life for straight murder."

Before the defense lawyers were able to adjust their thinking to the new specification, it was again amended to seek the death penalty. "Can't say I didn't expect it," Joseph said to Terry.

Neither Joseph nor Terry knew where the sex specification came from, but knew they had to deal with it. Regardless of the severity of the charge, the discovery process was slow and cumbersome—typically Thuman.

Numerous discovery demands were served, all of which Thuman either ignored or responded to inadequately. As a result Joseph and Terry were required to file several motions to compel requesting that Judge Crider order the prosecutor to comply with the requirements of rule 16 of Ohio's Rules of Criminal Procedure. This rule sets forth in precise detail the information to which a defendant is entitled.

Each motion had to be set for hearing and argument, which irritated Judge Crider because it interfered with her docket. She didn't like anything that disrupted the smooth flow of her day. The prosecutor predictably fought each, but was ultimately ordered to deliver at least the basic discovery information, including the autopsy report, photographs of the body and crime scene, scientific analysis and reports from the Bureau of Criminal Investigation. The Court made known her irritation with the defense counsel for filing so many motions, to which Joseph responded somewhat sarcastically, "You know, Judge, if Thuman would comply with the rule, we wouldn't have to be here. Do you suppose you just might be getting irritated at the wrong people?"

Joseph knew there was much more to be had, but Thuman was as obtuse as expected. The two defense lawyers met several times a week discussing every aspect of the case. They visited Jimmy in jail again and again without securing any additional information. Jimmy would sit in pathetic silence, head down, hair in his eyes, hands clasped in his lap. When pressed, his only response was a tearful "I can't remember...."

In order to get a better understanding of the events of the night June Westlock was killed, Joseph visited her home. He and Terry decided that a scale drawing would be invaluable in assisting the jury to visualize what transpired. So he sought and received reluctant permission from the Court to employ a local architect, Gene Tollan, to prepare a scale drawing. He had used the architect on several previous occasions.

Back at the office, Joseph said, "Della , would you get Gene Tollan on the phone for me?"

When she buzzed him, the elderly lawyer picked up the phone and, after explaining the purpose of the call, asked, "Gene, can you meet me at June Westlock's house about one o'clock this afternoon for a walk-through. You can get a feel of the place and decide how you want to proceed?"

"Sure, I know how urgent this is. You never call unless you need something yesterday. I'm sure I can rearrange my schedule and meet you there—no problem. But you'll have to get permission from the police for me to spend some time there with an assistant to take measurements. Okay?"

Joseph gave the architect the address and assured him he would get the necessary permission. Joseph and Terry were waiting in front of Westlock's home when Tollan arrived.. The house was still marked with crime scene yellow tape. Officer Stanford, the same officer who had been there the morning of the killing, arranged to let them in. He watched the group, but made no effort to interfere. Joseph was particularly interested in the utility room, where the body was found. He wanted to know about the available light source and, more particularly, the details of how the outside door opened into the room.

Walking through the house, he took notice that the basket of artificial flowers described in the police reports was still on the floor, as was the kitchen chair, the onions and potatoes. After checking the photographs of the crime scene with the current conditions, Joseph shared them with the architect.

"Gene, I want these items," gesturing towards the basket, the chair and other items in the photographs, "shown in your drawing. Ms. Westlock's body also. Please locate the body in your drawings just as it is shown on the police photographs. The drawings should all be to scale and on poster boards large enough for the jury to see—say from a distance of fifteen to twenty feet. If the State won't stipulate to the accuracy of them, you will have to testify that the drawings and the measurements were made by you or under your supervision. We need the entire house floor plan, the location of the furniture in the living room, the kitchen and the utility room, although I believe the dryer has been removed by the Prosecutor's Office. You can see where it was. The indentations in the linoleum will give you the measurements."

Tollan responded to Joseph's instructions, "I'm familiar with the procedure. Remember, we've done this kind of thing before, but never in such a high profile case. Hope I don't have to appear in court, but if I have to, I will."

Then turning to Terry, Joseph asked, "Have I missed anything?"

"I don't think so. We might want some rough sketches first so we can go over them with Jimmy. Oh, and we should have a plot plan showing the house location on the lot and the location of the outside light and things in the yard that might bear on the case. Don't want to take a chance and miss anything."

"Good idea. How soon can we get the sketches, Gene?"

"Is a week soon enough? We won't do the final drawings until you approve the sketches. Okay?"

"Great. Thanks. Give me a call when they're ready."

*   *   *

The balance of the week passed fairly quickly. Since there was little activity on the Westlock case—now called the Takas file—Joseph was kept busy by Della with routine office matters, most of which were handled by others in the office. On Friday afternoon Joseph was relaxing in his high-backed desk chair, feet propped as usual on his waste basket. He sipped at the Martini glass in his hand, watching those assembled in his office. Della was ensconced comfortably on the couch, also sipping her drink. The rest of the staff were in various states of repose. Joseph enjoyed Fridays with the office family gathered together. Everyone seemed to like each other, notwithstanding the occasional sibling uprising. Even the pigs blessed the group with friendly smiles.

The staff was anxious to listen to whatever progress was made in the Takas case. Terry rushed in, late as usual, joining them and accepting only a soft drink, diet at that—"Have a lots more work to do," he explained.

Joseph thought, *He works too hard. Needs to learn to relax.* With the Takas case under discussion, Terry reached for his briefcase and pulled out some eight-by-ten photographs. "Have you had a chance to look at the coroner's photographs of the wounds, Mr. Joseph?"

"Yes, I have. Why? Is there something in particular you want me to see?"

"Well, I'm not sure, but I have some blow-ups of the stab wounds. According to the autopsy report, several of the wounds were inflicted after Ms. Westlock was already dead. I noticed the wounds—they don't all look alike to me. It doesn't make sense—why they're different—don't understand it. But it seems to me we should look into it. It seems to be an area that the police and prosecution have ignored. Don't know if it will help, but who knows…." His voice trailed off.

"I know what you mean, Terry," Joseph responded. "I noticed the same thing and it's been bothering me too. That's why I asked Kathy Cobal to look at the photos. She's a resident at University Hospitals in forensic pathology. She is also a trained artist. She worked as a medical illustrator to earn money while going to school. She is pretty busy now, but agreed to stop by tomorrow morning to talk about the case. I have a good friend at University Hospital who told me about her. He also said not to take too much of her time—that residents hardly have time to sleep, let along get involved in a murder case. I assured him we just needed some help and wouldn't take up too much of her time if we could avoid it. I was going to tell you earlier, but you're so busy, I can never get you to stand still long enough to talk about anything," with a smile. "I assume you're available. I sent her a copy of the autopsy report and the photographs. I'd appreciate it if you bring your set of pictures with you in the morning. Okay?"

Terry, blushing, responded somewhat defensively, "Sure, Mr. Joseph. It really is interesting and, candidly, I don't understand it. Besides, you know I'm available anytime you want."

"Now, would you like a drink?"

"Like I said, just a diet soda. I still have some work to do downstairs."

"You young fellows work too hard. Isn't that so, Della?

Della responded with one of Mary's classic "Humphh"s.

The rest of the office staff gathered around Joseph's desk to look at the pictures. Each had a comment. Joseph listened patiently and was proud of the way everyone wanted to make a contribution. He knew how pleased they would feel with a satisfactory result, and how devastated if there were none. Joseph's chest swelled with pride.

With the conversation in full flow, Joseph heard the front door open. "Della, didn't you lock the door?"

"No. Stan Marten called and said he'd be stopping by. He said you gave him a call and invited him for a drink."

"I did? Getting old—don't remember. Is that him?"

Stan appeared at the office door and smiled. "Is this the way all law offices work? Maybe I chose the wrong profession."

"Come on in," Joseph invited. "What would you like to drink?"

Looking at Terry, Stan said, "Whatever he's drinking."

Joseph nodded for Della to bring Stan a drink and complained, "Can't understand this generation at all. Don't seem to mind ruining their brains with drugs of all kinds, but can't handle a man's drink."

"And how are you, Mr. Joseph?" Stan asked, changing the subject. "Talking about the Westlock case?"

"Yes, as a matter of fact we were," handing Stan the sheaf of photographs that were spread on his table. "See what you make of these."

Stan Marten studied them for a few minutes, saying, "I've seen these already. Is there something about them bothering you?"

"Yes, there is, Stan, but it's off the record so far. I don't want to see anything in the paper about it. Take a look at the wounds in these pictures," Joseph said. He then explained what Terry and he had noticed. "I've asked a forensic pathologist—well, she is doing a residency in forensic pathology—to come and take a look at the marks on the body and tell me what she thinks. In the meantime there is something I would like to get from you—some information. Terry and I've noticed that Thuman is being strangely silent and I was wondering if he had something up his sleeve that I don't know about."

"I can't think of anything, Mr. Joseph. I've tried to talk to him several times and he isn't saying much. For some reason he keeps putting me off. That isn't like him at all. He likes to see his name in the paper more than anyone I know. But some of his assistants don't mind talking to me. They say he's mobilizing his entire office on the case—not paying attention to much else. I've never seen anyone in the Prosecutor's Office so fixated on a case."

"Do you think I should be doing something else, Stan? Can you think of anything I might have missed?" Joseph inquired.

"If I know you, you've covered all the bases and are ready to try the case. Is there anything you want to tell me that I can print? Sure could use a good story."

"Nothing I can think of—except Jimmy's innocent. Can you think of anything else, Terry?"

Terry shook his head silently.

"If I think of anything, it's yours, Stan," Joseph said. "Now enjoy your diet whatever and let me finish my Martini. Kids…" Joseph said, shaking his head in wonderment.

*   *   *

On Saturday morning, as agreed, Terry stopped at Joseph's house to pick him up. Terry enjoyed the long, tree-lined driveway and the peaceful rural flavor of the place. He looked forward to seeing the deer and two fawns grazing near the tree line in the front yard, where they lived. He enjoyed it almost as much as Joseph. His heritage told him that he too belonged to the country and would get there as soon as he could afford it. There were no deer, squirrels, rabbits or other little beasties prancing, playing or eating there this morning, but Terry could see activity at the house. Mary was outside raising her flag and placing yard ornaments around—her cats sitting in the front window watched her every move. She called them her watch-cats. When she saw Terry parking his car in the turnaround, she asked, "Have you had breakfast yet?"

"No, ma'am. I don't often eat breakfast. My wife gets upset if I make too much noise in the morning. Doesn't want me to wake the kids until they have to get up."

"That's silly. You need a good breakfast," Mary instructed, shaking her head. She had as much trouble as Joseph did understanding this generation of kids. She said, "Terry, you come into the house and I'll fix you a decent breakfast," and walked Terry toward the house and in through the kitchen door. Terry followed obediently, as most people did when Mary gave instructions.

Joseph was in the kitchen drinking a cup of black coffee—the way he liked it. Mary pointed Terry toward a chair at the kitchen table and said, "Sit while I fix you breakfast."

Joseph complained, "We really don't have time. We have to be at the office before nine."

"The boy needs to eat. Now be quiet while I get him something," she said as she removed eggs, bacon and juice from the refrigerator and put bread in the toaster.

Joseph knew it was no use arguing, so he glanced at his watch. It was still early enough, so he suggested, "May as well make some for me too."

Mary responded with her patented "Humphh," but retrieved a couple more eggs from the refrigerator.

Joseph grinned as he prepared to take advantage of Mary's generous hospitality whenever guests were in her home. He hid his smile behind the morning paper so Mary wouldn't see how pleased he was. It pleased him that she wanted to, and did, make visitors comfortable in their home.

After consuming the extravagant meal Mary prepared, Joseph patted his belly and enjoyed the sated feeling. He and Terry arrived at the office a few minutes before nine. Kathy Cobal had already arrived and parked her car in the lot behind the office building as instructed. Leaning comfortably against the hood of her economy car, she smiled a welcome. Joseph greeted her warmly as he unlocked the building's backdoor and ushered her in. He noted that, since she had completed medical school and internship and was doing a residency, she must be close to thirty, yet the young African-American, dressed in tight low-rise jeans, black turtleneck sweater and tennis shoes, looked like a teenager. Tall and slender, she stood straight and proud, hair cropped short and neatly groomed. Her smooth and creamy skin was enhanced only slightly by cosmetics at lip and cheek. Joseph was impressed by her bearing and felt she would be an asset to the defense team.

After they were seated in Joseph's office, he asked, "Would you mind telling us a little about yourself?"

"Not at all. I've lived in Cleveland all my life, except for college. Went to Ohio State on a combination academic and athletic scholarship—ran track. Did my pre-med there. Was accepted into med-school at Case Western Reserve and was graduated from there four years ago. Did my internship at University Hospitals, residency in Akron General, and returned to University Hospitals as a fellow in forensic pathology. I have always been interested in the law and medicine—felt that is where I belong. While in the Cleveland public school system, one of my teachers noted that I had some talent in art so got me into the Cleveland Institute of Art for some early training. I am a pretty decent artist. That led to a job as a medical illustrator for a local publishing house. Even though I had scholarships, I needed money for books and stuff to get through school. Loans and the job as a medical illustrator carried me through. As I said, I am particularly interested in forensic pathology. That's why when you called the school, the Dean asked me if I wanted to review the file for you to see if I could be of any help. Seems he knows you pretty well and is anxious to help. Even though I am pretty busy at the hospital, he asked me to spend some time with you. I am kind of excited about working on a murder case too. I charge twenty-five dollars an hour for my drawings. If there is anything else you want from me—like testifying in court — we can work something out on the fees. Is that all right?"

Joseph and Terry were both immediately enamored by her soft voice and delicate delivery. She appeared relaxed and confident in herself and her abilities without being arrogant or overbearing. *A perfect witness,* Joseph thought, *I must be more than thirty years older than she is, and still don't have the self-confidence she does. It's got to be a generational thing.*

"Have you ever testified in court?" Terry asked.

"No, I haven't," she responded.

Terry continued, "Would you be willing to do so, if needed?"

"I would hope I don't have to because of the demands on my time, but if it's part of the job, of course I would do it. Wouldn't dress like this though. I do have some clothes that make me look like a professional," she replied with her endearing smile.

They all chuckled at the comment. Then Joseph asked, "Now, I sent you a copy of the autopsy report and the photographs I wanted you to look at. Would you review the autopsy findings and the photographs for us and tell us what they revealed to you?"

Immediately Kathy Cobal was all business. She drew out the copy of the autopsy report from her briefcase and spread it on the table before them.

"The autopsy protocol was prepared by the Cuyahoga County Coroner's Office. They're generally quite good. It indicates that June Westlock was a well-developed, adequately nourished Caucasian woman who appeared to be her stated age. She measured sixty-eight inches— that's five feet, eight inches—in height and weighed one hundred nine pounds. The report concluded that she had sustained a variety of injuries, some categorized as blunt-force injuries and some, the report says, were produced by an edge-pointed instrument. It makes me uncomfortable to comment on the work of a colleague, especially one who has had so much more experience than I, but I do take some minor issue with the autopsy report. It appears to me Ms. Westlock was stabbed or cut with more than one edge-pointed instrument—not a single instrument as it appears in the protocol. Maybe I noticed it because of my artist's eye. Anyway, I'll explain my reasons later.

"The blunt-force injuries noted are abrasions on the left cheek, the neck, the left shoulder and breast. This would seem to indicate that she had a physical confrontation with her assailant, but none of these injuries were medically significant. There were a number of superficial scrapes, some on her face, on the anterior or front of her trunk, on the extremities, and so on. Again, none were life threatening and it is difficult to tell exactly when she received them, although it is fairly obvious some were received during the fight with whoever attacked her that night—whether it be a person or persons."

Joseph was fascinated by the ease with which she reported these findings. "Tell us about the disagreement you mentioned with the coroner's report."

"Look at these pictures." The student fanned out the several glossy photographs Joseph had sent her. "These are blow-ups of the wounds suffered by June Westlock."

Joseph was pleased that Ms. Cobal personalized the victim.

"I noticed that the wounds did not all appear to be the same, so I asked a photographer to blow up or enlarge the pictures even further. There were fourteen stab wounds in all, one was at the base of the neck. It was three-eights of an inch in length and about an inch deep. There was one in the front of the neck, one in the right breast that did not enter the chest cavity. I'm not going to describe all of the wounds now—they are described in detail in my report—but you should know that there is a cluster of eight stab wounds in the abdomen, several of which actually penetrated to the abdominal cavity; however, very little blood was associated with these wounds. In fact, there was no bleeding into the abdominal cavity. Many of the wounds appear yellow. This means that most of those wounds were actually inflicted after Ms. Westlock died, or at about the time of her death. The most significant stab wound was in her back—on the left side—the entry wound was one-half inch in width, but penetrated deeply into her body immediately below the rib cage. It went through the left lung and struck the aorta. The aorta is the main artery, carrying blood from the heart to the rest of the body."

Joseph and Terry both sat silently, completely captivated by the young lady's lecture.

"That was the lethal injury. It was this wound and the fact that a number of them were delivered postmortem—that is after she died—and shaped differently that led me to believe more than one instrument was used. In fact, I believe there were three separate instruments. This wound—the one that led to her death—was from a very sharp, pointed blade with two edges. In other words, the wound was tapered on both sides. In fact, the wound was so deep the hilt or whatever else was at the base of the blade made a small bruise on Ms. Westlock's back. It left a mark like initials or a monogram. It looked like a circle with a letter in it that I couldn't make out—it wasn't clear enough.

"The second instrument, I believe, was like a kitchen knife that has one sharp edge and a blunt back—shaped like an elongated triangle. The third instrument appears to be like one of the blades of a pair of scissors. The triangle is more marked, not so elongated, and the blunt end more pronounced."

Joseph asked, "Could you draw a picture of each of the wounds, identify what instrument you believe administered it, and then draw a picture of the instrument itself?"

Yes, I can. In fact, I've already done that for my benefit—just sketches, but I think you can understand them," Kathy said as she drew more papers from her briefcase. "Here they are."

Joseph and Terry studied the drawings. Joseph finally asked, "Could you make final drawings of these and put them on poster boards? I would like to be able to place them on an easel to use as demonstrative evidence."

"Of course. Happy to," with her captivating smile.

Joseph and Terry thanked Ms. Cobal effusively for all the work she had done, gave her a check for the time already spent and arranged to pay for the work they expected her to do.

"Oh, by the way. There is something I hadn't mentioned yet. Almost forgot. There were three very small puncture wounds beneath the left breast of Ms. Westlock. It appears they were from a needle—like a hypodermic needle. They are in an unusual place—you know, where one wouldn't expect to find them if the deceased was injecting drugs or medication. They do not seem to be significant or relevant to the case at all. That is, they did not contribute to her death, but they made me think that Ms. Westlock did either shoot drugs occasionally, or had the paraphernalia for doing so. These needle marks appeared to be made before she died, but there is nothing to indicate that they were for the purpose of injecting drugs or any other type of medication—nothing was found at the site of the wounds. But they did suggest the need for a toxicology analysis. Samples of her body fluid—blood, urine, fluid from the gall bladder and stomach contents—were tested and found to be positive for marijuana, cocaine and benzoylecgonine, which is the breakdown product of cocaine. There were drugs in her system when she died—enough so that she was probably fairly high at the time of her death.

"She had a few needle marks on her arm where you usually find them in drug users—but not enough to signify she would shoot up regularly."

After she left, Joseph turned to Terry, "What do you think?"

"Wow! Everything she talked about is not only interesting, but I think vital to the defense—really important stuff—and she's beautiful. She'll make a great witness if we need her. Whether we use her or not, her drawings will be invaluable in your cross-examination of the coroner."

"What do you mean, my cross-examination? Aren't you going to do anything?" Joseph asked with a grin.

Terry responded, smiling, "Why do you think I asked you to be involved, old man? I didn't want to do everything. Myself." He was obviously getting comfortable enough with the elder lawyer to exchange an occasional barb. Joseph was pleased, but would never admit it.

Joseph glanced at his pigs. They too were smiling and, in fact, there smiles indicated they were pleased with the progress thus far. Joseph only hoped he could keep them happy.

"Joking aside, we need to talk to Jimmy again. Want to set up a meeting?" Joseph asked.

"Will do. We can see him first thing Monday."

*   *   *

The following Monday morning, Joseph sat in his office waiting for Terry. While he waited, he spread all three newspapers across his scarred desk. They were strangely silent. *Wonder why they aren't saying anything about the killing,* Joseph thought. *Seems like it should still be news. Unless the Prosecutor's Office or the police are sitting on something we don't know about. Maybe I should give Stan a call and see if he knows what's going on.*

Terry walked into Joseph's office and the two men—one young, tall and slender; the other old, short and plump—left to cross the square towards the Old Courthouse and jail, Terry chatting all the way. Joseph enjoyed the morning sun and the noise of the children arguing their way to school. Children, squirrels and birds belonged to the square and the day. Joseph was sorely tempted to sit on one of the park benches and just enjoy the morning sun. He didn't.

Arriving at the jail, the lawyers impatiently went through the usual security procedures before gaining access. Jimmy was waiting for them in the same cell. He was being kept out of the prison population. Many of the prisoners knew June Westlock, and, if not particularly friendly towards her, they had relied on her as a source of good feelings. As a result, Jimmy had been the subject of some fairly serious threats. There had been at least one fight—not that it was much of a fight, since Jimmy was incapable of protecting himself. The correction officers feared the other prisoners would take lethal action if Takas were allowed to remain in the prison community.

Terry and Joseph walked into the cell, noting that Jimmy had assumed his usual hang-dog posture on the cot that he had at their original meeting. Joseph thought, *He can't be comfortable.*

Shaking his head in wonderment, Joseph sat down next to Jimmy while Terry again perched gingerly on the seatless toilet after looking it over carefully.

Joseph said, "Jimmy, it would be a hell of a lot easier for me to talk to you if you would at least look at me," exasperation creeping into his voice.

Takas looked up for a moment, but his head quickly drooped. Terry, aware of Joseph's growing frustration, tried to lighten the mood by filling Jimmy in on what they had learned so far. Jimmy expressed no interest. If he hadn't occasionally glanced toward Terry, Joseph would have been convinced the young man heard nothing.

Joseph interrupted Terry's discourse and asked Takas, "Jimmy, has anything we've talked about refreshed your memory about the night June was killed?"

Jimmy answered with a brief negative shake of his head. *At least he heard that question,* Joseph thought.

"Jimmy, do you own a knife?" Terry asked.

Takas again shook his head negatively.

"Jimmy, for God's sake, we need some help! How often did you go to June's house? Did you know where she kept her knives? Have you ever used them? What did you do at her house? Come on, give us something," Terry pleaded.

Jimmy looked up at Terry through the hair hanging over his glasses. Then looking away again, he answered, "I was usually there when Clarence was around. They always had some good stuff—usually coke— you know, powder. June kept a razor blade, a needle and her stash in the linen closet in the hall by the bedrooms. She would get whatever we were going to use and bring it into the laundry room. She or Clarence would use the razor blade to cut lines on top of the dryer. Sometimes she'd have crack. We'd bust that up and smoke it with marijuana. They always had plenty of stuff. Sometimes she'd shoot up. I never did. When we got high, we would go into the living room and watch TV, you know, the music channel—it was always on. I never went back into the bedrooms because that was where her kid slept. Besides, Clarence was jealous. I don't know why he was jealous of me—she always had different guys over—they partied all the time—can't remember anything else—nothing," Takas whispered so softly it was difficult to hear.

"What about the bloody shirt?" Joseph asked.

"I don't remember...I can't remember..." whining.

Joseph exploded, "Jimmy, I'm getting goddamn impatient with you! We're busting our balls trying to help you and you're giving us nothing. I don't know if you're lying, frightened or just plain stupid!"

No response except for a sniffling sound coming from somewhere beneath Jimmy's hanging head.

Joseph looked at Terry. "Shit! Let's get the hell out of here! We're not going to get anything from Jimmy. We still got to... He's not going to help.... Looks like we got a lot more digging to do. Especially about the dryer."

CHAPTER SEVEN

The summer advanced slowly, Terry and Joseph doing their best to secure information from the police, the Prosecutor's Office and their client. The police, always friendly to Joseph, tried to cooperate. But, as expected, the Prosecutor's Office, obviously at Thuman's direction, continued its opposition every time the defense team made any effort to learn something—anything to help prepare a defense.

Rule 16 of Ohio's Rules of Criminal Procedure was designed by Ohio's Supreme Court to give both the State and the defendant equal footing at trial—to prevent trial by ambush. There should be no surprises. The new prosecutor either didn't believe it or didn't care. He wasn't about to abide by the rule unless forced to by the Court. This again resulted in a continuing slew of motions to compel on every issue and increased the cost to everyone—in Jimmy's case, since he was indigent, the State had to pay the entire bill. Judge Crider became more and more irritated with both the State and defense. Joseph stubbornly refused to back down, thinking, *Thuman makes no sense at all. The son of a bitch isn't going to get away with this. At least the judge is getting a little pissed at him instead of just us.*

The legal community learned, the hard way, that in the limited time Thuman had been in office, his philosophy was *If I charge someone with a crime, he's guilty! Winning is the only acceptable result—fairness be damned.* Thuman's single-minded hostility became more and more apparent at each hearing; and, for some reason, he was pushing for a quick trial. The prosecutor involved himself in every avenue of the investigation.

"He's always obstructive, but, for some reason, even more so in Jimmy's case," Joseph complained to Terry.

As the result of Joseph's persistence, the Court forced the office of the prosecutor to turn over what the defense team believed to be truly important information—a report from the Bureau of Criminal Investigation containing an analysis of the fingerprints and blood at the crime scene. But one of the pages was missing. Not understanding, Joseph called a friend at the Bureau, more commonly called BCI, and was informed that "Yes, there does seem to be a page missing from your copy. That is the page reporting a partial palm print on the dryer that had been removed from June Westlock's utility room. The print is the defendant's and it is superimposed on a spot of blood. We got the dryer and the prosecutor told us to preserve it for evidence in the case."

After receiving this information from BCI, the prosecutor called a press conference and couldn't wait to tell the media about his spin on the findings. "We found the smoking gun—that is, we discovered an absolute indication of guilt. The defendant's palm print is on the dryer found in the room where Ms. Westlock was killed. It was found on top of June Westlock's blood."

When Joseph learned of the statement to the press, the missing page gained importance. The missing page, Joseph learned from his contact at BCI, contained the phrase *The Criminalist doing the analysis of the blood-spot is unable to determine whose blood is beneath the print.*

Thuman's statement just wasn't true.

The criminalist from BCI added, "Not only are we unable to say with any degree of scientific certainty," using their style of witness-speak, "whose blood is beneath the print, we have no way of knowing when the print or blood was deposited on the dryer."

Hearing this, Joseph felt his face reddening and his anger stirring. He sputtered, "Goddamn it, Terry, this information is not only exculpatory, but vital to the defense. The State, according to rule 16, is obligated to provide exculpatory information to us."

Joseph was incensed that the report had not been given to him early on. "Terry, we have to file another motion to compel. I'm really getting tired of this shit!"

Joseph filed the motion and requested an immediate hearing. At the hearing, Joseph complained vehemently to Judge Crider, "For God's sake, Judge. This is probably the most important thing we've discovered so far. It completely removes the 'smoking gun' Thuman keeps talking about."

Judge Crider had called the prosecution team and defense lawyers into her chambers to hear the latest motion filed by the defense. The walls of her office were lined with bookshelves, containing not only law books, but figurines and photographs evidencing her love of cats. What could be seen of the walls was painted a robin egg blue—relaxing color—Joseph didn't feel relaxed. He was tired of fighting these battles. The windows overlooked the square and were covered by attractive drapes that attested to the judge's femininity. The judge, in response to Joseph's arguments, said, "Calm down, Mr. Joseph, before you have a heart attack. I'm not sure how important it is, but you are entitled to it. Why didn't you give the report to him, Harry?"

Joseph didn't appreciate the familiarity—the judge not only using his first name, but the diminutive of it. It was obvious she was much more friendly toward the prosecution than the defense.

Thuman, slouching in one of the judge's pattered upholstered chair, legs crossed at the ankles and tie askew, said, "Judge, the State doesn't believe the information exculpatory. But we did give him the BCI report. The page he's talking about must have been left out inadvertently. Besides, the victim was the only dead body in the room. Her blood was all over the place. No doubt the blood on the drier is hers—and the murderer's print is on the victim's blood."

"You're probably right, Harry, but give it to him anyway. No sense giving him more arguments for appeal."

Joseph, inwardly seething, but outwardly calm, replied quietly, "Thank you, Your Honor. Although I can't say that I appreciate your accepting Thuman's prejudging of the facts. You're supposed to be unbiased, you know."

The judge looked at Joseph and was about to say something when the prosecutor interrupted her. "I'll mail it to him, Judge."

Joseph stood abruptly, face red, "Like hell. We all know how undependable the mail process is. We'll walk over to your office and pick it up," indicating that he and Terry would accompany Thuman back to his office to get the report. "If it's mailed, we'll get it the second or third day of trial, or it'll somehow 'inadvertently' get lost in the mail."

Terry placed a calming hand on Joseph's shoulder. Joseph shrugged it off.

"Oh, never mind. I think Anne probably has a copy with her in the file. You can have it now," Thuman said ungraciously as Anne Dronke handed him a sheet of paper, that he passed to Terry, ignoring Joseph.

Terry leaned over to accept the document and whispered in the elderly lawyer's ear, "Relax, Mr. Joseph. He's an asshole, but isn't worth getting worked up over."

Joseph thought, *One good thing about Thuman's obtuse and obstructive behavior is that it makes me forget my feelings of insecurity. The boiling in my belly must put the butterflies to sleep.*

*   *   *

With the trial rapidly approaching, all of Joseph's office staff pitched in. Witnesses were interviewed and research done. Sheaves of paper containing witness statements and legal briefs were stacked, carefully labeled, on Joseph's desk for review. Joseph's perusal of each document resulted in additional instructions for the staff, all of whom labored for the benefit of Jimmy Takas—without being sure that he either knew about it or appreciated it. Joseph could not have been prouder of them.

Several witnesses refused to talk to Joseph's staff, saying that the prosecutor told them not to. This, of course, Thuman denied while Joseph seethed.

Although Takas was originally charged with straight murder, now as a result of the additional charges stemming from the prosecutor's contention that the killing was done while the assailant was attempting to rape the victim, Joseph and Terry were required to prepare and defend a death penalty case—much more complicated than a straight murder defense. In Ohio this requires a two-part trial—the first to determine guilt or innocence, and, if the defendant is found guilty, the second part is for the jury to consider whether or not the defendant should be put to death—two complete trials. Thuman was in his glory—not yet a year in office and he had his death penalty case.

*   *   *

Joseph was sitting at the breakfast table enjoying—well, probably not enjoying, but consuming—a late Saturday morning breakfast. He'd been up a good part of the night reviewing the Takas file. When he did fall asleep, he didn't sleep very soundly. His tossing and turning kept Mary awake a good part of the night as well. Joseph felt fortunate indeed that she was willing to prepare his breakfast for him, even though it was done in silence. Joseph could hear Mary explain to the cats how inconsiderate he was and how happy she would be when the trial was finished. "I can't understand why he gets himself involved in such a stressful case," she told the cats, ignoring the fact that she insisted he become involved. Joseph was smart enough not to remind her of this.

The trial was to begin next week and he wanted to relax as much as possible this weekend. His inability to look forward to a trial without major trepidation was not alleviated in the slightest by his victory in the earlier murder trial. He thought he could approach a new one without fear but finally realized, *Not true. How can anyone walk into a courtroom holding another man's freedom...or worse yet, someone's life...in his hands? Who the hell do I think I am? I can't do this....* Joseph could feel the fluttering in his stomach and the worms crawling beneath his skin. He was a wreck.

Mary, sipping her coffee, said, "By the way, your mother called while you were in the shower."

"Really, what'd she want?"

"Said she couldn't remember the last time you came to see her. Wanted to know if you were all right."

Joseph's mother was ninety-one years old and lived in an assisted-living facility nearby. She had some physical disabilities, but her mind was as sharp as ever, especially when explaining to Joseph how inconsiderate he was, forcing her to give up her house and move into a rented apartment. It didn't matter that they did feed her three times a day, clean her room, do her laundry and make her bed as well as provide her with all of the comforts she could possibly want or need, including a beauty parlor and bingo.

"You know I saw her twice this week. Had lunch with her Thursday. That's when Father O'Donnell comes to the home, has a little service and distributes Communion. The ladies all love him—even the ones that aren't Catholic. In fact, she insisted I go to the service with her and receive Communion. That's why God's so pleased with me and asked you to fix my breakfast. Did she sound like she needed something?"

As usual, Mary ignored his comments, but she said, "No. She just missed her baby."

"She can be a pain. But I understand her loneliness. Hope I don't live that long. I'll go see her later this morning, unless you have other plans for me. It's probably a good time since the Takas trial is going to start next week.. Actually Tuesday. Judge Crider always handles arraignments and pleas on Mondays—gets rid of the weekend stuff. "

Mary said, "I'll be working outside in the yard. Someone has to do the weeding. It doesn't get done by itself. I know you don't want to do it and there's nothing else you need to do. But I was hoping we could go to the mall this afternoon. Got to get some birthday presents."

She and Joseph had so many grandchildren, there was at least one birthday a month. Mary insisted on buying gifts for all of them and on taking the older children, especially the girls, shopping so they could pick out what they wanted. *Damn kids always want to go to Abercrombie or Victoria's Secret or some other expensive store to pick out stuff no one needs,* Joseph brooded silently.

"Well then, I can go for a little while this morning. I'll be back before noon and we can have lunch up at the mall, if that's okay with you," Joseph said.

Mary grunted her usual assent.

Joseph's mother would soon be ninety-two and made sure everyone knew it, was living in an assisted-living residence located in nearby

Mountain City. Joseph picked it after visiting all the facilities in the area when his mother fell and broke her hip on the same day her second husband died. Even though it was difficult for her to get around, her mind and mouth weren't affected at all by the injury. She enjoyed her suite of rooms, the delivered meals and almost daily bingo. She won frequently and was paid fifty cents for each win. She couldn't understand how she managed to win bingo money when she didn't have to pay for the cards. No matter how many times Joseph explained that it was included in the three thousand dollars a month he paid, she continued to believe her three- or four-dollar weekly winnings were profit for which Joseph should be appreciative, especially since she used it to contribute to her expenses.

"You want to go with me, Mary? We can do the shopping after."

"No thanks. You go ahead. You can just pick me up at noon and take me to lunch. We'll shop after that."

Joseph thought, *God, how I hate to shop. Got to keep her happy. At least I get to read while she wanders the stores. Can't understand how she can spend so much time looking.*

Joseph drove his small red truck to the home and parked in the small lot in front of his mother's unit. As he walked into the suite of rooms his mother occupied he noted she was dosing in the lift-chair Joseph and Mary bought for her. He knocked on the door as he entered.

His mother opened her eyes and looking at him said, "Who are you? What are you doing in my bedroom?"

Joseph turned and started to walk out.

She said, "Where are you going?"

Joseph looked over his shoulder, "You should never allow strangers in your bedroom."

"Come in, Pasquale." She was the only one to use his given name, unless Mary was really angry about something.

Joseph came in and listened to the usual list of complaints…his inattentiveness to her…his lack of consideration…his lack of appreciation for the labor pains by which he was delivered into the world…and, finally, his refusal to follow a career as a respected musician

100

instead of sneaking to law school and becoming an *avvocato*—"Who could respect a lawyer?"

Despite her constant complaints, Joseph enjoyed the visits. He helped his mother into her wheelchair and wheeled her to the sitting room, where other ladies sat and whiled away the afternoons they didn't play bingo.

There were eight or ten women living in the house and they kept each other company. Their antics amused Joseph no end. One of the women was confined to a Jerry chair—an upright chair with wheels. There was a small panel at the bottom of the chair upon which she could rest her ever moving feet. One of the aides forgot to insert the panel and the movement of the lady's feet started the chair rolling. The faster it rolled, the faster she moved her feet. Before Joseph could catch her, she rolled completely across the length of the living room, stopping just before plunging into the far wall. When Joseph got to her she said with a sweet smile, "My, it's breezy in here today."

Two other women occupied the sitting room. One, an elderly Teutonic lady with work-roughened hands, broad shoulders and hefty girth. The other, a sweet-looking, grandmotherly grey-haired wisp of a thing who suffered from Tourette's syndrome, a condition in which the afflicted has a tic-like disorder that manifests itself in several different ways. In her case it resulted in the constant repetition of vulgarities at the top of her voice. She would repeat over and over again words not acceptable under any circumstances—but she had no control over it—couldn't help herself. This afternoon, sitting in her wheelchair, her friend next to her, she repeated again and again words that Joseph wasn't even sure he knew the meaning of. The elderly German lady rose from her wheelchair, walked to her friend and, in her heavily accented voice, said, "Dat is enuff of dat!" and swung her ham-heavy fist into the back of her friend's head, knocking her from her chair to the floor, where she looked around stunned, as if to say, *How did I get here?* That was the only time Joseph saw her that she wasn't swearing at the top of her lungs.

The elderly lawyer spent the remainder of the morning visiting with his mother and her friends, leaving when lunch was served, feeling remarkably refreshed. Now, looking forward to next week's work, he returned home and to the chores he was sure Mary had assigned to him. The worms were gone and the butterflies quiet—hopefully settled down for a long stay.

When Joseph arrived home, he knew Mary would be outside. He walked through the garage and out the backdoor, looking toward their pond, that usually housed mallard ducks or Canadian geese along with several offspring. One goose had been injured and could only hop around on one leg. The others showed no pity on their crippled friend and pushed him away from the food Mary put out for them. Joseph could see Mary standing by the pond, hands on her hip and hair bobbing with her animated conversation. She was bawling the geese out and instructing them that there would be no further treats unless they behaved more charitably towards each other.

Joseph thought, *I certainly would obey her if I were them.*

Mary returned to the house, still talking to the geese over her shoulder. When she saw Pat, she said, "There are no chores we need to get to today. We may as well go shopping."

Joseph said, "I'll be happy to go shopping with you if we can stop at *Macaroni's* for lunch." It was on the way to the Fairlawn Shopping Mall and Joseph knew he could get a glass of good dry red wine, maybe Chianti, with his lunch. It would sustain him through the afternoon while Mary shopped. Maybe he could even get a bit of a nap on one of the benches while waiting for his loving wife.

Mary said, "Okay," bringing a pleased smile to Joseph's lips.

CHAPTER EIGHT

Monday, Joseph thought, *is the longest day of the year.* He did somehow work his way through it, with chores devised by Della at the office and Mary at home, even though all he wanted to do was to go over his notes on the Takas file several more times. He couldn't believe he was adequately prepared. No matter how much time he spent on a file, he never felt prepared.

After what seemed an eternity Joseph managed to get himself to the office early as usual on Tuesday morning, where he waited patiently for Terry. Della had already supplied him with his morning coffee fix and was comfortably ensconced in one of the client chairs, ready to take notes or instructions for the day's activities. On the floor next to her was the large wheeled briefcase Joseph would take with him to court. She had packed it meticulously in the manner she knew Joseph liked—each witness' file in a separate folder, pleadings and documents in a three-ring binder—everything labeled so he could find it without difficulty. He never could find anything, but it certainly wasn't Della's fault—they tried. He knew they would be taking with them much more than was needed, but the elderly lawyer was unwilling to take a chance and not have some required document with him in court. *With my memory* he thought, *I'm bound to leave something behind.*

Promptly at eight thirty Terry appeared at Joseph's door. "Ready, Mr. Joseph?" he asked.

"Of course," Joseph grunted as he pushed himself from his chair, using its well-worn arms for assistance. "Just help me with my coat. It's starting to get cold out there. But at least the sun is shining." Not unusual for an October morning in northern Ohio.

Joseph worked his way into a worn raincoat with the lining removed. He couldn't stand the feeling of being bundled up, so when Mary bought him the new coat and took it home from the store he took out and hid the zip-in lining. It found its way into a garbage can when Mary wasn't looking. He couldn't make her understand that he just didn't like heavy coats or linings. A few minutes of cold was a small price to pay for the comfort of wearing what he wanted to wear. His one concession to the temperature was the donning of an old-fashioned soft-brimmed fedora on his nearly hairless pate. Shunning gloves, he grabbed the extended handle of the briefcase and lumbered out the door—Terry following, his own briefcase in gloved hands, he was bundled into a neatly pressed woolen overcoat, plaid wool scarf wrapped neatly around his neck. *Bet he lets his wife dress him,* Joseph thought.

Joseph looked around the square as he stepped from the building and could find no squirrels or birds. The nude trees had shed their brightly colored leafs. Children were scampering across the square, moving quickly towards the school, located within a block of the square. *At least there's some life in town,* Joseph mused. The absence of those things that made life worthwhile…children's noises, birds, squirrels…because of threatening weather, always saddened Joseph. He glanced toward the porch of the Americana Hotel and noted the lonely rocking chairs and checker boards.

Hurrying toward the school crossing guard, Joseph asked Terry, "Are you ready to handle voir dire?"

"Yes. I worked most of yesterday on the questions to ask prospective jurors and developed a kind of profile of those we might want to keep on the jury. Just like we talked about."

"I'm sure it's fine, Terry. I have absolute confidence in you," Joseph said, not being as forthright as he might. He never trusted anyone to do a job as well as he.

"Good morning," he said to the school crossing guard—a young lady whose boyfriend he had represented some time ago. She was sweet—he was not.

She smiled back and held up traffic so they could cross the street. *Just like she does for the kids,* Joseph thought. He shivered as he approached the courthouse steps, wondering if it was the cold or the feeling of hopelessness that always accompanied him when about to begin a trial like the one they would be starting this morning.

Entering the courthouse should be the least of my problems, Joseph thought, starting up the granite steps leading to the front door. Suddenly he felt lightheaded and unsettled. He reached for the metal railing running up the center of the stairs and paused to collect himself.

A look of anxiety on his face, Terry asked, "Are you okay, Mr. Joseph?"

Joseph drew in a deep breath and said, "I'll be fine. Just a case of the jitters. It'll pass."

"I know how you feel, Mr. Joseph," Terry said. "I didn't want to get out of bed this morning. Certainly couldn't eat breakfast."

"Mary wouldn't approve," Joseph responded.

Walking through the front door of the courthouse, Joseph saw several local lawyers and court employees, along with a number of reporters, lingering in the lobby. It hadn't dawned on him—even though it should have—that there would be much interest in the case. In fact, he was surprised to see members of the media from Cleveland and Akron hanging around. He'd expected Stan Marten, since he was from the local paper, but not the big city reporters. Stan was there and Joseph smiled a "hello" at him. Stan returned the smile and asked pleasantly, "Anything to talk about this morning?"

"Morning, Stan." Joseph smiled. "Now, how could there be? We haven't empaneled a jury yet. That's what we'll be working on this morning. We'll see how it goes. But you can tell your readers," he said, loud enough for all the media representatives to hear, "that based on everything we've been able to learn so far, the police again failed to investigate the case adequately. We think Jimmy is innocent—the wrong man is on trial."

The television cameras were rolling and Joseph was satisfied he had provided a quick sound bite that would appear on the news channels later in the day . *Take that, Thuman,* he thought.

"Did you know that the prosecutor himself will be lead trial counsel for the State?" Stan asked.

"No, I didn't, but I kind of suspected he would. He has shown a surprising interest in this case. He can do what he wants. It's his office. Seems to have taken an awful strong personal interest in the case— unusual," Joseph responded thoughtfully. "But I guess he is getting his wish—a death penalty murder case."

"Any comment for publication?" Stan asked.

"You mean besides what we've already said?" Joseph laughed, adding, "Nothing other than Terry and I will be doing what we can for Jimmy. He's professed his innocence and we have no reason to disbelieve him. We'll represent him as best we can."

All the while they were moving towards the elevators. Cameras flashed as the doors closed, isolating Joseph and Terry with several others who had entered the elevator from the floor below leading in from the parking lot out back. Joseph guessed correctly that these were prospective jurors so he smiled politely and said nothing.

The second-floor lobby was filled with people. An armed guard sat at the desk to the right of the elevator with his back to the windows overlooking the parking lot. He was probably close to sixty, thick waisted, stomach hanging over his duty belt. Longtime Mills County deputy sheriffs considered too old to handle patrol were relegated to courthouse security. He and Joseph knew each other well over the years, often trading jokes, stories and gossip. He smiled as Joseph exited the elevator. The jail could be seen from the window behind the guard. Joseph looked to see if Jimmy Takas and his escorts were on the way. Terry had asked Mrs. Takas to bring civilian clothes for Jimmy—a suit, shirt and tie if possible—so he would not appear before the jury in prison orange. If he didn't have a suit, Joseph suggested, a nice long-sleeve button shirt and sweater.

Mrs. Takas assured the lawyer, "He'll have a nice suit with a white shirt and tie. It will be pressed and clean. My boy is going to look nice."

The guard, without leaving his chair at the table near the elevator, signaled to Joseph. When the lawyer walked over, the guard whispered, "He's in the witness room with his mom, dad and just one officer."

"Thanks," Joseph said and motioned Terry towards the room—a windowless ten-by-ten-foot box just outside of Courtroom One. The mahogany door was closed, so Joseph tapped lightly on it and opened it without waiting for a response. He and Terry walked in. The room was crowded and almost stifling hot despite the outside temperature. Joseph said hello to Jimmy's mom and dad and asked if they would mind excusing themselves for a minute so he could talk to the boy. He also asked the officer to give them a little privacy. The guard smiled at Joseph—another acquaintance—and said, "Sure, Pat." Ushering Mr. And Mrs. Takas from the room, he stationed himself just outside the door.

The room held four chairs and a small conference table, the top of which was about the size of an opened newspaper. Jimmy sat on one of the wooden chairs by the table looking down at his lap. He hadn't looked up since Joseph and Terry entered. Joseph placed his hand on the boy's thin shoulder and smiled down at him. The boy had on khaki wash slacks, clean and obviously freshly pressed, a blue sport jacket, white shirt and conservatively marked tie—obviously not clothes with which he was overly familiar—the collar of the shirt a little too large and the tie poorly tied. He didn't look particularly comfortable—but then it was unlikely anything at this time in his life would make him comfortable.

"Look at me, Jimmy. We all knew this day would be coming. You should be relieved. We'll be picking the jury today. I don't want you going in there with that hang-dog look on your face. Be attentive. Pay attention to what's going on. Be serious, because it is serious, but don't look frightened or smart ass either. This is like going to church and you should put on your best church face. Your mom did a good job picking out something for you to wear. You look nice. We don't want her to see you looking so dejected."

Joseph hadn't the slightest idea whether or not Jimmy understood anything he said, or if he even heard him. He just hoped to put him a little at ease. If nothing else, he didn't want his client to look guilty. A guilty look could convince a jury to convict more than anything a prosecutor might have to offer. Jurors often formed their opinions on the first day, and usually based on things that had nothing to do with the trial.

Terry added, "I will be asking the prospective jurors questions. Listen to the questions and answers. Try to look at each prospective juror. We want them to be your friends. When it comes time to decide whether or not we want them on the jury, we'll do that together. That is, Mr. Joseph, you and I will make those choices together. Do you understand?"

Jimmy nodded, but didn't say anything. Joseph and Terry both sighed, Terry adding, "May as well get this show on the road."

The three of them stepped into the lobby and moved to the first door on the left—the entrance to Courtroom One. The uniformed guard followed discreetly, Jimmy's parents right behind him. Jimmy, the lawyers and the guard proceeded toward the trial table while Jimmy's parents slid inconspicuously into the back row of pew-like seats at the rear of the courtroom. The low murmur of voices quieted as they entered the courtroom. All eyes in the room followed the lawyers and the defendant to the large wooden table positioned in front of and slightly to the right of the judge's raised bench. The three chairs at the table were on the side that faced away from the center of the room. Joseph seated himself familiarly in the first seat nearest the witness box, Jimmy next to him and Terry in the chair closest to the jury box. The guard seated himself on a wooden bench located against the wall behind the trial table allocated to the defense, and next to the door leading into the jury room—the room that the jurors, when finally picked, would occupy during breaks in the trial and in which they would ultimately deliberate.

Joseph looked across the vacant area before the judge's bench and saw, seated at a table identical to theirs, Prosecutor Thuman himself in the first seat. Behind him was his chief assistant, Anne Dronke, whose philosophy mirrored that of her boss. She was often characterized as a vicious, no-holds-barred street fighter. Seated behind her was Lieutenant

Richard Tell of the Milltown Police Department Detectives Unit, since he was the homicide officer in charge of the Westlock investigation. One police officer was permitted to sit at the table with the prosecutors throughout the trial.

Joseph looked around the courtroom and thought, *Judge Crider's choice of color for her office extends into the courtroom. She repainted the courtroom with a baby-blue color when she was first elected to the office. A good choice actually, since it sets off nicely the dark mahogany of the furnishings and trim.* The room was large and without adornment, except for the Great Seal of the State of Ohio on the wall directly behind the judge's chair, an American flag in a stand behind her right shoulder and the Ohio flag on her left. The windows, all along one wall on the west side of the building, were draped and covered by vertical blinds, kept closed most of the time—not so much to keep the outside out, but to keep those inside concentrating on the business at hand.

Wood beams and crown molding in the same polished mahogany as the bench and other furnishings in the room accented the high ceiling. Hidden lighting bathed the room with a soft glow, sufficient for reading without strain. All the wood was dark and highly polished, contrasting nicely with the light blue walls.

The jury box—oddly enough—was not located next to the judge's bench, but directly in front of it, forming an open square fenced in by the lawyers' tables, judge's bench and the jury box, leaving an open arena in which the jousting would take place, giving the jurors an excellent view of all that transpired there. It made Joseph think of the Colosseum, lions and Christians. The rear of the room contained three long pew-like benches on raised platforms so the observers could see everything going on in the courtroom. This morning, except for the two seats occupied by Jimmy's parents, the benches contained the defendant's "peers" called for jury duty—most of whom had no wish to be there—the prospective jurors.

The bailiff, an attractive lady of mid-years, dressed nicely in a pleated wool skirt and patterned pink wool sweater, approached Joseph and asked, "Is there anything you want to talk to Judge Crider about before we start?"

Joseph looked toward Terry, who shook his head, and responded, "No thanks, Nancy. We're ready," thinking, *It 's nice to see a lady dressed like a lady.*

Bailiff Nancy Short crossed the room and asked the same question of the prosecutor, who also responded in the negative. Sticking her head through a door to next to the judge's bench, she murmured, "We're ready, Judge."

Eileen Gillespie, the court reporter, took her seat at a small table directly in front of the judge's bench. It being her obligation to record everything said in the courtroom, it was necessary she be located in a strategic position.

At precisely nine o'clock Judge Crider, black robe flowing behind her, entered the courtroom and mounted the three steps to her bench, seating herself in a high-backed leather chair mounted on castors so she could roll easily from the end of her desk, where the witnesses would testify, to the other, where the lawyers would approach and present arguments on issues outside the hearing of the jury. Looking around the room over the reading glasses perched halfway down her nose, she asked, "Everyone ready?"

Without waiting for a response, she continued, "We are here in case number 99V-14562, the *State of Ohio versus Jimmy Takas.* The defendant is charged with the crime of aggravated murder."

This produced a collective indrawing of breath and an uneasy murmur from the prospective jurors, which Judge Crider ignored. Those called for jury duty were never informed of the nature of the case for which they were called until arriving at court.

The judge explained the charge and the function of the jury, briefly adding she hoped a jury would be picked "fairly quickly." She then instructed her bailiff to seat twelve people in the jury box. The bailiff did so from a list created earlier by pulling names at random from the jury roster. She then handed each of the lawyers copies of the forms each prospective juror prepared containing background and personal information, including previous jury experience and their attitudes on the death penalty.

Judge Crider explained that she, and each of the lawyers, would ask questions of the panel to determine their qualifications to sit on this particular jury. The venire—that is the group of people from which the jury would be picked—was chosen at random from the voting polls. The procedure of determining the juror qualifications was called *voir dire*. Most judges, including Judge Crider, when explaining the procedure, said the French words meant "to tell the truth." This always bothered Joseph. The words *voir dire*, mispronounced more often than not, literally translated meant "to see, to speak."

This process, by which a jury is chosen, is the only opportunity the lawyers and the prospective jurors have to actually look at each other, talk to each other and study each other to determine if, in their collective opinion, they can work together to get a fair trial for the client—at least that is how it is supposed to work.

The judge then, warming a little, smiled at the prospective jurors and went on to explain that if the questioning determined, for any reason, a juror could not be fair or impartial, or had a personal problem that would not permit them to give the proper attention to the trial, he or she may be "excused for cause." If there was no "cause" by which a prospective juror could be dismissed, each lawyer then had the opportunity to excuse a certain number of prospective jurors by what is called "peremptory challenges." That is, they do not have to state a reason for the challenge—it could be just a feeling that a particular person would not be favorable to that lawyer's side.

"In a case such as this," Judge Crider explained, "each side has six peremptory challenges. If you are excused in this manner, do not be offended. The lawyers have an obligation to represent their client to the best of their ability and do so vigorously. If they get an inkling one of you may not feel properly disposed towards their client, whether it be the State or the defendant, they are obligated to ask you to be excused. It is never personal.

"Now then," Judge Crider continued, "before we can ask any questions of you it is necessary that you be sworn to tell the truth in your responses." Then turning toward her bailiff, she added, "Nancy, please swear the venire in."

Once that was accomplished, the judge introduced the lawyers, the police officer at the State's table and the defendant, asking, "Do any of you know any of the people I have just named?"

Several of the prospective jurors raised their hands tentatively, one saying, "Mr. Joseph has done some work for my family."

When the judge asked, "Well, do you consider him your lawyer?"

"Not now, but, if we need more work done, we would go back to his office."

Judge Crider said, "You are excused. That doesn't mean you couldn't be a good juror, but we can't afford even the appearance of impropriety."

Several other prospective jurors knew of or had some casual contact with Terry, Dronke or Thuman and when asked, "Do you think that knowledge would cause you to be biased or more sympathetic to one side or the other?" elicited negative responses. She permitted them to remain on the panel and proceeded to ask each of the jurors the statutorily mandated questions necessary to qualify them as jurors—"Are you over the age of eighteen? Do you live in the county? Are you citizens of the United States? Are you under such pressure, health- or otherwise, that you cannot sit for the duration of the trial, which the Court reasonably believes should not be more than two weeks?" When she was satisfied that none needed to be excused for cause, she turned to the prosecutor and said, "You may proceed with your *Voir Dire*."

Prosecutor Thuman rose, told a little about himself and those at the table with him, and began talking to the jurors, asking questions designed to elicit information from them from which he could determine whether or not he wanted them on the jury. He wasn't supposed to, but took the opportunity to feed the prospects sufficient information about the case to establish some little bias or endear himself to them. Joseph could have objected, but knew he or Terry would do the same thing if the opportunity presented itself—so he sat silently. Trial lawyers always want the jurors to like them—it is difficult for a juror to vote against someone he or she likes.

Interesting, Joseph thought, *he's not leaving this part of the trial up to his number one assistant. Wonder why he isn't trusting anything to chance?*

When Thuman completed his questioning and "passed for cause"—that is, found no cause to dismiss any of the twelve jurors occupying the jury box—Terry took over questioning the twelve.

Joseph made notes on the forms supplied by the bailiff. None of the jurors admitted to having a bias or having pre-judged the case, although a number acknowledged they had read something about it. It was, after all, the first potentially capital case to be tried in Milltown since electrocution took the place of hanging. Several did suggest they would find it difficult to order someone put to death. This caused another long and rancorous argument between Terry and the prosecutor. Unfortunately, as expected, the judge sided with the prosecutor and that class of prospective jurors was dismissed.

Finally, towards the end of the day, Terry reviewed his notes with Joseph and they decided there was no cause to dismiss any of those in the box. They then talked about which of the persons occupying the jury box made them particularly uncomfortable and what peremptory challenges they wished to make. As the judge explained, each side could dismiss six jurors for no reason at all except that they just didn't want them on the jury. The prosecutor dismissed an elderly lady who admitted she had a son about Jimmy's age. The defense team "thanked and excused"a former police officer who believed in strict adherence to the law—drugs lead to killing.

So it went through the day with several breaks. Finally, at four thirty in the afternoon, Judge Crider said, "We have been going pretty steadily. I'd hoped we would have a jury empaneled by now. We will adjourn for the evening and resume at eight thirty in the morning. We will have a jury before noon," she stated dictatorially, "and opening statements will be concluded before we recess tomorrow."

She smiled towards the jury box, scowled her displeasure at the lawyers and swept from the bench, disappearing through her chamber door.

Joseph looked at Terry, including Jimmy in his smile, saying, "Not a bad day's work. I like what I see so far and hope we'll get a good jury tomorrow. See you then, Jimmy," as the guard approached. The guard discreetly waited for the prospective jurors to leave the room, then produced handcuffs, shackled Jimmy's hands behind him and led him out of the room. Jimmy would continue to be held in the local jail throughout the trial. His parents followed, obviously hoping for the opportunity to say goodnight to their son. The guard looked around to see if anyone was watching. Seeing no one of import, he kindly allowed Jimmy to give his mom a goodnight kiss. Joseph could see the tears silently running down her cheek.

*　　*　　*

The next day produced more of the same. Finally, with just two peremptory challenges available to the defense, Joseph and Terry conferred. "Is there anyone you are terribly uncomfortable with?" Joseph asked.

Terry looked at the jury, studied his notes for a minute and said, "I can live with this panel."

"Let's hope Jimmy does," Joseph responded, then leaned toward Jimmy. He had included Jimmy in all the choices thus far, but now said, "Jimmy, sit up and look at each of the jurors. Look at their faces. Take however much time you need. Then tell me whether or not you are satisfied with that person on the jury."

"Now, Mr. Joseph?"

"Yes, now."

Jimmy sat a little straighter in his chair and raised his face toward the jury. He brushed the hair from his eyes and, as instructed, looked at each. Some returned the look comfortably, some with more difficulty—but all looked at him. Joseph and Terry sat silently, as did the judge, although Joseph could tell she was getting impatient at the delay. Thuman, at his table, fidgeted but said nothing. Finally Jimmy took his eyes from the panel that was to decide his fate and whispered to Joseph and Terry, "I don't know what to say. They look all right to me."

Joseph nodded, placed an avuncular hand on Jimmy's shoulder and stood, saying, "Your Honor, the defense is pleased with the make-up of this jury."

Thuman still had a remaining challenge and exercised it by excusing an older woman who appeared as though she might be sympathetic to the underdog. Unfortunately she was replaced by another middle-aged woman who evidenced the same demeanor. Joseph chuckled to himself while remaining silent. He appeared no longer a part of the process—his demeanor saying, "This jury will give Jimmy a fair trial."

It was nearly noon when the jury of twelve was picked—six women and six men. The elderly woman, Joseph was pleased to see, occupied seat one—that is the seat nearest the prosecutor's table in the first row. Two of the men were retired Ford workers, although they didn't know each other, and were located in seats two and three. Seats four and five were occupied by a retired farmer and a pharmacist. An elderly black man sat in seat six, the seat nearest the defense table. Right behind him, in seat twelve, was a retired minister. Joseph was a little uncomfortable with him because his experience in the past led him to believe that even though Christianity teaches forgiveness, ministers tend to be less forgiving than some others—leaving forgiveness to God.

The balance of the back row was taken up by a grade school teacher in seat nine, a clerk in a local store in seat eleven and a stay-at-home mom in seat number ten. Two of the unmarried women worked for Eastern Insurance Company—but in different departments. It would be unusual for a jury empaneled in Milltown panel not to have at least one or more persons working at the largest local employer. They sat next to each other in seats eight and nine, quickly becoming friendly with each other in whispering conversation. The last, an accountant with a major drug company, sat in seat number seven. A diverse group that Joseph hoped would come to know, understand and look sympathetically upon Jimmy Takas.

Judge Crider decided two alternate jurors would be seated in case any of the chosen were unable to complete the trial. This was accomplished in short order and the jury sworn with the proscribed language, "Do you, and each of you, swear or affirm that you will well and truly try the issues in this case as you shall answer onto God?"

Standing and holding their right hands in the air, each muttered the appropriate "I do" response.

A break for lunch was ordered. "We will reconvene at one thirty. Please be prompt. But before you leave, you must, today and every day until the trial is over, leave and return through the jury room."

While saying this she pointed to the door behind the defense counsel's table that led into the jury room—a fairly large room around which all twelve could be seated comfortably in wooden armchairs. There were pencils and paper on the table and several chairs against the walls for the alternates. The room was furnished with a small refrigerator, a tiny sink, a coffee machine and an electric teakettle for those who did not drink coffee, as well as two bathrooms—one for men and the other for women. There were a number of magazines sitting on the sink counter for those times when the jurors would have to wait while things were happening in the courtroom they were not allowed to hear—but no daily newspapers were in evidence—and there would not be until the trial was finished..

The judge continued, "My bailiff, Ms. Short, will instruct you how to get in and out of the jury room when you report and leave daily. How you occupy yourselves in the jury room is your business and we will not interfere unless there is something you might need. If any of you have to make phone calls to let someone know you have been chosen to sit on this jury and will be involved for some time, she will make a phone available to you. You are now excused for lunch and Ms. Short can tell you where restaurants are. Please be back promptly. We will not feed you until you receive the case and then only if your deliberations take you through the meal hours. If you have any questions, please present them to Ms. Short. If she can't answer them, she will tell me and I'll provide whatever information you might need. Do you understand?"

Silent nods from all of the jurors acknowledged their understanding.

Terry and Joseph arose as the newly picked jurors filed from the jury box. When the jury room door closed behind them, Terry and Joseph walked from the courtroom. Stan Marten and several other members of the media approached, some shoving microphones into their faces. Stan asked, "What do you think of the jury?"

"Obviously we have no way of knowing, but they certainly seem to be good and sincere people," Joseph responded. "I think we will get a fair trial from them."

Thuman, eye twitching and obviously annoyed that the members of the media hadn't approached him first, responded with a crotchety "No comment."

CHAPTER NINE

Immediately on the dot of one thirty that afternoon, the door to Judge Crider's chambers opened and she entered the courtroom, still zipping up her black robe. She looked around the room and noted everyone in their appropriate place. Climbing the three stairs to her dais, she seated herself comfortably. "Good afternoon." She smiled, appearing much more pleasant than she had during the selection process. Apparently she felt the jurors were adequately impressed with the seriousness of the business at hand and could now relax a bit before starting the hard work expected of them.

The judge continued, "I hope everyone had a pleasant lunch. The first thing I am going to do this afternoon," she said, talking to the jury, ignoring the parties and lawyers sitting at the trial tables, "is give you a couple of brief instructions in the law you're going to need in considering this case. The Court, that's me, and the jury, that's you, have separate functions. You decide the facts in dispute and I will instruct you as to the law that applies. It's your sworn duty to accept the law as I give it to you. You are not permitted to change the law, nor to apply your concept of what the law should be. Do we understand each other?"

She paused, more serious now, and looked at each juror, waiting for their nods and murmurs of agreement.

The judge continued, "A criminal case begins with the filing of an indictment. The indictment is merely a piece of paper that informs the defendant he has been charged with a crime. The fact that it was filed may not be considered for any other purpose. As soon as the defendant enters a plea of 'not guilty' it is a denial of the charge and puts into issue every essential element of the crime charged."

The judge continued instructing the jurors on the legally required definitions of the Constitutionally protected rights of the defendant— such as the *presumption of innocence, proof beyond a reasonable doubt* and what *circumstantial* and *direct evidence* are. She closed these preliminary instructions with a discussion of the elements to consider when testing the credibility of witnesses.

She then added, "At this point in the proceedings the prosecutor and defense counsel will have an opportunity to address you in what is called opening statements. An opening statement is designed to give you a very general overview of what the case is about; that is, what they expect the evidence to show. Understand, what they say is not evidence unless I instruct you that the lawyers are entering into a stipulation—that is an agreed statement of a fact for your consideration. That doesn't happen very often and you don't have to worry about it unless it comes up, at which time I will explain to you what is happening. All you have to remember at this time is that nothing the lawyers say to you is evidence. It is sort of like commentators coming on before a President's speech telling you what he is going to say and then coming on afterwards telling you what he said. That doesn't mean you shouldn't listen to the attorneys. Their words are designed to help you to understand what is being presented from the witness stand."

She then turned toward the prosecutor's table and said, "Now, Mr. Thuman, if you are ready, please present the opening for the State."

Thuman stood and walked to the front of the jury box, hands folded in front of him, fingertips touching. He wore a plain dark grey wool suit with an almost invisible pinstripe, freshly pressed, trousers sharply creased. The knot of his tie, a muted red, was meticulously placed in the V collar of his white shirt, french cuffs holding gold-knotted links. His hair was carefully combed, but he was unable to command a lock to quit falling over his right eye even though he constantly pushed it back into place.

I certainly have an advantage being bald—never have to worry about hair getting into my eyes, Joseph thought. *He looks like he works in a funeral parlor. Bet his suit doesn't stay neat for long—looks like he sweats a lot.*

Thuman stood and approached the front of the jury box, a rapid blinking of his right eye partially covered by the falling shock of hair, and a nervous twitching of his mouth interrupting his flow. He took several deep breaths, calming himself, and said, "Thank you, Your Honor." Then turning to the jury, he said, "Folks, in this case, the State of Ohio will endeavor to prove beyond a reasonable doubt that the defendant," pointing to Jimmy with an accusatory glare, "did on the fifth day of May this year, in Mills County, Ohio, commit the offense of aggravated murder; that is, he intentionally took the life of June Westlock while committing or attempting to commit a felony—the crime of rape."

It wasn't lost on Joseph that Thuman intentionally refused to personalize Jimmy, but conversely made sure the jury would think of the deceased as a person by using her name.

Where the hell did that rape business come from? Joseph thought. *Nothing in the autopsy report supports it—no bruising in the genital area—no sperm. What the hell makes him think there was any kind of sexual activity? Does he know something we don't?*

"Folks, the evidence will show that on May fifth of this year this man," again pointing, "was driven by two things—lust and the quest for drugs—the need to feed his degenerate appetite for cocaine and sex." The dichotomy was lost on Thuman.

Pausing long enough for the jury to consider Jimmy's evil nature, Thuman picked up where he left off. " June Westlock's body was found on the floor in the laundry room of her home at 234 North Stubb Avenue. Right here in Milltown—right here in this peaceful town. She had been stabbed to death—many, many stab wounds in her slender, naked body—at approximately six thirty in the morning. Her estranged boyfriend, Clarence Knedder, found June's almost nude body. He called the police, crying, 'It's awful...Send a cop!'"

Thuman paused for breath, shaking his head theatrically at the enormity of the evil perpetrated by the defendant. "The evidence will show that on that date the defendant got off work, went to get a haircut, then went to *Tracks*, a local bar, ate, drank, danced, got pretty drunk and decided he needed drugs and sex. He went to the home of Miss Westlock, a single mother, and made demands on her. When she was unable or unwilling to meet his demands, he," pointing dramatically, voice rising accusingly, "killed her mercilessly!"

Thuman went on for the next thirty minutes seemingly more relaxed, beginning each change of thought with the appellation "Folks," as though the use of the word identified him with them, as one of the "common people." They together were going to decide this case and rid Milltown of such scum. He described in detail the evidence he would produce to establish that Jimmy had committed this heinous crime, admitting, "Miss Westlock may have been involved in drugs and other less than desirable activities, but she didn't deserve to die at the hands of this monster, who then fled to Florida to avoid the consequences of his acts."

When he finished, he scrubbed his hands across his face and said, "Folks, none of this is going to be pleasant for you, but the State will ask you to do your duty and," turning sharply and pointing his finger at Jimmy like a weapon, "convict this man!" After a dramatic pause, he lowered his voice and continued, "We will then ask you to consider whether or not he should be put to death for his acts." Turning his back, he clumped gracelessly towards his chair.

Joseph wondered, *Why's he so vehement? He's sure into this case. Can't believe anyone is so anxious to put someone to death. Guess it's part of his political agenda— get a major conviction and increase your political power.* He knew he could object successfully to the argumentative style and name-calling, but didn't want to give emphasis to Thuman's words. He shared his concern with Terry. "How come he's so worked up?"

"Don't know," Terry shrugged.

"Mr. Joseph," Judge Crider asked, "do you wish to make an opening statement at this time?"

The defense has the right to make its opening statement before any evidence is submitted at the beginning of a trial, or after the State has finished presenting its case, but before beginning the defense. Joseph was of the opinion that the earlier he talked to jurors, the better for his client. He believed it important for the panel to see a defendant as a person right from the beginning, and not the monster painted by the prosecutor.

"I'd like to address the jurors now, Your Honor," Joseph said, arising from his chair slowly and walking into the open square before the jury box. Looking over his shoulder apologetically, he added, "Sorry I have to turn my back on you, Judge."

Standing comfortably in front of the jurors, he began in a conversational tone, "Your Honor," looking over his shoulder, "Mr. Thuman," glancing towards the prosecutor's table, "ladies and gentlemen."

Although not appearing so, Joseph always felt nervous when first addressing a jury. A slight quaver in his voice and the shaking of his hand were hidden by clearing his throat and placing his hand before his mouth. He, too, was dressed in a conservative suit, white shirt and tie—shoes highly polished. Mary had picked the tie to go with his suit. His choice would not be nearly as acceptable. The suit couldn't hide his portly figure or the slump of his shoulders. He always intended to stand up straight, but never quite pulled it off. He relaxed into a comfortable slouch. The intimidating look he was accused of having when examining witnesses disappeared when talking to jurors. His habit of talking to juries conversationally relaxed both him and them. Before starting, he rubbed his hand across his almost bald head, mussing the remaining fringe. It gave him a bit of a teddy bear look.

He began again, "Ladies and gentlemen. It's always a little disconcerting to hear the judge say that the things the lawyers say isn't evidence. Of course it isn't. But then we lawyers come on and start telling you the entire story as we see it, just as though we are testifying from the witness stand. For that reason, it is really important for you to remember not only what you hear, but from whom you hear it. If it comes from witnesses, it's okay. If it comes from us, it's not." Joseph looked each juror in the face and smiled as he said this.

"What you have heard so far is a very positive and forceful rendition of a set of facts that the prosecutor wants to prove—to establish that

Jimmy committed this heinous crime. Yet, your job is to listen to the evidence presented from the witness stand and determine whether, as the prosecutor says, it points to Jimmy or, perhaps, somewhere else. It is easy enough to decide—as the police did in this case—that Jimmy is the killer; then look for facts that fit that decision. In this case, they made their decision on the basis of something Clarence Knedder told them—you know—the fellow that found the body. The circumstances of that are pretty strange." Joseph shook his head in wonderment. *I can be as theatrical as Thuman,* he thought.

"Knedder called the police, and when they came, he told them Jimmy was there that night. How did he know that? He told them Jimmy was there for drugs. Drugs, alcohol and casual sex are regular visitors in this community of people—a lifestyle we may not understand—certainly one we don't approve of—but one that is, today, unfortunately a part of our town."

Joseph, without pause, continued to review the facts he believed were consistent with the things the prosecutor had pointed out, and then added, "Sure, Jimmy, at first denied a drug connection with the deceased—he's no dummy—he knows drugs are illegal. But as soon as the police called to his attention that Ms. Westlock had been killed, he admitted the drug connection and cooperated with the police."

Pausing for effect, he continued, "That is, until they told him they didn't believe him. They told him, 'You killed June Westlock. We're going to send you to the electric chair or, at least, to prison for the rest of your life.' And yet, he voluntarily made statements. Even more important, something the prosecution failed, inadvertently or otherwise, to point out, Jimmy allowed the police to search his home, his car, and his person. Nowhere did they find anything that connected him with the crime. He allowed them to do whatever they wanted. He cooperated as best he could, and did so without complaint." The elderly lawyer appeared incredulous that the prosecutor would not make this information available to the jurors.

"What then did the police do? They say 'We don't believe you! You're a liar! You're a killer!'" raising his voice.

"Jimmy ran. It's not unexpected. Here is a boy with no record, no history of violence, no history of any behavior unlike the unfortunate decisions made by children of this generation. Of course he ran—he panicked. He is frightened, naïve, certainly not very sophisticated—the thought going through his mind, *They believe I'm a killer!* He made a stupid choice. Now, because of that stupid choice, the police quit looking at the evidence. They no longer asked, 'Who killed June?' They looked only at Jimmy—he ran, he must be the killer."

Joseph talked about the palm print, the blood, the evidence of several weapons, and the complexity of the evidence that would be presented. After several minutes, he closed with, "The State believes it solved this case. We believe the case is not yet solved and, of course, at the close of the case we will ask for an acquittal. In the meantime we only ask that you listen carefully to the witnesses—study carefully the evidence, and do all of these with an open mind until everything—I repeat, until all the evidence—has been presented." He then smiled a thank-you.

"Thank you, Mr. Joseph," Judge Crider said as Joseph returned to his seat. "Mr. Thuman, you may call your first witness tomorrow morning. We have worked hard enough today and since it is past four o'clock, we will adjourn for the evening. Remember, jurors, you are not to discuss the case with each other or anyone else until it is completed. Do not read the newspapers or watch the news on TV. Have a good night's sleep and we'll see you at eight thirty tomorrow morning."

*   *   *

As always, the media reported the opening statements along with everything else—the ebb and flow of a highly publicized trial can be followed by how it is reported. Joseph skimmed through and read parts of the article appearing in the following morning's Cleveland Plain Dealer. The headline read:

PALM PRINT, FLIGHT PROOF OF GUILT, MURDER TRIAL TOLD

MILLTOWN—Attorneys in the murder trial of Jimmy Takas laid down their strategies, with Prosecutor Harold Thuman vowing to prove Takas stabbed June Westlock as a part of a rape or attempted rape, while the defense attorney said the police arrested the wrong man.

Thuman, in opening statements in Mills County Common Pleas Court, characterized Takas as being "driven by lust and a quest for drugs." He said that investigators found Takas' bloody palm print in the laundry room, where Westlock's partially naked body was discovered by her sometime live-in boyfriend. Thuman said, "When confronted by the police, Takas fled the state. He was apprehended by the police in Florida."

Defense Attorney Patrick Joseph said, "The Police decided that since Jimmy ran, he must be the killer—and so quit looking." He asserted, "We believe the case is not yet solved." Joseph explained that Takas cooperated fully with the police, allowed them to search his home and car and yet was told by the police, "You're going to jail for a long time. Frightened, of course he ran."

The spectator seats in the courtroom were filled throughout the day with little disturbance; however, the bias of the respective sides was apparent. Several of the spectators complained to members of the media about the tactics employed by both sides.

And so day two ended. Joseph and Terry were not displeased; however, they knew that trials have flows—ups and downs. Good days are usually followed by bad. "Let's wait and see what tomorrow brings," Joseph admonished Terry.

CHAPTER TEN

After everyone had gathered in the courtroom, Judge Crider nodded at Thuman to call his first witness. "The State will call Tony Nuncio."

The bartender from *Tracks* took the stand and was sworn. After identifying himself, he responded to Thuman's questioning.

"I've known Jimmy Takas since we were in school together. He was at *Tracks* on the evening before June was killed. I don't remember the date, but I remember that night pretty well. Jimmy was in the bar most of the evening, ate dinner and had quite a bit to drink. He kept pestering me about when June was going to come in. She didn't. He was asking around for drugs—wanted anything—and even asked me to get him something. I told him I didn't do that shit and finally kicked him out."

Thuman asked, "About what time was that?"

"It was before closing. Maybe about one o'clock in the morning."

Joseph asked no questions of the witness, thinking, *He can only make Jimmy look bad.*

Acknowledging the judge's instruction to call his next witness, Thuman said, "Your Honor, the State will call Beth Westlock."

Joseph had moved for a separation of the witnesses—that is a request that the Court order all of the witnesses to remain outside the courtroom except when testifying. The purpose behind separation of witnesses is that one witness will not hear the testimony of another and be influenced by what they say—at least that's the intention of the procedure. Lawyers are well aware, however, that witnesses talk to each other in the lobby and rest rooms or coming and going to court. They share what they are going to say, what they did say and what happened in the courtroom—trying to keep their stories straight. They talk about what questions are asked and "what a mean son-of-a-bitch that lawyer is—trying to twist my words."

The Court is required to grant a motion for a separation of witnesses whenever it is made. Once witnesses have completed their testimony, they are permitted to remain in the courtroom during the balance of the trial, unless one of the lawyers says that a witness might be recalled. Often a lawyer will advise the Court that he intends to recall a witness, even if he has no intention of doing so, just to keep the witness out of the courtroom.

Nancy Short, the bailiff, walked to the door in the back of the room, stuck her head into the lobby and called, "Beth Westlock, please."

The dead girl's sister, Beth Westlock, walked into the courtroom and Bailiff Short accompanied her to the witness stand. Before seating her, the bailiff said, "Please raise your right hand. Do you swear or affirm that the testimony you will be giving in the matter before the Court will be the truth, the whole truth and nothing but the truth?" With the affirmative response, she seated the witness and adjusted the microphone, explaining, "Please make sure you speak into the microphone. Is that comfortable?"

The witness responded in a small voice, "Yes." Beth and her deceased sister, June, were enough alike that they could easily be recognized as siblings. Tall, slender and reasonably attractive, she differed from her sister only in hair coloring. Beth's hair was dark and worn long, swaying loosely past her shoulders. Her complexion, however, was quite fair—it rarely saw the sun. She was dressed in a T-shirt made of a silky light green fabric covered by a cardigan sweater of a darker green. Her skirt was of a tasteful length that Joseph knew was not normally worn by her. The ensemble was completed by hose and high-heeled shoes—not very practical for the time of year.

"Please state your name and spell your last name for the record," Thuman instructed, standing in such a way that the right side of his face was hidden from the jury. He wasn't blinking yet, but Joseph suspected it would come.

The witness leaned toward the court reporter and, in a small voice, identified herself and spelled her name. Prosecutor Thuman began his questioning standing behind his table, notes spread in front of him. He elicited from the victim's sister that she lived with her parents and worked in her parents' business, a bakery, and that her sister, when she was alive, also worked there.

Thuman then asked, "Did your sister ever say anything about Jimmy Takas?"

Joseph rose from his seat and said, quietly, "Objection, your Honor."

Thuman immediately asked for a bench conference. All four lawyers approached the bench at the side opposite of that occupied by the witness. They immediately began whispering their arguments in voices low enough that the jurors could not hear.

At a signal from the judge, Eileen Gillespie, the court reporter, followed and set her sten-o-type machine on the corner of the desk so she could record the arguments. Judge Crider then said, a trace of irritation creeping into her voice, "We are going to have some degree of order in my court. All four of you can come up here when we have bench conference, but only one of you on each side will be permitted to talk—that is, the one conducting the examination and the one that will be handling the cross-examination can argue. Decide right now who that will be and this will be considered an order. None of you will violate that order. Do we understand each other?"

All four nodded their acquiescence and Terry pushed Joseph forward. The judge listened patiently to Joseph, who said, "Your Honor, since I made the objection, may I be permitted to argue. We did intend, however, that Mr. Bernow would be handling the cross-examination of this witness. After this witness' testimony is completed, we will be happy to obey your order."

"Proceed, Mr. Joseph."

After listening to the arguments of both, Judge Crider said to Thuman, "It's obvious you're trying to get some state of mind information from this witness...like maybe the victim was afraid of the defendant...and you know it's not proper. Leave it be."

Joseph was pleased with the small victory.

Thuman returned to the witness and finished quickly, learning only that Takas had called the bakery and asked for June, but June didn't talk to him.

At a nod from Joseph, Terry rose to handle the cross-examination of the witness.

"Ms. Westlock, I'm Terry Bernow, one of the lawyers for Mr. Takas. I only have a couple of questions to ask you. How long have you known Clarence Knedder?"

"Maybe about ten years."

"What was his relationship with your sister?"

Surprisingly, instead of identifying Knedder as her sister's estranged boyfriend or the father of her sister's daughter, she said, "From what I understand, he was... I mean, she didn't want him around...they were... I mean—"

Interrupting her, Terry asked, "Why didn't she want him around?"

"Well, he was kind of bothering her."

Terry continued, "She was afraid of him, wasn't she?"

"It seemed like she was afraid of him, but—"

Still pressing Terry asked, "How many times did she express fear of Mr. Knedder?"

"A couple, I guess. We didn't talk about him much."

"And it's true, isn't it, that your sister never expressed any fear of," gesturing towards Jimmy, "Mr. Takas, did she?"

"Well, no."

Terry, knowing when to quit, thanked her for her testimony and sat down. One of the biggest mistakes a lawyer can make is to ask just one more question, when he should shut up and sit down.

"Any more questions, Mr. Thuman?" Judge Crider asked of the prosecutor.

"No, Your Honor. No more questions."

To the witness the judge stated, more kindly, "You're free to stay in the courtroom now if you want—or you can leave."

"Okay." She then walked to the back of the courtroom, past Mr. And Mrs. Takas, ignoring them, and took a seat between her mother and father, as far away from Jimmy's parents as possible.

The prosecution called its next witness, June Westlock's friend, Brenda Blanton. She testified concerning the deceased's movements on the evening she was killed—that she had visited her home and brought a birthday present to her daughter. Questioned by Assistant Prosecutor Anne Dronke, she testified smoothly and comfortably.

She's been well coached, Joseph thought, *dressed awfully nice too—not like I've seen her before. Thuman is doing a good job of coaching and dressing his witnesses.*

When Ms. Dronke said, "No further questions," Joseph stood and asked, Your Honor, may we approach?"

At the bench, Joseph said in a low voice, "Your Honor, I understand this witness made a statement to the police—a written statement. I would like to review it before I examine the witness. If the prosecutor would have made them available before the trial, it would save a great deal of this court's time."

After listening to Joseph and Dronke for a few minutes, Judge Crider addressed the jury, "Ladies and gentlemen, what we are doing at this time is reviewing a written statement, or actually a synopsis of a statement. When a witness has made a statement to the prosecutor or the police, defense counsel is entitled to see that statement after the witness has testified to determine whether or not there are any inconsistencies between what is in the statement and what the witness has said in court. That's what Mr. Joseph is doing at this time. So if you see the lawyers approach the bench after a witness has completed testifying, that is what is happening."

Actually the judge isn't supposed to see the statement either until the witness has testified. Joseph noted that the judge was apparently familiar with what was contained in the statement and wondered when she had seen it. For the time being he ignored the impropriety but wondered how many times the Court had had ex parte—that is, without defense counsel being present—conversations with the prosecution.

Joseph said, "Thank you, Your Honor. I do have a few questions of this witness." He returned to his place at the trial table. It put him within a few feet of the witness.

He began conversationally, "Ms. Blanton, I believe June Westlock was at your house the night she was killed. Is that correct?"

"Yes, that is true."

"And that's because it was your daughter's birthday?"

"Yes, sir."

"There were several people there?"

"Yes. That is June and her neighbor, Casey. She lives across the street from June. That is across the street from where June lived. Also, my daughter had a friend of hers for a sleepover."

"You and she talked about Clarence Knedder, isn't that correct?"

"Yes."

"And she told you he, that is Clarence, had been following her for some time?"

"Yes, for several weeks."

"And she was frightened of him?"

"Yes, that's true."

"She saw him the day she was killed, didn't she?"

"Unhuh."

"I take it that is a yes?

"Yes, sir."

Joseph continued in that vein for several minutes, establishing that June Westlock had seen Knedder watching her, that he was very jealous of her and getting more so. According to the witness, Knedder had been watching her for several days before she was killed. When Joseph completed these questions, he thanked the witness, saying, "I have no further questions."

Thuman had no redirect and so the witness was excused by the judge with the same admonition, that she was free to remain in the courtroom if she chose. She did, and took a place in one of the pew-like seats at the rear of the room, sitting next to Beth Westlock and several members of June's family—also as far as possible from Mr. and Mrs. Takas, Jimmy's parents.

Prosecutor Thuman called Casey Patterson next, June's across-the-street neighbor, to paint a picture of their evening's activities, adding nothing that Joseph didn't already know. She did admit, while being cross-examined by Terry, that she knew June and Knedder had been having problems that resulted in a court order the week before June's death that Knedder stay away from her and her house.

Terry asked, "And she told you she was afraid of him, isn't that so?"

"Not exactly like that…. We didn't talk about it much…. I just knew they were fighting and she forced him to leave the house. Everyone knew how jealous he was."

"And on the day she died, you knew Mr. Knedder wasn't supposed to be at her house?"

"Yes, sir."

"Yet you knew he was there that evening?"

"Not in the evening. He came to my house about two or two thirty in the morning looking for June."

"Thank you, I don't have any more questions."

The witness' husband was next called. He verified everything testified to by his wife, adding on cross-examination by Joseph that he had seen someone in June's backyard on the night she was killed. "There was somebody standing there…back there on the lawn…with Clarence."

Joseph asked, "Do you know who it was?"

"No…just someone standing there."

"Did that person say anything?" Joseph asked.

"No…uh-uh."

Joseph moved to a spot behind the jury box so that the witness would have to speak up to be heard. It is natural for anyone to look at the person who is asking questions. This way, while the witness was looking at Joseph, he would be looking directly at the jurors.

He then asked, "Was that person white or black?"

"Uh…I don't know. I couldn't see his face."

"But you described him to the police as white, didn't you?"

"Well, yeah. His hands were white."

"You also told the police, in your statement, that he was a large person—probably about six feet tall and well built?"

"Well, yes, sir. He was a big man—but not as big as me."

It was obvious to Joseph that the witness was instructed not to mention the presence of an unidentified white man unless asked directly. "Would you say he was about the size of, oh, say, Mr. Thuman?"

The prosecutor jumped to his feet. "Objection…objection!" right eye blinking and mouth twitching rapidly.

What the hell's he so excited about? wondered Joseph. *There's nothing wrong with the question.*

Judge Crider, without waiting for a comment from Joseph, said, "Overruled. Please answer the question."

"Yeah, that's about right."

"No further questions, Mr. Patterson. Thank you." Joseph was pleased that he would be able to argue later that the presence of another person suggested reasonable doubt.

"Nothing further," said Thuman, obviously upset by what had transpired. His reaction struck Joseph as being inexplicable.

The judge called a recess for the day and instructed the jurors and counsel to be in court promptly at eight thirty in the morning. She left the bench quickly. Joseph and Terry stood and waited patiently for the jurors to leave, then gathered their papers. Joseph leaned over to talk to Jimmy. "Not a bad day's work. It gives us something to talk about. Obviously you weren't the only one at June's house that night. If you can think of anything else that might be helpful, make sure you let us know. Work on your memory, please." Then adding loud enough for the police guard to hear, "We'll see you about eight fifteen tomorrow so you can tell us anything you might have remembered. Try to get a good night's sleep."

Joseph and Terry left with Jimmy, his parents following, making sure the last of the jurors were gone before descending in the only elevator. Reporters were hanging around, but Joseph and Terry ushered Jimmy's parents from the building and left without comment. On the way back to the office, Terry asked, "Do you really think it went well?"

"As good as we can expect. I think it gave us something to talk about when it comes time to argue. Now let's not think about it for a while—let me enjoy the evening."

It was starting to get dark earlier. Joseph was aware of the leaves gone from the trees in the square and knew that short skirts and sweaters would soon be replaced by slacks and winter coats. *It's a shame that people add clothing as trees shed theirs*, Joseph thought, wondering at the same time, *Is there some relationship between the word "leaves" and "leaving" that has to do with what happens in the fall? The only thing I really miss from my childhood is the smell of burning leaves in the fall. Wonder what they do with all the leaves.* These totally unrelated notions stayed with Joseph until he entered his building, followed by Terry.

Terry asked, "Is there anything we need to do tonight to prepare for tomorrow?"

"I don't think so. The State is still putting on its case and I think we've prepared our cross-examination of their witnesses as best we can until we see what they said in their written statements. Don't know exactly where we will be going until they finish. I've been trying to develop a theory of the case—but it's slow building. In the meantime, I just want to go home, have a Martini and dinner. If Mary doesn't have a bunch of stuff for me to do, I'll get to bed early and be ready for whatever tomorrow brings."

Then Joseph added, "You know, Terry, there's something bothering me. I don't know whether or not you noticed Thuman's blinking. It's only in his right eye and usually accompanied by a twisting of his mouth or stretching his neck. I went to visit my mom recently and there is a lady there suffering from a condition called 'Tourette's syndrome.' I read up on it the other day because of this lady—wanted to know what she was going through and if there is anything that can be done about it. It's a neurological disorder that manifests itself in different ways—in her case it's constant talking and using foul language. More commonly its symptoms are very similar to what Thuman is doing. It's sometimes treated by the use of an anti-psychotic drug—but mostly the articles say that reducing stress is the only thing that'll help. I notice his problem occurs only with some of the witnesses—and he pops a pill when he starts blinking. One of the articles said that *people with Tourette's syndrome often…experience considerable anxiety in social situations, and develop impulsive, aggressive and self-destructive behaviors.* Does that sound like our Mr. Prosecutor?"

Terry sat thoughtfully for a while, "I don't know, Mr. Joseph, but how can we use it in this case?"

"Oh, we probably can't. It's just an observation that maybe tells us a little about our esteemed prosecutor. I'm not a doctor and can't make a diagnosis, but it's so obvious I can't figure why no one else has mentioned it. I don't know that we can use it,"Joseph responded, "but let's think about it. Now I'm going home to relax with my drink."

"Okay, then," Terry offered. "I'll go home too. Promised my boy I'd watch his football practice if I could. He's playing safety on the junior varsity team. I'd like to watch. I didn't have much time to play sports when I was a kid. Glad he can. I guess he's doing pretty well."

Joseph responded, "My only athletic prowess is at the dinner table. Sure wish Mary could cook like her mother. Good night."

CHAPTER ELEVEN

Thursday morning dawned sunny, but not particularly warm. *Weather's catching up with us,* Joseph thought. He met Terry at the office as agreed, and the two men, one young and full of energy and the other old and tired, walked to the courthouse, spent a few minutes with Jimmy in the small conference room reserved for them, where they learned nothing knew from Jimmy's absent memory. As soon as they entered the courtroom, Thuman walked over to them and handed Joseph a piece of paper on the county's letterhead. It was addressed to Joseph and contained two names. "This is additional discovery we just learned about," he said curtly and walked away.

After reading the missive, Joseph motioned Judge Crider's bailiff over and said, "Nancy, I'd like a few minutes in chambers with the judge."

"I'll see what I can do," she replied.

Judge Crider told Nancy to usher all of the lawyers into her office. She was sitting at her desk, piles of papers and files before her, signing some documents. Joseph, Terry, Thuman and Dronke stood in front of her desk. Joseph said, "Your Honor, Mr. Thuman just handed me a piece of paper with the names of a couple of witnesses he intends to call...."

The judge sighed and then said, "Okay. You may as well sit down. What's the problem?"

There weren't enough chairs for all of them so Joseph sat in the chair nearest the door. Terry stood directly behind him. Joseph handed the judge the letter Thuman had given to him, and started to talk.

Judge Crider interrupted him and said to her bailiff, "Please get Eileen in here with her machine, I want this conversation on the record."

When the court reporter came into the small office, Joseph offered her his seat. As soon as she was seated and ready, Joseph began, "As you know, we always have trouble getting discovery from Mr. Thuman. It seems we have to fight with him about everything…. He loves to piecemeal discovery, counting on us missing something. Now he tells me there are two witnesses he intends to call that he," sarcastically, "'just learned about.'"

Judge Crider looked at Thuman, but before she could say anything, he began the blinking and stretching routine, then blurted, "Th…the ….the State just learned about these witnesses last night."

The judge said, "Now let's see. This case has been scheduled for more than two months, and you're just learning about your witnesses? What are these witnesses going to say?"

"Well, I don't know exactly except they really don't want to testify. They're both involved in drugs and don't want to be here. I know how Mr. Joseph feels, and I would have no objection to him having an opportunity to talk to these witnesses. I would never object to him calling a witness he just learned about so long as I was given an opportunity to question them before they took the stand."

"Sure," Joseph said with a look of annoyance on his face, "we have to fight to get anything from you and you are the first to bitch if we don't give you what you want. Give me a break."

"Again, what are they going to say?" Judge Crider insisted.

"The first will verify what has already been said about seeing Takas at June's house. The second will tell the jury that he and Knedder did drugs together—that Takas and June did drugs with them—that Takas gave June an eerie feeling and was always hitting on her—and lots of other stuff like that."

"How long have you known about these witnesses?"

"The first for some time now, but we only learned about the second one last night. The one who could put Takas at June's house about the time of the killing."

"Okay. Let's get on with the trial. Since you knew about the first witness for some time, he will not be allowed to testify. The second will."

"But, judge," Thuman began.

"Forget it. That's my ruling. Now let's get going."

Joseph, face red with anger, was ushered from the room by Terry. "Mr. Joseph, we got enough problems. Don't say what you're thinking."

*   *   *

Everyone gathered in the courtroom and the jury called, Joseph and Terry stood as the jurors took their seats in the jury box.

Judge Crider nodded toward Thuman to proceed, who intoned, "The State will call Andrew Little."

As the bailiff left the courtroom to find the witness, Joseph rose from his seat and said, "I really hate to interrupt the proceedings again, but there is something we need to discuss, Your Honor. I don't know if you want to do it at sidebar or if you wish to excuse the jury for a few minutes. It's not what we talked about in chambers."

Judge Crider glanced at Joseph. The look on his face indicated it was going to be more than a couple of minutes. "Okay, Mr. Joseph." Then to the jury, "We apparently haven't concluded our legal business. Why don't you go back to the jury room and relax for a few more minutes. The admonishments I have given you in the past about not talking about the case and so on apply. You will be called back as soon as we deal with whatever legal issues Mr. Joseph wants to raise." Saying this with a smile, she started to leave the bench and suggested, "Mr. Joseph, Mr. Thuman, would you like to join me in chambers for a bit?" as she nodded to the court reporter to follow.

Eileen, the court reporter, had just completed setting up, sighed and picked up her machine to follow the judge.

Joseph stood as the jury began to file out. He always extended the same courtesy to a jury that he did to a judge. Jurors, as fact finders, are an official arm of the Court and entitled to the same consideration afforded a judge. He instructed his clients to do the same, so Jimmy and

Terry arose with him. Once the jury had left the courtroom and the door to the jury room closed, he knocked on the door to the judge's chambers, and entered, followed by Terry.

"What is it now, Mr. Joseph?" Judge Crider said, her exasperation with Joseph clear on her face. She had unzipped her robe and sat behind her desk, her very feminine blouse a stark contrast to her apparel on the bench—and her mood.

"Well, Your Honor, you know we always have a bit of a discovery problem with Prosecutor Thuman," nodding across the room, to where Thuman and his assistant prosecutor, Dronke, sat. "This is—"

Judge Crider interrupted, "I know well your feelings about discovery. We just talked about it. What's the problem now?"

"Well, Judge, as you know, we made all the proper demands and motions for discovery. The witness Thuman just called lives in Atlanta. The State has flown him up here for the trial and, in fact, flew him up a couple of times before. He made a taped statement to Sergeant Dale. We have, several times, asked for copies of that tape. Thuman refused to make it available to us…"

Thuman interrupted, "I didn't have it, Judge. Sergeant Dale had it."

"Bullshit," Joseph interjected. You could have gotten it from Dale anytime you wanted, or you could have told him to give me a copy."

Judge Crider asked, "Didn't they give you a copy of the summary prepared by Dale?"

"Well, there are some problems with that, Judge. The summary is just Dale's interpretation of what the witness said. I am entitled to hear the witness' words. Even though I have a great deal of confidence in Dale and his integrity, his interpretation of what's on the tape is nothing more than hearsay. Incidently, how do you know about the summary? Have you been talking to the prosecutor about this case without us? I know you and Thuman are friends, but our client is entitled to fair trial. That's difficult enough without you two having ex parte conversations."

Terry blanched and rolled his eyes at the thinly veiled accusation, thinking, *We are in deep shit now.*

The judge ignored Joseph's query about the summary and her knowledge of it, saying instead, "You're right, Mr. Joseph, you can listen to the tape tonight after the witness testifies."

"What the hell good is that going to do? How am I supposed to cross-examine him on his statement? That's too late, Judge, and you know it. He's flying back to Atlanta tonight. Like I said, if there's inconsistencies on the tape, I won't be able to cross-examine on them."

"Too bad, Joseph," the judge said with some irritation in her voice. "The witness is going to testify and you can review the summary. If you wanted to get him on tape, you could have flown him here yourself."

"Sure, Judge. You know damn well the defendant is indigent," with no little indignation in his voice. "I can see you approving expenses for airline tickets for witnesses. Besides, the witness refused to talk, even on the phone, to anyone from my office because, he said, Thuman told him not to—"

"That's not true, Judge," Thuman interjected. "I told him he didn't have to talk to them if he didn't want to."

"Typical of his obstructionism, Judge. You known damn well how clear that message is. 'Don't talk to them—they are the enemy.'"

"Let's get on with it, Joseph," the judge said, clearly irritated with Joseph.

Heated by the judge's lack of understanding or concern, Joseph said, "I'm trying to get a fair trial for Mr. Takas, Judge. If you won't let me hear the tape before I conduct my cross-examination of the witness, I'll have to move for a mistrial."

"Overruled!" Judge Crider snapped, standing and reaching for her robe.

By this time Joseph was furious. "I know you spent most of your professional career in one prosecutor's office or another," Joseph chided, "but I'd hoped you'd outgrown the lack of compassion they dictate."

"Joseph," Judge Crider said, her face darkening, "You're pretty damn close to contempt. One more comment like that and I'm sure you'll regret it."

His face as red as hers, Joseph stood and said without any conviction, "That's not the only thing I regret, but I didn't mean any discourtesy,

Your Honor. But be assured, I will do everything I can to see Jimmy get a fair trial despite the stumbling blocks Thuman and the Court seem bound and determined to throw in the way."

Terry tugged on Joseph's arm. "Let's get out of here before you join our client in a cell," he said in a low voice.

*   *   *

Once again in the courtroom, with the jury present and obviously irritated at the delay—wondering what had taken so much time, Thuman took the spot usually occupied by Joseph when he examined witnesses. Little was sworn and Thuman began his examination with, "Mr. Little, I'm going to stand back here behind the jury so you will have to keep your voice up. That way the jurors and I can hear you. Okay?"

The jury couldn't see Thuman's nervous facial mannerisms that were readily apparent to Joseph and those at his table. *No wonder he took my usual spot,* Joseph thought.

"Yes, sir," the witness responded.

"Please tell the jury your full name and spell your last name for the record."

"My name is Andrew Little, spelled L-I-T-T-L-E."

"Where do you live, sir?"

"I live in Atlanta, Georgia."

Little was a tall man, six feet or more, thin, slightly round shouldered. Obviously in his late twenties, but already developing a paunch that was probably related more to poor posture than eating habits. A smoker, fingers and teeth stained brown by tobacco, he appeared uncomfortable not having something in his fingers. He found a pencil on the stand before him, picked it up and held it between the first and second fingers of his left hand—where the stain was most pronounced. He kept lifting it towards his mouth, fighting hard to keep from putting it between his lips. His greasy black hair was stringy and not disciplined. Balding, he tried to hide it by letting his hair grow long. It was a losing battle. All in all, not a very attractive person.

Thuman asked Little about his background. The witness had previously lived in the environs of Milltown, growing up in a small rural town in southern Mills County. He finished school locally and took a job right out of high school in Atlanta. After he left home for Georgia, his parents moved into a small house immediately across the street from June Westlock. They knew her but did not care for her very much, not approving of her lifestyle. Little was on vacation in the time frame coinciding with the week June was killed. He took his vacation in Milltown to visit his parents. On the night June was killed, Little and his parents had gone out for dinner at a nearby restaurant, returning home about ten in the evening. Little's father suffered from emphysema—a fate that probably awaited Little—so his parents retired as soon as they got home. Little decided to go out and "look for a little action."

"I might," he said, "see some of the people I knew when I lived here." Going from bar to bar, he ended the evening at *Tracks*. He saw Takas, whom he knew slightly from school, but didn't say anything to him— "Never liked him." He left the bar before Takas did and returned home, where, he said, he "sat on the front porch smoking a couple of cigarettes and drinking coffee."

Thuman then, in an effort to minimize the impact of his witness' background, asked, "By the way, Mr. Little, have you ever been convicted of a crime—a felony?"

"Yes, sir," lowering his voice, appearing repentant.

"What crime was that, Mr. Little?"

"Solicitation of prostitution."

Thuman knew that if he didn't elicit this information from Little, Joseph would. If he permitted Joseph to call it to the attention of the jury, it would appear Thuman was hiding something—a wise strategic move.

"Now then, while you were sitting on the porch drinking coffee, did you see anything unusual?"

"I don't know about unusual, but I did notice a car pull into the driveway of the house where the girl was killed."

"What did you see when the car pulled in the drive?" Thuman inquired in a tone implying he had never heard about this before—as if he hadn't discussed with the witness at length what his testimony would be.

"I saw two people get out of the car…a girl and a man…. They walked up to the house, she got out her key and unlocked the door…. They went in the front door."

"What, if anything, did you notice about the man?"

"Well, he was dark skinned. You know, like an Italian or a Greek," Little said.

Thuman continued, "Did you notice anything about the car?"

"Yeah. It was kind of grey."

Interesting, Joseph thought, *Jimmy's car was grey, but in the summary of his statement to the police Little originally told them the car was dark colored or black. Thuman coached him well.*

Thuman asked, "Did you see the man leave the house?"

"Yes, sir. He was in the house about a half hour." Then Little volunteered, "He left the house kind of quiet…closed the inner door like he didn't want to disturb anyone…looked around a little bit, then closed the screen door, like careful."

"What do you mean, 'looked around a little bit?'"

"Just kind of like this," craning his neck back and forth, "like looking up and down the street to see if anyone saw him."

"Objection," interjected Joseph. He had allowed Little to testify pretty freely, but this was too much.

Judge Crider, reluctantly, "Sustained. Mr. Little, you have no way of knowing what was in the person's mind. You can only testify as to what you saw."

"Yes, ma'am," contritely, and without waiting for another question, he continued, "He then walked over to his car, opened the door real careful like and closed it real quiet and left."

He was obviously well coached and would get in everything Thuman wanted. Thuman continued covering the same ground several times so the jury would have no doubt that the witness, even though he was unable to identify Takas, attributed guilty actions to the person he saw leaving Westlock's house.

After reviewing his notes carefully, Thuman finally said, "We have no further questions, Your Honor." Little had been on the stand for a little over an hour so far.

Jude Crider nodded towards Joseph and said, "You may cross-examine if you wish."

"Thank you, Your Honor. For the record, I would like to point out that the witness' taped statement is not here." Joseph wanted the jury to know that there wasn't a level playing field—he wasn't given all of the information to which he was entitled.

"Mr. Joseph. We covered this in chambers. Do you have any questions?"

"Yes, we do. It seems that even though we do not have the original tape, the summary prepared by Sergeant Dale shows some inconsistencies. I intend to cross-examine on those."

"Well, let's get to it," the judge said, impatience creeping into her voice.

"Thank you, Judge," Joseph said with feigned politeness, walking to a spot behind the jury—the same spot Thuman had occupied, carrying several papers. Joseph thought, *No way in hell he's going to usurp my space.*

"Mr. Little," Joseph began, "my name is Patrick Joseph and I, along with Terry Bernow, represent Jimmy Takas in this case. You are aware of that, aren't you?"

"Yes, sir," cautiously.

"My office has contacted you on several occasions, but you refused to talk to us, isn't that true?"

"Yeah. Mr. Thuman told me not to talk to you."

Thuman leaped to his feet. "That's not true. I told him he didn't have to talk to you if he didn't want to. I never instructed him not to talk to you."

"Is Mr. Thuman trying to impeach his own witness, Judge?" Joseph directed his question to the bench, ignoring Thuman.

Thuman was fuming, especially when the judge turned to him and said, "Mr. Thuman, you know you are to direct your comments to the bench and not counsel. Now, if that is an objection, it is overruled. You will have an opportunity to examine this matter further on redirect…if you want to." Then turning to Joseph, "Now let's get on with it." The judge was obviously losing patience with both. Joseph didn't care.

Terry, seated at the trial table and taking notes, tried to hide the smile on his face, as did several of the jurors. *Very good, Pat. Keep him off balance,* Terry thought.

Trying to make the witness less wary, Joseph brought him back to his original story, asking about the dinner with his parents, expressing sorrow for his father's emphysema, which required the witness to take to the porch in order to enjoy a cigarette. He then took Andy Little through his evening's adventures at the various bars—what he had to drink—whom he saw.

Little was beginning to get more comfortable. He relaxed back into the witness chair and spoke freely in response to the questions Joseph asked in a conversational manner, waving the pencil in front of him, still fighting the urge to put it between his lips.

Joseph then abruptly changed the subject, "If I recall your statement to the officers, you were looking for a woman with whom you could enjoy the evening?"

Little sat a little straighter. "Yeah."

"Any particular kind of woman?" Joseph asked, trying to remind the jurors of the witness' record, without being too obvious.

"No. Just looking."

"Didn't see anything you wanted?" Joseph asked.

"No. None of them I saw wanted me," the witness replied, growing more sullen.

"Now, let's see. You said you got home about one thirty in the morning?"

"Yeah, about that. I drove around for a bit before I went home."

Joseph, lightly, "Still looking for a girl?"

The witness nodded, adding, "I am a young man and always want…" stopping as though afraid he might have said too much.

"Didn't find any then?"

"Nah."

Again changing the subject, Joseph said, "Let's take a look at the summary of your statement to the police. Mr. Bernow will hand you a copy if you want to look at it."

"I already seen it," the witness said. Thuman had obviously provided him everything he needed.

"I want to ask you about a couple of things in there. First, didn't you tell the police that the man you saw leaving the Westlock house was a black man?"

"Well, it was dark, and he was kind of dark. Could have been something else," Little hedged.

Sternly, Joseph said, "Just answer the question," continuing slowly and emphatically, "Didn't you tell the police it was a black man?"

"Yeah," he mumbled.

Joseph repeated, "A black man? A Negro?"

The witness muttered another "Yeah."

"Speak up, Mr. Little. You are mumbling and I'm having a hard time hearing you. I'm afraid the jurors might not be able to hear you either. Now, your answer to the last two questions is in the affirmative; that is, you answered 'Yes' to both, is that correct?"

Little nodded. When Joseph began to insist on a verbal response, the witness reluctantly said, "Yes!"

Joseph paused long enough for the jurors to digest what Little had said, then asked, "The second question is, didn't you tell the police that the car you saw leaving the driveway of the Westlock home was black or some dark color?"

Little again tried to hedge, "Well, it could've been. It was dark out…it's hard to tell."

Joseph wasn't going to let the witness off the hook that easily. "There is a large light—a kind of security light—very bright—that shines in Westlock's drive, isn't there? And isn't there a streetlight right in front of your house?"

The witness again just nodded affirmatively to both questions. "In words, Mr. Little," Joseph insisted.

"Yeah…"

"Is that 'Yes' to both questions? The security light shining in the drive and the streetlight in front of your house?"

"Yeah…"

"Now back to the original question. Didn't you tell the police that the car you saw leaving the driveway was black or some dark color?"

"Yeah."

"Now then, you have had several conversations with the prosecutor, didn't you?"

"Yeah."

"In those conversations, did he tell you that the person charged with the crime was white and not black?"

"Objection," Thuman almost shouted.

"This is cross-examination, Judge," Joseph pointed out needlessly.

Judge Crider impatiently said, "Overruled. Answer the question."

"Yeah, he did."

"Didn't he also tell you that Jimmy's car was grey and not black?"

"Well, yeah, but—"

Joseph didn't want to ask any more questions on the inconsistencies at this time. He would save it for argument. He learned long ago that if you ask too many questions, you just give a witness an opportunity to explain himself, to the examiner's disadvantage.

"Thank you," Joseph said politely. Then without giving the witness a chance to relax, Joseph returned to the previous subject, "You said you were looking for a woman that night?"

"Yeah."

"Can you tell us what you like in a woman?"

The witness looked perplexed. "What do you mean?"

"Well, do you like blondes, dark hair, long hair, short hair, thin girls…? You know, what do you like?"

Joseph heard a chortle from the jury box, and a giggle behind him.

"Well, I like slender blondes with long hair, I guess, but anything would do," Little answered sarcastically.

"You wanted a lady that evening? You're a single man? You have needs. You saw Ms. Westlock that evening. It sounds like she is the kind of girl you like. In fact, the description you just gave us pretty well fits Ms. Westlock."

Little shrugged, a mild leer on his face.

The room reacted humorously to this old man's suggestive line of questions—the mood lightened.

Joseph waited for the room to quiet down. He then asked in a voice so low it barely carried to the witness box, "Now then, Mr. Little, you did find what you were looking for that night? It was right across the street from where you were sitting in the dark. You found what you were trolling for all evening, didn't you?"

The silence in the room was deafening. All the jurors' and spectators' eyes turned toward the witness, whose reddening face highlighted a look of guilt flashing across his face.

Ignoring the silence, Joseph, his voice quiet, "You visited Ms. Westlock that night, didn't you? You liked what you saw and walked across the street and…?"

Little did not respond, just repeatedly making a negative shake of his head, his face suffused with blood.

Wonder what he's feeling so guilty about, Joseph thought, *his actions or his dirty mind.*

After several silence-filled seconds, Little straightened in the witness chair, glared at Joseph and almost shouted, "No, sir, I did not."

Joseph mumbled under his breath just loud enough for jurors in the back row to hear, "I just bet."

"What did you say, Mr. Joseph?" Judge Crider asked, frowning at Thuman, who leaped to his feet. The judge waved him back into his chair.

"Nothing, Judge. Guess I was just thinking out loud."

"Well, do it more quietly. Now, do you have any more questions?"

"I don't think so, Your Honor. Let me check with Mr. Bernow and see if I missed anything," Joseph said as he gathered his notes and walked towards counsel table, where Terry and Jimmy sat. He wanted to take as much time as he could so the jurors could think about what had been said, and watch the witness squirm in his seat.

Leaning towards Terry, he whispered, "Did I miss anything?"

"I haven't the slightest idea, but this is a perfect spot to quit. There's no way in hell Thuman will be able to rehabilitate him. Great cross."

"Thanks," Joseph said, then turning to the judge, "We have no further questions, Your Honor."

Thuman couldn't let it rest. He tried for the next several minutes to rehabilitate his witness while the witness fidgeted on the stand. It was clear that Little wanted to be somewhere else—anywhere else. Finally, Thuman turned from the witness and walked back to his seat and growled, "No further questions, Judge."

Joseph was thrilled when Judge Crider said, "I think we have been going long enough. Let's call it a day. Remember," to the jury, "don't talk about the case to anyone, no newspapers, no television and do not form an opinion. We are adjourned till nine tomorrow morning."

Joseph and Terry spent a few minutes talking to Jimmy Takas before leaving him with the guard, trying to cheer him up and convince him that the trial was going well. Nothing they said seemed to penetrate the wall of gloom surrounding the young man. Head hanging, hair limp, eyes clouded, he was inconsolable. His parents were permitted to talk to him briefly, and they could do nothing to alleviate Jimmy's depressed state. Giving up, Joseph and Terry decided they may as well walk back to the office.

*   *   *

On the way, Terry asked, "You always seems to have an excellent ending to your cross-examinations. How do you know when to stop?"

"Well, Terry, let me tell you a story." Then paused. "One of my sons once said that I wouldn't be remembered so much for the stories I tell, but for the frequency with which I tell them. So if I told you this story before, don't interrupt—I want to tell it again."

Laughing, Terry said, "Go on. I'm sure I'll learn something."

"When I was in law school, one of my instructors said, 'Your legal practice will be dictated by the first client that walks through your office door.' He also said that it would probably be either a divorce or criminal case. Well, he was right, the first case I had was a criminal case. The mother of a young man I had known in high school hired me to represent her son. It seems he dropped out of school and had several run-ins with the law. He was charged with the crime of uttering. Uttering is trying to pass a bad check. The case was scheduled to be tried during Thanksgiving week. My client was being held in jail and so, when I arrived at the Criminal Courts Building in Cleveland—it was at East 22nd Street and Payne Avenue at the time—he was already in the courtroom. The bailiff told me the judge and assistant prosecutor wanted to talk to me in chambers. I walked through the door the bailiff pointed out. I was scared to death. The judge was sitting in his robes, feet propped on his desk. The assistant prosecutor was on the other side of the desk—feet also propped on the judge's desk."

Joseph chuckled at the memory and paused to catch his breath. Talking and walking were getting to be more of a chore every day.

"Anyway, the judge said, 'No one wants to be here during Thanksgiving week. Let's plead your client and go home.' I sat in the chair he pointed out and said nothing. After a few moments the prosecutor said, 'Look, I'll reduce the charge to an attempt and suggest he be sentenced to time served.' I still said nothing. The judge and prosecutor worked on me for several more minutes, offering more and more attractive plea agreements. Finally the prosecutor said, 'Look, I'll dismiss the charges if you agree your client violated his probation,' which, of course he had. I nodded in agreement. The judge said, 'Good, let's go into the courtroom and get it on the record.' We did. My client was thrilled and I was relieved to have the case behind me.

"Afterward, as we walked out, the assistant prosecutor looked at me and said, 'You are the toughest negotiator I've ever had to deal with.' I thanked him for the compliment and left. But the truth is, I really wanted to accept his first offer, but was so frightened I couldn't open my mouth.

I was literally scared speechless—couldn't say anything—too frightened even to nod my head. I was sure I was going to faint...had never been so frightened in my life. All the time I was in the judge's chamber, I couldn't have even told them my name if asked. But I did learn a gigantic lesson. You get a hell of a lot more out of a person—or a witness—by keeping your mouth shut."

Terry laughed and with the mood lightened, they continued to the office in companionable silence.

CHAPTER TWELVE

Even though Jimmy's mood dampened what Joseph believed they accomplished during the day, it did not keep Joseph from enjoying the clear, cold late afternoon. Looking around, he noted it was getting dark earlier. Since the checkerboards and rocking chairs had disappeared from the hotel porch, Joseph reflected, *Guess I'll have to wait until Spring before I get to sit with the duffers and learn how to play that game.*

"Terry, I don't think we have to review anything tonight. Today went well—probably better than we had any right to expect. I want to head home early, have a Martini and relax with a good meal. Oh, shit. Can't do that. Mary has a class tonight. She's into quilting and enjoys going to this fabric shop with our daughter. She probably won't get home until nine or so. Want to go over to the *Round Table* and have dinner with me?"

"Sounds like fun," Terry responded. "But I promised my kids I'd spend some time with them tonight. They like for me to play those video games with them…especially since I never win. Can't figure out how those things work. I haven't seen much of my family lately, and with a free evening, I'd kind of like to spend it with them—that is unless you really need to talk about the case?"

"No, I don't think so. We got everything in order. You go on home and enjoy yourself," thinking, *The only lawyers I know that make a great financial success are those that are married to their business instead of a wife and family. Doesn't bother me, I guess, never thought I'd get rich anyway. Seems Terry doesn't care either.*

They continued toward the office parking lot, Joseph and Terry moving towards the back entrance of the building.

"Mr. Joseph?" The elderly lawyer heard his name being called as he entered his building. He turned and saw Stan Marten. Stan had followed them from the courthouse. "I'd love to have dinner with you, if it's all right," Stan inquired, obviously having overheard Joseph's earlier invitation to Terry.

Joseph though about it for a moment, then nodded acquiescence.

They entered the office through the back, Terry going downstairs to his office and Joseph walking up the stairs to his, accompanied by the young reporter. "Della, anyone here?" he called.

Della, sitting at her desk, smiled a "Hi" to Joseph with a negative shake of her head as he walked past. "Everyone's gone for the day." She got up and followed him into his office.

He shrugged out of his coat, sat down and asked, "Anything I need to know about—or do?"

"Not really. Here's the mail. Nothing needs attention right now and I farmed out the work that needs attention. There's nothing the kids can't handle. There are a couple of new clients who insist they want to see the famous Mr. Joseph, but I told them you wouldn't see anyone until after this trial. I handled the preliminary interviews and there is nothing that needs immediate attention. You got to be proud of the kids in the office though. They have really pitched in and done a masterful job."

"Thanks. As always, it's obvious I'm not needed around here. Wanted to go home early and relax, but Mary's gone out. I'm going across to the *Round Table* and have dinner with this young fellow," pointing to Stan.

"Go ahead," Della said, "I'll lock up."

"Remind me to give you a raise," Joseph said as he got up to leave.

"Yeah, sure," Della said, using one of Mary's patented "Humphh"'s.

Stan and Joseph wandered across the square and settled in at the bar of the *Round Table* while waiting to be seated at a table. Joseph relaxed enjoying his Martini while Stan ordered and sipped on a coke. "Mr. Joseph, what was going on in the judge's chambers? When you guys got back in the courtroom you looked mad as hell. It looked like you were arguing something about discovery. Can you talk about it?"

"First of all, Stan, I am not a 'guy.' Can't figure why this generation uses such distortions of the English language. Not only is it unattractive, it's disrespectful. I hate it when waitresses call me 'guy,' and I don't want you to do it either. With your journalism degree, you should know better without me having to say anything."

Stan blushed and said, "I'm sorry. You're absolutely right. I have no excuse. It's just that, I guess, I hear it and repeat it. I won't do it again." Then getting back to the subject he asked, "Now what was that all about in there?"

"You're right, son. We were arguing about discovery. Thuman is always a prick about discovery—so I'm told. But apparently he is being more obstructive than usual. Terry and I can't figure out why. Anyway, getting back to your question, Ohio's Rules of Criminal Procedure provide that the State should, when the defense asks for it, give basic information about their witnesses, such as names and addresses among other things. In fact, your paper wrote an editorial on the subject, about Thuman and his unwillingness to provide discovery. Remember?"

"Yeah, I remember, and that's what made me think about it. What did he do this time?" Stan asked.

"When we got to court this morning, he handed me the names of two additional people he intends to call as witnesses. I kind of lost it and got into an argument with the judge about it. She lets him get away with murder—is that a pun?"

"I remember reading something about it in the *Cleveland Plain Dealer* recently. The City is paying some fellow more than a million dollars because he spent something like fifteen years in jail for a rape he didn't commit. Wasn't that about a problem with discovery?"

"Well, only partially. The prosecution didn't provide the defense with lab reports they were entitled to. DNA analysis revealed that the defendant couldn't have been the man that committed the rape. When the lab technician testified about his findings, it was substantially different than the information contained in his report. They also provided information to the victim to encourage her to identify the defendant as the man that committed the crime. The reports were never made available to the defense. Some time later, the defendant's family hired another lawyer, who made a public records request for all the reports this technician had made and found the discrepancy. The defendant was finally released from jail and sued the shit out of the city—rightly so. He got a big chunk of well-deserved money. It wouldn't be so bad except that the same thing happens time and time again—and prosecutors like Thuman just don't care. They want convictions."

"Does it really happen that frequently?"

"It sure does. The *Akron Beacon Journal* recently reported about a fellow who was convicted of felonious assault. It seems the victim and the defendant were involved in a bar fight—a not unusual happening. Anyway, the victim changed his story at trial and made it appear that the defendant was not only the aggressor, but beat and kicked him while he was unable to fight back. The story he told the police originally was quite different, but his statement was never made available to defense counsel. As a result the defense attorney couldn't cross-examine the witness about his earlier statement. So the jury never knew what the witness said at the time of the incident. One of the *Beacon* columnists wrote about it, complaining that ...*if Ohio required every prosecutor to share all evidence prior to trial, the defendant might not be sitting in prison right now. At the very least, the jury would have all the facts...*"

"Why doesn't someone do something about it, Mr. Joseph?"

"Ohio's Public Defender requested the Supreme Court to adopt an open-discovery rule and they almost did. The legislature killed it. Of course, they were lobbied very heavily by the Ohio Prosecutors Association. You got to realize that prosecutors have to get elected, as do judges, most of whom come from the ranks of prosecutors—they are primarily politicians and are willing to do damn near anything to get elected. They measure justice on the basis of their win-loss record. Justice becomes a contest—a trial—rather than a search for the truth. It disgusts me, but there isn't much I can do except keep pounding my head against that wall."

"It sure would be nice if the public knew about all this, Mr. Joseph."

"Of course they should and it's your job to tell them, but unfortunately most people just don't give a shit until it affects them or a member of their family. Now let's get something to eat."

*   *   *

Joseph was sitting on his glassed-in back porch enjoying a glass of wine when Mary got home from her sewing class. She and their daughter had enjoyed the evening together and wanted to talk about it. They sat at the round glass-topped porch table while Joseph poured a glass of wine for each, and refreshed his own. Sitting quietly in his favorite wicker rocking chair, Joseph listened to the conversation, enjoying the talk of things not involving someone's life or freedom, especially the talk about his granddaughters, thinking, *I am really proud of their achievements. At least none of them decided not to go to law school—smart girls.*

Feeling relaxed, he took inordinate pleasure in watching the cats trying to get to the birds through the glass—*Stupid cats.* Joseph knew the weather wouldn't permit many more evenings on the closed porch so he relished all of the good things there. After rinsing out the glasses and taking leave of their daughter, Mary retired to her sewing room, where she was working on another quilt, to be given to one of their children or grandchildren. Joseph poured himself another glass of wine, glanced through his notes for the morrow and dozed. A pleasant evening.

*   *   *

The next morning Joseph showered and dressed carefully…getting help from Mary in choosing a tie…picked at his toast and coffee and drove to the office. Pulling out of the garage, he again noticed the little brown rabbits that lived in his yard scampering around the flagpole. They were playing just the way children do, except there was no yelling or laughing—they made no sound. Children would have been laughing, screaming and making a ruckus—the bunnies did everything except for the noise part.

156

I wonder, Joseph thought, not for the first time, *why they can't make sounds. Doesn't seem to bother them—sure seems like they are enjoying themselves just the way they are.*

Joseph thought about these imponderable things all the way to the office and was glad for a respite from that which had been occupying his mind for the past several weeks. As usual, he was the first there. Thank God Mary relieved him of the obligation of feeding their house animals—she enjoyed doing it. Even so, Joseph had been assigned the task of putting out birdseed for the songbirds and peanuts for the blue jays before he left.

Waiting in his office for Terry, he wondered what Thuman would do next. He looked towards his pigs and asked, *What's he going to do?* They responded with their usual enigmatic smile. *You're no help at all,* Joseph mentally groused.

As soon as Terry got there, they took their familiar walk across the square, arriving timely in the courtroom, where the parties and spectators were gathered. Judge Crider called for and welcomed the jury, called the room to order and instructed Thuman to proceed. Joseph wasn't surprised to hear Thuman say, "The State will call Robert Draco."

Draco sauntered toward the witness stand, self-confident, a little over six feet tall, regular features marred by a somewhat flattened nose that appeared to have been broken more than once, and an old scar crossing his left eyebrow and extending down to his cheek. *Probably from a bar fight,* Joseph thought. Fitting his appearance, Draco was outfitted, pierced and tattooed in a manner that matched his lifestyle. His head was shaved in the latest fashion, a dark sheen to his skull—from one pierced ear dangled a silver lightning-bolt-shaped earring. He was dressed in a tight-fitting short-sleeved T-shirt from which well-muscled arms protruded, sporting a colorful tattoo that appeared to be the tail of a dragon, the body of which was hidden by the sleeve of his shirt. Some kind of rock band logo stretched across the T-shirt, clinging to his well-formed chest. Tight-fitting jeans and a leather belt with a fancy silver buckle completed the ensemble. Affixed to his belt was a chain attached to a wallet stuffed in his back pocket. Joseph wondered if the build was due to hard work, nature or pumping iron. Whatever, it was pretty impressive—and a little scary.

"Mr. Draco, please tell the jury your full name and spell your last name for the record," Thuman began in his usual manner.

"My name is Robert Draco, but everyone calls me Bub," delivered with a smirk. "My last name is spelled just like it sounds, D-R-A-C-O."

"If you don't mind, I will call you Mr. Draco," Thuman responded.

Draco shrugged his approval, then identified himself as being a neighbor of the deceased. "Lived around the corner from her."

The prosecutor then began asking questions concerning Draco's activities on the night June Westlock died, including his visit to Forge Street and his connection with Cockroach. When Draco began talking about his drug purchases, Judge Crider interrupted and told the witness to wait before answering the question and, with a gesture for the lawyers to approach, said, "Mr. Thuman, Mr. Joseph, please come here."

Motioning the court reporter to remain in her seat, Judge Crider, obviously irritated, said softly enough that her voice would not carry to the ears of jurors, "What the hell are you doing, Harold? You're asking this witness to incriminate himself. You've heard about the Fifth Amendment, haven't you? I'm going to advise him that he has the right to an attorney as well as the right to refuse to testify unless you grant him immunity from prosecution for anything he says on the stand. If you grant him immunity, I'll instruct him he has to testify. Do you understand me?"

Thuman started, "Look, Judge, he's been around the block a few times and knows his…"

The judge's frown stopped him. After a moment, obviously trying to think of some way to avoid the Court's demand, Thuman finally conceded, saying, "Okay, Judge. I'll grant him immunity," something Thuman was usually unwilling to do. Joseph wondered why he had given in so easily.

"Put it on the record," the judge instructed.

With some reluctance, Thuman did what he was told, whispering to the court reporter so the jury couldn't hear, "Eileen, let the record reflect that the State is granting immunity to this witness in exchange for his testimony in this case."

Thuman then walked to the witness, leaned over and explained quietly to the witness about immunity. Joseph smiled at Thuman's discomfort. It was clear to Joseph that the jurors were more than a little curious about what was being said. No one explained it to them.

Draco then went on to tell how he had seen June Westlock on Forge Street the evening she died. "It was at Cockroach's house and she probably bought whatever drugs he had available—that is, what I hadn't already bought. She did that a lot."

He then told the jury, without hesitation, "Later that evening she called me and asked if I had any crack or anything left. Takas was at her house, wanting something and being pretty insistent. She thought if she could get him something, he would go away. I had no intention of sharing anything with that little twerp and so told her I didn't have nothing. Takas come over to my house anyway."

Draco explained, "Me and a friend was sitting on the porch. It was nice out. Takas come running up the sidewalk wanting to buy some coke or reefer or something. I told him we didn't have none and he started to act, like, crazy."

"What do you mean?"

"He looked like he was crying and said something about he was going to kill himself. Like it was the last time we'd ever see him. He was real agitated. Something about a girl he was seeing or a girlfriend broke up with him and…shit, I don't know…he was just acting real crazy."

Thuman interrupted with, "What did you say to Mr. Takas then?"

"I was really getting pissed at him, so I stood up and started toward him telling him, like, get the fuck off my walk. Asked him why don't you and June go see Cockroach and get what you want from him?"

"Did he leave then?"

Smirking, "Yeah. In a real hurry."

"Can you identify Mr. Takas in the courtroom?" Thuman asked.

"Sure. He's the dude sitting between the old man and the other lawyer. He's wearing a grey jacket, glasses and a blue tie."

"Let the record show that the witness has identified the defendant," Thuman said.

The judge nodded her permission. "The record will reflect that the witness has identified the defendant."

Joseph ignored, but would remember, the comment about the 'old man.'

Thuman continued his questioning about the night's activities. It amazed Joseph that this witness' generation were able to hold jobs, sustain their lives and raise children, staying awake all night, doing drugs and other terrible things to their bodies and living the kind of life that is the figment of some crazy person's imagination. It seems Draco worked all day in construction, did drugs with his friends in the evening, stayed awake until the early morning hours.

"It was around three o'clock and I seen Knedder go in June's house. I called her home to warn Knedder someone was lurking around the neighborhood. I seen some guy going around by June's house. Thought he might be a narc—wanted to warn Knedder."

He said, "Knedder answered the phone and told me, 'I don't know where June is, but my little girl is asleep in her bed.'"

Of course, this was a surprise to Joseph. He hadn't been informed that Knedder had received a telephone call while in June's house—not surprising.

"Want a beer?" Draco had asked Knedder, and Knedder said, "Sure."

Draco grabbed a couple of beers from his fridge and walked out of the house. Knedder met him at the corner.

Thuman asked, "How did he appear to you?"

"Well, he was okay. Had a buzz going, but was all right. He was just Clarence, you know. Acted a little excited. Guess he was worried about his woman."

"Objection," Joseph interjected.

To which the judge responded, "Sustained. You can't testify as to what might have been in his mind."

The witness continued, "Then we walked across the street, where some dude was sitting on the porch. I thought it might be the guy was lurking around. Wanted to get a look at him. Clarence asked him, 'Did you see June?' and he said no. We talked for a bit, I learned he was from out of town and visiting his folks. We finished our beers and I went home. Clarence went back in the house, I think. At least he went round back of the house."

Thuman closed with, "When you said the reason you thought Knedder was excited, you were basing that on what you later learned about the death of June Westlock; isn't that right?"

"Yeah, I'd feel the same way myself."

"Your Honor…" Joseph protested.

Judge Crider, anticipating the objection, leaned toward the witness and said, "No editorial comments."

"Okay. I'm sorry," derisively, Draco said, obviously not contrite.

Thuman walked toward his seat, saying, "That's all the questions I have, Judge."

Judge Crider looked toward Joseph and inquired, "Do you have any questions, Mr. Joseph?"

"May we approach? I'd like to see any statement this witness made, Your Honor," Joseph said walking toward the bench.

Judge Crider looked toward the jury box and said, "Ladies and gentlemen, I think we'll take a break now. Remember, don't form any opinion on the case, don't discuss it until it's finally submitted to you. We'll call you back in a few minutes."

The jury stood and walked toward the jury room, Joseph and Terry standing politely until the jury room door closed, then together turned toward the bench. Thuman handed a copy of the witness' statement to Joseph, which he read, Terry reading over his shoulder.

Joseph turned to Terry, asking in a whisper, "Do you want to handle this asshole?"

"Nope. You do it and tear him one, 'old man.'"

After a few minutes, Judge Crider called the jury back into court. The jurors, now familiar with the routine, entered in an orderly line that would permit them to reach their seat without climbing over each other. Joseph and Terry stood respectfully waiting until the jurors found their seats.

Joseph, looking at Draco, felt a shiver traveling up and down his spine. He wasn't sure if it was in anticipation of the cross-examination or fear.

Certainly Draco's appearance alone would engender anxiety in the stoutest heart. Joseph thought as he walked towards his usual spot behind the jury, *What an arrogant bastard he is. He's one of the night people walking comfortable outside the law and proud of getting away with it. With all the reporters in the room, he is making the most of his fifteen minutes of fame.*

In spite of his dislike, Joseph address the witness in a steady voice, "Mr. Draco. My name is Patrick Joseph, one of the lawyers for Jimmy Takas. I'd like to ask you a few questions. You said you're working in construction, is that correct?"

The witness nodded affirmatively but the judge instructed, "You have to answer in words so the court reporter can get it all down."

Draco turned toward Joseph and said, "Yes, sir."

The judge continued, "You don't have to call him 'sir' if you don't want to, but you do have to answer in words so that Eileen can write it down."

Joseph interjected, "You can call me 'sir' if you want to. It's all right."

The jurors chuckled but the witness was clearly unhappy with the interchange, the expression on his face stating clearly that his pride would not let him be bested by this old man—*He ain't going to be putting me down,* he thought.

Joseph began the cross-examination slowly, wanting to make the witness feel safe and comfortable, inquiring into his employment and background, then, "You know someone named Cockroach, don't you?"

"Yeah, I know him."

Joseph, noting that Draco had mentioned his involvement with drugs only peripherally, wanted the jury to know exactly how much he was into drugs generally and particularly on the night June died. "He sells drugs, doesn't he?"

"I guess so. Everybody says he does," losing a little of his cockiness.

"You personally know he deals drugs, don't you? In fact, you buy from him, don't you?"

"Mr. Joseph," Judge Crider interrupted, "one question at a time."

"Okay, Judge," then to Draco, "He's your supplier, isn't he?"

"Well, yes."

Joseph noticed the "sir" was gone. He asked, "In fact, you bought from him on the night Ms. Westlock was killed, didn't you?"

A surly "Yes."

"What did you buy?"

"A twenty-dollar piece."

"Please explain to the jury what that is. We aren't all as knowledgeable about the drug trade as you."

Draco's face reddening, he answered, "A twenty-dollar piece is twenty dollars' worth of cocaine."

"Is that in powder form or what?"

"It comes in a chunk, but you…you know, can make it into powder."

"For what purpose?"

"To cut a line so it can be snorted."

"I assume that means to sniff it up your nose."

"Yeah."

"How many lines or hits can you get from a twenty-dollar piece?" Joseph didn't really want to know, he just wanted the jury to hear the kind of person the witness was and how willing and knowledgeable he was on ways to break the law.

The witness went on to describe how the drug was used. He explained that on the night June was killed, he made several lines from the cocaine he purchased and, with his buddy, consumed it all along with eight or ten beers. He had seen June about eight or nine o' clock that evening on the street where Cockroach lived and, in fact, had seen her on the porch of his house talking to him. He knew she bought some drugs. Apparently she used them all up because she called later to tell Draco that Jimmy Takas was at her house looking for drugs. She didn't have any left, so sent "him over to my house—the stupid bitch."

By this time, all his drugs had been all used up too, but even if they hadn't been, he wasn't about to share with that punk. He had known June for several years and had done drugs with her and Clarence on many occasions, "usually at her house."

He also explained that he was aware of the discord between June and Clarence—"she kicked him out of the house." He also knew about the

163

"peace warrant against him." But Clarence, like him, didn't pay too much attention to what the police wanted. They were always "a real pain in the ass."

The language produced a frown from the judge, but she didn't interrupt the testimony or reprimand him for the vulgarity, her demeanor saying that she wouldn't let it go much further.

Draco went on to say, "I seen Clarence was there the night she was killed. I called him at her house and he answered the phone. Wanted to warn him about someone hanging round the house—thought it might be a narc. Asked him if he wanted a beer, and he said, 'Sure.' I'd seen someone sitting on the porch across the street watching everything going down. I didn't know him. Wanted to let Clarence know about that too. Thought it might be the cops—could be the drug task force. They're getting pretty active in the neighborhoods, you know."

Joseph asked, "You and Knedder walked across the street and talked to that guy, didn't you?"

"Yeah. I was bringing a couple of beers to Clarence's house when he come up to the corner. I handed him a brew and we walked across the street, like to talk to the guy sitting there. Like I said, I didn't know him. He told us he was from out of town—just visiting his folks. We bullshit for a couple of minutes and then left. I walked back to my house and I guess Clarence went back to his."

Joseph asked, "And if I remember correctly, you said that he denied having seen June that evening, didn't he?"

"Yeah."

Joseph paused long enough to allow the jury to think about Little's earlier testimony, thinking, *Something else for final argument.* Then, seeming to shift gears, he asked, "Was Clarence's car in the drive when you went by the house?"

"No. I guess he parked down the street or around the block somewhere. Didn't want his car to be seen, I guess."

Joseph knew the response was improper so hurriedly asked, "You started snorting or doing whatever it is you do with your 'twenty-dollar piece' about eight or eight thirty, right?"

"Right."

"And started drinking beer about the same time?"

"Yeah, that's true."

"Now, let's see," Joseph asked, "you used up all the cocaine you bought by about ten or ten thirty and then kept drinking beer, or whatever, until one or two o'clock in the morning. I assume you do that fairly frequently. Doesn't that maybe get you pretty high? You know, maybe have some effect on your ability to appreciate what's going on around you? Maybe confuse you a little?"

"Nah. Cocaine don't hurt you," Draco smirked.

Incredulous, Joseph asked, "Cocaine doesn't hurt? How about cocaine and beer?"

"I'm still alive," Draco responded, reverting to his smart-mouth ways.

The judge interrupted with, "We can probably find some authorities that differ with you, Mr. Draco." She was obviously getting disgusted with this witness. Joseph was hoping the jury was too.

"Right." Draco wasn't making any friends.

"One last question, Mr. Draco. How long have you know Mr. Thuman?"

Before Thuman could offer an objection, the witness said, "I don't really know him personally, but I've seen him around…different places…. Don't think I've ever talked to him except about this trial."

"Talked to him about this trial, eh?" Joseph asked.

"Yeah."

"Did he tell you what to say?" Joseph asked innocently.

Thuman leaped to his feet, fuming, but before he could say anything, Joseph turned to the bench and said, "I have no further questions, Your Honor." He returned to his seat and sat down.

Terry was beaming. "Nice job, Mr. Joseph. If nothing else, you got Thuman pissed."

Thuman said, "I have no questions on redirect."

Judge Crider told the witness, "You can leave now. Or, if you want, you can stay in the courtroom and watch the rest of the trial." Then to the prosecutor, "Call your next witness."

Draco slouched out of the courtroom, face red, shaved head gleaming with sweat. He glowered at Joseph as he walked past his table. Joseph thought, *Oh well, another enemy. Don't make many friends in this business.*

Thuman and his assistant prosecutor were talking quietly at the trial table. Anne Dronke stood and asked the judge, "Your Honor, it is near the noon hour and our next witness won't be here until after lunch. Would it be a problem if we broke for lunch now and reconvened a little early?"

"I don't think anyone would object to an early lunch." Then turning to the jury, "Please remember the instruction about not forming an opinion or talking to anyone about the case. We can break now and be back at one o'clock."

With that, the judge left the bench and Joseph stood, hand on Jimmy's shoulder, waiting for the jury to leave. He leaned over Jimmy and said, "We'll see you in about an hour. We had a pretty good morning. How you holding up?"

Jimmy tried to smile, couldn't quite make it, but responded, "Okay," turned and gave a brief, unobtrusive wave to his mom sitting in the back of the room with his father. They had been there every day in the back row of pews valiantly trying to make a good appearance and hold back tears.

*   *   *

Travel agencies tout the New England states as the place to go if you want to see fall colors. Not true. Ohio's trees break into a riot of color every fall. Gold and red prevails just before the trees start to shed their leaves. Milltown's square has some of the finest old trees in the state and they always present a gorgeous face to fall. Usually Joseph was enamored of the colors and couldn't wait to get outside. Yet, as he and Terry walked towards their office he failed to notice them, grumbling under his breath.

"What?" Terry asked. "I can't hear you."

"Nothing..." Joseph started. "Yes, there is something. What the hell's wrong with these kids?" Anyone under the age of thirty-five was a kid to Joseph. "God blessed this Draco fellow with a gorgeous physique, handsome face and some modicum of intelligence, yet he throws it all away on drugs. The same thing for the so-called victim in this case. June Westlock did drugs and everything else that goes along with it—child out of wedlock—live-in boyfriends—drinking, smoking, living in the night. I just don't understand. They seem to love their children and surely don't want them to… Aw, shit…I'm sure my dad had similar thoughts about me and my peers.

"The young people in this country have all the advantages, except those in the direst of economic circumstances. They don't have to turn to illegal activities to earn a living. At the very least they can find entry level jobs to provide food…or rely on social agencies. The same isn't true in other parts of the world, where the governments don't offer any help to their people. Places like some of the villages in Columbia, where kids are only able to find work in the production of cocaine base…where they learn the business from their parents…where they need to do it to earn a living. I just don't understand our kids turning to drugs for fun…." His voice trailed off, clearly not understanding the type of mentality that permitted these night people to intentionally do damage to themselves.

"I don't think it's quite as bad as you think, Mr. Joseph," Terry offered. "I guess I'm a kid by your definition, but I don't think like they do. Growing up in an ethnic home didn't hurt. Discipline, respect and work don't leave much time or energy for the kind of life they live. I think they're in the minority—at least I hope so."

Joseph had to agree with Terry. He had two granddaughters who had already finished college—one teaching high school math in Florida and loving her job and students—the other working in a gymnastics academy. Both seemed solid, sensible young women—not allowed to call them girls in this politically correct world. Joseph was equally proud of his several other grandchildren, all of whom were doing well scholastically, participated in worthwhile activities and sports and appeared to be solid citizens. *Maybe the entire world isn't going to hell. There might be some hope for the world, what with my grandbabies and Terry's kids,* Joseph thought.

"Boy, I hope so too." Joseph growled. "Let's grab a bite and get back to try and cheer up Jimmy and his folks.

*   *   *

Returning to the courtroom, Joseph and Terry found Jimmy waiting. They talked for a few minutes, until Judge Crider entered and climbed the three steps to her seat. Looking around, she asked, "Everyone here?" After an affirmative murmured response, she said to her bailiff, "Please bring in the jury."

With everyone in place, Thuman said, "The State will call Clara Boyer."

Judge Crider nodded toward the bailiff. "Nancy, please get Ms. Boyer."

Now why the hell is he calling her? Joseph wondered. *She can't hurt us and maybe she'll be helpful. Oh well, let's see what he has up his sleeve.*

Clara Boyer entered the courtroom in response to Nancy Short's call. Joseph watched her walk to the witness stand. She was short, dark hair cut in what used to be called a pixie, a little on the plump side, yet rather attractive. She appeared comfortable with herself and took the witness chair as directed by the bailiff without fidgeting or obvious discomfort. Nancy then asked her to raise her right hand and droned the formula oath, the witness nodding and answering in the affirmative. Joseph wondered if she spent much time in a courtroom.

Anne Dronke, Thuman's assistant, walked toward the back of the room after the witness was sworn. Of medium height, stocky and with a boyish haircut, Dronke was dressed conservatively in a grey wool suit with muted red plaid markings. Her white blouse, buttoned at the throat, was adorned with a silk patterned, rather masculine tie. Joseph wondered if she tied it herself. She wore no jewelry except for small gold button earrings. She began the questioning with, "Please tell the jury your full name and spell your last name for the record."

The witness replied, "My name is Clara Boyer. That's spelled B-O-Y-E-R."

She was married, but separated from her husband, had four children and had moved back in with her mother. Her husband didn't support the kids but, the witness claimed, she held down two jobs as a waitress while her mother took care of her kids. She explained that this wasn't a burden on her mother, "She don't have anything else to do anyway."

There was nothing about this generation Joseph understood, thinking, *These kids seem to do that a lot—that is move in with their parents without a thought as to whether or not it's an imposition.*

Clara Boyer told the jury in response to a question that she had known June Westlock from the time they attended school together. "We were sort of friends." She knew Clarence Knedder too, but not as well.

"Did you ever see Clarence Knedder be violent towards Ms. Westlock?" Dronke asked.

"No."

"Did you ever see Ms. Westlock be violent towards Knedder?" Dronke continued.

"Well, she yelled a lot…like with foul language…she swore a lot," Boyer responded.

So that's what this is about, Joseph thought, *they are trying to downplay Knedder as a possible suspect—diminish our reasonable doubt factor.*

"Did you talk to her on the night she was murdered?" Dronke inquired.

"Objection, Your Honor," Joseph interjected, "no murder has yet been established."

The judge looked at Joseph over her half glasses and said, "Really, Mr. Joseph?"

"Well, Judge, we should follow the rules." Joseph had offered the objection to tweak the prosecution and let them know he was still in the courtroom. "Until evidence of a murder has been introduced, all we know is that Ms. Westlock is dead."

"Pretty technical, but correct, Mr. Joseph," Judge Crider reluctantly admitted. "Objection sustained."

"All right," Dronke began again, with little grace. "Did you talk to Ms. Westlock on the night she died?"

Joseph smiled at the assistant prosecutor and the jury. Several of the jurors smiled back. They seemed to get a kick out of the byplay.

"Yeah. She called me around midnight. She asked me what I was doing, and when I told her, 'Nothing,' she said she had a half, and wanted to know if I wanted to share it with her. I told her no, 'cause I was already asleep."

"When she said she had 'a half,' was she talking about cocaine?"

"She didn't use that word."

"But you knew that's what she meant, didn't you?"

"Yeah."

Joseph shook his head in wonderment. *Another beautiful person not worrying about screwing up her body or mind.*

Judge Crider called the assistant prosecutor and Joseph to the bench, "Ms. Dronke, I am sure Mr. Thuman told you about asking questions that require either immunity or a warning about self-incrimination, didn't he?"

"Yes, Your Honor," she responded and signaled for Thuman to approach. After a whispered conversation, Thuman went to the court reporter and reluctantly whispered, "We grant this witness immunity from prosecution in exchange for her testimony in this case regarding anything we may learn from her about drugs."

Once she was informed about immunity having been granted, the witness went on to tell how she, Clarence Knedder and Jimmy Takas were often at the house of June Westlock, doing drugs—usually cocaine— usually freebasing. She explained that freebasing was putting powdered cocaine in a small pipe and smoking it. "You have to keep a flame to it 'cause it wouldn't want to burn by itself...you know, it's not like tobacco."

Sometimes, she explained, they would cut lines of coke—that is take powdered cocaine and use a knife or razor blade to make a line so they could snort it up their nose. "Some people use a mirror to do this, but we always did it in June's laundry room on the washing machine or dryer. It worked real good. June kept the fixings in her hall closet."

Dronke continued her questioning. "How often did you do this?"

"Pretty often. You know, Clarence, Jimmy and June were always doing it and I guess I was there lots of the time, too."

"Do you know whether June ever called the police on Jimmy Takas?" Dronke asked.

"No, but she did call them on Clarence."

Joseph didn't think this was the answer the assistant prosecutor was looking for.

The witness continued, "Yeah, she said he'd come around and bang on her door or window and say things like 'You got a guy in there.' He was real jealous, you know."

"Would she let him in?"

"Sometimes she would and sometimes she wouldn't."

"Was she afraid of Clarence?" the assistant prosecutor asked.

Joseph interrupted with an objection, "How could she know what was in her mind?"

Before the judge could intercede, the witness turned to Joseph and said, "She told me she wasn't scared of him."

The damage done, Joseph smiled and sat back down. Pleasant surprise.

The assistant prosecutor turned disgustedly toward her boss as if to say, *She's no help at all.* When Thuman nodded, Dronke said, "No further questions, Your Honor."

Judge Crider looked at Joseph with a questioning glance to see if he intended to cross-examine the witness. Joseph said to Terry, "Go ahead. Get whatever good you can out of her. May as well take advantage of the opportunity."

Terry rose and walked towards the back of the jury box. When settled into the same spot reserved by Joseph, he looked at the witness, smiled and said, "Hi, I'm Terry Bernow. Mr. Joseph and I are representing Jimmy Takas. I have just a few questions, if you don't mind."

The witness looked at ease—apparently glad that this nice young man would be asking her questions instead of the old guy.

Terry asked about her work, and how long she had known June, Jimmy and Clarence. He then brought her through her testimony about the use of drugs in June's house—how many people—how often. He also secured from her a description of the house—small, ranch style, three bedrooms, kitchen, living room, and laundry room, with no basement and no attached garage.

Since the prosecution had downplayed June Westlock's fear of Clarence Knedder, Terry asked the witness to elaborate on an incident that was in the witness' statement to the police.

"Do you remember an incident when June called and asked you to pick her up at her house because of Knedder's behavior?"

"Objection," interjected Dronke.

"Overruled," Judge Crider said, "you opened the door to this line of questioning."

"Yeah, one night about a week before she died, she called me up and said, 'Clarence's out here and is acting crazy…he's banging on the windows and calling me names…he's waking up the whole neighborhood…I called the cops….'"

"Was there more than the one incident of this type?"

"Yeah."

"In fact, she told you she was scared enough that she bought a gun, didn't she?"

"Yeah," the witness almost whispered.

Terry continued in this vein for several minutes while the prosecutor squirmed, offering objections, most of which were overruled. Joseph really didn't care, the jury was getting the picture. He was pleased with the gentlemanly way that Terry was doing it. *He's going to be a good one,* Joseph thought.

On redirect, Dronke tried unsuccessfully to repair the damage, obviously regretting that she had called Ms. Boyer as a witness.

Finally giving it up as a lost cause, she dismissed the witness. She and Thuman then took turns calling several routine witnesses needed to establish the necessary technical elements of a crime—to show that a crime had been committed. But little, if any, direct light was shed on the killing. Finally the day ended, and with the judge's admonishment ringing in their ears, "Don't form any opinion on the case until its finally submitted to you, don't discuss it among yourselves or with anyone else—have somebody censor the newspapers for you—if you look at the paper…" the jurors left for the day.

Joseph was again pretty much pleased with the day's work and congratulated Terry on a job well done. He took his leave of Jimmy, nodded goodnight to Jimmy's mother and father with an encouraging smile and walked back to his office, looking forward to an evening of peace and quiet.

The elderly lawyer walked into his office and glanced at his pigs to see if they were smiling. Their expressions told him nothing. Joseph sank into his chair. He was tired. Terry followed and sat in one of the client chairs. He, too, was tired.

"Terry," Joseph said, "there is something bothering me. I can't figure Thuman. He is being more of an obstructionist than usual and seems awfully vehement about this case...more so than just his usual desire to get a conviction. I suppose it is because it's his first capital case since being elected—I don't know. That reminds me, there's something we should have picked up long ago—but for some reason didn't. Guess we were too busy. Anyway, do you think you have time tonight to stop at the police station on your way home and pick up a copy of their telephone and dispatch logs for the morning June was killed? We need to be pretty exact about the times things happened and the best way to get that information is from their logs. We should check the times before we cross-examine Dale. I expect he'll be their next witness."

"Yeah, I can do that. I'll knock out a public records request before I leave—I got one on the computer—and serve it on the dispatcher as soon as I leave. I'll give the Chief a call and let him know I'm coming. Should save some time. If they give me a problem, I'll get a hold of the Law Director. He'll tell them we are entitled to the information. But why do you want the records now?" Terry asked.

"I don't know. Something's bothering me about this whole thing. Maybe it'll give me a clue—at least it'll give me something to talk to Sergeant Dale about. But we do need to create a pretty accurate time schedule of what happened on the night June died. If nothing else, it'll make it easier for the jury to reconstruct the events of that night."

"Okay, Mr. Joseph. See you in the morning."

"Goodnight, Terry. It's a drink, dinner and sleep for me. I'm tired, my feet hurt, my back hurts, even my hair hurts," the elderly lawyer replied, feet on his waste basket and hands clasped behind his head.

Terry looked at Joseph. "You don't have much hair—can't be too painful." Over his shoulder, Terry noted the pleasant look on the face of Joseph's pigs.

"Smart-ass kids," Joseph mumbled with a smile.

* * *

Friday morning, as Joseph and Terry arrived at court, the bailiff told them that Judge Crider wanted the lawyers in her office. When they entered, Thuman was already there, seated comfortably in front of the judge's desk. Judge Crider said, "Mr. Thuman asked for this conference. What's it all about, Harry?"

The prosecutor started with, "Defense counsel made a public records request. The Milltown Police Department gathered the records he asked for. I reviewed them and excluded all of Knedder's juvenile record. The State is requesting that the Court instruct defense counsel not to ask any questions about Knedder's juvenile record. This is a formal motion and we want it on the record."

"We've already told you, we don't intend to ask any questions about Knedder's juvenile record," Joseph said in exasperation.

Thuman acknowledged the remark by saying, "Okay. I didn't recall you saying that, Pat, there is—"

Joseph would not ignore the familiarity, so said sarcastically, "That's okay, Mr. Thuman." He didn't like Thuman and had no trouble letting him know—in fact, wanted him to know.

Thuman frowned but continued arguing that defense counsel be precluded from asking questions on much of Knedder's record.

After a great deal of discussion and eye twitching on Thuman's part, Judge Crider ruled, "Pat, you may examine Knedder concerning convictions within the past ten years that are either offenses of moral turpitude or an offense of violence against Ms. Westlock."

Joseph wasn't pleased with her use of his first name either but could do nothing about it without appearing antagonistic. Nor was he pleased with her ruling. "A person's credibility is always an issue when he testifies. Felony convictions are relevant because they show that such a person has little regard for the truth," Joseph argued. He wanted free rein to examine Knedder on his entire relationship with both June Westlock and the police department.

The judge finally said, "You have my ruling, Mr. Joseph. Takas is on trial. Knedder is a witness—he is not on trial."

"He probably should be," Joseph responded heatedly, the muscles in his jaw tightening.

Judge Crider stood, dismissed them, saying, "You're really pushing me, Joseph. Anyway, it's nine thirty. We have a jury waiting."

Surprisingly, Thuman made no mention of the other information contained in the records supplied by the police department in response to the defense's request.

* * *

In the ordinary sequence of things, the next step in the trial should have been the calling of a police officer to establish the elements of a crime. But as a result of the argument in Judge Crider's chambers, Joseph wasn't completely surprised when Thuman stood, after all had gathered in the courtroom, and said, "The State will call Clarence Knedder."

Wonder why he's calling Knedder now instead of one of the police officers. Not too surprising, I guess. Probably wants to get a closer look at the records—see what I have in mind, Joseph thought, *but, what the heck, I'm ready for him. Might work out better for us this way.*

Knedder entered the courtroom. A tall black man with hair too short to twist into the dreadlocks he tried to sport, especially with the bald spot on top. He was well over six feet tall, heavyset, but obviously not in good shape—soft around the middle and slightly stooped shouldered. He had puffy cheeks and eyes so dark they were difficult to see in the blackness of his face. Shuffling toward the witness chair, he stopped, obviously familiar with the procedure. Without being asked, he turned toward the bailiff, raising his right hand, and waited for the oath to be administered. He'd been there before.

Thuman took his place next to the jury box and intoned the standard first question asked of every witness, "Sir, please state your full name, and spell your last name for the record."

"Clarence Knedder. It's spelled K-N-E-D-D-E-R."

"Mr. Knedder, this is a large courtroom. We have to make sure the jury hears everything you say. So, if you could, please keep your voice up. If I can't hear you, they can't hear you. I'll let you know."

Thuman was being extra solicitous, obviously trying to impress the jury with his kindness towards the man who had lost his live-in girlfriend and the mother of his daughter. He elicited from the witness his relationship with the deceased. Even though they had never been married, they lived together for a number of years and had a daughter between them. Despite the fact that he did not have steady employment, he worked at construction when he could, and was currently employed as a laborer for an excavation company. At the time of June's death, he was working at an auto body shop. He explained that on the day June died, he was at work until about six o'clock in the evening. He knew he wasn't supposed to be anywhere near June—one of the police officers had served him with a restraining order—but he drove by her house several times. She wasn't home, so he stopped at a local bar and had a couple of drinks. After leaving the bar, he drove by June's house again, but she still wasn't home, so he went to his sister's house—had a couple of beers, did some cocaine and smoked a little reefer.

Joseph was amazed how easy it was for the witness—all of the witnesses so far—to talk about their drug use. It didn't seem to bother them that it was against the law; in fact, they seemed pleased they could brag about their behavior with impunity. It was obvious to Joseph that Judge Crider had required Thuman to grant immunity to the witness before he had taken the stand. Joseph said nothing, but seethed inwardly at the relationship between the prosecutor and judge that led to conversations about the case to which he was not privy.

While Knedder was telling his story, Joseph glanced toward the jury box and wasn't surprised to see a look of disgust on the face of juror number six, the only black on the jury, expressing his displeasure as though saying, *It's difficult enough for a man of our race to gain respect without you shaming us like you do.*

All the jurors seemed as appalled as Joseph by the activities of all the witnesses thus far produced. *What the hell has happened to this town—my town—moved here so the kids wouldn't be exposed to this kind of crap. Is it a generational thing? Or it just a general letdown in morality? No respect for themselves or anyone else—sure am glad I'm at the end of my life instead of the beginning. Can't figure out how they can carry on with so little sleep—night and day people I guess.*

These thoughts played through Joseph's mind as he turned his attention back to the witness, Thuman and all the other younger people in the room. Then his eyes lit on Terry Bernow and he felt a little better—not much better—*Perhaps there is some savings grace...wonder if my dad felt this way about us. I don't think we gave him this much reason to.*

The witness went on to tell how he left his sister's house about three o'clock in the morning and went to check on June and his daughter, Shelley.

"You weren't living with June and Shelley at the time, were you?"

"No, sir. She'd kicked me out."

"After she threw you out, did you go back?"

"Oh, yes. Lots of times. We'd talk, and sometimes I'd stay the night. Sometimes she'd tell me I got to leave...depended on her mood."

The prosecutor changed the subject, "Do you know Jimmy Takas?"

"Yes, sir."

"Is he in the courtroom?"

"Yes, sir."

"Please point him out."

"He's sitting right there," pointing, "the little guy between those two lawyers."

Thuman turned toward the judge and asked, "Your Honor, can the record reflect that he has identified the defendant?"

Joseph said, "We will be happy to stipulate to the identification, Your Honor," trying to nettle Thuman and disrupt the rhythm of his examination.

The judge, ignoring Joseph, responded with, "Very well, the record will so reflect."

Thuman then secured from the witness a recitation of his relationship with Takas—that they had known each other for eight or ten years—did drugs together, usually cocaine and usually at June's house in her utility room. "He's real heavy into drugs. Booze, too. Don't never have his head on straight."

Thuman asked, "Can you tell the jury how many times you and Takas did drugs together?"

"Couldn't say."

"Well, was it more than ten times?"

The witness laughed, "Lots…just can't say how many. All depended. We'd sometimes go out together, pick up some stuff and go to June's house. Sometimes she had the stuff there. You know, we didn' keep a record. Just did what we did. We'd do some coke, or crack or marijuana. Once't in a while, heroin. Not too often, 'cause that's nasty stuff. Didn't snort too much either—makes your nose bleed and you gets sniffles all the time. Usually smoke crack in a pipe or tube or in a reefer."

Joseph couldn't help but shake his head in wonderment and looked at the jury to see their reactions. He was pleased to see looks of incredulity and distaste playing across their faces. Unfortunately, the same aversion to the State's witnesses probably applied to Jimmy as well.

Thuman got Knedder to describe a knife Takas owned that they sometimes used to cut the lines of cocaine at June's house. He said Takas had loaned the knife to him but he'd returned it some time ago—maybe a couple of months before June was killed.

"What, if anything, did Takas say to you when you returned the knife?"

"'Thank you.'"

"What, if anything did he say about how long you had it?"

"Nothing. He'd just thought he lost it."

Thuman then asked, "Now, the week before June was killed, you were told by the police to stay away from her home, isn't that true?"

"Yes, sir."

"Then why were you going to June Westlock's house on the morning she was killed when the police told you to stay away?"

Joseph thought, *This should be interesting.*

"Well, it just become a habit. You know, like checking on her and my little girl, Shelley. That's all it was. I mean, like I said, I'd go up sometimes and she'd...Sometimes she'd talk and let me in...sometimes she wouldn't."

"What happened when you went to the house that morning?"

"I walked in the backdoor. Wasn' nobody there."

"What did you see?"

"There was a chair in the middle of the kitchen floor—the wicker basket was turned over—potatoes and onions was on the floor. I kind of looked around, checked my daughter's room, peeked in June's room, didn't see nothing, so left."

How the hell could he look around and not see June's body if it was right there in the utility room? That's the door he said he used to enter the house, Joseph thought.

"Well, tell the jury what you did after you got into the house?"

"Well, I sort of spot-checked to see if they was in the house," hands gesturing as he answered.

Joseph, looking at the witness' waving hands, thought, *I have never seen such small hands on a man his size. His hands move like they belong to someone else.* Then, realizing what he said, thought, *He saw all the disruption in the house and didn't make a thorough examination. Bullshit.*

"Where did you spot-check?"

"You know, the bedroom, the living room, the baf-room."

Knedder went on to explain, in response to questions designed to draw him out, that he could see other people in the neighborhood. "I could see—like it was a nice night—other peoples in the neighborhood. Talked to some of them but no one knew where June was. One of the neighbors offered me a beer so I had one with him while we talked with some dude across the street. After, I went back to my house—went 'round to the backdoor by the utility room—went in that way. Looked in the bedrooms again—my daughter's room—June's room—my baby was sleeping and so I sat down and watched a little television. Then I called Jimmy Takas. He'd been with June earlier, I was told...so I gived him a call...asked him did he see June."

"And he told you what?"

"He said he'd seen her earlier and dropped her off."

"Anything else?"

"That was about it."

Knedder then said he left the house to get some cigarettes at a nearby convenience store, bought the cigarettes and drove back to his sister's house. After a while, still worried about June, he drove back to her house, went in the same backdoor and walked into the living room. Since the television was on, he sat and watched it for a while. About that time, Shelley woke up and called for her mother. Clarence said he went to her room and told her, "Mommy isn't home." She went back to sleep and, "It came to me to check the utility room. I went in there and lit the light—and there she was."

"Now," Thuman asked, "you hadn't seen her lying there before you turned on the light?"

"No, sir, it was dark."

"Tell the jury what you did see."

"She was lying there behind the door, flat on her back with her hands like above her head. Didn't look like she had anything on but her housecoat—it was all pushed up. There was blood all over." He gestured wildly with his hands and, his voice quavering, he covered his face with those tiny hands, slumping further into the witness chair.

"What did you do then?" Thuman asked in a faux sympathetic voice.

"Called the cops. They came and took me to the station. Kept me there a long time. Asked where my car was and asked could they search it. I told them okay and they took my fish-filleting knife out my car...and my clothes."

Thuman finished quickly, with, "Did you touch anything in the utility room?"

"I felt her cheek. She was cold. I didn' touch nothing else."

The jury sat quietly looking at the witness. There wasn't a sound in the room. Thuman, not wanting to break the spell, said quietly, "I have no further questions, Your Honor."

Judge Crider looked at Joseph, saying, "You may inquire."

Ordinarily Joseph preferred to begin his cross-examination as soon as the prosecutor completed the direct. In that way, the jurors would not have the opportunity to dwell on what the witness said. But knowing that Knedder had made several statements to the police, he felt it important to review them. As was to be expected, Thuman refused to turn the statements over until required to.

"Your Honor, as you know I have the right to review this witness' statement to the police before conducting my cross. I also understand he made a recorded statement. I would like to listen to that as well. It would certainly be less of an inconvenience to the jury, and Your Honor, if I'd been allowed to review them earlier."

"That's probably true, Mr. Joseph, but we try to follow the rules. The prosecutor doesn't have to make the statements available until the witness has testified." Turning to the jury, she added, "The statements and tape are rather lengthy, so rather than wait around in the jury room, we'll take a recess at this time. Come back about one o'clock—feel free to do some shopping or have a long lunch hour or whatever you need to do for a couple of hours—but remember, don't talk about the case or form any opinion until the case is in your hands, don't do any investigation. Report back to the jury room at one."

Joseph wondered how she knew the statements were lengthy—well, maybe not.

*   *   *

By one o'clock, everyone had gathered in the courtroom. Joseph had assumed his usual spot behind the jury box while the jurors filed in. He smiled at them as they gained their seats. Some returned the smile, while several made an obvious effort to avoid eye contact. This didn't disturb Joseph. He was aware that most jurors took their job very seriously and were reluctant to give the appearance of being friendlier to one side than the other. He would, nonetheless, maintain an amiable attitude, knowing from experience most people would eventually thaw out—it is always difficult to ignore a smile.

After everyone was in place, Joseph, a more serious demeanor spread across his face, studied Knedder for a few seconds. Beads of sweat were gathering on the witness' forehead. Knedder seemed to know what was coming and feared it for some reason. *Have to get him to relax a bit before I can really begin.* "Mr. Knedder, my name is Patrick Joseph. Mr. Bernow and I are representing Jimmy Takas in this case. Do you understand that?"

"Yes, suh," without expression.

"You know Mr. Takas, don't you?"

Again, "Yes, suh."

It didn't escape Joseph's notice that the witness was reverting to his usual street language—becoming his more normal self—the anticipation of stressful questions apparently making him forget the instructions received from the prosecutor.

"Is it fair to say that you and he had been fairly good friends over the years?"

"Yeah." He changed his answer a little, trying hard to do what he had been told to do.

"You and he have done drugs together, at June's house, isn't that so?"

"It was mine and June's house."

Joseph let it go for now, changing the subject. "Did you have a job on the day June was killed?"

"Yeah." He wasn't going to offer anything—just answer the questions.

"By the way, you and Mr. Thuman have talked on several occasions preparing you to testify in this case, isn't that true?"

Joseph could see Thuman begin to rise, eye twitching, while Knedder responded, "Yes, suh."

Back to the same response.

"Did he tell you what to say or how to say it?"

Thuman began to object and Judge Crider waved him back into his seat. "No, suh. He said to tell the truth and just to answer your questions without giving away too much."

Joseph could hear an amused sound coming from the jury. Everyone seemed to relax a bit. "Let's get back to your job," he said. "You were working at a body repair shop at the time Ms. Westlock was killed, weren't you?"

"Yes, I was."

"In fact, you worked most of that afternoon, and I understand you cut your hand at work that day, isn't that so?"

"Yes, suh. Cut my hand pretty bad."

"Cut it so bad, in fact, that it was still bleeding when the police came to Ms. Westlock's house, wasn't it?" Without waiting for a response, Joseph added, "And didn't the police ask you about it and put it in their report?"

"Yeah. I cut my finger. Like I said, it was a pretty bad cut. Bled for a long time. Was still bleeding that night. Had a bandage on it, but it was still bleeding."

Joseph changed the subject again, starting his attack by establishing the witness' credibility was, at best, questionable. "In your direct examination, you were asked about being convicted of the crime of filing a false police report, and you denied it."

"Didn't deny it. Said I couldn't remember."

"I have here a copy of the court record where you pled guilty to filing a false police report about a shooting. This happened about two years ago. Do you remember it now?"

"Yes, suh. Someone reminded me—brought it to my attention."

"The prosecutor, maybe?" Again Thuman took to his feet—right eye blinking spasmodically.

"No, just someone."

Joseph let it go. "Well, anyway, the court record is accurate, isn't it? You did plead guilty to filing a false police report—didn't you?"

"Yes, suh," sullenly.

"Seems it would be pretty difficult to forget it. That is, unless this kind of thing happens often to you." Then, before Thuman could object to the comment, Joseph added, "Do you often lie to the police?"

"No, suh," Knedder answered before Thuman, on his feet, was able to get his objection out. While Thuman was seating himself, Joseph continued. "But you did lie to them on, at least, that occasion?"

"Yes, suh," glowering, his expression conveying his dislike for the question and hatred for the questioner.

Again shifting gears, Joseph continued by asking the witness to describe the Westlock home, the entrances and the layout of the various rooms. He showed him the scale drawing of the house and the location of the furniture the architect he hired had prepared. After displaying the drawing on the poster board in such a way so the jury could see it as well, he asked the witness to identify it. Knedder did and was then asked to point out the room where he found June's body.

Pointing to the utility room and the sketched outline of June's body, Joseph asked Knedder to again describe how he entered the house on three occasions in the early morning hours through the rear door within inches of June's body, that he claimed he hadn't seen. Joseph asked the same question several times in several different ways so the jury could understand how ridiculous Knedder's story sounded.

Joseph had Knedder describe several more times the location of the backdoor—that it entered right in to the utility room. He talked about the light in the utility room, that was operated by a pull cord dangling directly over the head of June Westlock as she lay dead on the floor. He had Knedder describe the macabre gadget that was on the pull chain operating the light in the laundry room—a skeleton that shone in the dark. Joseph drew this picture out again, several times, so the jury could visualize the large black man lumbering into the house within inches of the body and claiming not to have seen it, even though it would have been impossible to light the overhead light without actually stepping on the body.

Finally, in response to Thuman's continuing objections, the judge said, "Asked and answered several times, Mr. Joseph. We get the picture. Please move on."

Joseph returned for a moment to the cut Knedder claimed he had gotten at work. "I think you told us you had a cut on your thumb that you got at work—is that right?"

"Yes, suh."

"And you were wearing a T-shirt at the time the police got to the house when you called them, isn't that so?"

"Yeah, it is."

"There were spots of blood on the T-shirt, weren't there?"

"Yes, suh—and I 'splained to the cops it got on there from my cut hand."

"What happened to the T-shirt?"

"I don't know."

"You mean, the police didn't take the shirt?"

"I said I don't know, man."

Terry, studying the faces of the jurors during Joseph's cross-examination of Knedder, was pleased with the looks of disbelief playing over the faces of several of them.

Joseph again had the witness describe in detail what he did on the evening June was killed—smoked some reefer and did a little coke—had a couple of beers—drove around and went past June's house several times—decided to visit June's house again—left his sister's apartment around three in the morning. "Everyone there was feeling kinda cool, but I was worried about June. She shoulda been with me. Didn' know where she was."

Joseph asked Knedder to describe the route he took. After going over the route, Knedder finished with, "I come up her street and went past the house...the curtain was blocked but the lights and TV was on."

"Did you pull in the drive?"

"No. I went past the house and down the block. Pulled into the parking lot of the Italian restaurant," pronouncing it "eye-talion," making Joseph wince, "on June's street."

"The restaurant is on North Wall Street, isn't it? Not on June's street?"

"Yes, suh, but they's a parking lot in back."

"Now, that's quite a way from June's house, isn't it?"

"Maybe about a quarter mile...."

"So you parked a quarter mile from the house and walked that distance over to June's house?"

"Yes, suh."

"Was there a car in the driveway?"

"No, suh."

"Was there a reason you parked so far from the house and walked to it?"

The witness fidgeted on the stand and after several false starts, "No...it's... I always park there."

"Perhaps it had something to do with there being a protective order that forbade you from going near June's house? Or perhaps you were involved in doing something there that you shouldn't?"

Thuman objected, but no one paid attention to it, including the judge.

Knedder offered no answer. Joseph allowed the silence to build and then elicited from Knedder how he walked across the backyards, rather than down the sidewalk, avoiding the streetlights, went to the back of the house and found the backdoor open, "almost all the way."

"Wasn't that unusual?"

"I didn' think anything about it at the time—the lock was busted—the wind could have blowed it open."

At Joseph's insistence, they reviewed again Knedder finding in the house an overturned chair, the tipped-over wicker basket, the onions and potatoes spilled on the kitchen floor...the television playing and lights lit, none of which seemed to cause him much concern. Knedder left the house at some point, returned to his car, went to a store, bought cigarettes and returned to his sister's house, where partying was still going on. He joined in the fun for a bit, but then "got to worrying about June," so went back to her house following the same routine—parking a quarter mile from the house, walking through backyards and entering the house by way of the backdoor into the utility room, where he "didn' see nothing."

The same items of disarray were present during his second visit—again the disorder not bothering him. He sat down and watched a little television and smoked a cigarette...then "stepped out the backdoor again to see if June was coming."

Even though all of this information had been presented to the jury during Thuman's examination, Joseph wanted it repeated in response to his questions so the jury could judge just how ridiculous it sounded.

After walking around the house he again returned—this time from the driveway side instead of across the backyard. He entered through the backdoor a third time—actually his fifth time through the door.

"Now, let's see. If my arithmetic is accurate, that is actually the fifth time you walked through the backdoor—into the utility room. Now again, you are telling this jury that you saw nothing, is that correct?"

"Yeah, nothing," getting more sullen—voice low and threatening.

Joseph ignored the implication and asked, "By this time, wasn't it getting light out?"

"Well, the sky was getting a little lighter—but the sun wasn' up yet."

"What next happened?"

"I went in to see my daughter. She was waking up a little...so I tol' her Mommy stepped out but would be back soon. She laid back down. Then it come over me to check the utility room. I went in the room and pulled the light string and saw June laying there dead..." placing his tiny fingers over his eyes and making sobbing sounds. Joseph saw no tears.

Ignoring the histrionics, Joseph asked the witness to make a mark on the scale drawing where the utility room light was located in relation to June's body. It was fairly obvious the witness would have had to stand on her head to reach it—Joseph made sure the jury was aware of this.

"Now, Mr. Knedder, in order for you to reach the light cord, it appears that it would be necessary for you to place your foot just about where Ms. Westlock's head was, according to the photographs the police took. Isn't that true?"

The witness just shook his head without answering directly, "I didn' see her, man."

Asking the judge if he could approach the witness, Joseph didn't wait for her permission but persisted, "Look at this picture, State's exhibit nineteen, I believe. See where Ms. Westlock's body is. Can you see the light cord dangling over her head? When you reached for the cord, did your foot come in contact with her head?"

"I didn' see her, man."

Obviously the witness wasn't going to make it any easier, and the elderly lawyer was getting tired. Still, there was more he wanted the jurors to hear. He wished he were in the courtroom across the hall. The bailiff there always had cough drops or hard candy in his pocket to supply needed moisture for Joseph's voice when involved in a lengthy cross-examination. Judge Crider's bailiff didn't have the same concern for this old man.

Joseph again changed the subject and had the witness tell how he told the police the location of his car and that he allowed the police to search it, finding what the witness described as his "filleting" knife.

Joseph asked the witness to describe the knife. "It's a small knife, about eight inches long, very sharp, used for fishing."

Joseph took the poster drawing made by Kathy Cobal, the young medical student and, showing it to the witness, asked, "Does the blade of that knife look like any of the knives shown on this drawing?"

Without responding, Knedder pointed to the single-edged blade with one blunt side. Joseph asked, "Your Honor, can the record reflect that the witness identified one of the knives on the drawing prepared by Ms. Cobal. I realize it hasn't been introduced in evidence as yet, but we will do that at a later time."

The judge, over Thuman's expected objection, said, "Okay, Mr. Joseph, so long as it is tied up later."

The elderly lawyer wanted to remind the jury of the kind of person the prosecutor asked them to believe. "Mr. Knedder, you use that knife for something more than cutting fish, don't you? Specifically, I am referring to your drug use. A knife is used to cut lines of coke, isn't that true?"

"Well, you can use a knife or anything sharp, like a razor blade or even a playing card. Anything...man...."

"And you've used that knife for cutting lines?"

"Yeah." As he fidgeted on the witness stand, it was clear Knedder wasn't comfortable talking about this—he was getting annoyed with Joseph.

"How do you do cocaine?"

"Snort it—smoke it."

"Smoking is called freebasing, isn't that true?" Joseph was getting an education too.

"Yes, suh."

"And you do that with crack cocaine, don't you?"

"Don't have to be crack—you can smoke the powder."

"Well, how do you snort cocaine?"

"Up your nose, man."

"What do you use?"

"Look, man, don' be stupid. You puts the powder on a smooth surface—mirror—piece of glass—or something like that. Use a knife, razor blade, playing card or somethin' to cut it into lines…take a straw—like a drinking straw—and sniff the cocaine through the straw up your nose." Clearly Knedder wanted the ordeal to end. He was getting more open with his answers in order to speed things up.

"How much coke do you snort each time?"

"Whatever we got."

"Ms. Westlock had everything at her house to do what you have described for us, isn't that true?"

"Yeah, man, she kept it in her closet."

"And you've done drugs with her and Jimmy Takas countless times at the house?"

"Yeah."

"After she kicked you out of the house, you were angry and would call to see if she had a man there or was doing drugs without you, isn't that true?"

"Well, I'd call sometimes, and yeah, I wasn' happy about being kicked out my house." His answers were degenerating more and more into the street talk with which he was more familiar.

Joseph attempted to ask questions about June Westlock's car, but the judge cut him short in response to Thuman's objections, ruling that the questions were irrelevant. Joseph argued with the judge about limiting his cross-examination, and made sure the record was protected for appeal, if necessary. The prosecutor and his assistant argued vehemently about Joseph's methods of cross-examination. Joseph was happy to get under their skin. He nonetheless reluctantly followed the Court's instructions and changed the subject. He wasn't going to let Knedder go yet.

"Mr. Knedder, you knew the police had served a court order on you not to go to the premises or be around June just two days before she was killed?"

"Yesss," sibilantly.

"But you went there anyway—in the middle of the night?"

The witness just nodded affirmatively, anger clear on his face. Judge Crider said quietly, "You have to answer in words, Mr. Knedder. But please move on, Mr. Joseph. I think you've covered this area enough."

Knedder nodded again, whispering, "Yeah." Joseph was glad the "filleting knife" wasn't available to the witness at the moment.

Joseph said, "Just a few more questions, Judge." Then to Knedder, "You went through the room where Ms. Westlock's body lay three or four times—within inches of her body?"

"Yeah—didn' see her."

"What race was Ms. Westlock?"

"She's white."

"How was she dressed?"

"She had on a robe—housecoat...."

"Was it open or closed?"

"It was on her laying wide open."

"Was her white flesh showing."

"Yeah, she was naked and you could see her body."

Joseph thought, *He had to see her body, if it was there, on his trips through the small utility room—had to!* and hoped the jury had the same thoughts.

"Mr. Knedder, if my math is correct you must have spent almost three hours at the house. You told us you first got there around three in the morning and you called the police around six in the morning, is that accurate?"

"I didn't give you no times."

"Well, you called the police about six o'clock and had been there several times from three on?"

"Yeah, that's so."

Joseph continued in a calm, quiet manner, "So if you were there from three in the morning until six, would that have been enough time for you to have killed Ms. Westlock?"

Thuman leaped to his feet. "Objection! Objection! Your Honor!" mouth working, eye twitching uncontrollably.

Before the judge had an opportunity to respond to the objection, Knedder said, "I didn' kill her, man."

Paying no attention to Thuman's efforts to get the Court's attention, Joseph, leaning toward Knedder and pointing his finger, raised his voice accusingly, "But you could have, couldn't you? You would have had more than enough time to kill her, isn't that true?"

Half rising from his chair threateningly, Knedder glared at Joseph with flashing eyes. "I said I didn' kill her!" his voice rising, as if volume alone would make his words more convincing, his small fingers flying.

Terry, at counsel table, stood, as did the uniformed police officer sitting on the bench next to the jury room door, in case intervention was necessary. Joseph could see several of the members of the jury tense up, expecting something to happen. Joseph, himself, was a bit concerned about his safety.

Knedder had been on the witness stand for several hours. Even though he refused to answer the last question, and several others, directly Joseph believed he had gotten everything he could from him. He wanted the jury to take with them his last question and the emotional response, so said quietly, "No more questions, Your Honor," and walked back to his seat thinking, *How's that for reasonable doubt?*

Terry nodded his approval, squeezing Joseph's hand as he walked past on the way to his seat, whispering, "You shouldn't take chances like that, Mr. Joseph."

Jimmy, in his usual slump, looked down at the trial table despite Joseph's instruction to appear interested in what was going on. He was clearly unable to do so, and hadn't even reacted to the tenseness that permeated the room.

Thuman wanted desperately to rehabilitate his witness, "I know you've been on the stand for a long time, Mr. Knedder, but I just have a few more questions."

He then had Knedder describe how he entered the house through the backdoor, stating that it was open only about a foot when he got there. He pushed the door open just enough for him to get through. He added that he wasn't looking down, he was looking towards the kitchen. On and on he went, using the exhibit Joseph had prepared. "The door wasn't open as far as it is shown on the exhibit, was it?"

"Objection, your Honor. Mr. Thuman is trying to lead his witness."

"Sustained."

"Well, how far was the door open, Mr, Knedder?" Thuman asked.

"Sure, Your Honor, now that he has instructed his witness how to answer."

"If that's an objection, Mr. Joseph, it's overruled."

"No, sir, it wasn'," Knedder responded, slumping further into the witness chair.

Finally the witness was through and Judge Crider was about to excuse him until Joseph said, "Just one more question, Your Honor."

Judge Crider sighed. "One question, Mr. Joseph?"

"Yes, Your Honor—something that was brought up on redirect."

"Okay."

"Mr. Knedder. When the police arrived at the house, the backdoor was chained shut. Did you lock it?"

There was no response. As the silence began to build and it became obvious Knedder was not going to respond, Joseph shrugged and said, "No more questions." He could have insisted on an answer, but was just as satisfied with the silence.

Without waiting for permission, Knedder left the witness stand. Joseph tensed as he felt Knedder pass behind him on the way out of the courtroom. The judge continued as Knedder shuffled out, "I think we've had enough for today. You all know about not forming an opinion or talking or reading about the case. Have a nice weekend, and we'll see you first thing Monday morning."

* * *

As they walked down the courthouse steps, Joseph said to Terry, "You know, I've been taking routine assigned felony cases for some time— nothing of the magnitude of this case—but representing indigent defendants. I really try to like my clients—identify with them so I can do a good job for them. Remember I told you about that young pedophile who thought I liked him. But more often than not, I don't like them at all. I am trying to feel close to Jimmy, but can't.

"Anyway, my clients are usually guilty of the crimes with which they're charged and I'd really prefer they not be acquitted. But I do defend them as zealously as I can because I have to. I live in this community and don't like the idea of criminals being on the street. But it's my job to see to it that the police and the courts do everything right—you know, see to it that the defendant's Constitutional rights are protected. The Constitution is the most important document that this country—or any country for that matter—has ever devised to protect all of us and guarantee our freedoms. Freedom, especially from a tyrannical government, was mighty important to our founders and should be to us. I don't want to represent scum and certainly don't want to be identified with them—but am."

"Well then, why do you do it, Mr. Joseph?"

"I guess I do it because someone has to, and I'm afraid if I don't, no one else will. Like I said, I rarely like my clients and am having a hard time liking Jimmy, even though I'm not convinced of his guilt. But I like even less the rest of the people involved—the witnesses—this guy Knedder— the deceased. They chose their lifestyle, centering around illicit sex, alcohol and drugs. How sad. The acronym for sex, alcohol and drugs— S-A-D—seems appropriate. I'm sure the jurors are also saddened by what they have learned in this case. These night people are demoralizing. I only hope it is not indicative of what our society is coming to. Sure am glad I'm at the end of my life and not the beginning...and that my kids are already raised."

Terry walked quietly along next to Joseph for while, finally saying thoughtfully, "Mr. Joseph, I think there are enough of us that the kind of people you're talking about will always remain a very small minority—at least, I hope so."

"Sure hope you're right, Terry."

CHAPTER THIRTEEN

Saturday morning, Joseph woke early as usual. Also, as usual, Mary was up before him. He stretched, put on an old pair of slightly worn jeans, a torn but favorite work shirt and old shoes. He looked from the second-floor bathroom window and saw Mary working in one of several flower beds in the backyard. Descending to the first floor, he saw that coffee was on so poured himself a cup. He was unable to face food that early in the day, despite his love of it from late morning on. Feeling unsettled by the trial and his inability to understand the attitude of the prosecutor and the fact that nothing seemed to hang together—it just didn't seem right—he left the house through the back porch door and called to Mary, "Morning, hon. Think I'll walk out back after I've read the paper, unless you want my help with the weeding."

Her responsive "Humph," along with a glance that told him he'd better leave her flowers alone, discouraged his help. He thought, not for the first time, that a single look from Mary could deliver more of a message than a priest's sermon at Sunday Mass.

He walked down the tree-lined driveway to the street, where the morning papers were deposited in different-colored boxes next to his rural mailbox. He was proud of the mailbox. During graduation week each spring, the seniors' pranks included driving past rural mailboxes and bashing them with a baseball bat from fast-moving cars. Joseph, tired of replacing his mailbox each spring, welded one up out of quarter-inch plate steel. It looked just like a store-bought mailbox. After installing it on a metal post set in concrete, he enjoyed the thought of the vibrations passing up the arms of the bat-swinging seniors in their fast-moving cars. Hadn't had to replace his mailbox in several years.

Finally getting to the street, he picked up one of the morning newspapers and read the headline:

DEFENSE LEANS ON VICTIM'S EX-BOYFRIEND

Pleased, he continued reading the article written by Stan Marten as he walked back to the house. *Stan is getting a lot of work out of this case,* Joseph thought.

MILLTOWN—In the culmination of several hours of questioning in Common Pleas Court yesterday, Clarence Knedder, the estranged boyfriend of murder victim June Westlock, several times denied murdering her. Jimmy Takas is charged with the murder of June Westlock, who had lived with Knedder for about ten years, though the two were estranged shortly before her murder.

Knedder found Westlock's body about six thirty Saturday morning after having visited the house on two or three occasions, looking for her.

Defense Attorney Patrick Joseph said to Knedder near the end of his questioning, "You were there long enough to kill her, clean the place up and leave, weren't you?" Over Thuman's objections, Judge Crider ordered the witness to respond. There followed several denials by an obviously distressed Knedder, who never responded to the question concerning the time element.

The article continued at length to rehash everything that had already been covered, but Joseph was not displeased. Dropping the paper on the porch table, he walked down the path to the barn, where he grabbed a shepherd's crook hanging on the wall beneath the overhang. He always carried it while walking in the woods. He looked in the disturbingly quiet barn, taking note of the four empty stalls he had built years earlier. Two had been occupied by horses, while a third was shared by two Nubian goats Mary had rescued. She learned that when petting zoo goats, because of their size and age, became potentially dangerous to children, they were put to death and sold to Akron Zoo to be fed to the carnivores. Mary was outraged and went to the manager of the petting zoo, where two goats were scheduled for disposition. The administrator tried to explain, "Well, ma'am. They're too dangerous to be with the children. There's nothing else to do with them."

She would have none of this and demanded she be permitted to take the goats home with her. "You will not destroy them," she insisted. "I'll buy them." She'd pay whatever he wanted. Few could stand up to Mary when she made up her mind.

After negotiating a resolution, Mary left the zoo with two young goats in the backseat of her almost new car. By the time she got home they were already named Billy-the-Kid and Alexander- the-Goat…two new additions to the Joseph household. Joseph hated to admit it, but he enjoyed them almost as much as she. They grew rapidly, but always maintained the same playfulness they had as kids. With their exuberance, they certainly would have been a danger to small children.

Billy had no horns and Alexander only one—the attempt to de-horn him only partially successful. They got on well with the horses, eating the weeds in the pasture and leaving the grass for the horses. They loved rose-bushes, thorns and all. What they did not like was being confined, no matter how big the pasture; they wanted to be outside the fence. Not that they wanted to go anywhere, just be outside.

Billy loved to go for long walks in the woods. Joseph would take him, fixing a lead around his neck and laying the line over his back, not bothering to hold the other end. Billy never strayed further than the distance of the lead—apparently being unaware that no one was holding the other end. All of the animals were now gone and Joseph felt the loneliness of the quiet. The barn dog, now old and hardly moving, would try to accompany Joseph on his walk, but wouldn't be able to stand the strain. Joseph locked him in a stall. The black dog lay on a bale of straw in appreciation, tail slapping the bale once or twice before his eyes closed in sleep.

Joseph closed the door to the barn, picked up the shepherd's crook, walked past the pond, through the back pasture and into the woods.

About fifty feet into the woods was a clearing, where several of the animals once housed in his barn were buried, their grave marker an old bathtub Joseph filled with goat feed for the deer. Joseph thought about how he missed the animals as he gazed on the grave. He missed Billy most—missed his following him on their walks in the woods. Billy-the-kid was never concerned about where the path led—just that he be allowed to follow the path delineated by Joseph's wanderings.

Joseph began to relax—his woods always relaxed him—and thought about the goat's simple approach to life. *Maybe there's something to that. Maybe it's what I need to do with this case. Just follow the path and see where it leads— not try to direct it. Such a nice day, bet Mary would like to go to the mall, grab a piece of pizza and shop. Can't understand her fascination with shopping, but bet there are lots of things about me she can't understand. Don't know why, I'm such a nice, simple guy.*

Amused with his thoughts, Joseph wandered back to the house, getting there just before noon. "Mary, want to go to the mall?"

"I'll have to change clothes." Her usual comment. She wouldn't be seen dead unless she was dressed properly for the occasion.

Joseph went in the kitchen, heated a cup of coffee in the microwave and waited for Mary to get ready. He would never admit it, but he actually wanted to go to the mall, too, so he could pick up a paperback novel, sit in the food court, read and munch on something Mary would never otherwise permit, and watch people while Mary shopped.

*   *   *

Regenerated by the relaxing weekend, Joseph backed his ancient truck from the garage and started down his long driveway to the road. He noticed his same little brown rabbit friends playing in the yard that were there the other day. Joseph wondered again why rabbits were one of the few animals made by the Creator without the ability to make sounds except in extremis—then the sound was awful. Joseph brooded about the unfairness of this as he drove to the office, then shrugged, thinking, *Wish I had answers to these weighty questions. Oh well, may as well prepare myself for the day and not worry about the bunnies' problems—except it would be nice if some people were as silent—awful lot of people communicate too much.*

As usual, he arrived early at the office. While waiting for Terry, so they could walk to the courthouse together, he perused the paper—nothing interesting. Another gorgeous fall day, children running through the square on their way to school, yelling, pushing and doing all the things young animals do in preparation for adulthood. *Sure hope none—or at least very few—of them turn out like the animals I've seen in court this past week.*

"What do you suppose is next?" Terry asked Joseph as he walked through the door into Joseph's office.

"Don't know, but Thuman has to get to the police and coroner pretty soon."

Terry reported, "I went to see Jimmy this weekend. He's a little more talkative. But still insists he can't remember anything that happened after he got to June's house that night."

Joseph responded thoughtfully as they started walking across the square towards the courthouse, "I guess I'm having a real hard time accepting that. I don't have a very good feeling about this case—wish I did," then, after a moment's silence they reached the courthouse steps. Joseph, grabbing hold of the railing, turned to Terry, paused, and said, "You know, Terry, the big difference between this case and the murder case I tried last year?"

"No, Mr. Joseph. What?"

"In that case, I could really identify with my client. She was a nice lady caught up in a situation most of which wasn't of her making. I was really emotionally involved, and thrilled at the result. Can't seem to get worked up quite the same about Jimmy. I feel sorry for him—he is rather pathetic—and I can't really believe he is capable of the terrible things that were done to June. But like I said before, I just don't like him. I know it's not important, but it would be a hell of a lot easier if I could work up some feelings of affection for him. I really like his mom and dad—they don't deserve a son like him—too bad he's the only one they had."

"I know what you mean, Mr. Joseph, but we can't let that get in the way of doing our job."

By this time they arrived at the top of the courthouse steps. Joseph sighed, "You're right, Terry. Let's go. We won't know what's on Thuman's mind until we go in."

When they got upstairs they found the courtroom full. All the weekend newspapers had covered Joseph's cross-examination of Knedder. The articles suggested that perhaps it wasn't such an open-and-shut case as the public had been led to believe. This brought out the court watchers and some of the local lawyers. Joseph couldn't figure out why the feelings of nervousness that usually accompanied his court appearances hadn't made their presence known until now. He couldn't believe he was getting used to it. Seeing the crowd in the courtroom and hall, he felt a return of the remembered feeling of unease. The butterflies were just waiting to make themselves known.

Working their way through the crowded room, Joseph and Terry sat in their usual spot at the trial table, one on each side of Jimmy, who was already seated—his guard unobtrusive on the bench against the wall. The jury would walk past him on their way from the jury room to the box. By this time many of the jurors had come to know the officer and smiled at him pleasantly.

Once everyone was in place and Judge Crider called the room to order, Thuman announced that the State would call Sharon Walls, the dispatcher on duty the night June was killed. As she approached the witness stand, Joseph noted how young she looked, a petite brunette wearing a loose-fitting yellow sweater and what Joseph believed to be a too short skirt made out of some kind of jean material. Her reddish brown hair was tied back in a ponytail, tight curls spilling out of the decorative rubber band holding it in place. She had an attractive smile that dimpled one cheek. If asked, he would have had to admit she was cute—sort of like a kitten.

Sharon Walls explained that she had been a dispatcher for the Milltown Police Department for about a year before May 5, the night the call came in about June Westlock. She was working the midnight shift and received the call at six twenty-five in the morning. It was near the end of her shift. She looked at her copy of the log sheet as she responded to the question.

When asked, "What did the caller say?" she read, "*Please send the cops…it's awful…please send the cops.*"

Answering further, she said, "I tried to get more information out of him, phone number, name, and so on, but he didn't answer any of my questions. I didn't need him to give me the information because I knew where the call came from. The address and phone number are shown on the computer screen. I was just trying to keep him on the phone—you know, get him to talk so I could get more information."

"What time did you send an officer out?"

"Sergeant Dale was standing right there at my desk. I signaled him over and whispered that the caller was really upset—he'd said something awful happened. He saw the address on the screen and whispered that he knew the house. He'd go right there. There was another uniformed patrolman on station—Rob—Rob Stanford. He said he'd get his cruiser and follow Sergeant Dale to the house."

"What time did they arrive on the scene?"

"I still had the caller on the line when I heard Sergeant Dale's voice over the phone. So I knew that he arrived on the scene at six twenty-eight. I noted the time on my log. He got there just three minutes after leaving the station. I hung up the call then."

When Thuman had no further questions, Terry, handling the cross-examination, asked the witness if she recorded everything that transpired on her log sheets, "such as time the call comes in, how you respond and whether or not an officer is radioed."

She responded, "I record everything. That's what we're trained to do," and showed a copy of the log sheets to Terry. Terry noted the times and information contained. He asked the witness to identify the copy as being a true and accurate copy of the record kept in the ordinary course of business and prepared by her. Upon her affirmative response he asked to have the copy marked as a defense exhibit. He then asked the Court to instruct the witness to leave the copy with the court reporter until it could be admitted. He thanked the witness, had her excused and enjoyed the look of confusion on Thuman's face.

He walked back to counsel table and showed the log to Joseph. Pointing, he whispered, "You're right, it's exactly like she said. The time frame puts Knedder in the house until past daylight. He had to see her."

Thuman and his assistant called several more witnesses to trace the activities of June Westlock on the evening and morning she was killed. Cross-examined by Joseph and Terry, they told them nothing that they had not already known.

Finally, after the noon break, Thuman called Sergeant Dale, who, after going through the routine drill necessary to qualify a witness, explained he was the shift commander for the Milltown Police Department on the night June was killed, confirming the testimony supplied by the dispatcher. Joseph thought, *It's no wonder jury trials take so long. We treat the jurors like they are complete idiots, telling them over and over again the same old shit with different witnesses. It's as though we can't believe they are more than three years old and can only learn by rote—repetition. It's got to be boring as hell for them.*

Dale repeated how he was in the dispatcher's room when the call came in. When the dispatcher signaled him over and whispered, "Sounds like someone's dead or hurt real bad," he told her he recognized the address and would take the call. As he started out of the building, he saw Patrolman Rob Stanford and told him to grab a cruiser and follow him to the house. Within minutes, he arrived at June's house, where he found Knedder crying in the living room. Knedder recognized Dale as a police officer and pointed towards the back of the house. As soon as Dale walked into the utility room, he saw June Westlock's almost nude body lying on the floor in a pool of blood. He was sickened because of the amount of blood on the floor and because he had known June so well. There was no doubt in his mind that she was dead, yet he took the time to kneel on the floor next to her and try to locate a carotid pulse—there was none.

When Dale returned to the living room, Knedder tried to say something to him. Dale wouldn't allow him to talk—he didn't want any admissions made until Knedder was properly Mirandized. Less than two minutes had passed since he arrived at the house. Dale was still standing in front of Knedder, when there was a knock on the front door, followed by Officer Rob Stanford walking into the living room. Prosecutor Thuman followed him in. Dale asked Patrolman Stanford to read Knedder his Miranda rights. In the meantime, he took hold of Prosecutor Thuman by the arm and accompanied him outside of the house. He didn't want the crime scene compromised before the detective in charge of homicide investigations arrived. He was polite but insistent and heard Stanford reading Knedder his rights and taking him into custody. Knedder offered no resistance.

Dale explained that people began gathering in front of the house while he was standing there with Prosecutor Thuman, but he allowed no one in. As the first senior officer on the scene it was his obligation to secure the crime scene. He explained to Mr. Thuman that since it was a crime scene, it had to be preserved until the homicide unit had completed its investigation. He was sure Prosecutor Thuman was aware of that and had no desire to contaminate the scene or obstruct the investigation.

Thuman asked, "Were there lights on in the house when you arrived?"

"There was a lamp lit in the living room and the television was playing. The overhead light in the kitchen was on. So was the one in the utility room, where the body was."

When Thuman completed his examination of Sergeant Dale, Joseph began his cross-examination by asking the witness to take a look at the dispatcher's log sheets. He did so thoughtfully and, after a moment, handed them back to Joseph, saying, "They appear to be in order."

Joseph then asked the officer, "When you saw Knedder in the living room of Ms. Westlock's home, he was crying or, I think your words were 'He was upset,' is that correct?"

"Yes, sir," politely.

"Did he say anything to you?"

"Yes, he said, 'Someone broke in here and killed June.'"

"And then did he just point to the back of the house?"

"No, he just said, 'Utility room,' and when I started towards the bedroom area, because I wasn't sure where the utility room was, he pointed the right direction out to me."

Dale then described the items of disarray he found in the living room and the kitchen, as had several of the earlier witnesses.

Joseph then asked, "Sergeant, can you tell us please the sequence in which people arrived at the house from the time you got there—who came and when?"

"I can't give you exact times, but I was the first there, at about six-thirty in the morning. A few minutes latter Officer Stanford and Prosecutor Thuman arrived. Next came the life support team. That was fifteen or twenty minutes later. At about the same time, Lieutenant Richard Tells arrived and began taking pictures of the deceased and the crime scene. Then, maybe an hour or so later, some family members came, but I wouldn't let them in so as to protect the scene."

When he had completed his questioning, Joseph was surprised to hear Judge Crider say, "We will break for the day. Remember my admonitions," repeating them again as though it were impossible for the jurors to actually remember them.

Joseph looked at his watch and wondered how the day had gotten away from him. He looked at Jimmy, after the jury filed out, and asked, "Now that we've been going for several days and you have heard what all the witnesses have had to say so far, do you remember anything else?"

"I really don't, Mr. Joseph. There are some hazy flashes, but I can't put it all together. I'm scared. What's going to happen?" He seemed to shrink further within himself.

He'll soon disappear, Joseph thought.

"We don't know, Jimmy. But Terry and I are doing what we can to get to the truth. Keep faith. Now, smile at your mom. She's more frightened than you."

Jimmy tried unsuccessfully to smile at his mother as he was led from the room.

*   *   *

Joseph was getting tired. *I'm getting too old for this,* he thought. *Office, court, office, home, drink, dinner and listen to Mary report her day's activities. That's the only thing that keeps me sane—that and the animals—nonjudgmental—always glad to see me—and, of course, the pigs. Their smiles are not pleasant today.* These disconnected ruminations wandered through Joseph's mind as he sat on a bench in the square, legs splayed, eyes closed, enjoying the warmth of the sun, that would soon be replaced by winter's chill, waiting for Terry. He could hear the children shrieking as they climbed on the World War II cannon memorial marking the north-west corner of the square—an instrument designed to bring death during wartime, now a playground for the children bringing life to it. The noise warmed his insides as the sun warmed his outside. *Getting so I don't like the changes in the weather as much as I once did. It seems the older I get, the colder I get.* Terry had agreed to meet him at the park bench this morning before trial started for the day.

Terry crossed the street, coming from the parking lot behind the old *Reporter* building and trotted up to where Joseph was sitting. He wasn't even out of breath, which Joseph had a hard time understanding. It was eight thirty and they were due in court within the hour.

"Terry," Joseph said, "Will you handle the motion in limine?" He was talking about a request filed with the Court asking that the State be limited in introducing certain evidence the defense believed was not proper, or would have the effect of creating unreasonable prejudice on the part of the jury. The motion would have to be heard and considered by the Court outside the presence of the jury.

"I'll be happy to, if that's what you want. I researched it last night and this morning, but could find no cases on point. I think we have a decent argument. At least making the motion will preserve the issue for appeal— if we need to file one."

Walking across the street to the courthouse, they discussed the points that should be raised in the argument. After everyone had gathered in the courtroom, without the jury present, Judge Crider asked, "Do I understand there is something you wish to call to my attention, Mr. Joseph?"

Terry rose from his seat, moved toward the center of the bench, and said politely, "Your Honor, we have a motion in limine to discuss."

He moved back towards the trial table and picked up a sheaf of papers. Referring to them, he continued, "Behind the prosecutor's table there is a drier that was removed from the decedent's utility room and brought into court. We understand they intend to introduce evidence of a partial palm print that is supposed to belong to Mr. Takas that was found on a drop or smear of blood on the surface of the machine. We know that the State is unable to determine on whose blood the print is superimposed. Or, for that matter, when the print and blood were deposited on the piece of laundry equipment. The possible remoteness in time could lead to confusion of the issues in this trial. Certainly the unfair prejudice to the defendant outweighs any possible relevance."

Terry paused and then reminded the judge, "If you recall, Your Honor, Knedder testified he'd cut his hand and visited the home of the deceased both before and after she was killed. Perhaps it's his blood—and perhaps the print was placed there that evening or earlier, long before Ms. Westlock was killed. In fact, the police report said Mr. Takas had several cuts on his hand when interviewed—the cuts received days earlier at work. Perhaps it's his own blood the print is on. For all these reasons, the lack of relevance, the remoteness in time and the unfair prejudice, we respectfully request that the fingerprint evidence not be allowed."

Thuman was on his feet before Terry had seated himself, eye blinking and mouth working. When he calmed himself sufficiently, he said, "The State vigorously opposes the motion in limine. Although it's true we could not identify the blood, there is only one dead body in the room and her blood is all over the place. The drier was just a couple of feet from the body. We know Takas was in the house that night. Again, even though we cannot say exactly when the print was placed there, we know it must have been that evening—or morning. The jury is entitled to look at all the evidence and draw whatever inference from it that common sense dictates."

He drew a breath as though to present further argument, but the judge waved him back to his seat. "It's obviously not remote in time. The defendant's bloody print is in the room where the girl was killed. The jury is entitled to know that. Everyone knows what a good housekeeper Ms. Westlock was. It's unlikely she would leave a bloody fingerprint sitting around. The motion in limine is denied. Let's go!"

Forgetting that Terry was arguing the motion, Joseph stood and said with apparent irritation, "For God's sake, Judge. There is no evidence before the jury as to the quality of Ms. Westlock's housekeeping. She could have been a slob for all we know. How can the Court even suggest that the drier was clean, had no blood spots or fingerprints before the killing?"

Joseph stopped for a breath, but before he could say any more, Judge Crider interjected, "In the first place, Mr. Bernow is arguing the motion—not you, Mr. Joseph. In the second place, you heard my ruling."

How many prosecutors do we have to fight? Joseph thought not for the first time as he seated himself without apology. Terry joined him at the trial table, placing a calming hand on the elderly lawyer's shoulder.

*   *   *

Thuman, appearing smug at the minor victory, said, "Your Honor, once the jury is collected, the State will call Officer Rob Stanford."

Stanford, a nice young man, whom Joseph had met on a number of occasions, took the witness stand, appearing serious—yet acknowledged Joseph with a brief smile. He was probably in his mid-twenties, of medium height and slender, with broad shoulders and arms that threatened the sleeves of the uniform shirt he wore. Hair dark and neatly combed…dark brown eyes bright with the knowledge that he was doing the job he always wanted to do. Born to a police family, they were as proud of him as he was of the job he held. Joseph had no doubt he would tell nothing but the truth—oath or not—while testifying. He was the kind of reliable and honest witness Joseph enjoyed, no matter for whom he was testifying.

After having the oath administered and the routine matters out of the way, Anne Dronke asked a number of questions that elicited again the same basic information the jury had heard ad nauseam. Patrolman Officer Stanford was working the third shift, nine at night to seven in the morning, on the night June Westlock was killed. He was on station getting ready to close his shift when a call came in by someone asking for help at the Westlock residence. Sergeant Dale, also at the station, took the call and, on his way out, asked Stanford to follow him. Stanford secured his police cruiser and followed, arriving at the Westlock house about two minutes after the sergeant. As he exited his cruiser, he met Prosecutor Thuman on the front lawn. The two of them entered the house together. Sergeant Dale asked Mr. Thuman to wait outside and then instructed Stanford concerning his duties.

Stanford went on to explain that he entered the house, saw Knedder— a man he knew from other police contacts—sitting in the living room with his face in his hands "appearing as though he were crying."

Sergeant Dale told him to look in the laundry room where, "I saw a female previously known to me as June Westlock laying on the floor. She was obviously dead, skin very pale, not breathing, eyes slightly open. There was a great deal of blood on the floor. She had on some type of housecoat or bathrobe...I think it's called a negligee...it was a dark color...all bunched up near her head and neck...but I couldn't see if she had anything on underneath it. I checked for a carotid pulse, but could feel none."

The officer then went on to explain how he read Knedder his rights, placed him under arrest and subsequently transported him to the police station. Before doing so he secured the scene and looked through the house. He saw Shelley Westlock sleeping in the first bedroom he came to, and then went into the second bedroom. No one was there.

Terry conducted the cross-examination of the young police officer and asked if he had observed the backdoor, that led from the outside into the utility room.

"Yes, sir. I did. The backdoor was locked by a chain. The lock itself apparently was broken and the door was secured with a chain lock."

"Was there blood on the door?"

"Yes, sir. There was quite a bit of blood on the doorknob and on the door itself near the chain. There was blood on the chain as well. And I believe there was some on the wall too—near the door."

"Did you see blood in the kitchen or anywhere else in the house?"

"None that I seen."

Terry then asked, "Now, Officer, did you happen to notice any blood on Mr. Knedder's T-shirt or trousers?"

"Nothing I really noticed. His clothes weren't clean and all I noticed is that what was on them looked more black than blood color."

"Well, doesn't blood darken, as it dries? If you know."

"Well, yes, I think so."

"Thank you, Officer. Did you notice whether or not Mr. Knedder had a bandage anywhere on his hand?"

"Yes, sir. He had a bandage on his thumb."

"Do you remember, was the bandage clean or dirty like his clothing?"

"I don't remember."

Joseph was pleased with Terry's cross-examination. He made the jury aware that Knedder had blood on him and a cut on his hand. *Reasonable doubt…maybe?*

"Oh, by the way," Terry asked as he started back toward his seat, "When you arrived at the house, where did you see Mr. Thuman?"

"Objection," from Dronke, "relevance."

The Court said, "You're probably right, but let him answer."

The officer thought for a minute, and responded, "He had pulled his car up behind mine and exited his vehicle before I was out of mine. He was on the lawn and walked toward me. I waited for him and we walked to the house together."

"Thank you, Officer," Terry said and sat down.

Joseph smiled his pleasure.

*   *   *

After excusing Officer Stanford, Thuman called the homicide detective in charge of the investigation, Lieutenant Richard Tells. He had been sitting at the prosecutor's table throughout the trial. The rules permit the presence of a police officer as the State's representative in a criminal trial—just as though he is a party to the litigation. Joseph wondered why Milltown's police department had a homicide unit. He could only recall two murders in the past several years.

Joseph knew the lieutenant well. He'd been a police officer for many years, first serving with the Mills County Sheriff's Department and later as a detective with the Milltown Police Department. His training was extensive and Joseph knew he was honest and intelligent, even though he had a distinct bias when it came to criminal trials—a worthy adversary. The lieutenant was shorter than average, but well built and healthy looking. Face unlined…for some reason the stress of his job left him unmarked. He was clean shaven and had slightly grizzled dark brown hair cut short and neatly combed. His clothing, obviously not expensive, but neat and conservative, was appropriate for a police officer's income. He wore no jewelry except for an inexpensive watch and a plain gold wedding band on his left hand.

In response to questioning by Thuman, he described how he arrived at the home of June Westlock, took charge of the investigation, talked to Officer Stanford before entering the house, instructed the officer to secure the scene and permit no one else entry. He then entered the home. In addition to police and life support personnel on the scene, Clarence Knedder and June's daughter were in the house. He had a brief conversation with the "civilians" there and asked Officer Stanford, who had returned to the scene after transporting Knedder to the station, to remove them from the home. Lieutenant Tells had known both the deceased and Mr. Knedder since both were familiar figures to the police.

Tells then described in detail, using the stilted police report language, his findings in the house—the disarray in the kitchen—the crushed onions and potatoes on the floor—the tipped furniture—the cover of the phone box knocked off and lying on the floor—a mussed throw rug between the kitchen and utility room. He had diagramed these items on a sketch he made as well as preserving them on video tape. He was asked to look at the scale drawing prepared by the defense and asked if it appeared to display accurately what he had seen. He replied that it did.

He described, in response to a question, what he had seen in the utility room without emotion, in the same manner used to describe the inanimate objects found elsewhere in the house.

The officer went on to say that "the assistant county coroner had not yet arrived." The lieutenant observed Ms. Westlock's body, but did not touch her, and concluded, "It was obvious she was dead. The body had started to set in rigor, which means that the muscles had started to harden and stiffen," he explained. "Her hands were at the level of her shoulders, her elbows at her side. She was nude. Her legs were straight, but her right leg was at a slight angle from her body, pointing towards the water heater."

The officer related the balance of his findings to the jury, looking directly at, and talking to them rather than his questioner—obviously testifying at jury trials was as routine to him as his other work. The lack of emotion in his description lent emphasis to the horror of his findings.

"Were you present when the assistant coroner arrived?" Thuman asked.

"Yes, sir, I was."

"Please tell the jury how the body was removed from the scene?"

"After the assistant coroner pronounced her dead, June stayed with us for a couple of hours, so I could collect whatever physical evidence was there, make sketches and measurements and photograph the scene."

His use of the deceased's first name sent chills down Joseph's spine.

"Then when she was released to the funeral home, I watched as her body was removed. The lividity and the compression marks on her body were consistent with her having died where she lay."

"Lividity, sir. What is that?" Thuman asked, as if he had never heard the word before.

"When someone dies, their blood no longer circulates through the body. Gravity will cause the blood to settle in the lowest part of the body, where it leaves a purplish cast to the skin. At the place where the body rests on the floor, compression marks are formed. That's because the body weight pressing down will pinch out the blood in those areas, leaving the skin whiter—without color. Those are called 'compression marks.'"

He went on to tell of the wounds he observed—the multiple stab wounds on her chest, stomach, back and rib cage—the marks on her neck and shoulders—the defensive wounds in her hands.

"What do you mean by defensive wounds?"

"When someone is being attacked they try to defend themselves by putting up their hands—to ward off a blow—the cut and stab marks on the hands are considered to be defensive wounds. That's what they are called."

"Judge," Thuman said, "we'd like to show the jury the video tape the lieutenant took."

Joseph rose from his seat and said, casually, "We have no objection, Your Honor, but would like to talk about it for a minute."

"Okay." Then to the jury, "We have to set up the equipment in the courtroom, so why don't we take a short recess now. Usual admonitions. Just wait in the jury room. We'll have you back shortly."

After the jurors had retired to the jury room, Joseph said, "We are aware that the Court is going to allow the jury to see the tape. We only asked that a portion of the tape be edited out—that part which is a closeup of the Mother's Day card, signed, *Love, Shelley.* I believe Mr. Thuman has made an edited tape, at my request, and we ask that it be used. The jury need not be informed of the part that is deleted—in fact, I really don't want them to know—it would make an emotional situation that much more so. Also, I would like to thank Mr. Thuman for his cooperation—in this if nothing else."

"Okay, Mr. Joseph. The jury will be informed that the tape is a fair and accurate depiction of the crime scene. Does that satisfy you, Mr. Joseph?"

"Well, yes, as far as it goes. Now, for the record, the defense has a general objection to the showing of the tape at all. We believe that the prejudice far outweighs any probative value."

The judge said, "I reviewed the tape and do not feel that it is prejudicial."

"Oh, and one other thing, Judge. The defense requests that the audio portion of the tape be turned down so that the jury can't hear Lieutenant Tells' editorial comments or any of the remarks he made while doing the taping. If any explanations are required, Mr. Thuman can ask questions after the tape is seen. Or even interrupt the tape if he feels it important."

"I think that's fair, Mr. Joseph. Harold, make sure the audio is turned down sufficiently so the jury can't hear anything the lieutenant or anyone else at the scene said."

Joseph sighed, returned to his seat without asking permission, and slumped into his chair. He turned to Jimmy and whispered, "We're going to be looking at a rather lengthy video tape showing June's body and the house. Just take it easy. I know how difficult it is, but don't worry if you show emotion—like tears or sadness. Just don't act out."

After the jurors returned and everyone was in their place, Judge Crider called for silence in the courtroom and addressed the jury, "We're going to play a tape for you. It is a videotape that Lieutenant Tells took at the scene of the crime and again a couple of days later. It isn't pleasant to watch, but I don't think it will unduly affect or influence you. While the tape is being played, Prosecutor Thuman may ask Lieutenant Tells to explain some of what you see. After the tape is finished playing, Mr. Joseph may cross-examine on it." Then, after a pause, in which the judge looked at the jurors to see if there were any apparent problems, she said, "You may proceed, Mr. Thuman."

"Before we start the tape, Judge, I need to ask Mr.— I mean Lieutenant Tells a couple of questions."

"Proceed."

"Lieutenant, have you taped crime scenes before?"

"Yes, sir."

"Have you reviewed this tape?"

"Yes, sir."

In order for photographs or videotapes to be introduced into evidence, it must be established that they fairly and accurately portray what they show—a formula dictated by the Supreme Court. "Lieutenant Tells, is the videotape a fair and accurate representation of the subject matter depicted in the videotape?"

"Yes, sir, it is."

As the tape began, Joseph could hear the jurors settling into their seats in the darkened room, preparing to watch the tape. The sound of their breathing indicated that at least a few of them were somewhat apprehensive.

The tape began mildly enough, trailing across the front yard and the front of the Westlock home and showing the address, numerals affixed to the mailbox on the stoop. As the camera entered the front door, the overturned flower basket could be seen. Lieutenant Tells was asked, by Thuman, to identify briefly the things that were being shown and about which the jury had already heard from him, and in the testimony of others. The tape panned to the overturned chair, the vegetables strewn on the kitchen floor, moving inexorably towards the utility room and the body of June. Before entering the utility room, the tie from Ms. Westlock's robe could be seen. Then bloody marks appearing on the floor and wall were visible and, slowly turning the corner, the camera showed June's body. It lay as she was found in the dishabille testified to by several witnesses.

Joseph could hear the sound of indrawn gasps, as if the room had been holding its collective breath. In response to Thuman's questions, the lieutenant continued his description of what was being seen in a voice uninfluenced by emotion. The lack of any apparent strong feeling emphasizing the horror of what the jury was viewing. Closeups displayed vividly the wounds and bruises. The only emotion aroused by the exposed breasts and genitalia was sympathy for the deceased. Each item in the room, as well as articles of June's clothing, was pictured showing how they were splattered with flecks of blood. The body was rolled over by a man whose face was unseen, showing the marks of lividity and compression earlier identified.

The tape seemed to go on forever—sobbing could be heard from the back of the room, and perhaps from the darkened jury box as well—but it took less than forty-five minutes to play. Lieutenant Tells' responses to questions delivered by Thuman were taken down by the court reporter, a small light on her table making her face and sten-o-type machine stand out in an eerie glow. It made real the crime scene, the disarray of the house and the marble-white body of June Westlock laying pathetically in her own blood. There was nothing sensual about her nudity.

Ringing in Joseph's ears were the sounds of crying coming from the back of the courtroom, where the Westlock family gathered to observe the trial. At the opposite end of the pew-like seats, Mr. and Mrs. Takas sat—both crying silently—tears streaming. After the first few minutes of the tape, Joseph noted Jimmy was unable to look—eyes downcast—

shoulders slumped—pathetic despair. Joseph found himself moved to tears as well, even though he had studied the tape several times. He glanced across the room at Thuman and wondered why he had the only dry eyes in the room.

The film taken the day following June's death showed the balance of the house, including the closet where the drug paraphernalia—a mirror, razor blade and drinking straw used for snorting—was kept, the bedrooms and bathroom, none of which appeared disturbed except for Shelley's room, where the bed was unmade. A picture of Shelley had also been taken and Joseph believed it was done for the purpose of arousing sympathy—as if anything else was necessary to accomplish that end. Outside the backdoor, there was what appeared to be footprints in the still wet grass—prints that followed the route Knedder said he took as he entered the yard and the house. In the closet of June's room, there were, in addition to her clothing, articles of men's apparel.

When at last the screen went dark, Judge Crider cleared her throat and said, "We'll take a brief recess," and left the bench, forgetting to recite the normal admonition to the jury.

Actually, Joseph didn't want the detective to be on the stand any longer than necessary. He didn't want the jury to dwell on the tape. He said to the judge as she was entering her chamber door, "Your Honor, I don't have any questions of Lieutenant Tells. Perhaps we can excuse him."

She turned to the lieutenant. "You're excused. You may remain at the State's trial table for the remainder of the trial if you wish." Then to the jury, as they were filing out, "It's almost noon. Why don't we take our lunch break now. Be back at one thirty. Same admonitions apply."

CHAPTER FOURTEEN

After lunch all of the participants settled back into the courtroom. Joseph wasn't happy to see how quietly the jurors filed into their seats. It was unfortunate, from his point of view, that they had the opportunity to brood on the vivid pictures of the decedent for so long without anything else to interrupt their thoughts.

As soon as the judge called the court to order, Prosecutor Thuman stood and said pompously, "The State will call Doctor Jonathan Shieve."

Why the hell is Thuman such a stuffed shirt? Doesn't he know how to relax? Joseph wondered.

Again the routine of swearing in the witness and having him identify himself was accomplished. "My name is Doctor Jonathan A. Shieve. My last name is spelled S-H-I -E-V-E, and I am a pathologist with the Office of the Cuyahoga County Coroner."

Although Joseph knew several of the pathologists who worked for the Coroner's Office in Cleveland, he had never met Dr. Shieve. The office, under Dr. Gerber, had an excellent reputation, but Joseph had heard nothing particularly good or bad about Shieve. In fact, the only time he had seen the names was on the autopsy protocol. He wasn't impressed with Shieve's appearance or presentation. *Bet no one ever calls him Johnny, or even John. Probably doesn't let anyone call him anything without using his title. He's as overblown as Thuman—a good pair.*

The doctor was of medium height, a little taller than Joseph, but much heavier in the chest. A full head of very grey, very wavy hair that appeared to receive much attention from the doctor, although there was a scattering of dandruff on Shieve's dark blue jacket. Joseph thought, *If I had hair like that I'd treat it pretty nice too—probably should use Head & Shoulders a little more often.* Shieve's face was heavy and jowly, eyes blue but not lively, florid face and mottled nose of a man not reluctant to have a drink or two before and after dinner. *At least my before-dinner Martinis haven't left their mark on my nose—yet.*

The witness told the jury that the body of the decedent had been referred to their office for autopsy since Mills County didn't have the wherewithal to do the job adequately. He then pretentiously outlined his qualifications and educational background.

"I am a graduate of the University of Philadelphia Medical School. After receiving my MD and completing my internship, I did a residency in pathology at Belle Mount Hospital in St. Paul. I served a couple of years in the military and returned to Belle Mount Hospital, where I began the private practice of pathology. When I returned to the Philadelphia area, I practiced privately for a few more years. At the same time I served as deputy coroner for that county, until I was elected to serve as coroner for a couple of terms. I was offered a position with the Cuyahoga County Coroner's Office in Cleveland, Ohio, several years ago and was pleased to accept since I had decided not to seek reelection to the post I had held. When I came to the Cleveland area, I did a fellowship at University Hospitals in Cleveland in forensic pathology. Forensic pathology is the use of medical studies in resolving criminal matters. I soon became a full-time member of the Cuyahoga County Coroner's Office in Cleveland."

Pompous and pedantic, thought Joseph. *Wonder how well the jury likes it. I know if I were on the jury I wouldn't want anyone talking down to me like that.*

Thuman continued, "Are you licensed to practice medicine in Ohio, Doctor?"

"Yes, I am, and have been since the mid seventies."

"What are your duties with the Coroner's Office?"

"My duties include the viewing and examining of bodies as they are received in the Coroner's Office, receive information and reports from the police agencies involved, view the disrobed body and determine whether further investigation—an autopsy—is required. I have probably done several thousand autopsies, although I don't know the exact number."

It's obvious he has testified a number of times before. He knows the questions before they are asked, Joseph thought.

"It is my understanding, Doctor, that the purpose of an autopsy is to determine the cause and manner of death, is that correct?"

The question was leading and objectionable in that form, but Joseph decided to let it pass. He didn't want to interrupt—yet.

"The *cause* of death is defined as the disease process or injury that initiates the series of events that ultimately lead to the death of an individual. The *manner* of death is the fashion in which the cause came into existence. If the cause of death is the result of natural disease, the manner of death is 'natural causes.' If violence contributes in any way to the cause of death, then we have to decide whether the violence is the result of an accident, suicide or homicide. Once we make that determination, we assign the manner of death as being one of those; that is, accidental, suicide or homicide."

The prosecutor asked the assistant coroner to explain how an autopsy is performed. The doctor described the method utilized in unnecessary detail, talking about disrobing the body, examining the nude body in its entirety, making a Y-shaped opening in the torso of the deceased, removing all of the internal organs, examining them in a systematic fashion, testing body fluids, cutting and microscopically examining tissue from various parts of the body. He talked to the jurors as though in a classroom—he the teacher, they not very bright students.

The heavy eyes of several jurors attested to the fact they had recently indulged in a hearty lunch. That, and the witness' droning voice, was a sure cure for insomnia. Joseph was impressed that the members of the jury worked so hard at staying awake. A good jury.

"Did you have occasion, Doctor, to do an autopsy on the body of June Westlock?"

"Yes, I did."

"Please tell the jury and the Court when and where that was performed and what findings it produced."

"The autopsy was performed at our offices in Cleveland, Ohio on the morning after her death. June Westlock appeared to be a well-developed, adequately nourished young woman consistent with her stated age of thirty-two years. She measured sixty-eight point five inches; that is, five feet, eight and one-half inches tall, and weighed one hundred eighteen pounds. The examination revealed a variety of injuries—some blunt-force injuries and some produced by a sharp instrument. I have with me a number of photographs that would more clearly illustrate for the jury the injuries that I discovered."

Thuman then asked the court reporter to mark the photographs for identification, which Eileen did, and then she returned them to Thuman. He studied them as though he had never seen them before. Joseph knew Thuman had hand-picked the photographs he wanted the jury to see. Joseph had his own set and looked through them as the witness identified the ones Thuman handed him. The elderly lawyer picked duplicates of the photographs from his stack and made a separate pile of those not used by the prosecutor. He would possibly use some of them later.

Question after question from the prosecutor resulted in the doctor's explanation of the wounds shown in the photographs. Several times the doctor pointed to examples of what he referred to as blunt-force injuries, which he described as "bruises, scrapes and tears of the skin.

"However," he added, "some of the scrapes could have been produced with the point of a knife being dragged across the skin."

The witness went on for several minutes describing in minute detail the size, location and extent of the blunt-force injuries. Joseph hoped that, because of the numerous examples coupled with the lack of emotion in the witness' voice, the jurors were becoming, at least, a little desensitized to the terrible trauma suffered by June Westlock.

The assistant coroner then began talking about the injuries produced by an "edge-pointed instrument." Joseph noted that the witness kept using the singular when referring to the edge-pointed instrument. He wondered why this was so, when it was fairly obvious, to him anyway, that more than one instrument produced the wounds described.

Thuman interrupted Joseph's thoughts when he asked, "Your Honor, may we show the photographs to the jury so they understand more clearly what the doctor is describing? He could hold up the photograph or go and stand by the jury box to testify about the wounds."

Judge Crider began, "I don't care—"

Joseph stood and asked if they could approach moving towards the bench before the judge could respond, "Your Honor, we object to that. So far the witness has only described wounds that are superficial in nature and none of which were lethal. Showing them to the jury before they are admitted into evidence—if ever—would be grossly prejudicial."

Waving Joseph silent, Judge Crider said, "The Court has instructed the prosecutor to lay a foundation about the photographs. Then he may show them."

Laying a foundation requires that when a photograph is offered into evidence, it must be first established when and where the photograph was taken and that it fairly and accurately reflects that which it depicts. Although the procedure seems simplistic, it is especially true today with the advent of digital cameras and computers being able to create photographs that have no relationship whatsoever to reality. Nevertheless, Joseph wondered, *When did she give the prosecutor those instructions about these pictures? Is she still having ex parte conversations with him?* Then turning to Terry, Joseph whispered, "How many adversaries we got?"

Terry shrugged.

After laying the necessary foundation, the prosecutor suggested to the witness that he take the photographs and move forward—toward the jury box. The witness did so, trying to balance the photographs and his notes. He didn't have enough hands. Joseph graciously said, "Feel free to use the corner of our table," which drew a dirty look from both the witness and the prosecutor.

The doctor again began talking about the wounds, describing some of them as "stab wounds" and some as "incised wounds," explaining the difference "A stab wound is usually deeper than wide. In other words, it is usually the width of the implement, and could be as deep as the instrument is long. An incised wound, on the other hand, is longer than it is deep. The instrument is dragged along the skin and produces a cut that is longer than it is deep."

He described clusters of wounds on the abdomen, breast, neck and back, some of which extended into organs of the body that could lead to death, but that "a number of the wounds produced very little bleeding or discoloration. That indicates that they had been delivered postmortem— that is, after or at about the time she died."

The doctor continued, "The most significant wound was on the left side of her back. It measured one-half inch in length, penetrating deeply into her body, passing immediately below the rib cage, then upwards through the diaphragm, through a lobe of the left lung and passing completely through the aorta. The aorta is the main artery of the body, that carries blood to all portions of the body. This," showing one of the exhibits, "would be the lethal injury. That means the one that caused her to die."

How stupid does he think they are? Joseph wondered.

The prosecutor began to ask more questions about other findings not reflected in the photographs. The witness had been standing in front of the jury for some time and asked, "Is it all right if I sit down now?"

"Of course. Sorry I was so inconsiderate. I was just fascinated by what you were saying."

"Object to the editorial comment, Judge," Joseph said without smiling.

The judge mildly reprimanded the prosecutor, "Mr. Thuman…" shaking her finger.

In the meantime, the witness returned to the witness stand and sank gratefully into the seat. He apparently didn't like to be on his feet for any length of time. He responded to additional questions that there was "the presence of cocaine" in June. He then explained how he examined her vaginal cavity, mouth and anal cavity, finding no presence of sperm or injury except for "a small, rather meaningless scratch near her vagina. I cannot clearly state when or how it was produced."

Joseph thought, *That resolves the death penalty problem,* and smiled at Terry, including Jimmy Takas. Terry smiled back—Jimmy was not responsive. Clearly he was unaware of the hurdle they had just overcome.

The doctor concluded, "The cause of death is multiple—twenty-three stab and incised wounds of the trunk and extremities with organ perforation that resulted in exsanguination—bleeding to death. The manner of death is homicide."

Thuman continued with the witness for another hour, asking the witness to identify the clothing Ms. Westlock was wearing, the relationship of the rents in her garment to the wounds on the body, the length of time it would take for her to have died after suffering the lethal blow and the approximate time of death. The doctor testified that she died between one thirty and three o'clock in the morning.

By this time, the witness, Joseph, the Court and the jury were obviously exhausted—almost bored to tears. When the prosecutor finally said, "No more questions," the judge sighed and added, "We will take a recess at this time before the cross-examination begins. Remember my admonitions," she said and stole from the bench.

Joseph and Terry stood waiting for the jurors to exit. "Pretty dogmatic. Want to take him, Terry?"

Terry smiled. "Nope, he's all yours."

Just as Joseph and Terry were starting to leave the courtroom to step outside and grab a breath of fresh air, the judge called them back. "It's snowing like hell out there. An early snowstorm has hit the area and the Governor has declared a state of emergency. I guess the roads are something awful. I'm going to release the jury for the weekend with instructions not to read the papers or listen to the news in addition to the usual instructions. We'll start early Monday morning. I'll ask Judge Clarke to handle my Monday morning docket. I know it's a little early, but I think we could all use the break."

Joseph objected for the record, saying, "It is unfair for the jury to hear only the direct examination of the assistant coroner without the defense having an opportunity to cross-examine him. They will hear nothing contradictory for the entire weekend and… Well, it is just to the defendant's disadvantage."

Actually Joseph didn't care and was anticipating with some relish the time off. Judge Crider ignored his argument and ordered everyone to be back in her room at eight thirty Monday morning.

It had been a grueling week and Joseph looked forward to the weekend.

*   *   *

As Joseph and Terry walked across the square, people could be seen rushing from the surrounding businesses and offices to their cars. "Looks like everyone is going home early," Joseph commented.

The square was buried in soft wet snow—perfect for making snowmen or snowballs. It was piling up on the trees, making pyramids on the streetlights and finding its way into Joseph's shoes. The change in the weather struck so suddenly, no one was prepared for it. Not too unusual for Ohio at this—or any—time of the year. Nevertheless, it was beautiful, even if unexpected so early in the year. Della and the rest of the staff waited for Joseph's return. He decided to forego the usual Friday cocktail hour and told everyone to go home. Everyone left but Della.

"Are you going home, Pat?" she asked.

"Yeah. May as well. I'm not going to miss my Martini though. Going to have it at home."

"There is nothing here that needs attention. I can check the mail tomorrow morning if you want. Everything else can be on hold until next week."

"Thanks, Della. Don't bother to come in tomorrow. I'm not. Enjoy the weekend, such as it is. As always, you make me look good."

The roads, trees and lawns were all snow covered…the large beautiful flakes falling softly to the earth, covering everything in sight with a clean, fresh, virginal look . Every year it was the same thing…Ohio drivers forget how to drive on winter roads over the summer, and the first snow fall results in either careless fender-benders or overly cautious drivers.

Joseph shook his head in wonderment at the inexplicable way humans behaved when facing the unexpected, and drove carefully in his old four-wheel-drive pickup truck. He arrived home before the world darkened. As he entered his long, sloping drive, he noticed the tracks of several deer crossing into the adjoining woods. What with all the new construction in the area, the poor things were daily losing more and more of their habitat. Joseph thought to tell Mary of the tracks but refrained. He knew she would have him out in the weather providing feed for them. He was too tired.

When he entered the house from the attached garage, Mary was already feeding the inside animals. "Would you mind walking down to the barn and feeding Old Dog tonight? I've been so busy, I haven't gotten to the barn yet."

Joseph acquiesced, knowing it would be a waste of time to argue—besides, he wanted to spend a few minutes with his old friend before locking him in the barn. He knew the dog was lonely since the horses and goats were gone. Joseph felt a bit lonely too. He always liked being with the outside animals in this weather. He remembered how the horses and goats would cluster in the barn for warmth and greet him gratefully. He would don a pair of barn shoes he kept in the garage and, without changing clothes, walk down the path to the barn where he was always welcomed by a raucous combination of goat, horse and dog sounds. He would tell the larger animals to be patient while he greeted the then much younger Old Dog and gather their food.

By the time Joseph changed his shoes and walked to the barn, Old Dog approached cautiously with a swaying tail, just getting close enough to be noticed. The old fellow was reluctant to show affection, but Joseph knew he wanted attention. Squatting, he petted the large black dog, who stood still to enjoy the touch. The dog's tail expressed his appreciation as he walked towards his bowl.

The memories were vivid as Joseph dug into the metal feed bin for Old Dog's food. He used the same bin he had used to keep the grain for the horses and goats. While he filled the dog's bowl first, the remaining animals would rush to their own stalls, waiting for their feed boxes to be filled. It baffled Joseph how they knew which stall was their own. It was as though they could read the names carved into the wooden plaque above each. He would have to feed the goats next. If he didn't they would lock the horses out of their stalls and eat their food. The pleased munching sounds relaxed Joseph as much as his evening Martini. Joseph was startled, and slightly dispirited, by the vividness of the memories. So he petted Old Dog for a few minutes and talked nonsense to him, resulting in a pleasant switching tail.

Joseph locked the old fellow in his stall and turned to leave the barn. On his way out, he stopped at the feed bin and filled an open box with a combination of horse and goat feed and carried it to the old apple tree standing in front of the barn. The deer often visited it to pick off the apples left behind for them. He placed the box under the tree and went into the house. *Mary would have made me do that anyway. No sense having to get dressed once I've made myself comfortable.*

Removing his outside clothes in the garage, Joseph entered the house to the smell of cooking. He went upstairs to change, finally secured his Martini and settled himself at the table in the large old-fashioned kitchen with his drink and newspaper, reading glassed perched on the end of his nose, prepared to listen to Mary's day's activities, a feeling of warmth flowing through him that he could not attribute solely to the Martini.

After dinner, he settled to do some reading while Mary worked on a quilt she was making for one of the grandchildren.

*   *   *

Monday morning arrived too soon for Joseph. He checked the bedside clock. It was six thirty, the time he usually wakened—hadn't set an alarm in years. The other half of the double bed was empty. Sighing, he knew Mary was already up and feeding the inside animals. He rolled out of bed, remembering the time, long ago, when he could just bounce up. He felt around under the edge of the bed with his feet and stuffed them into an old pair of worn slippers, reached for the ratty bathrobe hanging on the bed post, shrugged into it and tied the belt loosely around his stomach.

Mary had been trying to throw it away for years, but he kept retrieving it from the rag bin.

Following his usual morning routine, he showered, shaved and brushed his teeth. He used a waterpik instead of floss—*can't get that damn string between my teeth*—finally shuffling from the bedroom and down the stairs. He smelled coffee. The coffee, along with a slice of toast and orange juice, were waiting for him at his place on the kitchen table. Mary was sitting at the table sipping a cup of coffee and lackadaisically petting one of her cats.

Joseph began his breakfast munching on the toast he didn't want and talking to Mary. He mentioned, "I've got to cross-examine the coroner from Cleveland today. Must have done it ten or twelve times during the night. Wish I could do as good a job when I'm awake."

"Don't talk with your mouth full."

"He's kind of the key to this case. I know there were several weapons used in the killing of June—he insists there was only one. Don't know why he's so obtuse."

"Don't worry about it. The jury will figure out what the truth is."

"Wish I could be as confident as you."

"Humphh…"

After finishing breakfast, Joseph dressed carefully in a soft brown wool suit, military striped cravat tied neatly beneath the collar of his white oxford cloth shirt. He felt he looked good, but knew it wouldn't make much difference by the middle of the day. He kissed Mary on her nose, threw a dog biscuit to the inside dog, left the house in his old pickup and drove to the office, arriving before anyone else. *Sure hope Mary remembers to feed Old Dog. Probably will when she sets out the birdseed.*

He and Terry arrived at court at the time dictated by Judge Crider, to discover that Dr. Shieve had not yet arrived. Judge Crider said, "I believe he has been detained by the roads and weather, even though they have cleared up considerably since Friday. We received a call from his office saying he would be a bit late. Mr. Thuman would like to use the time, while waiting for Dr. Shieve, to have the photographs taken by Lieutenant Tells identified and introduced."

Joseph knew it would have to be done sooner or later, so offered no objection. He did, however, want to take the opportunity get in a dig. "No objection, Judge, but it would be nice if the prosecutor would quit having those ex parte conversations with the Court about this case. The defense would like to be included in at least some of those conversations."

The judge glared at Joseph, but could say nothing, knowing he was right. Joseph was aware he wouldn't be getting any favors from her, but didn't care—wouldn't have anyway. *How many prosecutors?*

After about two hours of reviewing and arguing about photographs and other exhibits—necessarily done outside the presence of the jury, everything Thuman introduced was admitted into evidence. Joseph and Terry weren't surprised. At this point, Judge Crider interrupted the arguments and announced, "My bailiff informs me that Dr. Shieve is in the lobby. We will take a five-minute recess and start his cross-examination."

The jurors had been cooling their collective heels in the jury room all morning and were undoubtedly getting impatient. Thuman left the courtroom and stepped out into the lobby. Joseph knew he would be chatting with the assistant coroner, bringing him up to date on what had happened and reminding him of the State's spin on the evidence. A few minutes later the judge returned to the bench and called the room to order.

Joseph, standing for the jurors, waited until they were all seated, then walked to his usual spot behind the jury box to begin the cross-examination he had been anticipating—the feeling of inadequacy moving with him. He felt a slight tremor in his hands as he thought, *How can I possibly cross-examine this well-trained professional in his area of expertise? He has shown his bias—how can I get the jury to see it?*

"Dr. Shieve, my name is Patrick Joseph. Terry Bernow and I are representing Mr. Takas in this case. I understand you have been an assistant coroner for many years—fourteen years, I believe. And as such, you are a student of forensic medicine, isn't that correct?"

"Well, one's exposure to the problems related to medical law really commences with one's training. When I served in the Armed Forces, there were a number of medical examiner type cases—and at the hospital where I trained—"

Joseph could not let the witness control the examination or ramble on, so tremulously interrupted, "Doctor, you have been trained in forensic medicine, isn't that correct? That calls for a simple 'yes' or 'no' answer."

Joseph could feel the judge and prosecutor glaring at him, but the doctor responded, "Yes, I have."

"Thank you. Now, would you please tell the jury what the term 'forensic' means?"

"Well, it simply means, in this instance, the application of the principles of pathology to the investigation of crimes. Forensic pathology is investigating deaths occurring suddenly and unexpectedly. Such deaths may be due to natural disease or some form of violence—whether that be accident or homicide."

Joseph continued, "Is it then fair to say that your exclusive practice of medicine...in your entire career...has to do with the study of problem-solving as it is related to crimes or potential crimes?"

"That is a fair statement, sir."

"So then you have had a great deal of experience in that area."

Smiling with a failed attempt at humility, the assistant coroner responded, "You can say that." None of the pomposity had left the doctor—he still felt in control.

Joseph was beginning to feel more comfortable. His extensive preparation kept him on track despite the doctor's partiality. "Doctor, the skin of the human body is classified as an organ, isn't that true?"

"It can be so considered," the doctor equivocated.

"Well, is it, or it isn't it?" Joseph persisted.

"Medically speaking, it is," the doctor answered.

Joseph continued, "As the surface or covering of the body, part of its function is to protect the body, isn't that so?"

"It is the external protective barrier." The assistant coroner was beginning to relax as well since the discussion was within his realm, while Thuman fidgeted, wondering where Joseph was going.

"Is it safe to say, Doctor, that the skin has a certain amount of elasticity?"

"It does."

"Then as such, Doctor, isn't it true that it will usually take the shape of an object that pierces it in a straight line?"

"That's only partially correct," the doctor responded. "The skin does contain elastic tissue, and there are lines or grains that have been described by a man named Langer. Physicians practicing general surgery or plastic surgery are more familiar with Langer's lines than the layman—or even myself." The answer came in a manner that said, *I know a hell of a lot more about this stuff than you do.*

Joseph was ready. "Doctor, are you referring to the discovery of Carl Ritter Von Langer, the Austrian anatomist that studied the structural orientation of the fibrous tissue of the skin sometime in the 1800s, that forms the natural cleavage of the skin?"

"Yes, I am. Again, this is more familiar to surgeons."

"Langer mapped the lines, didn't he, Doctor?"

"Yes," Shieve snapped. "But I don't think that someone who stabs someone else would be familiar with those lines."

"But you should be, shouldn't you, Doctor, so that you can tell if an entry wound takes the shape of that which penetrates the skin or is distorted because it crosses one of Langer's lines?"

Thuman was getting impatient and a little nervous—feeling out of control. His eye blinking and his mouth working, he rose from his chair, saying, "Objection, Your Honor. This can't possibly be relevant. I think Joseph is just showing off."

Instead of addressing the Court, Joseph turned to Thuman and said, "Showing off, huh? It might be helpful if you did a little studying before trying to blow smoke at the jury."

Judge Crider banged on her desk, "Both of you—quiet. Your comments should be addressed only to the bench and you both know it. Now, Mr. Joseph, are you going somewhere with this?"

"Why yes, Your Honor," Joseph replied innocently. "Just a few more questions will tie it all up nicely—if Mr. Prosecutor will refrain from interrupting the witness."

The judge waved him back to his spot, adding, "You may continue without any more asides."

Joseph turned back to the witness and asked, "Do you remember the question? It was whether or not you could tell if the entry of an implement would leave a distorted wound if it crossed one of Langer's charted lines?"

The witness did not respond. Joseph waited for a pregnant moment, then asked, "Doctor, can you tell us whether or not you took into consideration Langer's lines when you examined the size and shape of the wounds you identified for the jury?"

Again, the doctor did not answer, so Joseph pressed., "Did you, Doctor?"

A reluctant "No."

Joseph shrugged. "In the protocol that you have identified for the jury as your autopsy report, you made an effort, did you not, to describe, measure carefully and identify the characteristics of each of the many wounds that pierced Ms. Westlock's body?"

"I did," he answered, wondering where this was going.

"And you described the wounds in several different ways. For example, you said several were round like a needle, some sharp at one end and blunt at the other, some sharp at both ends. Is that true?"

"Well, yes." Guessing where Joseph was going, he added, "That describes only the wound, not the instrument inflicting them."

"Thank you for the editorial comment, Doctor," sarcastically, "but we'll get to that in a minute.

"Now, Doctor, you do agree, do you not, that the first wound we talked about—the round one—is consistent with an object like a hypodermic needle, don't you?"

"Yes."

"Then is it safe to say you are satisfied that at the very least more than one object was used in the stabbing of Ms. Westlock?" the elderly lawyer asked placidly.

The question produced a reluctant "Yes" from the doctor.

"Part of your training—and one of the objectives of your job—is to make a real effort to determine what type of weapon created the wounds you identify on a decedent?"

"Yes, that's true, but it isn't an exact science—"

"Yet, you did measure and describe in your report the precise dimension and shape of each wound you found on Ms. Westlock? Even though we know you made no effort to determine whether or not the wound was distorted by the structure of the skin."

"Well, yes, I did. But again, it isn't an—" Then reluctantly, "Yes, you are partially correct. Injuries produced by a particular instrument will, to some degree, reflect the shape of that instrument."

"Thank you, Doctor. That is precisely what I have been trying to get out of you."

"Mr. Joseph," Judge Crider interjected, "you need not make editorial comments either."

"Sorry, Judge. I guess I've learned from this witness," which produced a scowl from the judge and a few titters from the jury.

"Now, Doctor, I have here a chart that we will identify later. But on it are several drawings of wound shapes and instruments that would produce such a wound shape. In other words," pointing, "this slightly elongated oval shape has next to it a drawing of a double-edged knife. Do you see that?"

"Yes."

"And this shape, with one sharp end and one blunt end—sort of like an elongated triangle—has next to it a single-edged blade. Do you see that?"

"Yes, I see it, but—"

"My question was just do you see it. Nothing more need be added at this time. Now, Doctor, if you would look at your protocol and find, on page twelve, the description of one of the wounds."

"Page twelve?"

"Yes, page twelve, where you describe the wound as having a sharp end and a blunt end," Joseph explained patiently.

"I see that."

"Good, Doctor. Is that consistent with the drawing I have shown you of the wound produced by a single-edged knife?"

"No. It isn't."

"It isn't? Why, it looks just like it to me."

"Well, the wound on the body had the blunt edge on the superior access and the sharp edge on the inferior access," the witness hedged.

"You're saying, Doctor, that the wound is just the reverse of what is shown in the drawing. Okay, then let's say that the person administering the wound turned the knife around in his hand, would that satisfy you? Or perhaps, we could turn the drawing upside down, would that satisfy your concerns?" producing some titters from the jurors.

Judge Crider frowned them to silence.

The witness sat mute, face getting redder and sweat breaking out on his forehead. Finally he said, "I still believe that only one weapon—except for the needle—was used on the deceased."

"Why is that, Doctor? Is that what the prosecutor wants you to say?"

"Objection," yelled Thuman and Dronke simultaneously, both jumping to their feet. The jurors turned their eyes from the witness to the prosecution table and saw faces equally red and angry, Thuman's eye twitching uncontrollably.

Judge Crider snapped, "Sustained. That's not a proper question, Mr. Joseph."

"This is cross-examination, Judge, and I believe I'm allowed to show bias. I trust you're not limiting my cross-examination of this witness," he suggested mildly. He wouldn't back down and really didn't care whether or not the jury heard the answer. Putting the thought in their mind was enough.

"You heard my ruling, Mr. Joseph. Move on!"

Joseph continued in the same vein, going over each wound described and measured in the coroner's report and comparing the shape and size to the drawing his medical illustrator had developed.

Again and again the witness tried to evade the question—insisting that only one weapon was used whenever he could. Joseph wouldn't allow him to draw that conclusion, continuously pointing out the size and shape of each wound as described in the autopsy protocol prepared by the witness in his own handwriting. "Well, Doctor, you examined her body, did you not?"

"I believe I was there and examined her body," sarcastically.

"And in each instance you made the observation as to the shape and size of the wound."

"I wrote down what I observed, and said what that was here in court, but let me tell you again that such observation is not entirely reliable."

"Are you saying, Doctor, that your examination of the body is not reliable? Is that what you're saying?"

"No...no...that isn't what I said at all. I said that I gave my best judgment of the shape of the defects."

"Well, then, at least in this instance, your observation is consistent with that wound having been made with a double-edged knife?"

"Yes," the doctor finally conceded, sighing and sinking lower into the witness chair. He had enough. He wanted the questioning to end and Joseph to go away, even if it meant making concessions he didn't want to.

"Now then, Doctor, you have admitted thus far that there were at least three weapons—the needle, a single-edged knife, and a double-edged knife that could have produced the defects you found on the deceased?"

"Yes. But my best judgm—"

"Your Honor, please instruct the witness to just answer the questions. It sure would save all of us a lot of time."

The judge said nothing, the witness interjecting in a small voice, "It's a difficult thing—"

Joseph said in a conciliatory manner—he didn't want the jury to start feeling sorry for the witness—"Of course it's difficult, but you've been doing this for many years—and are well trained in the field."

"Doesn't make any difference. It's as difficult today as it was twenty years ago."

Joseph thought, *Maybe the jury is starting to get the idea that this witness isn't the best example of most of the highly trained conscientious pathologists in the Cuyahoga County Coroner's Office. He's just second rate. I don't want it to reflect on his office—just him.*

"Doctor, can we conclude that your findings are consistent with more than one weapon—in fact three different weapons could have produced the wounds you identified?"

"Yes," stiffening his back and sitting up straighter, "but it's also consistent with one weapon having been used."

He wasn't going to give up either. The look on the face of some of the jurors indicated to Joseph that they were not convinced by the witness' stubborn reluctance to give up the party line. They were quickly losing respect for this witness.

Joseph wasn't quite ready to quit. He felt the need to destroy the witness now, but to do it with finesse so that no one would feel sorry for him. "Since you're so insistent that only one weapon was used, Doctor, can you explain how a single-edged knife could produce an oval-shaped wound—one with sharp edges on both aspects? Would it require placing the knife in the wound, drawing it out and returning it to the same wound after turning it around?"

"No…no…It would merely require drawing the sharp edge of the weapon across the skin and then plunging it into the body."

"If that were so, Doctor, the superior aspect of the wound would be abraded and the inferior a stab wound. Isn't that so?"

"Well, yes, but if it was done carefully enough…"

No one laughed at the witness' discomfort, but his performance had approached the ridiculous.

The witness slipped lower in his chair—his posture that of a dejected man. "I just did the best I could…. If you could tell me how to do it better, I would…."

"Doctor, I'm not here to tell you how to practice your profession, I'm ju—"

"Whoa, whoa," interjected the judge. I think it's time for a break. We have been going on for some time and I think we could all use a break.

Remember, don't form an opinion…" and she left the bench without finishing the admonitions. Obviously she intended to give the witness a chance to catch his breath and compose himself.

The jurors stood. Joseph remained standing behind them watching as they filed out. Some smiled at him, some looked unhappily at the witness.

After the recess the witness returned to the stand—he didn't look any the better for the time spent in the men's room trying to refresh himself. Joseph still had one or two questions about the wounds, getting the doctor to say that the killing wound was consistent with having been administered by a weapon with two edges—similar to a letter opener as drawn on the defense exhibit, which was quickly accomplished.

There was another area Joseph wanted to cover. "Doctor, you described some of the cuts on Ms. Westlock's hands as being defensive cuts, did you not?"

"Yes."

"We don't have to repeat what that means, I am sure the jury remembers. But what I'd like to know is, did you do any scrapings under Ms. Westlock's fingernail to determine if she had scratched her assailant?"

"I found no reason to scrape her nails."

"But isn't that standard procedure when one suspects a decedent had been involved in an altercation with her assailant?"

The witness repeated, "I found no reason to scrape her nails."

"If there had been traces of skin under her fingernails, would you have been able to identify the assailant through the use of DNA tests?"

As if in a trance he repeated, "I found no reason to scrape her nails."

The jury had to know that the failure was inexcusable. "Doctor, you are Board Certified in forensic pathology?"

"Yes."

"And I am sure you are familiar with Deshee and Eckert's celebrated three-volume work on forensic medicine?"

"Yes. I have a copy in my office."

"Have you read it?"

Before he could answer Thuman objected and the judge said, "Sustained."

"Well, do you use it as a reference work?"

"Occasionally."

"Have you ever used that section of the book that says it is very important to do an examination of the hands, fingers and nails, giving particular attention to the presence of foreign particles that might indicate a deceased's attempt to resist an assault?" Holding up a book in his hand, Joseph asked, "Do you want me to read it to you?"

"No...no...that's not necessary. I wouldn't be surprised if it says that," the doctor said, but dogmatically, "I found no reason to do a scraping."

"Doctor, you're not here as a partisan witness, are you?"

"I'm not sure I understand your question."

"Forget it. We're getting close to the time you can leave, Doctor. There are just a couple of more things we need to talk about."

Since the witness had established for the jury that the deceased was wearing her nightdress when she was stabbed, Joseph wanted to show that the robe she was wearing over it when she died did not contain the same rents or tears. This would mean she either didn't have it on when stabbed or that it was opened. The last time she had been seen by any of the other witnesses and by Jimmy Takas, the robe was closed and tied. The doctor verified that there were no tears in the robe.

Lastly, Joseph wanted to establish that there was no physical evidence of recent intercourse—let alone rape, as Jimmy was charged. The doctor testified, "I examined the ovaries, fallopian tubes, uterus and vagina, both internally and around the external area. There was no evidence of the presence of spermatozoa or any abnormalities of any kind. I examined the anus, mouth and vaginal area to determine if there was any evidence of recent intercourse or sexual activity and found none. No sperm, no semen and no male acid phosphatase. Nothing to indicate sexual activity."

"Thank you, Doctor. I have no further questions."

Joseph returned to his seat feeling exhausted, but pleased at what had been accomplished during the cross-examination. *Let's see if Thuman can rehabilitate him.* Terry looked pleased.

Thuman tried, but all he could get was the dogmatic repetition of his arbitrary position that only one weapon was used despite the fact it was not supported by his findings or the photographs. He said what Thuman originally wanted to hear, but was unable to convince anyone—not even himself—as to its truth. No one looked as though they would take him seriously. The fear of every trial lawyer is realized when a witness is not believed in one area; his entire testimony becomes suspect in the collective minds of the jurors. *How can you believe anything coming from someone who lies about even one thing?*

Joseph heard a sound in the back of the courtroom. He turned toward it and saw Stan Marten moving towards the door. Stan stopped, turned towards Joseph, smiled and gave a thumbs up sign. Then hurriedly left. Joseph thought, *Well, he's got his story for tomorrow's paper. Hope he does his usual good job.*

*   *   *

Thuman sat down, obviously dejected, eye blinking and mouth twitching. He leaned over to Anne Dronke, his assistant, and whispered, "You take the next one. I'm tired."

Ms. Dronke stood and said, "The State will call…"

The State then produced a series of witnesses who should have been called earlier since it is important that a story be told in the chronological succession of events in order for jurors to develop a clear picture of the incident. Sometimes it can't be done, but lawyers should always be careful not to call witnesses out of order just for the convenience of the witness; even so, it is often done for physicians or other professionals who have busy schedules. It is never helpful to the trial lawyer—a lesson Thuman just learned well. In any event, the State was now going into the happenings on the night June Westlock was killed..

The first, the attendant on the ambulance from Mills County General Hospital, explained that he arrived a little after six thirty in the morning and immediately entered the house. When he was shown the body of Ms. Westlock, he felt for a carotid pulse and, feeling none, decided not to start cardiopulmonary resuscitation. It was obvious she was dead. "She was mostly nude and her body was cool to the touch and showed lividity. Her arms were already stiffening in rigor."

On cross-examination Terry secured nothing useful except that the witness had no problem seeing the body of June Westlock lying on the utility room floor; and that the backdoor was closed and chained. "It was dark in the room, but there was adequate light to see the body."

The next witness was the physician called to the scene by the Emergency Medical Unit. He arrived at approximately seven o'clock that morning and was acting as Mills County Assistant Coroner, since the coroner himself was not available. He found the same things as had the prior witness, except that he checked for pulse and respiration. "Finding no sign of life," the witness said, "it was my responsibility to pronounce her dead at four minutes after seven that morning."

On cross-examination, Terry obtained from the doctor that it was he who "wanted to send Miss Westlock's body to Cuyahoga County Coroner's Office for a full and comprehensive examination and autopsy, which I felt we were not capable of doing in Mills County."

The witness was on the stand for quite a while because he ventured an opinion as to the time of death, yet performed none of the tests described in the manuals for arriving at that determination. He testified that she had died sometime between midnight and four o'clock in the morning. The time frame could have been reduced had the appropriate tests been utilized.

Of some significance, he did testify that the victim's hands were not 'bagged' to preserve any evidence of skin scrapings beneath her nails that may have been attributed to her attacker. Generally it is standard procedure for plastic bags to be placed and secured on the hands of an assault victim to preserve such evidence. "I guess I just forgot to do it."

And so ended what Joseph considered the most successful day of trial.

CHAPTER FIFTEEN

The next morning, Joseph read in the *Milltown Reporter* about the testimony of Dr. Shieve under Stan Marten's byline, and the banner **MEDICAL EVIDENCE CONTESTED IN TRIAL**.

MILLTOWN—Defense attorney Patrick Joseph questioned the precision of determinations made by medical investigators in the stabbing death of June Westlock. Joseph represents Jimmy Takas of Milltown, who is on trial in the county Common Pleas Court for Westlock's murder. The defense attorneys challenged the ability of two medical witnesses to identify the weapon used and the time of death.

One witness, Dr. Jonathan A. Shieve of the Cuyahoga County Coroner's Office bristled at Joseph's line of questioning, but had to acknowledge he couldn't identify with certainty the time of death or the weapon used. The prosecution has not produced the murder weapon.

In his opening statement, Joseph said Westlock's murder is not yet solved. The prosecution claims Takas killed Westlock while attempting rape. Joseph was able to secure from Shieve that his autopsy produced no evidence of rape or sexual activity. Shieve stated that Westlock's death was caused by numerous stab wounds, the most serious to her back, piercing the victim's aorta, causing internal bleeding that lead to exsanguination—bleeding to death. Joseph questioned the shape, length and depth of the wound, asking if the type of weapon could be determined with certainty. "These things are not black and white," Shieve said, "it's just a best judgment."

Challenged by Joseph as to the methodology of determining the time of death, Shieve said, "Calculating the time of death is fraught with difficulties. There is no absolute way to determine time of death."

Attorney Terry Bernow asked similar questions of Mills County Coroner, that resulted in the same type of hedging responses.

Joseph had lost track of the number of days spent in trial. Fortunately, Della did not. She kept the office going, only asking questions of Joseph when absolutely necessary. At the end of a day, she would wait patiently in the office for his return and put in front of him letters, checks or documents that needed signing—which he signed without reading. He had absolute confidence in her. She gave orders to the others in the office like a mother. Even the lawyers and arrogant clerks who were fascinated with their own importance—after all, they would be lawyers soon—were sufficiently afraid of her that they jumped to their tasks. Joseph thought, *I'm not really needed around here—or at home for that matter.*

"How's it going, Pat? Are you all right?" Della asked solicitously. Everyone else had gone for the day. She and Joseph were sitting in companionable silence, he with his feet up as far as they would go and his eyes closed, Della in one of the client chairs, papers and files stacked in front of her.

"I don't know," he sighed. "We finished with the doctors today and Thuman will put one of the cops back on to get in all of their physical evidence tomorrow. Bet they finish within the next day or two—but I'm tired—too old."

"You look tired. Why don't you go on home. I'll lock up."

"I would if I had the energy. Let's just sit for a bit."

Della quietly picked up the files and moved to her office, just outside his door, closing it quietly behind her. She busied herself at the desk, waiting for Joseph to catch his short nap and leave. Terry stuck his head in and asked if he could talk to Joseph for a couple of minutes. Della said, "Only if it's really important. He's exhausted."

"Nothing that can't wait until tomorrow. I'm going now. Tell him goodnight for me."

Joseph had heard the whispered conversation outside his office door and roused himself enough to put his feet to the floor. Swiveling around in his chair, he looked at his pigs. They returned the look, smiling as usual, but studying him carefully.

Lumbering to his feet, he called, "Time to leave, Della. Let's get the hell out of here."

* * *

Somewhat refreshed by a good night's sleep, following one of Mary's special dinners, which included one of her delicious apple pies, Joseph was ready to take on whatever Thuman had to offer. Mary was without a doubt the best pie maker in the world. It was the only area of cooking in which she could compete with her mother. Joseph sorely missed the pork chops Mary's mother made on Sundays. Food well prepared and served always improved Joseph's mood.

By arrangement, Joseph met Terry at the courthouse. Together they went to the little conference room reserved for them and their client as early as possible. Jimmy was already there with his constant guard companion. "How you doing, Jimmy?" Terry asked.

"Okay, I guess. It's kind of hard listening to everything in there and not knowing what's gonna happen to me. I feel bad about June. Hearing what she must've gone through is awful. If I did that, I deserve to die."

This was about the longest speech Jimmy had delivered since the trial began.

"Are you remembering anything?" Joseph asked.

"Not really. I see blood…I see June with her back to me…I feel myself being really mad…but I don't see nothing else…. I just don't know…" By the end of the sentence, Jimmy was crying, hands over his eyes—real tears falling.

Joseph wished he knew what truly happened. He also wished with all his heart that he could say something to set free the poor, wretched soul.

He could not, so said to the guard, "Would you mind taking him to the bathroom before you bring him into the courtroom so he can wash his face and catch his breath? We'll be in there waiting."

The guard, sympathetic and friendly to Joseph, nodded and led Jimmy from the room.

Moving into the courtroom, the elderly lawyer chatted quietly with Terry, noticing the rows of seats already filled. The Takas family at one end of the pews and the Westlock family at the other. They never talked or looked at each other. If one family member's glance happened to make contact with that of a member of the other family, hoods dropped over their eyes and their expressions blanked as though staring into space. Joseph hurt for both families, even though it was clear the Westlock family had little love for him.

The prosecution team was already in place and Lieutenant-Detective Tells was in the witness chair. The judge entered the courtroom and called for the jury. Everyone seemed to be moving and talking slowly this morning.

Judge Crider nodded for Thuman to proceed. His assistant, Anne Dronke, stood and began asking the detective to identify certain objects, photographs, and various pieces of physical evidence the prosecution wanted admitted. Joseph allowed things to proceed for some time, until the State attempted to introduce a shirt that had been obtained from Jimmy Takas' house.

"Your honor, I have to make an objection at this time."

"Please come to sidebar, Mr. Joseph."

"As Your Honor knows, the shirt was taken from Mr. Takas' house because it does have a bloodstain on it. But it was determined that the blood was not that of the victim. Clearly the shirt is not relevant and will only lead to confuse and bias the jury."

"Well, Mr. Joseph, I am sure you will be able to bring out on cross-examination that BCI determined the blood was not that of June Westlock. Since it was taken by the police, the jury is entitled to see it."

"For God's sake, Judge. You know damn well that the jury isn't going to remember what any of the technical witnesses says—they'll just see the shirt and make assumptions that certainly won't be fair to Jimmy."

241

"Don't use that kind of language in my courtroom. You heard my ruling. Let's go."

How many prosecutors?

On and on it went. Knives of all types found at various places—the Westlock home, Knedder's car, Jimmy's house—were brought in, none of which were identifiable as the murder weapon. The judge allowed them in.

Again Joseph arose to protest. "Your Honor, I must object. The prosecutor is bringing things into the courtroom that are clearly not relevant and never tied in to the killing of Ms. Westlock.. He is bringing them in bags marked with his assumptions. It is unfair to Mr. Takas for the jury to be allowed to consider those assumptions without any evidence in support of them."

"Mr. Joseph, I told you not to state the reasons for your objections before the jury. If you have something to say, do so at sidebar. Objection overruled."

"Then may we approach.?"

"No. I have ruled."

"May the record reflect a continuing objection," then mumbling under his breath, "to your bias."

"The record will reflect your objection. But if you want me to hear something, you will have to speak louder."

"I will—if I want you to hear."

Animosity getting out of control, Terry feared Joseph's temper and knew he would have to calm him down. He whispered, "For a guy that says he scared to try these cases, you're getting pretty feisty. Take it easy. Your face is red all the way to the top of your bald head. Do you want me to handle the cross-examination?"

"No, I'll do it." Then pausing to breathe more deeply, he added, "But you're right, of course. I am really getting pissed."

Joseph walked slowly towards his spot behind the jury, calming himself, then looked at the witness, "Lieutenant Tells, seems like you been there for a long time. I'll try to make it short, but I do have a few questions. You said that when you first entered the Westlock home, you saw Mr. Knedder, who you knew, is that correct?"

"Yes."

"How did you know him?"

"He's been around for years and everyone in law enforcement in this town knows him."

"Can you tell us why he is so well known to the police?"

"Objection sustained, Mr. Joseph."

"I didn't hear an objection, Your Honor."

"You heard my ruling."

Joseph changed the subject, thinking, *It must be pretty obvious to the jury that Knedder is a bad guy. No way the judge is going to let me get it in. Guess this is the best I can do. May as well move on.*

There were pictures of ashtrays in the living room where Knedder sat when the police arrived. Joseph asked how many cigarette butts were in the ashtray—how many un-smoked cigarettes in Knedder's pocket—was a count done? It wasn't. He asked about the mercury vapor light that lit Westlock's backyard—he asked about the swing of the door into the utility room that came within inches of Ms. Westlock's head—all of which the Detective answered exactly as Joseph wanted.

Then he asked, "Lieutenant, you found an address book beneath the phone in the living room, did you not?"

"Yes, that's true."

"Did you find any other phone book in the room—such as a city directory?"

"No, that was the only one we found."

"You recall Mr. Knedder's testimony about finding a couple of numbers—the neighbor and Jimmy Takas' in the phone book when he made calls that night."

"Yes."

"Would you please look through the phone book—that is the address book you found—before you and see if you can find a number for Jimmy?"

"You want me to do that now?"

"I would have thought you had already done it," Joseph suggested innocently, still drawing a frown from Thuman and the judge, "but if you haven't, we can wait while you do it now."

The detective paged through the address book, finally looking up and saying, "It ain't there."

Joseph continued, "You didn't check the telephone for fingerprints, did you?"

"No."

"The chair that was obviously thrown across the kitchen floor had metal parts—did you check those for fingerprints?"

"No, sir."

"Did you do a count of the number of cigarettes in the ashtray and the number of cigarettes in the pack in Mr. Knedder's pocket to see if the total amounted to what should have been in the new pack he said he purchased?"

"No, sir."

"Did you check to see how much light entered into the utility room from the mercury vapor light in the backyard when the backdoor was open?"

"Well. There was some, I can't say exactly how much."

"Did you have any trouble seeing Ms. Westlock's body when you walked in to the utility room?"

"Well, no, but it was kind of dark. The backdoor was closed."

"You didn't open the backdoor to re-create the situation described by Knedder, as though walking in to see if you could see the body that was within inches of the door?"

"No, sir."

"The men's clothing you found in the house, did you make any effort to determine its ownership?"

"Mr. Knedder said they belonged to him."

"Did you check to see if they were his size?"

"No, sir."

The witness was questioned and re-questioned again and again by both the prosecutor and Joseph—Joseph's questioned designed to show the inadequacy and incompetence of the investigation. He hoped that some of the answers, and more particularly the questions, created reasonable doubt in the mind of at least one of the jurors. Lieutenant Tells as the officer in charge of the investigation was excused after several hours on the stand. He returned to the prosecution trial table.

Judge Crider, after a brief recess, said to Thuman, "Call your next witness."

Anne Dronke rose and called the local doctor who had signed the death certificate. He actually knew nothing about the case, hadn't seen the body, and hadn't visited the scene. He signed the certificate based on information supplied by third persons who talked to the police and the Cuyahoga County Coroner. Joseph guessed that he was called only to prove that June Westlock was dead, which seemed ludicrous to him. So out of curiosity he asked, "Doctor, why was it necessary for you to sign the death certificate, particularly since you had never seen the deceased and knew nothing about her injuries or death?"

"Well, it is the only way for a death certificate to be issued. The deceased can't be buried without a death certificate."

"Thank you, Doctor, I have no more questions," Joseph said, while thinking, *God save us all from bureaucracy and bureaucrats,* but to perfect the record, added, "May we have a sidebar, Your Honor?"

At sidebar, Joseph said, "I move that the entire testimony of this witness be stricken—particularly that portion of it that relates to the time of death as included in the death certificate. It is an effort on the part of the State to establish the time of death to coincide with Mr. Takas' presence at the scene. The basis for this motion is that the witness' entire testimony is founded on hearsay, not his personal knowledge. He assumed certain things to be true because that was what someone else told him. In fact, it's the worst kind of hearsay because the information he obtained is from third persons—not even from those that secured the information. Knowing he was wasting his breath, I would ask that the jury be instructed to disregard any of this witness' testimony; and that the death certificate not be admitted into evidence."

"Overruled."

How many prosecutors?

*　　*　　*

While waiting for the next witness to be called, a voice from the rear of the courtroom could be heard, "Your son raped my daughter—ain't you proud of him?"

There was no response except for the sound of shuffling in seats. The members of the jury craned their necks to see what was happening—everyone looking toward the Westlock side of the room, whose occupants were staring at Jimmy Takas' cringing parents.

Judge Crider immediately excused the jury for a brief recess. She stayed on the bench as they filed out. As soon as they left she said, "Before the next witness is called, I want to talk to the spectators. So far you have been behaving properly, coming and going quietly in the courtroom—showing proper regard for the legal process. You have been quiet and respectful in the courtroom—as you should be. But it has come to my attention that there have been some comments passing back and forth between some of you, and now I heard a totally inappropriate remark. I won't have trouble in my courtroom and I won't have trouble in the hall outside of my courtroom. If you folks can't behave, I will do what is necessary to see to it you do. That includes clearing all of you spectators from the courtroom, findings of contempt and possible jail time. It could also result in a mistrial, which would require we do this all over again with some of you being permanently excluded from the courtroom. If that's what you want, so be it. Your behavior so far has been fine. Let's keep it that way. Do I make myself clear?"

Though her demeanor was polite, no one doubted she meant what she said. Without waiting for a response from the crowded courtroom, she said to her bailiff, "Call the jury back please, Nancy."

The next several witnesses were police officers to establish the chain of evidence from the crime scene to the Bureau of Criminal Investigation and the criminalist from BCI. In a criminal trial the State must be able to show an unbroken chain of any item of evidence from the crime scene to the courtroom. This is called the "chain of evidence." If an item can't be accounted for in this unbroken chain, it must be excluded from the trial. In this case, the chain was being used to establish that Jimmy Takas' fingerprint and partial palm print were found in blood on the drier in Ms. Westlock's home.

The criminalist, during his testimony, did make it clear, however, "We were unable to ascertain whose blood was on the drier beneath the print. Nor can we say how long the print had been there."

That was the best Joseph could hope for; however, it did give him the opportunity of again objecting to the print and blood being entered into evidence. He knew his objection would be overruled, but he was protecting the record for appeal, if necessary. One of the most important tasks for a criminal defense lawyer is to protect the record. Failure to do so is considered a waiver of a defendant's Constitutional rights—something which Joseph would never do.

After all of this was accomplished, the State called Jimmy's employer at the time of the incident. He testified that Jimmy had been in his employ at the time June Westlock was killed; and, in fact, Jimmy worked the Monday and Tuesday following the death of Ms. Westlock. "Jimmy came to work on Tuesday and left with the police. He called me later that day and said he had to take a few days off. He never returned to work."

On cross-examination, Joseph had the witness tell the jury that, as Jimmy's immediate supervisor, he thought his behavior on the Monday following June's death was perfectly normal. Then on Tuesday, he began to appear like he was getting upset about something, but didn't say what. That was the last day he worked. Joseph also secured from the witness that Jimmy had several cuts on his hand—always did—because of the nature of the work.

Again, this witness was only on the stand for a short time. It being the middle of the afternoon, the judge asked Thuman if he had any more witnesses. "Just one, Your Honor."

"Well, let's get to it."

"The State will call Laura Takas."

Joseph would have loved to object, arguing that Laura Takas had been the wife of the defendant and thus anything she had to say would be privileged—a spouse cannot testify against her husband—unfortunately, they had been divorced, and he knew her testimony was going to be allowed. This had been argued out earlier. Of course, the judge ruled in favor of the State. Again, though, the elderly lawyer objected—to preserve the record.

Thuman decided to ask the questions of Ms. Takas himself. Joseph knew it was going to be hurtful for Jimmy, so he whispered to Jimmy, "Take it easy. Don't let it get to you no matter what she says. Okay?"

Jimmy just nodded, saying, "I'm all right." Joseph wasn't convinced—Jimmy didn't look all right.

"Ma'am. Please state your full name and spell your last name for the record." Thuman was standing on the far side of the jury box so the witness would have to keep her voice up.

"My name is Laura Takas. T-A-K-A-S."

Her blond hair hung loose, falling over her face. From time to time she automatically pushed it back—it never stayed there. Slight of build, she couldn't have weighed one hundred pounds. She was so small, she could hardly be seen in the witness box. It appeared that was the way she wanted it. Uncomfortable about being there, she continually glanced apologetically Jimmy's way. He didn't notice. Dressed in a simple house dress, she was clean, plain and pitiful. Very pretty in a childish way…didn't look at all like the mother of two.

"I'm standing way back here so that if I hear you, the jury will too. Okay?

The witness nodded an affirmative response.

"That's the other thing. You have to answer in words so the reporter can get it all down, okay?"

It was obvious to Joseph that Thuman's eye-blinking was exaggerated, because he was excited about this witness.

Thuman then asked Mrs. Takas to talk about her marriage to Jimmy, their children and their divorce. She explained to him, "We are still friendly, mostly because of the children. Jimmy has always been a good father and made most of his support payments—even giving me extra money when he has it. He visits the girls as often as allowed. They love him and love to be with his mother—their grandmother."

Thuman then asked about a telephone call made by the witness to Jimmy shortly after the death of June Westlock.

"Which call are you talking about?" she asked. "The one where I told him about the sergeant wanting to talk to him or the one when we talked about the girls?"

"Why don't you tell us about both?" Thuman said.

"First, after the police called me to ask Jimmy about the night June died, I called him at his mom's house and told him they wanted to talk to him. He said, 'Okay.' Later, I wanted to tell him not to see the girls for a while until things got cleared up. Jimmy has visitation rights with our girls. I called to tell him I didn't think it was safe for him to see the kids at this time. He agreed and said that I should just tell the kids he was sick that weekend and would see them later—like, he could pick them up the following weekend. I said, like, that was fine 'cause things should cool down by then."

"Did you talk about anything else during that conversation?" Thuman asked.

"Well, we just wanted to talk."

"Did you have any more telephone conversations with him about that time?"

"Yes," very quietly.

Thuman, eye working, said, "Please keep your voice up. Tell us about that call?"

"He called me towards the middle of that week. He was crying and very emotional. 'They think I killed her,' he told me, and he said he was gonna commit suicide—you know, like, kill himself."

"Do you know where he was calling from?"

"He said he was where we had taken our last vacation together—that was in Florida, we took the girls to that Disney place—so I asked, 'Are you in Florida?' and he said he was."

"What else was said?"

"I was, like, trying to talk him out of killing himself so asked why—what was the matter. He went, like, you know, 'They said I killed her and I don't remember nothing like that and they're gonna kill me. I'm just gonna do it myself—can't stand this...' and he was crying all the time. He said he remembered there was blood on his shirt, so I asked him about a knife. He said he didn't know about no knife. He just woke up that morning and had blood on his T-shirt."

"Did you ask him about the shirt?"

"Yes, I asked where the shirt was and he said he didn't know. That maybe his ma had washed it."

"Do you know if it was ever found?"

"No. I told the police and they searched his house. There wasn't any bloody shirt there."

"Did you hear from him again?"

"Yes—about a week later."

"Tell us about that call."

"Well, I was just glad he wasn't dead. He hadn't killed himself and sounded a little better. I told him about the article in the newspaper and that they said he was wanted for June's murder. He asked me to read the article to him—so I did. And he said, 'I guess they'll be coming for me. I'll probably see you soon.'"

"Did you tell this to the police?"

"Yes, Lieutenant Tells," and she nodded toward the detective sitting at the trial table with Anne Dronke, "kept asking me about talking to Jimmy. So I told him about the calls."

"Did you tell him everything?"

"No—not everything." By this time Laura's voice was getting softer and her breathing more shallow. Joseph could tell she wasn't far from tears. She kept looking toward Jimmy and when she caught his eye, mouthed, "I'm so sorry."

Thuman, showing a little compassion for the young lady's obvious discomfort, which was totally out of character, said, "I have no further questions."

The Court ordered a brief recess so the witness could compose herself. The jury was called back within five minutes and Joseph began his cross-examination. He avoided looking at Jimmy, but could tell from the sounds he was making his emotions were close to the surface.

"Mrs. Takas, I'm not going to keep you very long. I just have a couple of questions. You know my name is Pat Joseph, and Terry Bernow and I are representing your former husband. You and I have talked before, haven't we?"

"Yes, sir. I came to your office when you asked me to. We talked about the case."

"Thank you. Now, I would like you to tell the jury about your marriage to Jimmy."

"What do you mean?"

"Well, tell us about your children and how Jimmy got along with them.?"

"We had two girls. They loved their daddy and he loved them. He saw them frequently even after we were divorced. He supported them pretty good, but he didn't always have work and was a little behind in his payments. But he always tried to make up for it and give us extra when he had some."

"Can you tell the jury, was Jimmy kind and gentle towards the children?"

"Oh, yes. He always enjoyed being with them and they with him."

"Do you have an opinion as to whether or not it was in Jimmy's character to kill Ms. Westlock.?"

"I'm not sure what you mean, but Jimmy couldn't hurt anyone. He wasn't that kind of person. Until I got the phone call from the police and talked to Jimmy, I couldn't believe it. When he talked to me about the shirt, I began to wonder—but I still don't believe he could have done it. I didn't want him to see the girls then, but that was because I was scared of what someone else would do, not Jimmy."

"Did you every doubt Jimmy?"

"Well, when he ran away, I did wonder a little. Not so much about June, but about his gonna kill himself. He was crying a lot on the telephone and said he was gonna kill himself. He just broke up with his girlfriend…he'd been doing a lot of drugs…he drank too much.…"

"And you were aware of that?"

"Yes."

"And was he having trouble with his parents?"

"Yes, sir."

"And were you aware of that?"

"Yes, Jimmy told me about it."

"And you had just told him he couldn't see his children?"

"Yes, sir."

"And he told you the police suspected him of committing a murder?"

"Yes…" Her voice faded as she recalled the buildup of problems Jimmy was facing at that time.

"And is it fair to say it was the combination of all these things that caused Jimmy to run away?"

"Yes, I believe it was," the tears falling freely as she looked towards Jimmy with obvious sympathy—her heart breaking for him.

Joseph thought, *She still loves him. Drugs kill more than people*, and shaking his head sadly, he said, "No more questions, Your Honor," and sat down.

Thuman leaped to his feet and began asking questions before Joseph had settled himself.

"Ms. Takas, has the defendant ever struck you?"

"Objection, your honor," Joseph said. "There have been no questions concerning their relationship. I avoided that line of questioning in order to avoid any embarrassment to this witness."

"Mr. Joseph," Judge Crider said, "how many times do I have to remind you not to argue your objections before the jury. Objection overruled."

Joseph shrugged and returned to his seat, mumbling beneath his breath, *It sure would be nice if she treated me and Thuman the same.*

"I'll restate the question," Thuman said, obviously so excited he made no effort to hide his twitching eye from the jury. "On cross-examination you were asked about the kind and gentle nature of the defendant," to which the witness nodded.

"Were there any occasions when he directed violence towards you?"

"Well, yes," the witness whispered, looking towards Jimmy as if to say, *I'm sorry.* Then added, "We've had one or two arguments that got pretty heated and he did slap me once."

"No more questions," Thuman said, sitting.

Joseph arose slowly from his seat and remained standing at the trial table—not taking his usual stance behind the jury. "Ms. Takas, I'm really sorry that we have been forced to talk about this." Ignoring the judge's frown, he continued, "The incident you're talking about—when Jimmy slapped you—that was as a result of Jimmy finding out about an act of infidelity on your part during your marriage to him?"

Her whispered "Yes" was enough to embarrass everyone in the court. The jurors didn't want to look at Laura Takas as she sat sobbing in the witness seat, but they did glance at Jimmy—their faces reflecting sympathy or, at least, a little more understanding.

"I have no more questions, Your Honor."

Judge Crider told the witness she was free to leave. As Laura Takas was leaving the room, she walked behind Jimmy and placed a hand on his shoulder, mouthing again, tears streaming down her childlike cheeks, "I'm sooo sorry."

Into the silence that permeated the courtroom, Judge Crider said, "Ladies and gentlemen, we seem to have reached a good stopping place. It's almost four-thirty, so we may as well quit for the day. Remember, don't form an opinion until the case is finally submitted to you and don't discuss the case or allow anyone to discuss it with you or in your presence. We'll see you back here at eight thirty tomorrow morning."

Joseph stood as the jury shuffled out. Jimmy tugged on Joseph's coat sleeve. "Mr. Joseph, Mr. Joseph, I have to talk to you."

"Okay, Jimmy. But not now. I think the State is going to rest. I don't think we want to put on any witnesses, but Terry and I will have to consider our options and what is the best trial strategy. I also have to work on my final argument. I'll have Terry come see you as soon as we are out of here. Now, smile at your mom and dad—try to relax. I'll be real busy tonight so Terry will come and see you. You let him know what you want and he'll call me later. I'll see you tomorrow."

"But, Mr. Joseph, I really need to talk to you," Jimmy whispered.

The elderly lawyer had never seen Jimmy so animated, so he patted his shoulder. "I promise to talk to you before court tomorrow. You talk to Terry tonight. He'll be in touch with me. Let's go."

* * *

Joseph gathered his papers and walked slowly from the courtroom—he was the last to leave. Even though it was not yet five o'clock, the sky was beginning to darken. Leaving the building, he held his briefcase in one hand while grasping the center rail of the steps with the other. There were twelve concrete steps down to ground level and he felt every one. He was tired. His mind working as he trudged slowly across the square to his office, he failed to notice the lack of people on the street or the laughing children in the square—the things in which he usually found particular joy. He didn't even wonder that the crossing guard had already gone for the day.

Entering his building through the front door, he walked into his office without calling for Della—unusual. Standing in the doorway of his office, he was too tired to walk behind the table he cherished, instead slumping onto the leather couch and propping his feet on the oak coffee table in front of it. He glanced at his pigs—their smiles sympathetic.

*　　*　　*

Sliding into a sleep-like state, he thought, *Have to prepare my argument—too much needs to be said—they have to understand.*

Ladies and gentlemen of the jury, he thought, sinking into the soft leather of the couch. In his mind's eye, he studied the face of each juror—faces he would never forget. Standing directly at the center of the rail separating himself from the jury, he looked toward where the female jurors were clustered. Moving slightly toward them, he began, *We have heard a bruising and vehement diatribe by the prosecutor, telling you how you must find Jimmy Takas guilty of this most heinous crime. I understand the prosecutor thinks he is just doing his job, but there is so much more we must do before we can render judgment in this case. There is a certain morality by which we raise and teach our children to be respectful, decent adults.*

Joseph moved to his right and looked at the male jurors, saying, *There is a certain morality by which we raise and teach our children before we can say that they have grown to adulthood as responsible contributors to society.*

Moving further to the right and standing directly in front of the black, male juror, he said, *There is a certain morality by which we raise and teach our children before we can say how proud we are of them as representatives of our society or culture.*

Della opened the door to Joseph's office quietly and saw him resting peacefully on the couch, hearing only soft zzzz's. Backing from the office, she closed the door, thinking it was the first time in weeks he looked at peace. He needed his rest.

In Joseph's dream, he moved back to the center of the jury box, resting his hands lightly on the rail and sighed, *I don't think we can ever understand the cast of characters that appeared before us during this trial. Night people—people who live for drugs, alcohol, sex, personal gratification—people who feel no responsibility...have no respect for themselves or society. People who in my day would have been called dregs—the lowest of the low,* saying all this while watching the faces of the jurors. His mind's eye told him that heads were nodding and faces showed understanding.

Joseph straightened and, in a louder voice, said, *None of this is to say that June Westlock should have been treated as she was—none of this is to say she should have been so violently murdered—none of this is to say that the person who murdered her should go unpunished. But we must keep in mind that we cannot treat lightly the responsibility of the State to establish beyond a reasonable doubt who is responsible for the killing. Just because the people involved are less than the model citizens we would like them to be, this does not relieve the State from doing its job properly.*

The elderly lawyer began in his mind to talk at length about the various characters who had the opportunity and motive to kill June Westlock. *It is not our job here to decide who killed June. But it is certainly a question that each of us wants answered. I must admit, however, that those words keep playing in my mind like lyrics of a well-known tune—Who killed June?—Who killed June?*

Body relaxing more and more into the old leather couch, Joseph's dreams deepened. *Who killed June? he asked. Who hated her enough to take her life? Who had a motive? Who had the opportunity? Was Jimmy the only one? Or was it one of the other seemingly endless cast of characters we have heard about during this trial?*

Clarence Knedder, vehemently jealous of June, seems the most obvious. In fact, he was the first person the police suspected. Why and when that suspicion was discarded, we will never know. He admitted on the witness stand that he had some problems with the truth, especially where the police are concerned. We learned that he has a violent streak to his nature, so much so that June was frightened of him and, in fact, had secured a peace warrant—a court order that he not come within five hundred feet of her or her home. An order he consistently ignored. He admittedly drove back and forth in front of her house time and time again. On the night she was killed he came to her house in the wee hours of the morning, parked his car a half mile from her house so it wouldn't be seen, stole through the backyards and entered the house through a backdoor—a door he claimed had a broken lock. He then told us he went through that backdoor five times within inches of June's head but didn't see her. He told us he saw the house in a condition of dishabille, with baskets, vegetables and chairs strewn around—none of which caused him to be suspicious enough to look around thoroughly. That story is impossible to believe! with a great deal of force.

He also told us he touched nothing in the laundry room, and yet, when the police arrived they found the backdoor chained. How did that happen? There are just too many holes in his story. Did he kill June? You saw him on the witness stand and learned from his own mouth he certainly had the time to do it—no matter how vehemently he denied it. Don't his words alone tell us that there is reasonable doubt in Jimmy's case? glancing at the black juror with sympathetic understanding, knowing the embarrassment he was feeling about the road a member of his race had taken—feeling shame even though he had nothing to do with the dishonor Knedder brought.

Joseph then, in his mind, talked about Andy Little, who, with a sexual criminal record, claimed to have seen everything while sitting on his parents' porch across the street—who had that evening searched from bar to bar for a lady with whom to spend the evening, describing what he was looking for. The description, coincidently, matched perfectly that of the deceased.

Let's look a little further in an effort to answer the question—Who killed June? Andy Little, with an admitted sexual criminal record, was looking for female companionship on the night June died. What was most interesting in his testimony was how much of what he said in this courtroom differed from the statement originally given by him to the police. What is more surprising is that the changes coincided precisely with the prosecutor's theory of the case. A coincidence or an intentional act by a man that has little regard for the truth? What did Mr. Little have to hide? Did his search for sex from a woman that looked like June move him to June's doorstep? Did she reject him?

Did such rejection give him a motive to do her harm? Did he fear that his acts during the wee hours of that night, along with his record, might come back to haunt him? Was there a motive? Certainly there was opportunity. Did he kill June? But of more importance to you and your job, do his testimony, evasions and lies create reasonable doubt as far as Jimmy is concerned?

Settling more comfortably in his sleep, his thoughts or dreams turned to another witness, Bub Draco. He talked about him to the jury, describing him—*A neighbor who was upset with June because she had sent Jimmy to his house. In the middle of the night he wandered over to June's house for some unexplained reason "to talk with her" and had a beer with Knedder.*

He talked about Cockroach, June's supplier, and the many "friends" she welcomed to her house to make use of her generosity in providing recreational drugs. He could not provide motives or names, but such people were neither stable nor adverse to breaking the law.

Or was there some stranger we have not heard about amongst the many acquaintances of her ilk that may have had reasons we may never understand to kill June? Again, we are not obligated to solve the case—the only question we must answer is, do these facts provide reasonable doubt as to whether or not Jimmy is guilty of this heinous crime?

Turning slightly on the couch, his mind shifted gears to the wounds on poor June's body, so he talked about the three different types of wounds found, and how some of them were delivered after she died. *So much confusion,* he argued, *is not amenable to the simple answer the State demands—that you convict Jimmy Takas of this crime.*

Joseph heard a soft snort and realized it was his own snoring that awakened him. Thus far, he felt the argument he dreamed made sense, but he knew something was missing. He lay there awake for some time, thinking about what he may have missed that the jury must know about. Just as he began to doze off again, he remembered.

How many other unanswered questions are there? The coroner tells us there were defensive wounds on June's hands. She must have struggled with her assailant. The textbook of the pathologist tells us it is extremely important to examine the fingernails of the victim for foreign particles. The coroner tells us, 'I saw no reason to scrape her nails.' Why? It is common knowledge that fingerprints often point to an assailant.

Remember that the lieutenant told us none of the items strewn around the kitchen were examined.

Also unanswered—how and who locked the backdoor? Where was the telephone book that Knedder said he used to find Jimmy's number?—and on and on. Was no effort made to answer these questions because they didn't fit the State's theory?

Now we must address the most damning piece of evidence. Not the bloody shirt we haven't seen. Remember, Jimmy's ex-wife talked about blood on a T-shirt. We heard from Jimmy's employer, who testified that Jimmy had cuts on his hand almost every day from the work he did. Blood on a T-shirt is neither unusual nor incriminating. But the State has told you how Jimmy's bloody fingerprint or palm print on the dryer is incriminating. And it could be. The most significant thing about that though is the State's inability to say whose blood lay beneath the print. We know Jimmy was there many times to do drugs—we know they did drugs on that very same dryer—we know Jimmy's hand was cut that night—we know Knedder's hand was also cut and bleeding that night. The State has not—and cannot, according to its witnesses—tell you exactly when that print was placed on the drier.

Now then, if such evidence is consistent with guilt, it is equally consistent with innocence. If an innocent explanation is available, the State has failed to prove its case beyond a reasonable doubt—and you must acquit.

*   *   *

Joseph was brought back from his musing about what he considered a very satisfactory final argument by the sound of a muted conversation outside his door. He recognized Terry saying, "Mrs. Raven, I really need to talk to Mr. Joseph," and Della responding, "He's resting. I will not disturb him. Call him later."

Joseph pushed himself up from the couch, walked to the door, and said, "It's all right, Della. Come on in, Terry. I feel pretty confident tonight. In fact, I wanted to talk to you about our strategy. I don't think we need to put on any witnesses. All of the exhibits we prepared have been made available to the jury. I don't think there is anything we want to add. Reasonable doubt..." Joseph's voice trailed off as he observed the expression on Terry's face. "Terry, what's wrong?"

"Mr. Joseph, you won't believe this," Terry began before Joseph could re-seat himself. He was so agitated, he had difficulty getting words out. "Jimmy wants to change his plea to 'guilty.' His ex-wife's testimony got to him. He couldn't stand what she was put through. He said he still doesn't remember that night, but doesn't want to be convicted of aggravated murder...if we can work out a deal for straight murder, he wants to take it...."

"For God's sake, Terry, did you try to dissuade him?"

"Yes, sir. He wouldn't talk to me about his decision. He said he made his mind up and just didn't want to talk about it. He expects us to do what he wants. In fact, he said if we don't, he'll fire us and ask the judge to appoint different lawyers."

"We'd better go talk with him. See what the hell is going on in his mind," Joseph said.

Terry responded, "Don't think it'll do any good. But we got to try."

Della said, "Go ahead. I'll lock up. Everyone else is gone anyway. See you tomorrow."

Joseph turned to his secretary, knowing there was no way to express his appreciation for her loyalty. "Goodnight, Della. Thanks for everything."

Della let Joseph and Terry out the front door and locked it behind them. Joseph, finally taking notice of his surroundings, saw that the snow had melted and the temperature was much more pleasant than it had been for the past several days. The only people on the square were those heading for the deli or the arcade for a drink before going home. It was too early for dinner customers at the *Round Table*. Terry said nothing as they hurried across the square. Joseph didn't want to use his breath for conversation—he was in a hurry to reach Jimmy.

At the jail, they went through the routine procedure to gain access. "Hi, Wanda. We need to see Jimmy. Will you call us in?"

"Hi, Mr. Joseph. I'm just getting ready to leave but I'll get one of the CO's to let you in. How's Mrs. Joseph? Still making those quilts?"

"Yep. Won't quit until she has one for each of her grandbabies—and they keep coming."

By this time, one of the correction officers had arrived to escort Terry and Joseph to the third-floor walkway. He asked if they wanted Jimmy removed from the community area for private conversation.

"No," Joseph responded. "We'll talk to him in the walkway. If you would, though, please keep the others in their cells so they won't bother us."

Several other prisoners in the area called, "Hi, Mr. Joseph."

"How's it hanging?"

"See me before you leave, need to talk to you."

Joseph waved to all of them with a smile, saying, "Can't tonight. Too busy, but I'll see you soon."

When they had some little privacy, Jimmy began , "Mr. Joseph, I—"

Joseph waved him off. "Mr. Bernow told me what you want to do. I don't want you to say anything. I won't ever make a prediction about what a jury will do, but I got to tell you, we have a good jury and they've seemed sympathetic throughout. I do know it is impossible for you to be convicted of aggravated murder—the elements aren't there. Judge Crider will have to grant a rule-29 motion and dismiss that part of the charge. She'll allow the jury to consider the charge of straight murder and there is a chance you will be convicted of that—but chances are good that you will be home before Thanksgiving. In fact, in my mind, you have better than a fifty-fifty chance of spending the holidays with your family."

"I really don't care, Mr. Joseph. I've been here several months now. The food is regular. I can watch television—don't have to worry about anything. I've dried out and don't even crave drugs or booze no more. There's drugs here all the time if I wanted them, but I don't touch them. I just don't want no more of this—want to do my time and get out."

"When you say, 'do my time,' you do know that the minimum sentence will be fifteen years to life?"

"I know—and don't care."

"Jimmy, for God's sake, don't say anything more tonight. I want you to think about what I've said—you've got a pretty good chance of getting out, and you can't be convicted of anything more than what you want to plead to—we'll finish this conversation before court tomorrow. Think about your daughters and not being able to see them grow up. Think about your parents and what they've gone through for you. Just think about everything. Talk to your mom and dad before you make up your mind. See how they feel about it—listen to them. Promise?" almost pleading.

Joseph paused to cath his breath and finally said, "Terry and I will see you in the morning—about eight thirty. Good night."

Jimmy started to say something. Joseph shushed him. "I said good night," turned and walked away, Terry following without saying a word.

As they walked from the jail, Joseph turned to Terry and said, "Want to stop for a beer, before we go home?"

Terry declined, "I promised my kids I'd be home for an early dinner and play some basketball with them tonight. They want to go to the rec center and always enjoy beating me. As a matter of fact, I enjoy it too. It relaxes me and makes me forget the daily shit. But if you think we need to talk, I'll go with you. Don't know what there is to talk about though."

God save me from a family man, Joseph thought as he trudged his way across the square to the parking lot behind his building, where his beat-up pickup truck waited. *I'll just have a Martini when I get home. Tonight I need one.*

*   *   *

Joseph woke earlier than usual the next morning. As he struggled up from his twisted bed clothes, he saw Mary sitting on the edge of the bed looking at him.

"My goodness, Pat, I didn't get a wink of sleep. You tossed and turned all night. You were mumbling and carrying on so it scared me half to death. I tried to wake you up a couple of times, but you'd go right back to sleep and start all over again."

"I think I'm as tired as you. If I did sleep, it sure wasn't restful. I presented my final argument to the jury at least a dozen times in a dozen different ways. I don't know if I'm ever going to be able to deliver it though—if I can't convince Jimmy… He wants to change his plea. I'm not sure why. He still insists he has no memory of that night. There is so much reasonable doubt in this case, Terry and I don't think we even have to put on a defense—"

Mary interrupted with, "I'm going down to start breakfast. Why don't you just get dressed. Don't worry about it—everything will work out—it always does…"

God, I wish I had her faith. Everything is so simple for her, Joseph thought as he started through his morning routine. While dressing, he yelled down the stairs to Mary, "Don't bother with breakfast for me. I'll grab a coffee and bagel at the deli. I want to glance through the paper before I see Jimmy."

The deli was crowded with early arrivals, but Joseph was able to find a table in the corner, where he could spread the *Reporter* before him while munching on a buttered bagel. As usual, Stan hadn't missed a thing and covered yesterday's testimony.

MILLTOWN—In the most emotional testimony thus far, the ex-wife of Jimmy Takas, who is on trial for the murder of June Westlock, tearfully recounted a telephone conversation with Takas the day after the killing. Shaking and with tears falling freely, Laura Takas said the call was very emotional and that "Jimmy said he wanted to kill himself." She testified that he had no memory of the incident; however, woke up and had blood all over his T-shirt. Shortly after saying that, Laura looked at Jimmy, seated several feet away from her at the defense table, and said, "Jimmy, I'm so sorry."

Prosecutor Thuman pressed her, asking, "Why did you say that?"

She responded with "He's the father of my children and I still love him. I can't believe he would hurt anyone," and then burst into tears.

In other testimony, more than 35 pieces of physical evidence were presented to the jury, including a bloodstained doorknob, chain, several knives, photographs of the deceased June Westlock, her bloodstained clothing and an assortment of other items found in the house where June was killed. The prosecution insists that Ms. Westlock was killed as a part of an attempted rape; however, the State's pathologist testified there was no semen found in or on Ms. Westlock and there was no evidence whatsoever of sexual activity.

Even though a number of knives have been introduced into evidence, none have been identified as the murder weapon. Lieutenant Richard Tells, the detective in charge of the investigation, and Sergeant Hilary Dale, of the homicide unit, both testified that they searched the entire house, including the roof and gutters of the house and several houses in the neighborhood as well as all the catch basis and sewers in the vicinity, finding nothing.

It is anticipated that the case will get to the jury by the end of today or tomorrow.

*　　*　　*

Terry met Joseph at the deli and shook his head no when Joseph asked if he wanted anything. They walked across the square to the courthouse and met Jimmy and his parents in the small conference room next to the courtroom. The room was hot and close, not designed to contain five people. Sweat broke out on Joseph's forehead as he tried to talk what he considered sense to Jimmy.

"Jimmy, listen to what Mr. Joseph is saying. He is honest and knows best," Jimmy's mother implored. His father sat silently, not knowing what to say to his only son.

The four of them sat in silence while Jimmy shook his head, "My mind is made up. I want to plead guilty—just make the deal for me that I told you to."

He listened to their arguments, face stoic. It was the first time Joseph had seen Jimmy so resolute—his mind made up. After spending as much time as they could with Jimmy, his mom and dad, they entered the courtroom. Terry Bernow asked Judge Crider's bailiff, "Nancy, could we see the judge in chambers before she starts this morning's session? It's important."

"I'll ask."

A few minutes later, the bailiff called the defense and prosecution teams into Judge Crider's office. "What is it now, Mr. Joseph?" impatiently.

Reluctantly Joseph began, "Your Honor, we might be able to work out a plea agreement. Since the State is unable to prove aggravation, Mr. Takas is prepared to enter a plea to simple murder in exchange for a sentence of fifteen years to life. I have to say I've tried unsuccessfully to talk him out of this. He has made it very clear to us," pointing to himself and Terry, "and his decision is against our advise. Last night he told Terry and me that was what he wanted to do. I persuaded him to wait until this morning, sleep on it and then talk to his mom and dad. The guard was kind enough to give them a few minutes alone in the witness room this morning, and even though they tried to talk him out of it, he still wants to change his plea. He continues to maintain that he has no memory of the night, and personally, I believe there is sufficient reasonable doubt to acquit him."

With Joseph's mouth still open to add more, Thuman interrupted and said, "Judge, the State will accept his change of plea and recommend the sentence, if it's all right with you."

Joseph noticed that Thuman's eye wasn't blinking and his mouth wasn't twitching, and thought, *Even though he's anxious to get a conviction, he seems awful happy about Jimmy's decision to plead.*

The judge looking incredulously from Joseph to Terry, said, "It's certainly all right with me, but I have to say I'm amazed. Joseph, I have never known you to cave like this. Are you sure you can't talk your client into finishing the trial?"

Shaking his head negatively, Joseph said, "Believe me, Judge, I tried. His mom and dad tried, Terry tried. He is adamant—I'm just not sure why, except that he did say he still loves Laura and couldn't stand seeing her put through what happened on the witness stand. He just wants it finished."

At Joseph's response, the judge continued, "If that's what you both want, it's a done deal. Now go on into court. I'll have Nancy bring in the jury. But first, let's get the court reporter in here. I want this all on the record."

When all gathered in the courtroom, Judge Crider entered, robes flowing around her. After calling everyone to order, she said, "For the record, the Court has been informed that the defendant wishes to change his plea from 'not guilty' to 'guilty' to the charge of murder. The State of Ohio is willing to dismiss the charge of aggravated murder. The Court will accept the plea if that is everyone's wish."

"The State is willing to accept the plea and dismiss the aggravated murder charge," this from Thuman, who was unable to keep the pleasure from creeping into his voice and spreading across his countenance. Joseph refused to look at Thuman, not wanting to see the satisfied smirk he knew was playing across the face of the prosecutor the elderly lawyer never wanted to see again.

"As I explained to the Court in chambers, Your Honor, we spoke to the defendant this morning and he expressed his wish to change his plea. He explained to me that the testimony relating to the blood on the T-shirt, the print on the dryer or washing machine, whichever—that he knew he was there that evening and, although he has no memory of the event, believes he must be responsible for the death of Ms. Westlock. And he now wants to change his plea. Terry and I must inform the Court, however, that the change of plea is against the advise of counsel. The defendant told us that if we wouldn't go along with his wishes, he would fire us and ask the Court to appoint substitute counsel. I am sorely tempted. "

At first the room was silent, the jurors and observers appeared stunned. Then members of the media stormed from the room. Chaos broke out. Judge Crider banged her gavel but it took several minutes for order to be restored. Finally Judge Crider asked, "Is that your wish, Mr. Takas?"

"Yes, ma'am," in a quiet voice.

"Before I can accept your change of plea, I will have to ask you some questions. You will have to answer those questions yourself, but you may discuss them with your attorney if you want. Please stand before the bench."

Usually a judge dismisses the jury before accepting a change of plea. Judge Crider did not. The jurors having lived with the case for so long and listening to so much emotional testimony, she determined they had a right to see the case through to the end. Joseph had no objection.

Accompanied by Joseph and Terry, Jimmy walked to the bench and stood before the judge. Joseph noticed that it was the first time Jimmy was able to look anyone in the face during a conversation. He stood as tall as his slight frame could manage and the glassy look disappeared from his eyes. In fact, Joseph noted, Jimmy looked almost happy. *Happier than I have ever seen him*, Joseph thought. *In fact, some of the little boy look I remember has come back—well, if not happy, satisfied.*

The judge proceeded through the prescribed litany. "What is your true name? Are you a citizen of the United States? Are you represented by counsel? Have you talked over your case with your lawyers? Have you had enough time to discuss it with them? Have you told them all the facts and circumstances surrounding your case? Are your satisfied with the representation they provided? How old are you? How far did you go in school? Are you now or have you ever been adjudged mentally incompetent?" all of which questions he answered appropriately.

At this point, Joseph interrupted with, "Your Honor, we did have a psychiatric evaluation done that indicated to us Mr. Takas was, because of his heavy involvement with drugs, operating under a drug-induced psychosis at about the time of the killing; however, there has been no adjudication of mental disability."

The judge ignored Joseph's comments and asked, "Do you understand what's going on , Mr. Takas?"

"Yes, ma'am."

She then continued with her questioning, "Do you know what you are charged with? Do you know the punishment? Do you understand you do not have to change your plea? Do you understand you will be giving up several Constitutional rights if you change your plea? Is this plea voluntarily?"

And on and on for several more minutes, to all of which questions Jimmy again answered appropriately.

Judge Crider finished with, "How then do you plead to the charge of murder?"

"I plead guilty," the word resonating through the silent courtroom.

"The Court will set sentencing for one thirty this afternoon." Then to the guards, "Please take Mr. Takas to the jail and return him to the courtroom at that time."

Turning to the stunned and silent jurors, she explained the conversation that was had in her chambers that morning, ending with, "This, therefore, discharges you of your duty. We appreciate it, and I am sure it will make your holiday much better. For the Takas and Westlock families, the holidays will not be pleasant, but, at least, a resolution is final. Your jury service is now over. Have a Happy Holiday."

Joseph and Terry stood while the jurors silently filed out of the room. Neither the older nor the younger lawyer wanted to leave, knowing that they would be inundated by questions from members of the media waiting just outside the courtroom door. Opening the door, Joseph could see Thuman, chest out like a pouter pigeon, stuttering happily for the reporters and posing for the photographers. His voice would be heard on every television station in the viewing area that evening.

Joseph tried to steal past, but Stan stopped him. "Hi, Mr. Joseph. Is there anything you want to say?"

"Not really, Stan. But thanks for asking. Terry and I are pretty tired and will want to digest what has happened before there is much we can say. Incidently, off the record, I am still not convinced Jimmy killed her. It is totally out of character. I just don't know…" his voice trailing off as he walked past the elevator, rejecting it in favor of the stairs—knowing the elevator would be filled with people he didn't want to see. Terry accompanied him, as dejected as he. Joseph thought, *The pigs aren't going to like this.*

CHAPTER SIXTEEN

The jury was gone, Takas was sentenced, and it was past Joseph's usual dinner hour. He wasn't hungry anyway—just wanted to sit in his office and stare at his pigs. They were, as usual, smiling—an enigmatic smile Joseph couldn't read, but he was sure there was at least a little sympathy for him and contempt for the system that seemed to have failed Jimmy. Terry had walked back to the office with Joseph, but asked, "If you don't mind, Mr. Joseph. I would like to go home for a bit. Haven't seen much of the kids lately, except for last night. That was the first evening I spent with them in several weeks and my wife said she would like me to have dinner with them. If you need me, just give me a call. I can be back in five or ten minutes."

Joseph waved him away, saying, "Go on home. Enjoy your wife— enjoy your kids. I know you haven't seen much of your family lately and you must be as tired as me. I'll call if I need you."

Joseph called his wife and explained to her what had happened in court that day, not wanting her to see it on the news before he broke it to her. Properly understanding, she asked, "When will you be coming home, Pat?" sympathetically.

"Not for a bit. I want to catch my breath and see if there is anything I have to do at the office. Don't bother to wait dinner. I don't think I could eat anything now. I won't be too late."

Jimmy Takas had been removed from the courthouse and returned to his cell awaiting transportation to the receiving center at the state prison in Lorain County. He would be processed there and assigned a permanent location within six or eight weeks.

The phone rang on the elderly lawyer's desk. "What the hell," he muttered, "Della knows I don't want to talk to anyone now." Thinking it might be Mary again, he picked up the receiver. "Hi, honey. Did I forget something?"

"Well, hello to you too, sweetheart," a masculine voice answered with a chuckle.

"I thought it was my wife calling." Joseph didn't recognize the voice immediately and started, "Who...?" and then, "Oh, hi, Sergeant. Didn't know who it was at first. Guess I'm tired. What can I do for you?"

It was Sergeant Hilary Dale. Joseph recalled that Dale had not been in court during the change of plea or, for that matter, at all that day. The only representative of the police department present at trial was Lieutenant Tells.

"I know it's late and you probably want to go home for dinner, but I hoped I might catch you in. There's something I'd like to talk to you about. I think it's important. Can you meet me at the deli in a few minutes—maybe grab a cup of coffee? I'm at the station now and can be over there in a couple of minutes."

The police station was a block off the square, just across the street from the new Municipal Court Building. Since the deli was directly across the square from Joseph's office, walking they would both get there about the same time. Joseph asked, "What's it about? Is it about the trial? The trial is finished, you know. Jimmy changed his plea today. I assumed you would have heard the news by now."

Dale ignored the questions and asked, "I heard, but can you meet me?"

Joseph paused, knowing that Dale wouldn't bother him unless he believed it important, and said, "Sure. See you in a couple of minutes." He called Mary to tell her he would be a little later and sent Della home. Everyone else had already gone. He knew they all wanted to commiserate with him, but didn't know how, so thought it best to just leave him alone.

The elderly lawyer tried to smile at his pigs, but didn't feel like smiling. Since their return smile was inscrutable, he paid no attention to them, ignoring their ambiguous response. He shrugged into his coat, walked out of his building, locking the front door behind him, and proceeded across the square. It was a quiet evening, but nice. The only others using the square were the little squirrels looking for nuts long gone from the trees. The quiet and solitude didn't bother Joseph. He enjoyed it. His path across the square was illuminated by the old-fashioned lamps set high on ornate poles, glowing with a soft golden light. It took just a couple of minutes to traverse the square, circumnavigate the gazebo and cross the street to the deli. It was still open. He and Sergeant Dale reached the entrance at the same time. They chose a booth near the rear and ordered coffee from a tired waitress. No one else was in the diner.

Joseph was not in the mood for small talk, so as soon as the coffee came asked. "What's this about, Sergeant?"

"Please call me Hil—short for Hilary—that's what my friends call me. Don't have many in my kind of job. Most everyone calls me Dale. Wish they wouldn't."

Joseph was amazed at the police officer's sensitivity. He had never thought of him as having, or wanting, friends. He was just a tough cop with a reputation of being good, persistent and honest.

"Okay, Hil. Now, what can I do for you?" Joseph said, a little more conciliatory.

"Well, it's kind of a long story, if you got the time."

"Go ahead. Got nothing but time now that the trial is over. Can't say I'm very happy about it."

"Well, there's been something about this case that's been bothering me for a long time. I heard the testimony by the assistant coroner out of Cleveland that there was just one weapon used to kill June." His voice shook a little when he mentioned her name. Joseph knew the officer had known and was paternally fond of the murdered girl, who was young enough to be Dale's daughter.

"Well, I saw the original wounds and it didn't look to me like they were all inflicted with just a single weapon. The good doctor's testimony made no sense to me and it really bothered me. I studied the drawings that girl did for you and Mr. Bernow. They made sense. I helped with the investigation and there wasn't no weapons found at the house. We found Knedder's fish knife in his car—but it didn't match any of the wounds. We looked around a lot, but there was just nothing there. Asked myself, where could they have got to? Didn't get no answer. But you know, Clarence was there long enough to have cleaned out the house. Hide things where we could never find them. We got to Jimmy Takas pretty quick and found nothing at his house, in his car or on him. I just couldn't come up with a satisfactory theory of the crime."

This was the longest speech Joseph had ever heard the sergeant make. The entire message was delivered in such a way that it made Joseph think Dale was reconstructing the events in his mind while verbalizing them for Joseph's benefit.

"I've kind of felt the same way about it, too. Something really odd about the case but nothing I could really put my finger on," Joseph offered.

Dale paused and took a sip of his coffee—black, the same way Joseph took his.

"Go on, Hil." Joseph remembered to use the name by which he wanted to be called.

Dale smiled, then began seriously, "I have to talk to the lieutenant about this, but he isn't on duty tonight. I'm working the night shift and he'll be in first thing in the morning. I'll get a chance to talk to him then. I think this is important and am talking to you off the record for now—until I have an opportunity to talk to Lieutenant Tell."

"Well, what is it, Hil?" Joseph's curiosity was aroused.

"There was the thing, you know, the thing that happened that morning that made no sense at all. I couldn't understand why Thuman showed up with Officer Stanford. Rob was at the station with me and practically followed me to June's house, arriving within no more than two or three minutes of me getting there. Since we were both on station at the time, the dispatcher didn't have to send out a call for assistance. She wouldn't have tried to reach any of the other officers until I called the killing in and asked for detectives."

Dale then added with a quizzical expression on his face, "I asked Thuman how come he was there. He told me he heard the call on his scanner. I didn't think anything about it at the time and, in fact, it completely slipped my mind until just the other night. You had Mr. Bernow file a public records request for the police logs for that night. They included the dispatcher's log and notes. Before he would let me give them to Terry, Thuman told me to review them—I guess he forgot what he told me that night, or thought I forgot it. Anyway, I looked at the logs and found there no record of a call going out."

Dale pulled a sheaf of papers from his pocket and laid the dispatch log on the table between them. Pointing, he said, "See, these are the entries the dispatcher made that morning. There is no record of a call going out from her. It could not have been on the scanner."

"I noticed that," Joseph said, "but wasn't sure what it meant, especially since I had no way of knowing about the conversation you had with Thuman."

"Then," Dale continued, "I waited for the dispatcher that was on duty that night to come in. It was several days latter—she was on vacation—and the trial had been going on for about a week. Anyway, I showed her the logs and asked if she remembered that morning. She said she did. It was the first murder case she had anything to do with. So I asked her if she had put the call out on the air. She thought about it for a minute then told me she was sure she hadn't. 'There was no reason to,' she said. 'You and Rob was both on station.' She checked her dispatch log and told me that if she had, it would have been recorded. She is very exact in recording everything that happens on her shift. I believed her."

Dale paused for another sip of his coffee. It was growing cold, so he signaled for the waitress to warm it up. She refilled both cups.

"I wasn't sure it was important, but it made me think. I remember how Thuman wanted to get into the house that night, and he was kind of pissed when I wouldn't let him in. He involved himself in the investigation with the detectives right from the start. In fact, Lieutenant Tells said he was getting to be a real pain in the ass. Wanted to know everything that was happening and reviewed everything that went to BCI. All along I was thinking how great it is to have a prosecutor that takes an interest in our work and wants to prepare his case so thoroughly—not like that one we had before."

When Dale paused again, the quizzical expression reappearing and his brow wrinkling, Joseph asked, "What does this mean to you, Hil?"

"I'm not exactly sure, but it's real strange. Thuman didn't do anything outright improper and didn't try to mess with the evidence. He just made sure we was doing everything right and helped us look for things that pointed to the defendant. He was bound and determined to get a conviction, and didn't want anything to stand in the way. It kind of scared me because he was so…I don't know the word…maybe persistent in wanting to hang Takas. It was like June was a friend and he took her killing very personal. Maybe that's it—I just don't know. But I thought I should talk to you about it because it's been bothering me and I think you should know. I'm only sorry I didn't get it to you before the trial ended."

"Wished you'd said something earlier. Not sure if it's going to make any difference now," Joseph said, "but thanks for calling it to my attention. Don't know what good it will do, but thanks anyway. I might be able to talk Takas into filing an appeal on the basis of newly discovered evidence…" suspicion starting to build.

They both stood, Dale insisting on paying for the coffee and Joseph dropping a dollar bill on the table for the tired waitress. Both the police sergeant and Joseph left the restaurant together, Joseph crossing the street toward his office, since his truck was parked behind the building. Dale turned in the direction of the station. As Joseph crossed the square, he glanced at the building housing the Prosecutor's Office. Although most of the building was dark, he noticed a light in the second-story office of Harold Thuman. For some reason not clearly apparent to him, he decided to visit Thuman, knowing it was a stupid thing to do without someone else present. He kind of assumed Thuman wouldn't be alone in the office. Moving past his building, he entered the recently built bank building on the corner, that housed the Prosecutor's Office. The bank was closed, but the street door was open to the elevator lobby that led to the upper stories. Joseph ignored the elevator and mounted the stairs to the second floor. He walked past the darkened reception area towards the back of the building, where the light was shining beneath Thuman's door.

The elderly lawyer tried the knob. It was locked. Knocking lightly on the door, he heard, "Who's there?"

Joseph replied, identifying himself, and heard, "Just a minute," muffled by the door. Footsteps approached and Thuman opened the door. He was still dressed in the clothes he had worn in court, the jacket hanging on the back of his desk chair, his tie loosened and the collar of his sparkling white shirt opened. His hair mussed as though his fingers had scrubbed through it several times. "What do you want? Your client's already pled guilty. Do we have something else going that we need to talk about?" right eye blinking, mouth working.

Joseph wondered, *Why is he still nervous?* He said, "No, I don't think so. "I just wanted to talk."

"Well, what do you want to talk about?" mouth still working.

"I just had a cup of coffee with Sergeant Dale. He had some interesting things to tell me—thinks about which I wasn't aware," Joseph began as he entered the sparsely furnished office.

It was a large square room with no pictures adorning the wall—only a framed diploma from Capitol Law School in Columbus—the only remaining totally night law school in Ohio—and the Certification from the Ohio Supreme Court that Thuman was licensed to practice in Ohio. Joseph noted that the license was issued three years after the date of graduation and wondered if Thuman had to take the bar exam several times before passing. The desk was the plain green metal of government-issue origin, as were the client chairs. The desk chair was the same, except that it was on casters. Joseph shook his head in wonderment. The austere appearance was a far cry from the luxurious office Thuman's predecessor had occupied. There were no comfortable chairs or couch.

Joseph seated himself on one of the straight backed chairs before the desk. Thuman took his seat behind the desk. "Again, Joseph, I asked, what do you want?" Thuman stammered.

"I was wondering if you could explain something Dale told me. It seemed there was a kind of discrepancy in the dispatcher's log. It reported there was no call from the dispatch office that night that went over the air. Dale asked her about it, and she confirmed that there was no need for a call to go out since both he and Officer Stanford were on post. Yet, you told Dale you heard the call on your scanner."

As Joseph was saying these things he watched Thuman closely. Thuman began to sit straighter in his chair—his face reddening—his fingers working. He reached into his desk drawer and his hand closed on something Joseph couldn't see. He began to rise. "I had hoped no one noticed…" he began. Then, after a brief pause, continued with, "She must have made a mistake and forgot to log what she had done. I'll see to it that she is properly reprimanded."

*   *   *

It was almost two o'clock in the morning. Jimmy Takas, driving carefully, as drunks do, pulled his car into June's driveway. June Westlock hopped out of the car and walked quickly toward the front door. Reaching for her key in the pocket of the robe she wore, she quickly unlocked the door. Opening it, she walked into her house and tried to close the door behind her. Jimmy jumped from the driver's side of the car and, staying right behind her on the walk, stopped her from slamming the door, pushed it open and followed her in. He wasn't going to let her get away with doing him the way she had. He was able to function well enough even though still in a self-induced alcoholic state—he was drunk so often that he was able to do many things while in that condition, most of which he never remembered. He was also beginning to sober up a little because of the sick feeling that came when he didn't get the drugs he needed.

He pushed June through the door and into the living room. Before she could catch her balance, Jimmy reached the hallway linen closet, where she kept her fixings. Reaching up to the top shelf and pulling off the dish towel beneath which she kept her supplies, he reached in and found nothing except a needle attached to a syringe. June never used it— Clarence sometimes did. Jimmy turned to June, holding the needle in his hand, "Don't you got nothing here?"

"I been telling you all night. There's nothing here and I can't get nothing tonight."

"Well, I'm gonna get something for my troubles," Jimmy growled, reaching for the tie on June's robe. She had nothing beneath it but a short nightie.

June didn't want any fuss—she was afraid her daughter would wake up. She said, "Sure, Jimmy. Come on back in the living room." Anything to keep him quiet and send him on his way.

There was no light in the living room, just the television playing quietly in the corner. It was left on all of the time. June walked to the couch, opened her robe and lay back, beckoning to Jimmy seductively. He stared at her stark white body and walked toward her as though in a dream. He was in too much of a hurry to disrobe, so just unzipped his trousers and climbed clumsily on top of June. Nothing happened. He worked feverishly, but was unable to arouse himself. June waited patiently, but after a short while couldn't keep from smiling, and then began to giggle at Jimmy's discomfort. Jimmy was unable to penetrate her at all—he had nothing with which to penetrate her.

"Don't laugh!" he almost screeched, but June couldn't help herself. He was standing in front of her in an awkward state of dishabille, pants around his ankles, underwear torn, completely flaccid, no evidence of sexual ability or desire. His face a deep red—apparently all his blood congregated there instead of where he needed it—hair mussed—eyes wild—glasses down on the end of his dripping nose— a funnier sight June had never seen. She now laughed aloud, unable to control herself.

Jimmy was furious. He slapped her and grabbed her by the shoulders with a strength he didn't normally have, leaving bruises near her neck. June had enough, she pushed him away. Jimmy looked around and could find no weapon to use on her. He saw the hypodermic needle he'd dropped on the floor while searching the closet—it was the only implement handy. He grabbed it and jabbed at June, striking her on and beneath her bare breast, two, three times. June slapped him and said, "That's it, Jimmy. I'm gonna call the cops now."

As she walked toward the phone, Jimmy straightened his trousers as best he could and walked quickly to the front door. He opened it, looked out and, seeing someone sitting on the front porch across the street, walked casually to his car, started it and backed out into the street—drunkenly careful.

*　　*　　*

June smiled to herself at the memory of Jimmy's discomfort but was angry enough to punish him for his behavior, especially for sticking the needle in her breast—it hurt like hell. She reached for the telephone and, dialing a number from memory, waited through several rings. Finally the phone was answered by a sleepy voice mumbling, "Hello."

"Harry, is that you?" June asked.

"Of course it's me. Who the hell is this?" He didn't need to ask. There was only one person who called him Harry, no matter how many times he instructed her otherwise.

"It's June, Harry. I need you...now!"

Fumbling for the clock on the bedside table, he squinted at it. It read a little after two o'clock in the morning, "For God's sake, June. It's the middle of the night. I've told you not to call me at home. I want you, I'll call you. Now let me go back to bed—I'll stop by tomorrow—first chance I get."

"No! I want you to come over...now!"

He tried to put her off, but she would have none of it. After a few minutes of argument, he acquiesced, saying, "I'll get dressed—be there in about fifteen minutes," knowing he must do her bidding. She could make plenty of trouble for him if he didn't. *Gonna have to do something about that, and damn soon!* he thought.

Sleeping nude, he didn't bother with underwear or socks, but slipped on a pair of jeans, an old sweatshirt, loafers and a jacket. Pulling his car out of the attached garage, he drove to June's house, parking around the corner on the street. He approached through the backyard. He knew the backdoor lock was broken, so entered by way of it. He called, "June, what's so goddamn important you need me in the middle of the night? How many times I tell you, don't call me?"

"Yeah?" Standing in the doorway to the utility room, kitchen light on behind her, her robe opened, nothing visible underneath, June pointed toward her crotch and making a mocking seduction bump, said, "You call anytime you want some of this, and expect me to be ready." Her voice getting more shrill, "You call anytime you want some blow, or a joint, you bastard! You expect me to have everything you want, but don't want me to call you. Fuck you!"

She stalked into the kitchen, robe flapping. She turned toward him and pointed at her breast, where the puncture mark was almost invisible, and her neck, where a red mark was starting to form, "Look what he did to me! I want you to fix him right now. Make him stay away from me like you did with Clarence. He got to learn he can't do me like this. You got to fix it!" almost screeching.

Harry looked at her and saw a spot of blood on her left breast, and one beneath it. "Calm down, June. I'll do what I can. Now tell me what happened? Who you talking about? Did Knedder do this to you?" he asked.

"No. Jimmy Takas. He came here tonight. Said he was looking for Clarence. I tol' him Clarence don't live here no more. He didn' care—wanted drugs. Drunk, as usual. I didn' have nothing. He was really flying, so I took him by Cockroach's—he wasn' there. No one around had any pot, coke or crack—nothing. I told him, but he wasn' satisfied. Came back here and tried to jump me but couldn't get it up. I laughed at him. He grabbed my needle from the closet and stuck it in my tit—three times. Now you call the cops. You get him tonight—I want that son-of-a-bitch."

"Look, June," right eye blinking, mouth twitching, "be reasonable, I can't do anything tonight. I'll talk to the police—have you make out a report tomorrow—you can file a complaint—"

"I don't want to file no report. I want the bastard in jail tonight. You can do that. You better..." she threatened.

He tried to reason with her, but she was rapidly growing beyond reason—quickly losing control. Finally, "Okay. You won't help me, I'll take care of it myself. I'll call nine-one-one and tell them you're here. I'll tell them all about how you use me and how I feed your habit. You and your fuckin' politics—let's see how many votes this gets you!" She was becoming hysterical and Harry knew she would do what she threatened.

"June, wait—"

But there was no stopping her. She ran for the telephone on the small table next to the couch in the livingroom and reached for the phone. The television played softly in the background. Harry followed, grabbed her arm and said, in a voice he hardly recognized as his own, "You're not going to ruin me! I can't let that happen! It won't happen! I've worked to hard for you to spoil everything!"

He began to feel as though he were outside his body, watching himself on a movie screen. Nothing was real. The actions were those of someone else—not him. All of a sudden the phrase *seeing red* had real meaning to him. He saw everything through a red haze. He could see clearly, but everything was unrealistic—dreamlike—colored over by a crimson film.

He saw someone grabbing her by the neck and shoulder, slapping her face and pulling her away from the phone. He saw someone picking up the letter opener lying on the little telephone table. It had a knife-like blade and came to a sharp point—the edges sharp. He heard a voice that sounded like his own saying calmly, "You aren't going to do this to me, June…."

The person he was watching plunged the letter opener into her back so hard it went in all the way, leaving a distinctive mark on her back from the decorative hilt.

She looked over her shoulder at him, shock taking the place of anger on her face, quickly replaced by terror. It was the first time she ever felt fear for her life. She turned and ran through the kitchen toward the back of the house, knocking over a wicker basket in the corner of the living room, strewing artificial reeds from it, trying to reach the outside door in the utility room she knew so well. Harry saw himself jumping over the basket, almost losing his balance, grabbing the back of a chair sitting next to the kitchen table. It fell, spilling potatoes and onions from the table onto the floor. June reached the backdoor, but before she could pull it open, Harry was on her, grasping her by her shoulders and striking her again and again with the small blade. "You won't ruin me.... I worked too hard.... You won't ruin me...."

June fell to the floor in a pool of blood. She tried to cry out. He held his hand over her mouth, her eyes wide, staring. He could feel her screams pulsating against his palm—no sound. She clutched at the hand covering her mouth, clawing with her nails and drawing blood. She needed air. He struck at her hands with the sharp edge of the letter opener to make her quit, watching carefully as the look in her eyes slowly changed from terror to a silent plea for help. He still didn't remove his hand. The light faded from her eyes and she lay sprawled across the floor, her robe open, limbs askew, eyes open, accusing. Her body convulsed once, and she was still.

Harry looked down at her, rising slowly to his feet. A flush of feeling passed though him—almost like an orgasm—sensual but not sexual. He spent a moment enjoying the feeling of elation. He checked to see if there was any blood on him. Oddly enough there wasn't, except for his hands. He went into the kitchen past the chair lying on the floor, rinsed his hands in the sink, drying them on a paper towel, thinking, *The bitch really clawed me—doesn't matter, the scratches will heal pretty quick.* He took the towel and the letter opener with him as he walked out the backdoor, being careful not to touch anything or step in the pooled blood. He didn't bother to pull the door closed behind him.

Walking to his car, he saw a black man he recognized as Clarence Knedder sneaking through the backyards, just as he had, and enter June's house through the same door he had just exited. He wondered, *What's he doing here? Supposed to be an order keeping him away.* He watched for a couple of minutes, but no lights came on in the house. He stayed where he could watch the house for a few more minutes, then returned to his car, waiting to see what would happen next. Everything was quiet, so he drove to a nearby closed diner and threw the paper towel into the trash receptacle in the back parking lot. The letter opener was kind of pretty. He decided to keep it.

* * *

Clarence Knedder lumbered through the backdoor of June's house, wondering briefly why the door was open. He was still a little high—it snowed regularly in his life—cocaine leaves one a bit paranoid. Reaching for the dangling light chain, he kicked something soft. Looking down— his eyes were accustomed to the dark from sneaking around in the night and with the little light shining in the kitchen window from the neighbor's yard—he saw the outlines of a startling white body lying on the utility room floor. He knelt, reached out and felt hair, then a face. Because of his familiarity with her, he knew immediately it was June. Her face was still warm.

"June, June, what happened, baby?" Reaching further, he could feel her naked body. "What you doing like this? I know that som-bitch, Jimmy, was here. You been cheating with him."

Anger built in him. "How can you do me like that?" Reaching to lift himself from the floor, he took hold of the top of the dryer with his small hands—felt a pair of scissors that June had left there—grasped them in his hand. "How can you do me like that wi' our baby in the house?"

Overcome by anger and despair he struck her dead body again and again with the scissors, tears streaming down his face, "How could you?" He couldn't understand why she wasn't bleeding. He stumbled into the kitchen, grabbed a knife from the utensil drawer and returned to the still body. "Why don't you move?" he yelled. "Move, damn it," and struck her several more times with the kitchen knife. Nothing. She didn't move, just lay there limbs akimbo.

After several minutes, he calmed down, looked at his shirt, saw blood on it and ripped it off—scrubbed his tiny hands with it as though it would clean away the acts they committed. He opened the backdoor, looked around and, seeing nothing, left. Running to where he had parked his car behind a restaurant on the next street, he saw a garbage can in back of one of the houses he passed. Lifting the lid, he dropped his shirt and the knife he still held in the can, replaced the lid and returned to his car. He thought for a minute, *Oh, shit. I forgot the scissors.* He silently returned to the house, picked up the scissors where he dropped them, and brought them to the garbage can as well. He had some not too clean clothes in his car. Since

June kicked him out he often lived there. He pulled an old, dirty sweatshirt from the backseat and slipped it on.

He sat in his car without starting the motor—thinking about June and her cold body lying there in the house they'd once shared. He thought about his little girl, who wouldn't have a mommy now. Overcome with grief he cried, howled and beat his hands on the steering wheel. "How could she? I thought Jimmy was my fren'. I can't leave her like that."

After several minutes, he left the car and walked back to the house. He again entered by way of the backdoor and, without looking at June's body, walked through the kitchen and into the living room. Dropping onto the couch, he felt confused and didn't know what to do. He wanted a smoke and reached for his cigarettes. They must be in the shirt he had thrown away. Feeling desperate without his smokes, he again left the house the same way he entered, being careful to close the door behind him. He went to his car, couldn't find any cigarettes there, so drove to an all-night convenience store near the uptown square. He pulled into the lot, got out of the car, went into the store and purchased a pack of cigarettes. Hands shaking, he tore open the pack and lit a cigarette. As he left the store, he saw a policeman he knew. They nodded at each other casually and Knedder left.

He returned to June's house, walked in through the backdoor, and again closed it behind him, being careful to engage the chain since the lock was broken. He didn't look at June's body lying there now so cold, walked into the living room and sat on the couch. He smoked another cigarette, and another. Finally, he picked up the phone and dialed nine-one-one. When a lady answered, he began crying again, "Please send the cops! It's awful! Please send the cops…."

He held the phone and could hear the lady talking but couldn't make out the words. He couldn't talk—choked up. Soon he heard a thumping on the front door. He carefully replaced the telephone in its holder, covered his face with his hands and sobbed out loud as he heard the door opening.

*   *   *

Thuman, driving aimlessly around town, slowly began to return to his body—it was almost like coming down from a cocaine high. Thinking about the night's activities, he drove back toward June's house. Although it seemed like only a moment had passed, when he looked at his watch he realized about three hours had gone by since he left June's house. As he approached her street, he heard a siren, then saw a police car pull up and stop in front of her house. A young officer he knew as Rob Stanford walked toward the front door. Harry pulled his car behind the police cruiser, got out, met the officer on the lawn and followed him onto the front stoop of the house, where they were met by Sergeant Dale.

*   *   *

Watching Joseph intently as he sat across the desk from him, Thuman sat up straighter and asked, "What are you planning to do?" in a voice much calmer than Joseph expected.

Thuman, Joseph noticed, still had his hand in the top drawer of his desk. He watched as the prosecutor withdrew from it a letter opener. It had a crystal handle and a shiny stainless steel blade about four or five inches long with an extremely sharp point—the blade edged on both sides. Joseph thought for some reason it looked familiar, a bit like the drawing that the young artist made for him. Thuman held the point against the forefinger of his left hand while his right hand spun the grip, the crystal handle reflecting the light in an almost hypnotic way. Thuman stared at Joseph for several seconds awaiting his response—his face expressionless—his demeanor calm.

Staring at the letter opener in Thuman's hand, Joseph noted the letter *W* enclosed by a circle on the small cross-bar at the base of the blade, or hilt. It tickled his memory of a conversation with the young medical resident telling him that one of the stab marks had penetrated so deeply that the pressure of the hilt left the mark of a letter she was unable to decipher in June Westlock's skin.

Joseph asked as casually as he could, "That is an unusual letter opener. Where did you get it? It was June's, wasn't it?"

Thuman didn't respond—just kept twirling the opener, its point now on the blotter on top of his desk, his hand on the crystal handle, the light making bright flashing patterns as Joseph's eyes were drawn to it. As if in a trance, Joseph said, unnecessarily, "You killed her, didn't you?" The elderly lawyer wasn't feeling calm or relaxed—but the sound of his own voice, so calm, so normal, surprised him

"What choice did I have? She was going to talk about me—tell lies. Sure, I occasionally use drugs—everyone does. It's not as though I was breaking the law—I have to know about these things—it's my job to prosecute criminals—the people elected me to do that and I will— nothing can get in the way of that—I was called to rid the world of this trash. She was trash, you know—no good—lived with a black man—had his baby—no good. She spread drugs around and even got me started on them. She even spread her legs for me—and, I guess, anyone else that wanted her." He chuckled at his own play on words, chortling, "Spread drugs...spread legs..."

Then immediately his face resumed the complete lack of expression he had maintained throughout the conversation. "I couldn't help myself— it was her fault—she was beautiful, but so evil," his voice rising but without inflection. He was preaching to himself, justifying his actions— he had no choice—God directed him.

Joseph sat quietly. He was really curious, and wondered why he didn't feel more frightened—Lord knows he should. "Then why have you worked so hard to convict Jimmy when you knew he didn't kill June?"

"But he did kill her. He was the one that started it all. He came to her house. When she wouldn't get him the drugs he wanted—needed—he tried to, but couldn't fornicate with her. When she laughed at him, he stuck a needle in her chest. If it wasn't for him, June wouldn't be dead— it's his fault she's dead. He had to be punished."

Thuman continued to stare at Joseph without expression except for the rapidly blinking eye and a twitch as the corner of his mouth. His hands moved constantly, playing with the letter opener, obviously trying to make a decision. Finally he sighed and started to rise up from his chair. *My God, he's big*, Joseph thought.

"You know, Mr. Joseph, I've never liked you. You're as bad as the people you represent. You're just like them. Using tricks and your smooth ways to get them off. The world will be better off without you…" moving slowly around his desk.

He's convincing himself that I have to die. He's going to kill me. I've just tried two murder cases and now I'm going to be murdered because of it. I can hear Mary saying, "I told you so." Why don't I feel frightened. No way in hell I can protect myself. Joseph's mind turned to a phrase he remembered from Ecclesiastes , *He sets the time for birth and the time for death…the time for killing and the time for healing. Is this my time for dying? Guess it doesn't really matter—I'm old—but Mary will sure be pissed at me.*

Joseph got to his feet as Thuman moved closer to him. "How will you explain my body?" he asked, thinking, *I can't fight him—I have to talk my way out of this.*

"I'll know what to say," as he lunged toward Joseph. The elderly lawyer tried to back away, tripping over the chair on which he was sitting. The chair clattered to the floor. Joseph crabbed backwards, trying to avoid Thuman's grasping hand. Thuman was swinging the blade, trying desperately to make contact with Joseph. Joseph held his hands out and the blade nicked one of his wrists, drawing blood. The thought raced through Joseph's mind. *This is what the coroner calls "defensive wounds."* He couldn't believe he was thinking so clearly of extraneous things when he should be thinking about how to escape from this madman.

Thuman calmly followed, walking toward Joseph as he rolled across the floor and crashed into another chair, upending it. Thuman's face was expressionless, his eyes empty. *There is nothing in there,* Joseph thought. Thuman was in no hurry—just trying to complete a slightly unpleasant task. He couldn't seem to understand why Joseph didn't cooperate. "Stay still, old man. You're just making this harder on yourself," his voice as impassive as his face.

Joseph tried to get to his feet, but Thuman was on top of him, holding him down. The blade descended again, striking Joseph in his quickly raised arm. It hurt. This time Joseph yelled, "Get the fuck off me!"

As Thuman raised his hand for a second blow, they both heard pounding on the door. Thuman stood erect, holding the collar of Joseph's jacket in his hand, the other upraised with the letter opener prepared to strike. The door crashed open—Dale rushed in, followed by Terry Bernow.

Thuman, without blinking or emotion, said, "Thank God you got here. He was trying to kill me."

Sergeant Dale said calmly, "Okay, Mr. Thuman. Now, give me the knife. Let him go." He approached Thuman with one hand outstretched, the other beneath his jacket, where he carried his weapon.

Terry ran to Joseph's side and helped him to his feet. "Are you all right?" Then, seeing the blood, "We got to get you to the hospital."

Joseph swayed and suddenly felt his legs go weak and his vision fade. He tried to keep his balance, but found himself sitting on the floor again, back against the wall. He knew Terry was talking, could see his mouth moving, but couldn't understand the words.

Terry knelt beside him and said, "Mr. Joseph? Pat, can you hear me? Are you all right?" and looked to Dale for help. Dale was occupied with Thuman and could offer no assistance.

Joseph took a deep breath and, sitting up straighter, felt his head clear. "What the hell. Did I faint? I've never fainted in my life. I'm all right. Help me stand up." He looked at his hand and the tear on his suit jacket. "I suppose we'd best go to the hospital. But I have to call Mary first. She'll be mad as hell if I don't let her know I'm all right. Will you let her know where we are? I think I fainted—that's the first time I did that—I'm all right. By the way, what are you doing here? How did you know?"

Terry held on to the ashen-faced lawyer and helped him into the chair, after righting it. He said, "I was walking across the square back to the office. I forgot something I needed. I saw you and Dale walking out of the deli. I asked him what was going on. He told me about the conversation you and he had. I tried to catch up to you—you know, to go back to the office with you, when I saw you going into the prosecutor's building instead. It frightened me and I began to run after you and yelled for Dale. I guess he heard me and thought it a good idea to follow. We were coming up the stairs when we heard a crash. The only light in the building was coming from under Thuman's door. When we knocked and heard nothing, Dale told me to get out of the way so he could bust the door down. Thank God."

While Terry was making his explanations to Joseph, Dale placed handcuffs on Thuman's wrists and called the station for a cruiser, saying to the dispatch operator, "Send a cruiser to Prosecutor Thuman's office. Call Lieutenant Tell and let him know I need to talk to him as soon as possible."

They started to walk out the door. Stan Marten was standing in the darkened hallway. "Hi, Mr. Joseph. Is there something you want to tell me?"

Thuman, being led out past Marten, looked over his shoulder at Joseph, eye working, mouth twitching, neck straining, trying to reach into his pocket and withdraw some money. He said, "Dale, get the money in my pocket—give it to Joseph." Then to Joseph, "You're my lawyer. Everything we talked about is confidential—privileged communications, you know—lawyer and client."

Joseph, not believing what he was hearing, responded, "Yeah, right," while thinking, *I'd have to ask Mary anyway.*

EPILOGUE

Pat Joseph sat in his office as his habit commanded, feet propped on his waste basket, hands clasped across his rotundity, staring out the front window at nothing in particular. He had arrived at the office, early as usual, before anyone else. He could see the square, virginal white in blemish-free snow, the old-fashioned street-lights wearing cone-shaped hats of snow. He thought, *How beautiful, except where are the little animals and the kids? The kids will show up.* The children would appear shortly on their way to school, running, making music with their screams, creating snow angels and throwing snowballs at each other and any hapless adult who wandered into their play area—the winter jacket of snow would disappear from the World War I cannon. *Unfortunately the animals won't make an appearance—they must have found somewhere warm to sleep,* Joseph thought. He waited patiently to see how much change the children would make in the short half hour of their presence.

He craned his head around, glancing at his pigs—their smiles showing placid contentment. Nothing exciting had happened in the past several weeks since the Takas trial was finally ended and disappeared from the newspapers. He recalled in vivid detail the conversation with Mary when he returned home the night of his confrontation with Thuman. He desperately needed to tell her his side of the story before the morning papers arrived. She was waiting up for him at the kitchen table when he got home and, unasked, placed a glass of warm milk in front of him.

"Mary, I know I did a rather stupid thing…" he began hesitatingly, then described his conversation with Sergeant Dale.

"As I was returning to my office, I saw a light in Thuman's office. For some reason, I felt compelled to tell him about my talk with Dale. I went into the building and up to his floor. There was a light shining under the door and I could hear him in there, so knocked…" The elderly lawyer then described as delicately as he could what had transpired, downplaying the risk to him.

"Dale and Terry followed me into the building and came busting into Thuman's office just at the right time," Joseph continued.

Mary listened placidly while Joseph explained in detail the circumstances and his thought process. He began to feel unreasonably content, thinking, *Mary isn't going to get mad. She is just happy I'm home and all right. This isn't going so bad.*

Joseph then finished with, "That's exactly what happened, Mary. So after we take care of the necessary details, Jimmy will go free after all, and Thuman will take his place. I'm sure Mr. and Mrs. Takas will be appreciative. They'll probably say something to you at church. Aren't you happy?" he asked with a silly look of expectancy on his face, thinking, *I can never figure out why Mary says people find me intimidating—she is a master.*

Mary sat quietly for a long minute, looking off into space. She didn't look at Joseph where he sat at the kitchen table, a tentative smile on his face.

Mary took a deep breath and began quietly, "Of course I'm happy for Jimmy and his folks and I'm glad you're home safe. But you are without a doubt the stupidest person on the face of the earth…taking such chances…I never…" then she took off nonstop, for a full ten minutes describing in detail Joseph's careless, feckless, irresponsible behavior, unmindful of his responsibility to her, the office and his family—ending with, "How could you…?" then breathless and without waiting for any response, shook her head, left the kitchen table, picked up one of the cats and disappeared up the stairs.

That didn't go so bad, Joseph thought. He called the dog and they walked out into the backyard. After the dog completed his day's business, Joseph returned to the house, locked up, turned out the lights except for a nightlight that Mary insisted be lit for the cats, climbed the stairs, readied himself for bed and crawled in, looking at Mary's unmoving back. He wasn't going to chance another diatribe, so turned out the light, lay down and tried to sleep.

The newspapers had a field day reporting again and again the happenings of the final night of trial, reiterating at length the story of the killing and the potential perpetrators and the unexpected conclusion. There wasn't much else in them for the most of three weeks.

Joseph and Terry immediately moved to withdraw Jimmy's "guilty" plea and requested a new trial. Judge Crider granted the motion, declaring a mistrial. She demanded that all parties appear in her courtroom that afternoon for a conference. An assistant prosecutor—the elected prosecutor being unavailable—appeared on behalf of the State. The judge insisted that a visiting prosecutor be brought in from a neighboring county. She also required that Jimmy Takas be brought back into court. The participants took the same seats they occupied during the lengthy trial—Jimmy looking somewhat confused. Jimmy's parents were seated in the same pew they occupied throughout the trial—the Westlock family was not present. The balance of the courtroom was filled with members of the media and television cameras.

The judge addressed the participants in open court, reciting for the record the substance of the motions and everything that had been brought to her attention. Peering sternly over her half glasses at the prosecution table, she said, "I think it imperative that you declare your intentions forthwith. Do you intend to retry Mr. Takas or do you intend to dismiss the charges?"

The visiting prosecutor had spent the morning closeted with the Milltown Police Department. So, without conferring with one another, he rose and said, "Your Honor, the State has no intention of retrying the case against Mr. Takas. We move that the Court enter a dismissal at the State's request. The matter of Prosecutor Thuman will be considered by the grand jury this week."

The judge turned toward Jimmy and said, "Mr. Takas, the charges against you have been dismissed. You are released from custody. Unfortunately you will have to return to the jail for the release papers to be executed. It shouldn't take too long. The Court would like to apologize to you and your family for what you have been put through. But I must point out that you are not without some responsibility. Your drug and drinking habits contributed to June Westlock's death. In fact, I have never seen a less desirable group of people in my courtroom. I trust, but am not convinced, that you have learned a great deal. I hope I never have to see you in this courtroom again." Then, gathering her robes around her, she left the bench.

Members of the media, who had waited impatiently during her fulmination, tore from the room to report what had transpired to their respective editors.

Jimmy was soon released to his parents and the three of them showed up in Joseph's office, offering effusive thanks. Joseph was pleased, but his question to Jimmy, who refused to look at him, "Why in the world did you want to plead guilty?" produced no response other than a shrug.

Thuman was indicated and entered a plea of "not guilty by reason of insanity." Pat Joseph was not his lawyer.

Fini

Printed in the United States
73225LV00007B/25-36